I Wish for You

Camilla Isley is an engineer turned writer after she quit her job to follow her husband on an adventure abroad.

She's a cat lover, coffee addict, and shoe hoarder. Besides writing, she loves reading—duh!—cooking, watching bad TV, and going to the movies—popcorn, please. She's a bit of a foodie, nothing too serious. A keen traveler, Camilla knows mosquitoes play a role in the ecosystem, and she doesn't want to starve all those frog princes out there, but she could really live without them.

You can find out more about her here: www.camillaisley.com and by following her on Twitter.

@camillaisley
www.facebook.com/camillaisley

By The Same Author

Romantic Comedies

Standalones

I Wish for You
A Sudden Crush

First Comes Love Series

Love Connection
I Have Never

New Adult College Romance

Just Friends Series

Let's Be Just Friends
Friend Zone
My Best Friend's Boyfriend

I Wish for You

(A Happily Ever After Romantic Comedy)

Camilla Isley

This is a work of fiction. Names, characters, businesses, places, events and incidents either are products of the author's imagination or are used fictitiously. Any resemblance to actual events or locales or persons, living or dead, is entirely coincidental.

Copyright © 2015. Pink Bloom Press
All rights reserved.
ISBN: 0996556125
ISBN-13: 978-0-9965561-2-5

Dedication

To my parents, for making me love reading

And to my husband, for making me love

One
The Day After

I rush back into the building and hide pressing my back against the wall and out of sight of the revolving glass doors. As I flatten my palms against the cool marble, I can't help the heavy breaths that make my chest bob up and down. Did they see me? She did. I'm sure I caught a flash of evil blue eyes looking my way before I retreated into my office's building. Before she kissed him. James. My James.

I abruptly wake up thanks to the racking sound of my alarm clock piercing deeply into my skull. I come to a sitting position and silence the damn thing, slamming my right hand on the off button.

Was it a dream? *No, it was real.* As my comatose brain regains consciousness, I experience a stream of increasingly awful emotions. It starts with a choking pain, immediately followed by fear, anguish, and a strong wave of nausea. Ouch, heartbreak sucks!

I lie back on the pillows, trying to abate my squeamishness. Sugar, my black and white rescue cat, decides this is a good moment to jump on my belly and meow for his breakfast.

"Not now, baby," I say, pushing him aside. "I need five minutes before I get up."

No. No. No. I don't want to get up and go to the office, not today, *please*, not after what happened. I'm not ready to face Vanessa. Not while I look awful, and I'm being optimistic.

After spending the whole night crying, my eyes will be horrendously puffy-red and my skin ghastly, in-between a putrid mustard and greenish coloring. There will be no mistaking my utter state of distraught. Damn! I can already picture the evil grin of triumph on her face. Of course, she's going to mask it as one of her best I-want-world-peace beauty pageant smiling faces, pretending nothing's wrong.

I hate it when someone is vicious, and I'm the only one who can see it because they pretend to be the kindest and most caring person in the world. Well, she's the kind of two-faced poser who manages to make people feel in the wrong even when it's *her* delivering a sucker punch to their stomachs. She does it with such grace and poise that no one ever dares argue or be angry.

She must know exactly how badly this hurts for me. *Yep,* now many of the little nasty remarks she's been making in the past months about the guy she was dating begin to make sense. She seemed to take my unconcerned responses as a personal affront. Maybe she thought I knew! Well, from my reaction yesterday it must have been pretty clear I didn't. Wait a second, how long has she been doing it? When did she start? Did she say dating? Did she use the word boyfriend?

Oi.

Picturing James and Vanessa in a committed relationship, makes my heart skip a beat. I gasp for air. Wow, this hurts... this physically hurts! There's this huge ball of pain in my chest that expands all the way down to my stomach. I can hardly breathe and I'm dizzy. Lying back on the pillows is not helping. My heart is beating so fast I can't suck in air, and I feel trapped. Yeah, trapped in my horrible, disastrous life.

I need to calm down. I'm just having a panic attack! Aha! Mark the roots of a problem and then find the solution. What did Dr. Oz say? Ah yes, I simply need to take deep, profound breaths: air in, air out, in... and out...

Gradually, my respiration returns to normal and I'm able to inhale and exhale properly. What should I do next? Clearly, I can't go to work in this state. The mere thought makes me sick. Well, sicker than I already am! Wait, sick... I am ill! This is my way out. I'm going to pull a sickie. Genius!

I haven't taken one illness leave in the five years that I've been with my company. Surely no one is going to suspect me, and it's not going to affect my career too badly. I mean, it's just one day. Yes! I just need the one day to calm down, regroup, and think of a strategy for what to do next. Of course, she will guess why I'm not there today. Oh, screw her! She can think whatever she likes.

Where is my cell phone? I need to put on my glasses because without them, I am basically blind. Usually, I do that on autopilot before even opening my eyes. So I can pretend I can actually see, but I guess today my routine went out the window. I grope the nightstand, grab the glasses, and put them on.

Ah, this is better. I scan the bedside table for any trace of my cell but it's not there. Instead, nicely perched next to my table lamp, there is an innocent-looking Sugar. I follow his not-so-innocent gaze to the floor and finally spot my mobile lying discarded on the carpet. I grab it before I change my mind and dial the office's number, all the while shaking my head at my vindictive cat.

"Good morning, you've reached Crispy Koob Corporation." Instead of hearing Michelle's voice, the company's receptionist, I am redirected to voicemail. "Our offices are open Monday through Friday, from 7 a.m. to—" I end the call.

This is weird. The answering machine is never on during the week; they only turn it on for weekends and holidays. Hold on a second. What day is it today? I look at my phone's screen and there it is, the sweetest writing ever:

Saturday, May 16

Yes! *Yes*! This means I have not one, but two full days before I'll be forced to face the world. This is so much better. I'll have time to recover, think a little, and craft a plan.

Duh, why am I always this dumb? What made me think it was a weekday? As my self-questioning goes on, I spot the culprit standing right there on my night table—the abominable alarm clock. Why the hell did it wake me on a Saturday? I never—and I swear never—turn on my alarm clock on weekends. I mean, sleeping in is the best part of the weekend, so why…

Bizzzzzt.

The doorbell rings, interrupting my train of thought. Who's at my door this early on a Saturday morning? Surely it's not going to be any of my friends; they all went away on a couples' weekend. I was supposed to go, but I wasn't really in the mood for being the only single person in a romantic cabin lost in the woods amidst three perfect examples of fairytale-like happily ever after. Of course, in that moment, *that* seemed the worst possible scenario for me. I certainly didn't foreshadow what heinous threats would await me in the city.

Why didn't I go? Anything would have been better. *Anything*. Now I wouldn't be in so much pain; I would still be in oblivious bliss. Well, ok… I still wouldn't exactly be in very high spirits, but at least I would not find myself in desperate, hopeless awareness! What do they say? What the eye doesn't see, the heart doesn't grieve over, right?

Anyhow, back to present. Who can it possibly be? No one ever visits me unexpectedly. I don't have intruding neighbors. The landlord never shows up, unless of course, you're late with the rent (even if it's merely by one day and definitely a genuine mistake on your part, as you forgot there are only twenty-eight days in February). And the handyman is a fugitive in hiding, unfindable for the life of you… so, who's left? Awk, I gasp. Could it be…? My stomach does a double flip. No, I won't even allow myself to go there. Those things only happen in movies, not real life…

Bizzzzzt. Bizzzzzt. Bizzzzzzzzzzzzt.

The buzzer goes off again in such an annoying way that any hope that might've been rising in my heart is promptly dissipated as only one person in the world could think that buzzing people this way is funny. My mom.

Now it all comes back to mind. Why my alarm clock was on, and another reason why I said no to the weekend gateway. I promised my mom to accompany her to the flea market. The flea market? Really? Am I in this state of misery for a stupid flea market?

I ponder telling her that I'm not well and that I don't want to go. But if I do, she will come up anyway to check on me and she will plant herself in my apartment for the rest of the day. I should just go, be done with it in a couple of hours, and have the rest of the weekend for myself.

I get up, crawl all the way to my tiny entry hall, and push the intercom button.

"Hi Mom, did you find any parking?"

"Hello, dear. Yes, I got lucky. I've found one of those two-hour off-street parking spots."

I live near Lincoln Park on the north side of Chicago, finding an available car spot on the street is a rare stroke of luck.

"Great. I'll be down in just a sec."

"Do you want me to come up?"

"Actually, I didn't have time to make coffee, so would you mind going to the Starbucks across the street and getting it for the both of us? I'll meet you there."

"Ahhh, always trying to get any second of sleep you can, huh? Alright, don't keep me waiting too long."

"No, Mom, I just need five minutes. I promise."

Since I'm nowhere near ready, the second I release the buzzer button I rush back into my room to dress at top speed. My mom was right in saying I always try to sleep until the last minute; I'm definitely not a morning person. On the bright side, after years of waking up late, I've acquired the useful skill of being able to get ready as fast as the flutter of a butterfly's wing. Anyway, the coffee shop across the street is always super busy on Saturdays, so it will take her at least fifteen minutes to order, pay, and for the coffees to be ready, which is plenty of time for me.

I select my favorite pair of stretch jeans, a classic plain white T-shirt, and an old pair of Converse. This is one of my all-time favorite casual looks; it makes me always look good and never goes out of style. I don't have time for a full shower, so I quickly wash my face and other body parts, brush my teeth, and arrange my brown hair in a bubble bun. A small, ridiculously poor-looking bun, as my hair is so thin that not even folding my ponytail over twice accomplishes much of a volume. I don't have the time to do a sock bun, which usually helps a little.

Of course, Vanessa has great hair! Long, silky, *and* voluminous. Bitch! Oh, forget her! I'll deal with her later. Mmm, deodorant, a bit of perfume, clothes, shoes… et voilà, I'm ready to go.

"Meeeoowww." Oops, just one more thing to do. I select one of Sugar's premium feline meals and serve it to the prince of the house who shows his appreciation by purring loudly.

Before exiting, I grab my maxi bag and the biggest pair of sunglasses I own to try to conceal my puffy eyes. I don't hope to maintain the secret from my mom for very long because she's going to notice. Somehow, she always does. I just want to postpone the interrogation for after coffee.

As I shut my building's heavy glass door behind me, I spot my mom coming out of the coffee shop holding two big cups in her hands and looking around for me. Despite the situation, a big smile spreads across my lips and a surge of affection rises in my chest. I love my mom. I wave and run toward her. We hug tight, and I gladly take my cappuccino.

"Darling, what's wrong? Have you been crying? Something happened?" she immediately fires worried questions at me.

Ouch, I should've known I didn't stand a chance, not even for five minutes.

"No, Mom, I'm ok. Don't worry," I state unconvincingly.

"So you haven't been crying?"

"Yes. I mean, no! I don't know."

"You don't know?" She is silent for a moment. Then she sighs, deeply inhales, and asks the question. "Is it still about James?"

I flinch at the "still" in her question and say nothing in response, bracing myself for what's coming next; something I've already heard not just from my mom, but pretty much from everyone I know. In fact, here it comes pronto.

"Sweetheart, it's been more than a year. I know it has been hard, but the time has passed for you to move on."

I keep my silent treatment going.

"You are young, smart, and beautiful—you will find someone else. You just have to stop thinking he was the only one for you. It's just silly. The world is full of—"

And here I snap.

"I am not silly," I almost shout. "He was the love of my life—he is the love of my life. You don't forget the love of your life. Not in a year, not even in ten years. You never forget. NEVER!"

It's her turn to be quiet. After my little outburst, we walk in silence until we reach the car.

"I'm sorry, darling." She stands beside her door, not opening it. "I didn't mean to say you were silly or to hurt your feelings."

"No, Mom, I'm sorry. I didn't mean to snap that way. It's just that everybody keeps telling me how I should feel... and well, I just feel the way I feel, and I can't do anything about it."

"Ok, I will not do it again. But would you please tell me what happened this time? Did you see him?"

"Yes, I did see him."

"How was he?"

"He had his hair shorter," I reply evasively.

His soft curls were no longer visible, a pang of longing crosses my chest. She probably had him cut it.

"Did you talk?"

"No, he was... he was busy," I say, my voice slightly cracking.

Silence on both sides. She's giving me time to elaborate.

"Was he with a woman?" she finally asks, when I don't offer anything further.

"Mm-hmm."

"Do you know her?"

"Yes," I confirm. "And that's the worst part—I don't just know her. I see her every day and I hate her!"

"Oh hush, darling, you don't hate anyone. It's such a horrible thing to say. And just because this person is going out with James, it doesn't mean you have to have all this, well… animosity for her."

"Oh, Mom! Would you please stop being ever trusting in humanity? Not everyone deserves the benefit of the doubt. And Vanessa most certainly doesn't!"

"Vanessa? Not that nice girl you work with."

"See, this is exactly what I'm talking about," I say, exasperated. "She isn't nice, or sweet, or even polite… she just pretends to be. She's pure evil, and I hated her way before I saw her with James!" She winces at the word "hate." "Yes, Mom, hate. Because that's what it is."

"I find that hard to believe. When we met her, she seemed so genuine."

"Well, yes, she's very good at pretending," I reiterate.

"What did you do when you saw them?"

"I panicked," I admit, flushing. "I froze in the middle of the street, turned around, and ran away."

"Did they see you?"

"I'm pretty sure *she* did."

"So, is there something serious between them?" Mom asks.

"Mmm… that, I don't know. But I'm sure she'll fill me in first thing Monday, enjoying every minute of it," I whine. "And she's going to flaunt it in my face every single day after that. She has already tried, only I hadn't noticed because I didn't know."

"Oh darling, I am sure she can't be that bad."

"Mom, haven't you been paying attention?" I ask rhetorically. "I told you she's a wolf in sheep's clothing."

"Ah well, anyway, what do you plan on doing, sweetheart?"

"I don't know yet, Mom, and I don't want to think about it right now. Can we just enjoy the market and not talk about it anymore?"

"Sweetie, I'm sure everything will turn out all right," she says with a big, loving smile, finally opening the car for us to get inside and head toward the market.

Two

A Little Coffer

We are going to the Randolph Street Market, a European-style indoor and outdoor antique market located in the historic West Loop neighborhood of Chicago. It is one of the largest and liveliest urban antiques market in the USA. My mom adores it.

We don't say much on the ride there. I stare out of the window most of the time, admiring the skyline of my city, which I never tire of. Upon spotting the rusty elevated railroad of the central line, I also think I am glad Mom came with her car so I don't have to use public transportation... at least for one day. Traffic is not too bad and we get there in good time. Luckily, there's a cheap valet service, which means we won't need to circle around for an hour to find a spot or pay thirty dollars for a two-hour stop.

"So Mom, what do we need to find today?" I ask her as we exit the car.

"Well," she answers, while handing over the keys to the valet, "I need to find a corner wrought-iron rack for my vases. With different layers like a stair, but sort of rounded."

I take her arm under mine and we jump into the search of the numerous stands displaying all kinds of antiques. The market is bursting full of people and sounds. There are some vendors shouting to attract the attention of passers-by, others vivaciously negotiating with their customers, and the general chitchat of shoppers enjoying the market's colorful display on this sunny day. A live band is playing traditional bluegrass music on a side stage, adding more verve to the already kinetic-energy filled environment.

Weird and wonderful treasures may hide in this labyrinth of objects from all eras, but a lot of it just looks like heaps of rags and old junk for sale. We pass a giant stand completely covered

I WISH FOR YOU

in mounds of bric-à-brac, porcelains, vases, plates, and, to my utmost disgust, even an old chipped chamber pot. It was no doubt something used by royalty given the evident finery, but it's still a used chamber pot. Ewww.

Despite this, the more we walk around, the more I am enticed by the atmosphere of this place. My skepticism begins to evaporate, leaving me free to feel the pull of all these objects, of the lives that have been lived in them. Moving forward, I get more and more fascinated by the diverse array of vintage fashion, art, fresh flowers galore, jewelry, and decor stalls showcasing eclectic artwork and crafts. I am particularly taken by an old rusty booth displaying antique charcoal sketches. It transports me into a bohemian Paris, so I spend a long time leafing through them, imagining the secret history behind each one together with my mom.

After that, we wander around for about an hour. We have fun deriding the vast selection of plaster Snow Whites, old scratched toys, and various knick-knacks, and admiring the magnificent display of wood furniture, vintage accessories, and art from the fifties—one of my favorite decades.

As we're walking, a movement of the crowd separates me from my mom, pushing me against a cart of used shoes and her toward a lopsided scaffold acting as a stage for a bunch of colorful, old-fashioned furniture. This place is way too packed for me. I am becoming all sweaty and sticky, which is even less to my taste.

"Mom!" I shout. "I am moving over there to the side lane."

"Okay!" she shouts back, "I just want to have a look there." She points at the rear end of the furniture stall.

I give her the thumbs-up and push my way out of the crowd. When I finally manage to disentangle myself from the coils of this anaconda of humanity, I spot a drinking fountain at the end of one of the lateral alleys and head there. In my present overheated status, it appears as inviting as an oasis in the desert.

I reach it with a few quick steps and quaff as much fresh water as I can without choking.

I already feel much refreshed, and since there is nothing else to do, I slowly find my way back to the uncongested part of the market. As I poke around lazily, looking for an unknown object, two men are bargaining over an old fire fender, the bygone music of a lost opera plays from an ancient phonograph being tested, and the air seems infused with a mystical atmosphere.

I am attracted by the smallest stand. A very old lady is sitting behind it in a rocking chair, an odd hat obscuring her face almost completely. On each side of the stand are two vertical panels, and dangling from them is the most amazing collection of bizarre objects. The horizontal surface of the cart is covered by an amazing array of cute little boxes; jewelry cases, I think. I am particularly drawn to one, and I grab it to have a better look. It's made of some kind of metal, maybe brass. It's really shiny and beautiful, all carved with small opaque stones attached on each side and a roundish, protruding grip on the top.

"I see you have been chosen!" the old lady says out of the blue with a shrill, croaky voice.

She startles me so much that I almost drop the little case.

"You are a very lucky young woman, my dear," she continues, standing up. She seems completely unaware of my recent distress. "After today, your life will be changed forever."

"Mmm, yes. Sorry, I was just looking," I say, putting back the box.

This old lady must be nuts.

"Oh no, no. This will not do! It chose you, now it is yours," she insists.

"Eh. No, really, I was just poking around. I don't want to buy anything, thanks."

"Nonsense, nonsense, my dear." She shakes her head vigorously while retrieving the little box from the cart and offers it to me again, outstretching her arms in front of me with a pleading expression.

Her face is a crisscross of deep wrinkles that give her such an air of frailty that she's making me feel sorry for her. I begin to think it would be easier to just buy the damn thing and be done with it. Granny here is either wacky, or she has the best selling strategy I've ever seen. I am about to ask her how much it is when I am saved by my phone ringing. I grab it from inside my maxi bag and answer right away. It's Mom.

"Sweetie, you have to come and help me," she says. "I've found my rack, but I need you to carry it out of here."

"Where are you, Mom?"

"Still at the furniture stall—do you remember how to get here?"

"Yeah, sure. I'll be there in a sec."

"Sorry, I have to run. Maybe next time," I say to Granny, glad Mom gave me a real excuse to escape.

I wave goodbye, turn around, and step away before she can trap me again. She mumbles something after me, but with all the surrounding noise I am already too far away to hear what it is… and, honestly, I don't care.

***

By the time I get back home it is already six in the evening. Mom insisted on having lunch together after the market, which took longer than I expected, and after lunch, I had forgotten I had a hair appointment, to which I added a mani-pedi and some beauty product shopping. I decided to load my weapons for Monday and at least try to appear my best, even if I feel the opposite inside.

Overall, the day went a lot better than I would have anticipated this morning. Well, except for nagging thoughts of James and Vanessa occasionally creeping on me unexpectedly and knocking the air out of my lungs, leaving me breathless for a second or two every time.

When I finished with the pampering, it was already five-ish, and since I had no intention of cooking tonight, I went to my favorite Chinese takeout and grabbed some dinner to enjoy at home in sad loneliness. So, right now I am entering my apartment with my steaming to-go order in one hand, a huge bag of beauty products in the other, and I'm just about ready to sag back into darkness and self-commiseration. I deposit the food on the kitchen countertop and drop my maxi bag on the floor where it lands with a heavy thud.

Damn, my shoulder is sore! I must stop carrying everything around in my purse. I promise myself I will do an inventory check after dinner to see if there's something I can take out. After changing into some comfy clothes, I decide to eat at the bar of my L-shaped open kitchen. I set all the little white food containers on it and pull out two stools, one for me and one for Sugar. Once I break my chopsticks, I am ready to start.

I share the occasional shrimp or chicken treat with my furry friend, who is thrilled whenever he gets to eat my food… or human food in general. I don't know why; does he feel more involved? I should study feline psychology. Once he has had his fill, he strolls away to drink some water from his pet fountain. I know, he's spoiled rotten. He then disappears, probably to find a soft spot to sleep. Sometimes I wish I were a house cat; their life seems far more uncomplicated.

After just a few minutes of peace, I hear worrying meowing and clinging sounds coming from behind the counter. I lean forward to check what's going on, only to find that the little pest has scattered the contents of my bag all over the place and is enthusiastically playing with it. Quite the opposite of sleeping. My feline empathy is off today. In particular, he is attacking a little bundle that I don't recognize.

I hurry around the kitchen island to salvage whatever it is that Sugar is butchering and snatch it away. To my utter

I WISH FOR YOU

surprise, I find myself holding a small, nicely wrapped package whose origin is a complete mystery to me. I weigh the enigmatic parcel in my hands for a while before unwrapping it. It is quite heavy; no wonder my shoulder was so sore! What could it possibly be? I carefully undo the cover, recognizing immediately what lies beneath. It's the jewelry case from the flea market; the one the creepy old lady insisted I should buy.

This is impossible! I didn't buy it, and sure enough, I didn't steal it. I perfectly remember putting it back on the stand and then running away to catch up with Mom. The old lady was never near enough to drop it in my bag, nor would she have had the time to wrap it so carefully. Then what?

Ugh! Now I'll have to go back to the market tomorrow and try to explain it all to Granny. Just what I needed!

Well, nothing I can do about it now. I am just going to finish my Chinese food, not thinking about stupid boxes magically materializing in my bag. But honestly, how can you not think about an ancient-looking little box that has magically materialized in your bag? It is impossible! I quit trying at once. I set aside my unfinished food and begin my examination of the object.

It certainly is very nice and, judging from the quality of its embellishments, very old. The metal is cold to the touch and has a golden shine to it, but it can't be solid gold! I peek at it more closely. The stones that appeared opaque this morning now seem changed; they are almost translucent. Someone must've cleaned this thing. Probably the same someone who put it in my bag.

I wrap my fingers around the little knob at the top, undecided. Finally, I gather my courage and open it. I gasp as I see... nothing. It's empty! Well, what was I expecting? I am being silly right now; even my heart is beating faster for no reason at all.

I close it again, turn it around in my hands a couple of times, and play a little with the knob on top, which suddenly turns producing a loud click. I study it for a second; the little knob seems to be attached to some sort of gear mechanism on the lid. I lift the cover again.

Argh! A nasty puff of dust just blew in my face, almost choking me. This is what I get for fooling with obscure objects I shouldn't have in the first place. Where did that dust come from? It wasn't there a second ago.

I need some water to ease the itchiness in my throat. I'm heading to the fridge when something odd catches my attention out of the corner of my eye. An even louder gasp escapes my lips when I turn around to check and find a man comfortably settled on the living room sofa. I don't know if I am more stunned by the fact that there is a stranger sitting on my couch, by how he is dressed, or by the fact that he must be the most gorgeous man I've ever seen.

He has dark, chin-length hair, deep blue eyes, and a fair complexion. He is sitting, but I can tell he's tall. *Very* tall. He must have some sort of costume on because he looks like an English gentleman from the eighteenth century.

The man is wearing a double-breasted dark blue tailcoat with large gilt buttons that are unbuttoned. The coat opens on a figured silk vest that is tightly fastened over a white and perfectly ironed and starched high-collared shirt, which is complemented by a creamy silk knotted cravat. His pants are a pair of tight fall-front breeches made of pale yellow buckskin that have an orderly line of three covered buttons at the knee. His footwear consists of black leather Hessian boots adorned with golden tassels. As if this wasn't enough, he's fully accessorized with black gloves, a gold-mounted cane, and a black top hat.

I am so dumbfounded that when I open my mouth to speak, nothing comes out, so I close it. I try to speak again, but nothing happens. I must look like a fish underwater. Now I understand when they say how fear can completely paralyze you. He stands up, and I instinctively withdraw until my back is pressed against the fridge. He really is tall, at least six feet two.

"My lady," he announces, "I am deeply sorry if I have startled you. May I introduce myself?" Then he bows. Yes, a full gentlemanlike bow.

"So you *are* British." It's all I can come up with when I find it in me to speak.

"That would be technically correct. However, I would rather be addressed as English, if you please," he states with extreme politeness, coming toward me.

"Stay where you are." I try to make it sound like an order, but it came out more like a plea.

"As you bid, milady," he says, sitting back on the couch.

"Who the hell are you?" I ask, exasperated.

"Arthur, your most humble servant. Pleased to meet you, my lady."

"Lady who? How did you get into my apartment?"

"I believe you summoned me."

"I didn't summon anyone!"

"Did you not turn the Wheel of Destiny and open the Coffer of Fortune?"

"I didn't turn any destiny thingy, or open any fortune widget," I say angrily. "Listen, I've no idea who you are or what you're talking about. I just think you're some kind of weird lunatic dressed funny who somehow has broken into my apartment." Admittedly, a very good-looking lunatic.

Ally, get a grip. Ogling psychotic burglars… Have I sunk so low?

"But the Coffer of Fortune is right next to you!" he protests, pointing at the jewelry case.

"What are you saying? That by opening this stupid thing, I somehow magically summoned you to my apartment?"

"That would be accurate."

"And why exactly?"

"I am enslaved to the coffer and eternally cursed to grant the wishes of its owner."

"Ah, well. You should have said so in the first place. Now it all makes perfect sense. You're the genie of the lamp, arrived here to grant my wishes," I say ironically.

"Djinn are merely a myth, ancient legends created by men in the hope of—"

"Enough hocus pocus for me!" I briskly interrupt him. "I don't know who you are or what you want, but I am asking you to leave right now or I'll call the police!" I grab my phone and dial 911.

"Oh, I am most apologetic. Were you planning on visiting someone tonight? This police friend of yours? Have I made you late?"

"You are completely crazy! This is the last time I ask you nicely. Please get out of my house now!"

"My lady, the only way you can rid of me is by letting me grant your wishes."

"I've had enough of this—I am calling the police!" I press the green button on my phone.

"911, what is the nature of your emergency?" a metallic voice comes from the speaker.

"I see I have to resort to extreme measures," the lunatic says.

"Hello, my name is—" I begin to say.

BANG!

My living room is transformed into an African desert. The hardwood floor has been replaced with high dunes of fine, warm sand that my feet start sinking into. The furniture is gone, the kitchen is gone, even the walls are gone. I am standing in my PJs in the middle of the freaking Sahara. I gape at the view astonished, my mouth dangling open. The English gentleman is quietly sitting cross-legged on my couch, nonchalantly rotating his cane in the air, except the couch is now positioned atop an orange sand dune. Poor Sugar is meowing pitifully while he struggles to climb up a sand pile, leaving a trail of small paw prints behind him.

I look back at the stranger who is eying me from under his cylinder hat with an amused, challenging smirk.

"Miss, I am sorry I didn't get your name." The metallic voice comes from my phone, which I'm still solidly clenching in my right hand. Still mesmerized, I press end.

"Ok. You've made your point," I say, still a bit dazed. "By the way, I'm Ally," I add, as an incredulous smile spreads on my lips. "Ally Johnson."

"Very pleased to meet you, Miss Johnson."

Three
Rules

I am super excited. This is the most incredible thing that has ever happened to me. Some extra supernatural powers are exactly what I needed right now, and the timing is perfect. Then again, who wouldn't like some magic solution to all their problems?

I detach myself from the fridge and move into the living room, still feeling some sand grains slipping among my toes. Sugar escaped out of sight the moment my apartment went back to normal. Poor baby, he must be stressed. I, on the other hand, am hardly able to contain myself. I have so many things to ask my new magical friend. What was his name? Ah yes, Arthur.

He hasn't moved from his comfortable position on my sofa, and he seems impatient. In fact, as soon as I sit in the armchair in front of him, he starts talking in a matter-of-fact tone, as if nothing particularly out of the ordinary has happened.

"Now that your initial resistance is overcome, Miss Johnson, we need to discuss rules," he says. He takes off his hat and gloves and places them carefully on the empty seat next to him.

"Wait a minute, slow down. What rules? I have like a million other questions."

"All your questions will find an answer in due time."

"But I want to know now!" I protest. "Like, are genies the only magical creatures? Or are there also vampires, werewolves, elves, gargoyles, fairies, witches?"

"There are no such things."

"So the lady at the flea market wasn't a witch?"

"I do not believe so."

"But she knew about the box and she put it in my bag."

"The coffer has its own ways—the lady you are talking about was probably under its magical influence."

"So you are the only magical creature in the whole world?"

"I believe I am the last one, yes."

"Last one? How many were there? What kind?"

"It is a matter of little importance at present," he states curtly, flaring his nostrils in annoyance. "Miss Johnson, I feel obliged to explain the instructions you have to follow first," he continues. "I judge it might be wiser to do it at once, before dwelling on other things. Will you please allow me?"

"Oh, that. Don't worry, I already know everything. I aroused the genie so I get three wishes—no killing, no resuscitating the dead, and no love spells. I saw the cartoon."

"I am not aware of what a cartoon is, and as I explained before, I am not a Djinni."

"What are you, then?"

"I don't presume to fit in any particular category, milady."

"Are you at least human?"

"I was human once, and I am in human form presently. However, it is not worthwhile to bore you with my history," he adds politely.

Mmm, it's not for *my* sake he doesn't want to talk about his story. So I drop the subject for now, but I will get to the bottom of it, eventually.

"Okay, but since you will not tell me anything, I'll keep calling you Genie."

"I do not suppose you could call me by my given name."

"Tsk, no. Too boring."

"I foresee you are going to be one of the difficult ones."

"Why, how many have there been before me?"

"Many."

"*How* many?"

"May we delay the interrogation for a more convenient time and keep our interests focused?"

"Okay," I give in reluctantly. "But only for now."

"Marvellous. Shall we get started?" he asks hopefully.

"Okay. So do I get three wishes?"

"No. You do not."

"That's not fair. The one time I get a genie I don't get three wishes. Why do I always have to get crappy deals?" I whine, disappointed.

"I do not believe this is suitable language for a lady," he says with contempt.

"What century are you from?" I retort. "There is no more aristocracy rubbish in this one."

"To this purpose, I meant to ask. Pray, tell me what century is it now?"

"Twenty-first," I answer curtly.

"Blimey!" he exclaims, utterly bewildered. "I have never been absent for so long—more than two centuries! I need to query—Did Napoleon lose the war?"

"Napoleon? How old are you?"

"Considerably old compared to the typical human life. Many hundreds of years."

"I guess there'd be no point in asking how many exactly."

"I would prefer to amuse myself with your curiosity for a little longer."

"And *I* am supposed to be the difficult one."

"I admit I can be pretty stubborn myself," he concedes.

"You don't say."

"Hmm, so has he won or lost?" he asks again.

"Communication is a two-way channel—you tell me something, I tell you something. Tell me how old you are, and I'll tell you everything about Napoleon."

He seems torn between the two options, pondering a little longer before announcing his decision. "I think it best we leave idle topics for later. There are a few things you had better be aware of."

"All right," I surrender. "Go ahead, tell me all I need to know."

"Very well—very well, indeed. First of all, I am going to grant you five desires."

"Five! Whoa! That's awesome. It's—"

"However, some restrictions apply."

He seems quite exasperated by my constant questions and interruptions. Maybe I'll just be good and sit here nice and quiet.

"There are rules that cannot be contravened," He keeps going. "I usually prefer my charges to write them down."

"No, don't worry. My memory is good."

"If you cannot write, there is nothing to be ashamed of. I can write them down for you. Are you at least able to read?"

"What?" I shout back, affronted. "Of course I can write! What do you think I am, some kind of illiterate, ignorant person?"

"Please accept my deepest apologies, Miss Johnson—it pains me to have offended you. In my last era, it was not unusual for common people to be analphabets, and since your house does not appear to be of much stature, I simply assumed—"

"Let me be perfectly clear," I cut him short. "I'm not sure what kind of grandeur you're used to, but insulting a person's house is not a great way to apologize, not even to common people." I totally air-quoted common people.

I then get up with the most indignant face I can master and go to fetch a notepad and a pen. Once I have them, I return to the living room and sit down again, maintaining an air of high countenance.

"Are you ready, milady?" he asks with extreme politeness and a perfect poker face.

I suspect he's having fun at my expense.

"Yes!" I say acidly.

"Let us commence, then. As you already said, I do not kill, I do not resuscitate the dead, and I cannot make someone fall in love. But also be advised that I cannot make people fall out of love."

"What do you mean?" I ask, confused.

"Let us imagine, for example, that you were in love with a man, and that this man was in love with another woman."

He makes an infinite pause and observes me with a knowing stare that makes me very uncomfortable. As I start awkwardly shifting positions in my chair, he resumes his explanation.

"I simply could not dissipate said sentiment, as true love is sacred and it is not to be tampered with."

"Ok, no falling out of love," I repeat as indifferently as I can, scribbling it down on my notepad.

"You cannot ask for extra wishes."

"Yep, pretty basic," I say, unimpressed.

"All wishes must concern you in some way or another."

"That is to say…?"

"For example, you could not wish for Napoleon to lose the war. By the bye, has he lost?"

"Yes, he *has* lost! He died alone in exile and misery. Are you satisfied?"

"Ah, ah. I knew old Wellington would take him down." He laughs contentedly. "But back to us. Where was I?"

"Wishes must be self-centered." Not bad, this one; no one can accuse me of being selfish for not asking for world peace. "Wait a second, does this mean that I can only use magic on myself? Or I can use it on others as well?"

"As long as you do not break any rule, you can use your wishes as you see fit."

"But if I can use it on others as well, how do you determine if a wish is about me or not?" I ask, a bit puzzled.

"Let's say, for example, that one of your dear ones was challenged to a mortal duel."

"Not very likely these days," I say.

"Likely or not," he continues, unfussed, "you could wish for that person to win the duel, or not to get injured or die during it. On the other hand, if he was a soldier you could wish for him to never die in battle. However, you could not wish for no one to ever get wounded or die in a duel ever again, or for wars to have no more casualties. The magic has to affect you in some way or other."

"Mmm. So, for example, could I wish for my best friend to have smaller boobs, like right now?" I am not being a bitch here; she hates her abundant D size, even though her boyfriend would probably kill me if I did something like that.

"I am not exactly sure what boobs are. Anyhow, to make anything happen to someone else you need to be in their proximity. But in theory, yes, you would be able to express that sort of wish even if it does not involve you directly because it is about someone you know."

"Makes sense. Anyway, I'll have you as a consultant if I'm ever in doubt. Anything else?"

"Ah, yes. You cannot ask for immortality."

"Oh, I hadn't thought of that, but it sucks!"

"Trust me, eternity can be very tiring," he comments mysteriously.

I want to ask him to tell me more, but there's no point, so I patiently wait for him to re-start with his list of rules.

"No time travelling."

"But why?" I complain, disappointed. I've always been fascinated with the past and, lately, obsessed with the future. Time traveling was definitely going to be one of my wishes. Stupid rules!

"Actually, it is very simple. Time only exists in the present—it comes and goes in the blink of an eye, leaving no vestige to come back to."

"Whatever." I shrug, annoyed.

"This also means you cannot ask to learn the future or to travel there. It has not happened yet, thus it does not exist."

Go figure. I make a face and add it to the list.

"Can I at least teleport myself?" I ask, struck by a sudden inspiration.

"From one place to another in the present? Yes, you may ask for that."

"So, could I also ask to teleport other people?"

"Yes, exactly—it is another good example. You may ask to have a particular ability and ask to be able to use it on others. As long as you are near them it would work."

"Cool! I'll think about it. If I was able to teleport myself, I could see the whole world. I would never have to take a plane ever again. Wow!"

"What is a plane?"

"A machine that flies."

He gives me a blank stare.

"With people inside," I further explain, "you know, to move from one place to the other faster."

"Mankind can *fly*?"

"Mm-hmm."

"How marvellous."

"Yep. Can we get back to my wishes now?" I ask eagerly.

"I am glad to have you interested at last."

"So, are the rules over? Can we start?"

"Hmm. No, they are not. A few more remain."

"Bummer. Go ahead, then."

I feel as if I were a child again. Whenever I had a new toy, especially if it was a cool electronic one, my dad wouldn't let me use it before we read the whole instruction manual. I couldn't wait to try my new game, but no, I had to listen to endless boring instructions instead. And here they keep coming.

"You cannot ask for all my powers."

"Ok."

"You cannot wish me free of my curse."

"Have you been cursed?" I stare up at him.

"Yes, as I told you before." His face becomes a mask of pain and regret.

"Sorry," I say sincerely. "I must've been over-excited by the whole situation. I didn't hear you. What happened? Who did it?"

"I do not wish to talk about it." His tone suggests that I'd better back off, but he can't just say something like that and then refuse to talk about it!

"Is the curse unbreakable, or can it be broken in some other way?"

"It *can* be broken somehow, but I most certainly was not told how."

"We could try to find a way, though, right?"

"I've tried before. Nothing has ever worked."

"That doesn't mean we have to stop trying."

"Trust me, it is a painful endeavour, made of false beliefs that never prove truthful."

"I'm sorry," I mumble. "It must've been hard for you. But we can stay positive and keep hoping. Something will come up, I'm sure."

"Hope is a good breakfast but a bad supper," he comments cynically, shaking his head at my optimism.

From his bitter tone, I get the impression that the topic, once again, is making him uncomfortable. I'm sure he will be more ready to open up once we get to know each other better, so I'll let it be for now. But I'm not giving up. If there's a way to free him, we just need to find it; he simply needs some faith.

"Genie—" I try to lighten the mood by changing the subject. "Can I give one of my wishes to someone else? I mean, as a gift?"

"Absolutely not, and this is the last rule." A note of strain is still audible in his words, but he seems relieved that the conversation has moved on. "You cannot speak to anyone about me, the wishes, or the coffer. It would make it all disappear the moment you voice your first word."

"Ugh! I hate to keep secrets, and I'm not very good at it, either," I grumble.

"I am afraid you will have to keep this one."

"But when I am done, can I pass the coffer on to someone else and make them discover its secret?" I ask hopefully. "This way I would not need to break any rule. I wouldn't be telling anyone. Can I do that?"

"No, most definitely not."

"Why?"

"The coffer has its own will. When you are finished with it, it will go to whoever it sees fit. Ahem, here I was, thinking I had finally found my liberator... whereas you are already trying to hand me down like one of your possessions."

"I—" I blush vividly, looking down in mortification. "That's not what I... ummm..." I stutter. "I wasn't really... I mean, associating the two things in my head, I..." I look at him and see that he's messing with me; he's hardly suppressing a grin. "Oh, forget it!" I tell him, my face still very red.

Upon being discovered, the genie roars with laughter at my embarrassment. He's even more gorgeous when he's not sulking. I only wish it wasn't at my expense.

I look at him morosely. "Are you having fun?" I ask pointedly.

"Please excuse my incivility—I could not resist the temptation." He chuckles. Then, still grinning, he asks, "Is all that we discussed clear?"

I nod grudgingly and look down at my pad to do a mental recap.

RULES

No killing
No resuscitating the dead
No falling in or out love
No extra wishes
Wishes must be self-centered
Proximity rule for magic on others
No immortality
No time traveling :(
No future telling :(

Teleportation ok
No Genie superpowers
No freeing the genie
No telling anyone anything
No gifting the coffer
Note to self: investigate Genie's curse, age...

Even with all these stupid rules, I can still do a lot of damage. I smile in satisfaction, anticipating my first wish.

Four
Mirror, Mirror

I feel sorry for the genie. I mean, being cursed probably isn't easy. And he must have been really lonely, spending two hundred years alone in that box.

"Do you need to eat, sleep, take a shower, or whatever?" I ask him, trying to be nice.

"I am very fond of eating and drinking, indeed. However, I've been dormant for two hundred years, so I am not in a hurry to rest," he replies matter-of-factly. "Anyhow, why would I be in need of a rainstorm?"

"A rainstorm?" I repeat, perplexed.

"You asked if I needed to *take* a shower."

"I meant to wash yourself," I explain, rolling my eyes. "Like taking a bath."

"That would be most refreshing if it is not too much trouble to warm the water."

"The water comes out already warm."

"From the well?"

"No, from the in-house plumbing. I'll show you later." I drop the issue. "Do you need to eat? I have some Chinese leftovers."

"Chinese?" he asks, skeptical.

"You know, I don't have a horde of cooks to prepare you delicacies."

"Nothing to worry about—I can conjure food in case of need."

"So you can use magic even if I don't wish for anything?"

"For minor things, yes, I can."

"Minor things like what?"

"Food, for example."

"Gosh, you are infuriating, you know?" This is the last time I try to be friendly with him. "I should kick that British derriere of yours."

"I would not attempt such a thing if I were you."

"Why?" I challenge him. "Will you kick back?"

"No, I would never lay hands on a woman. But, I should advise you not to touch me when we are alone. I have been told it could prove a most unpleasant ordeal."

"Like what?" I ask, and impulsively reach for his arm.

My fingertips freeze on the spot, and the most gelid shiver passes through my entire body. I retrieve my hand as quickly as I can, blowing on it to warm it. It was like touching liquid ice and having it soak underneath my skin.

It takes me five good minutes to stop trembling. Definitely an experience not to repeat.

"That was horrible!" I say as soon as my teeth stop chattering.

"I did warn you." He gives me the eighteenth century's version of "I told you so."

"Nothing could have warned me of that! Anyway, I need something hot. Would you like some infusion? Or do you only drink tea? 'Cause I don't have it," I retort nastily.

"Not to worry, I can make my own," he replies smugly.

This genie of the box is really annoying. I should just wish my wishes and get rid of him.

"So, how does this work?" I ask, purposely changing the subject. As I start to clatter with the pots in my kitchen, I add, "Can people see you? Hear you? Or am I the only one?"

"It depends. Actually, it is for you to decide. There will be circumstances in which you'll need me with you, but not visible to others. And vice versa."

"Mmm, good. And will you look like this…?" I ask, circling my index in the air around him. "When you are visible to others?"

"That is also for you to decide. I mostly prefer to go around as myself, but I can assume any human form you will need me to," he replies tensely.

"Ok. And when you are visible to others if someone touches you will they freeze to death?" I want to make sure none of my loved ones will experience the bone-chilling touch. I am barely recovering from it now, thanks to the soothing warmth of my honey-vanilla chamomile.

"No, they will not."

"And if I touch you in public? Do I still get to freeze?"

"No, you do not."

"So why can't I touch you right now?"

"It is a rule."

"A very stupid one! Why should I risk freezing to death if I bump into you by mistake?"

"It was put in place to avoid improper interactions."

"What improper interactions?"

"You know… the romantic kind."

"Yikes, no chance in hell. No offense." He's really attractive, but personality-wise I don't like him one bit.

"None taken."

"Since we're clear on this point, can we change this rule?"

"I am afraid not."

"That's crazy. Who's deciding all these rules, anyway?"

"The same person who cursed me," he replies gloomily.

Oh no, oh no. Back off, reverse gear. We have a funereal suffering face again. I'd better change the subject quickly to avoid further mood-worsening.

"Anything else I need to know?" I ask.

"Yes. As I am your servant, you may command me to return to the coffer and summon me again when necessary." He still sounds rattled.

"Aha! So I can get rid of you anytime I want?"

"Yes, you may." His reply is strained.

Okay, not the best of times for jokes.

"Don't worry, I'm not evil. I'm not going to do that, I promise." I smile, trying to soothe him.

He doesn't say anything, but he seems relieved.

"Very well, now that we've sorted out all the boring stuff, can I express my first wish?"

"I beg your pardon?" he asks, surprised. "Do you not need at least a night of rest before you decide?"

"Oh no, I've wanted this all of my life—I don't need to think about it for a minute longer. I want to be able to shapeshift like Mystique in *X-Men*!"

"Forgive me, I am quite at a loss here. I do not know what you mean."

"Wait, wait." I am too excited to pay him any attention. "I also wish to make others change if I want it."

"I dare say I do not quite understand your desire, Miss Johnson. I do not happen to be acquainted with this Lady Mystique you are referring to. Anyway, there is a procedure to follow in order to—"

"Oooh, you know nothing! Why couldn't I get an up-to-date genie?"

"I apologise for being such a disappointment to you, milady. I—"

"Don't get all touchy with me again." I cut him off. "Just tell me what I have to do."

"I was not about to—"

"Stop whining and tell me the procedure." I air-quote *procedure*.

"Very well," he replies, still offended. "All you have to do is to state clearly what your desire is and pronounce the incantation *Avra Kehdabra*."

"Abracadabra, really? Are you messing with me?" I ask, very skeptical.

"Not Abracadabra, *Avra Kehdabra*. These are very ancient words, never to be disparaged. They behold immemorial powers."

"Abracadabra?"

"Avra Kehdabra! It means 'I will create as I speak.' Please be serious about this—it is of the utmost importance. You have to *believe* the words for them to work."

"Okay, okay. No need to get all worked up. I am very serious. Can you repeat it one more time?"

"Avra Kehdabra."

"Abrakedabra."

"Avra Kehdabra."

"Avrakedabra."

"It is two words. Avra…"

"Avra."

"Kehdabra."

"Kedabra."

"Almost. Try to pronounce it like me. Kehdabra."

"Kehdabra."

"Good! Now the two together. Avra Kehdabra."

"Avra Kehdabra."

"Perfect!"

"Uh-uh." I clap my hands happily.

"Now you may proceed and express your wish. Remember, state what you desire and immediately after, say 'Avra Kehdabra.'"

"Avra Kehdabra. Okay, I've got it. Can I go?"

"Yes."

"Crap, this is more stressing than I thought." I shake my hands forcefully to try to calm down. "Okay. Here I go. I wish to have the power to change my body and others' as well, whenever I want, in any way I want, just by thinking about it. Avra Kehdabra."

CLINK.

"What was that? Did I do it right?"

"Yes, you did. That was the little wheel on the coffer turning—it will do so for every wish you express."

"Come with me," I say in a shrill voice.

I WISH FOR YOU

I am so impatient I am about to drag him by the arm, except that I remember the horrible shivering that would come from it. So I signal for him to follow me instead. I almost run to my room and start peeling off my clothes in an excited frenzy.

"Oh," he exclaims, visibly reddening when he joins me. "I apologise, milady. I didn't mean to intrude on your privacy."

"Don't be silly, Genie, come in!" I beckon him to enter the room. "Don't tell me you're shy. You seem to be blushing a little."

"I am most certainly not blushing, I simply did not anticipate that you were about to show me your nudities."

"Oh, come on! You must have seen a woman in a bikini before... *or not*. Anyway, in this century this—" I say, pointing at my underwear, "is a perfectly appropriate attire, at least for the beach."

I position myself expectantly in front of my wardrobe that is perfect for the task, having two huge, mirrored sliding doors and a line of spotlights on top of it, which I turn on.

"Your lamps are truly luminous," the genie says. "What kind of oil do they utilise?"

"Oil?" I ask, puzzled. "These are electrical."

"Are you burning amber, then?"

"Amber? No! I'm not burning anything," I say, exasperated. I don't have the time for a physics class, plus I am not exactly an expert. "There are these little electron-thingies," I try to explain. "They run in the wire and make it become luminescent somehow."

He stares at me blankly.

"I'll update you on the modern world later," I say impatiently. "Tell me how this works. What should I do?"

"Ah, yes, yes. Of course."

He still seems a bit distracted by my lack of clothes, or is it the electricity thing? Who knows? I wonder if he still thinks like a man, if he has the same longings...

"All you have to do is concentrate," he explains, "and visualise what you want."

"Just like that?"

"Yes."

"No more gibberish?"

"It is not gibberish. I beg you, these are ancient incantations toward which you need to pay the utmost respect."

"Whatever. Am I good to go?"

"Yes, just concentrate."

"Ah. Let's the fun begin." I stretch out like an athlete before an important game. "You can sit down if you want—this is going to take a while."

"Do not worry about me, milady, I crave a bit of a stretch myself."

"Okay, suit yourself. Here we go."

First of all: hair. I concentrate hard on the mirror. I want double the hair, double the thickness.

SWISH.

I feel a gentle prickle on my scalp, and WOW! It worked! I lean closer toward the mirror, still incredulous. This is the best! For the first time in my life, my hair isn't fine and limp, but lush and voluptuous. I can't stop running my hands through it. Let's make it even better.

I concentrate again, imagining my hair like those of models in TV commercials, all shiny and soft. Let's also make it an inch longer. Screw today's haircut, I can finally have long hair.

SWISH.

Split ends be banned.

SWISH.

"This is awesome," I say, beaming toward the genie.

"You appear radiant," he flatters me.

"Thank you." I make a small curtsy. "And this is just the beginning."

"I am glad you are enjoying yourself."

"Genie, it's amazing. Now, let's get rid of another kind of hair," I say enthusiastically.

I focus again on the mirror, picturing all the hair from my legs, arms, armpits, lips, and bikini-line, gone forever. Even the ingrown ones.

SWISH.

I feel the same warm prickle as before, but this time it's all over my body. I gently caress my skin. This is a dream come true! No more waxing, no more shaving, and no more ingrown hair that makes my legs a match for chicken skin. I sit on the bed to examine them better; they never looked this smooth, not even after an hour of torturous scrubbing. By the end of this, I am going to be perfect.

"Is hair such a vexation for you?"

"Ah, yes! It is—*was*—so annoying. But isn't it the same for men and having to shave every day?"

"Yes, yes indeed. I forgot how harassing it could get. I have not shaved for a long time, you see."

"So you get it. For girls it's the same, especially now. You'll understand the first time we go out. There's a lot more of skin showing these days compared to your time."

"I most definitely cannot wait to witness such a display."

"Back to me now, you wily old fossil. Let's get rid of all the cellulite as well." Not that I have much, but still.

Eyes on the mirror. I imagine my skin tight, smooth, spotless, and orange-peel-effect free.

SWISH.

"Ah, ah, ah." This time, the tingling is so universally spread that it makes me tickle badly.

"Is everything all right?"

"Yes, it was just a funny sensation," I reassure him.

Let's continue the hard work here.

"I want my eye circles gone."

SWISH.

"I want to lose five pounds."

SWISH.

"Wow! Let's make it seven."

SWISH.

"Super wow!"

"Satisfied?"

"This is the best! The best ever!"

Now I try to imagine how my body would look if I went to the gym every day.

SWISH.

Ouch! I went too muscular, and my body turned professional bodybuilder. I should tone it down a little.

"Hey, what do I do if I want to revoke my latest change?"

"Were you planning on boxing?" he replies, eying me, evidently amused.

"Can I go back or not?" I ask, quite alarmed at this point. I don't want to be a female version of Arnold Schwarzenegger for the rest of my life.

"Just think about yourself five seconds ago."

POOF.

I am back to my unmuscular self. Let's try this again. I concentrate, picturing a Gwyneth-Paltrow-in-Iron-Man-III kind of body.

SWISH.

Et voilà. This is more like it. My limbs are fit and toned. My abs are tight, my buttocks round, and my saddlebags are vanquished forever. It's perfect... no gym ever again.

Is there anything else I need to fix? Ah yes, nails and eyebrows. Since I had them done today they're perfect, but I want them to stay that way always. Teeth whitening. And maybe I could pop my boobs up a notch as if I was wearing a push up all the time. Ok, I could also inflate them a little.

I add these final adjustments and admire the result in the mirror. I didn't need a major makeover or anything, but I was full of all those small defects that can drive you crazy and require a lot of work to be kept in check, or that can't be helped at all. Like my limp hair. Now I can get rid of the endless array of beauty products sitting in my bathroom, even the new ones I've bought today.

I am jubilant. I'm the best I could ever look while still being myself, and I feel wonderful. Ready for war.

"What do you think?" I turn to the genie.

"You seem mostly the same to me, except your skin seems to be glowing."

"Thank you, Genie, that's exactly what I was aiming for."

"You are a jot too skinny, if I may say."

"Well, Genie, you know what they say… you can never be too rich or too thin." Which, so to speak, brings me precisely to my second wish.

Five
The Second Wish

I study my reflection a little longer... *it is* perfect! I am a photoshopped version of myself, only a real 3D version. The only flaw is the glasses. If only I could get rid of those as well... Wait a moment, could I?

"Genie?"

"How can I assist you, milady?"

"When I wished to be able to change my body, does that mean I could cure a medical imperfection?"

"If it requires a physical change, I don't see why not."

"Uh-uh! So how do I do it?"

"First, what is it you need to do?"

"I need to fix my mole-like vision."

"Do you know what kind of intervention that would require?"

"Not exactly."

"I would suggest reading some sort of medical writing on the subject before attempting anything. Do you possess any such thing?"

"No."

"We should probably wait until tomorrow then, go to the local hospital, and see if they have a medical library we can access."

"Yeah, sure," I say ironically, opening my laptop and turning it on. Once again, no time to explain modern technology to him.

I open Google and type myopia.

I click on the first result, scroll down the page, and read:

Myopia, or nearsightedness, is a defect of the eye that causes a difficulty in focusing on faraway objects... blah, blah, blah...

I WISH FOR YOU

"That would work too," the genie comments from behind me. "Interesting instrument. How does it work?"

"Later." I don't want to be rude to him, but again, I am busy. No time for an A.I. class, plus I've just found the good stuff.

I keep on reading.

***

"It worked," I exclaim enthusiastically an hour later, admiring my perfectly in-focus reflection with no glasses on. "Hey, Genie—" I turn around to attract his attention. "Do you prefer blondes or brunettes?" I tease.

Now that my image is fixed, I want to play around a little.

"Both have their merits," he replies noncommittally.

"Come on, be a sport! Blondes or brunettes, this is the question."

"As I said, both bear their fascinations." He's finally relaxing, losing some of his uptightness. "Nonetheless, I've always found dark colourings more endearing."

"Hum, let me see." I mull my options with my arms crossed in front of me and my index finger pressed on my lips. "You mean something like this?"

SWISH.

I turn into a Penelope Cruz-y version of myself. With long dark ebony hair, a slightly tanned skin tone, and almost black eyes.

"You… that… ahem…" he stutters, stupefied.

"Has the cat got your tongue?"

"I simply was not expecting anything the like of your transformation. It caught me absolutely unprepared," he says, regaining his austere composure.

"If you say so," I retort skeptically. "What about redheads?"

SWISH.

I give myself flaming copper-red hair, fair skin, and bright aquamarine eyes.

"Do you like freckles?"

SWISH.

I add some cute little freckles to my nose and cheeks.

"I am afraid I do not dote on red hair," he says, in a strange tone I can't quite place.

A shadow of gloom passes over his face—very fast, almost imperceptible. He hides it immediately as if he was used to keeping his emotions from showing on his face. He didn't want me to notice.

I suspect there is more about redheads to be investigated. But I'm sure there'd be no point in asking openly, as he doesn't seem eager to answer questions on the subject... or any subject, for that matter. I am sure that if I did ask, he would just tell me I have a fervent imagination. My only option is to store all my questions for later, be patient, and wait until the fruit is ripe to collect it.

"What about blondes?"

SWISH.

I turned my eyes a deep blue, and shining golden hair arranged in soft waves reaches down to my waist.

"Suits you perfectly, milady," he says, still a bit ruffled.

Ignoring his attitude, I go on to try every possible physical combination I can think of. I try being taller, shorter, with more curves, fewer curves, or no curves at all. I experiment with every hair color, style, and length imaginable. From long, straight, cotton-candy-pink hair, to a full afro head. I am so excited that my squealing has reached an only-dog-hearing point. I might have done a victory dance as well along the way.

When I run out of options to change myself, I transform into a bunch of celebrities just for fun. At one point I even turn into Mystique herself, with yellow eyes, orange flaming hair, and blue-scaled skin. It scares the genie so much that he almost falls from his chair. He *did* sit down after about an hour of my shape-shifting game.

"I am glad to be the source of your amusement," he says with a bit of contempt after my little prank.

"Oh, come on. You've been stuck in a box by yourself for two hundred years. You could use a bit of fun, no?"

"You are quite in the right." A small smile finally surfaces on his lips. "But could you please oblige me nonetheless and transmute back into a more human appearance? I feel I've had enough fun for today."

"I guess blue skin is not your cup of tea after all."

SWISH.

I am myself again. Well, my greatly improved-self. I am going to keep this look for the next whatever years… no wrinkles for me. Eventually, I'll have to age myself a bit, but not until I am fifty or something. I could always say it is a family trait to age well. Most people will think I'm hiding a very good plastic surgeon and don't want to admit it, but who cares?

Sugar chooses this moment to reappear from his hiding place. He sniffs the genie suspiciously and then jumps on the bed, tilting his head sideways and uttering a single meow.

"What? You're in for a makeover as well?" I ask, scratching him behind the ears.

"Meow."

"I'll take that as a yes. Let's see how a pedigree suits you."

I turn him into a couple of different breeds. He seems to enjoy being a Maine Coon the most, but when he starts chasing his tail around because he doesn't recognize it, I turn him back into his usual shape and pick him up for some cuddling.

"What time is it?" I ask, more to myself than to the genie. "Crap, it's almost one in the morning! Time flies. I only have time for the second wish before we go to bed."

"What?" the genie shouts, aghast.

"What, what?"

"In hundreds of years, this is the first time one of my charges is so flippant with her wishes. These are unique gifts bestowed on you by a higher power. It was outrageous enough for you to express a wish within five minutes of having discovered your good fortune, but to use two in a matter of hours… it is unthinkable."

"Is there a rule about not expressing more than one wish in a day?"

"No, there is no specific rule, but—"

"No buts, stop right there." I raise my hand, palm forward, to silence him. "If there is no particular rule on the topic, I would like to express my second wish now so that we can have an early start tomorrow. Monday is only one day away. I don't have a clear plan yet, and I don't want to lose any precious time tomorrow."

"What sort of plan are you in need of?"

"Never you mind. Do I go as before? I state the wish, and after say abracadabra?"

"Avra Kehdabra."

"Yeah, yeah, I know. So?"

"Technically, yes, but I beg you, milady, to reconsider your decision. Once the wishes are spent, they are forever lost, and there is no turning around."

"Do you see me regretting my first wish?"

"No, but it has only been a couple of hours. Maybe in the future, there will come a time when you will regret your choices of today."

"Or maybe I simply know what I want. Or maybe you're scared I will use up all my wishes in one week, and you'll have to go back to your box right away."

"This is the most infamous, most outrageous accusation." His face becomes all red and puffy with an expression of pure indignation, which is so sincere that I feel sorry for him. "Never in all my years of service have I been slandered to such a level of ignominy. I, who was only trying to advise you, who was looking out for your best interests, who—"

"Okay, okay, you are the purest of heart. Genie, let me tell you, you're too sensitive."

"You were accusing me of ignoble behaviour. I will not stand indifferent when my reputation is being besmirched in such a vile way. Upon my honour…"

I am trying to keep a straight face while his pompous monolog keeps going and going about honesty, morality, and decency… This genie is really a piece of work. I concentrate hard not to burst out laughing, which I know would only get me a longer sermon.

When he's finally done, I try to smooth his feathers a little by professing my total, untainted faith in his integrity, and then ask, "Can we proceed with my wish now?"

"If you are absolutely certain."

"I am."

"Could you at least tell me beforehand what the desire is?"

"Does it make a difference?"

"Yes, it would help me in advising you better."

"All right, I need a financial boost."

"I see. First beauty, and now wealth."

"And what is it exactly you see?" I ask, irritated. "Are you getting all judgmental on me?"

"No. I understand that attractiveness and prosperity could prove to be two very precious weapons for a woman with a purpose. May I ask what would yours be?"

"Him… no, not yet, not until I have a clear idea myself."

"Very well. You know what to do, then."

"Okay. Here I go."

I take a deep breath.

"I wish to always have all the money I need and much more, anywhere, at any time, forever. Avra Kehdabra."

CLINK.

The noise of the little metallic wheel turning comes from the other room, the faint sound clearly audible in the quietness of the night.

"I know you don't sleep, but I need to. I want to get up early tomorrow." I sigh; it'll be the second time this weekend. "So, if you don't mind, I'll show you how the shower works and then go to bed."

"So very kind of you, milady."

We move to the bathroom, which is an en-suite that also has a second door leading to the hallway. I know, it's weird, but it's useful. This way the genie will be able to exit without waking me up or come into my bedroom while I sleep.

"So." I show him the wonders of modern plumbing. "You turn the tap to open the water. The more you turn to the left, the warmer it comes."

He plays with it, fascinated. "This is brilliant!" he comments, amazed.

"Have fun with it," I say, opening my cabinets to find some fresh towels. "You can use these to dry yourself when you're done."

"Milady, you are most kind."

"Hush, it's nothing. So, are you sure you'll be fine sleeping on the couch or wherever?"

"It is my first night in the world after a long absence—I will try not to waste it in sleep. However, be reassured that I am perfectly capable of taking care of myself."

"Ok, you can borrow one of my books if you get bored," I say, exiting the bathroom. I consider telling him he could watch TV but think twice about it as it would trigger too many questions I am too tired to answer. "Good night, Genie."

"Thank you, milady. I wish you a good night."

I leave him playing with the sink faucet and stroll back to my room where I immediately sag on the bed like a potato sack without even brushing my teeth.

I curl up in a ball under the soft duvet and Sugar, who was already fast asleep on the bed, slightly adjusts his position to mine, purring. Exhausted, but somewhat heartened, I close my eyes, lulled by the soothing sounds of the running shower and purring cat, feeling hopeful about the future for the first time in over a year.

Six
Morning Bliss

I had the weirdest dream last night. I fantasized that I had found the genie of the enchanted lamp, and I had awesome superpowers. Gosh, that Chinese food must've been radioactive or something... it felt more like hallucinating than dreaming. Time to open my eyes, literally, and get back to reality. I reach for my glasses on the bedside table and put them on in autopilot mode.

Oh, this is weird. I still see everything out-of-focus. Do I have to see the ophthalmologist again so soon? I went less than a year ago, is this normal? Am I going totally blind? Could I still be under the influence of the yucky Chinese food? Can Chinese takeout make you blind? If a rare, transmitted-via-rotten-Chinese-takeout disease exists, it completely figures I'd be the one to catch it!

Why do I always have such bad luck? Why? I drop my head to my knees, discouraged. Ouch! Bad move, bad move. Never drop your head onto anything if you're wearing glasses. I take them off and lower my head on my knees again. What can I do blind, battered, and abandoned?

Oh, perfect! Now I also need to pee badly. I hope I can manage to get to the bathroom even if I don't see anything. Come on, Ally, use any sight you've left, put one foot in front of the other, and reach... the potty! Uh-huh, freedom! I could rally the Scots with my motivational thinking. Ok, let's get going...

Miracle! I can see. Oh wow, how stupid am I? It was just morning foggy vision. Or the aftermath of Chinese food poisoning. Who knows? Whatever. Posterity will judge. No eye doctor after all. I hate having people fool around with my eyes, even when it's me putting in contacts, which I wear whenever I'm in public.

Wait a second, something weird is going on. The glasses are still in my hand, but I see perfectly. I put them on... foggy vision. I take them off... 20/20 vision. I repeat this operation several more times with the same result. This is the weirdest thing.

"I am glad to find you already awakened, milady."

"Aaaarrrghhhh!" I scream, and gracelessly tumble to the ground.

"Forgive me, milady. Did I frighten you?"

"You scared the crap out of me!" I bark back sourly.

"That is unmannerly talk for a lady."

"Don't act so damn civilized. Not after you've just crept up on a half-asleep, unsuspecting person."

"I just wanted to tell you that I have prepared you breakfast. Whenever it pleases milady, you can join me. I will wait in the other room," he replies stiffly and leaves.

Oh. Now I feel sorry for the genie. He was just being nice. Ah, the genie! It wasn't a dream after all. I did find the enchanted lamp! Well, it looks more like a jewelry case, but who cares? I have superpowers. And I can ask for three more wishes! I can't believe it!

I get up from the floor and check myself out in the mirror. Yes, I definitely have superpowers. No way would I have such a perfect body without supernatural help. And I am rich, too. Yay.

Okay, I'd better go make up with the genie or he might stay cross with me all day. He can be hypersensitive for someone who has been around for so long.

I go to the other room and... Wow! Instead of walking into my living room, it's like I've entered a scene from Sofia Coppola's *Marie Antoinette*.

Every flat surface is covered with culinary wonders. The breakfast table is nicely laid for two with the cutest china set ever (definitely not mine), accompanied by two matching steaming kettles. I guess one is for tea and one for coffee. Pyramids of cream puffs, macaroons, mini muffins, and tiny croissants are beautifully arranged on cake stands next to the pottery set, and they appear so inviting my stomach growls loudly. Also, on the kitchen island, there are orderly rows of porcelain platters holding flamboyant pastries, multicolored tarts, éclairs, and pies. The other side of the countertop is covered with bowls filled with grapes, nectarines, cherries, and all kinds of berries. And on the floor, there is a selection of delicacies for Sugar arranged in matching china bowls.

I take all of this in, cringing at the way I reacted a few minutes ago. The genie is leaning against the stovetop with his arms crossed over his chest, looking at the floor sulkily.

"Genie, this is amazing! When did you do all of this?"

"It was but a meagre effort on my part," he replies, clearly still offended.

"Genie, I am sorry for yelling at you. I am not very friendly when I wake up, and you scared me to death. I am truly very sorry, can you forgive me?" I make sure to use my most honeyed tone. If this doesn't work, nothing will.

"It is I who should be forgiven, milady. I should not have invaded the privacy of your room, and I too possess an awful temper. Centuries of trying have not taught me yet how to be levelheaded—it must be the royal blood that runs in my veins."

"Wow, you were a prince then. A king?"

"I already said too much."

"A duke, perhaps?"

"Would you prefer tea or coffee, milady?"

"So you're just going to ignore me. Asking you a question is like beating a dead horse."

He smiles slyly but doesn't say anything.

I am becoming more curious every passing minute. Who is this genie? What happened to him? If he's not willing to tell me more, I'll find out on my own. I know that he is centuries old,

English, and of royal blood. His name is Arthur... could he be *the* King Arthur? Please, a genie is already enough! I don't need to believe in Camelot and the round table as well.

Oops. I must've zoned out for a while because King Arthur here is eyeing me suspiciously.

"Hm, coffee would be fine."

"Coffee for the lady," he enthuses, pouring me a cup.

"You know, you didn't have to do all of this."

"Milk?"

"Yes, please. It must've taken you all night."

"Not at all. Sugar?"

"Yes. You know there is no way I can finish all this stuff by myself."

"I was not sure about how you usually break your fast, milady. And I thought you might have a social gathering planned, it being Sunday."

"Oh, Genie, if you weren't already here, they should invent you. Anyway, breakfast is more of a quick deal these days."

I begin to devour everything within my reach. Mmm, these pastries are delicious... and I can eat as many as I want. Ha—I am not going to get fat. The loud purring sound constantly coming from the floor tells me Sugar is enjoying the surprise as much as I am.

"Sit down, King Arthur, don't stand there looming over."

"I beg you, milady, not to joke about my lineage," he replies gravely.

"You need to loosen up a bit, you know."

"Speaking of kings," he says, "pray tell me: who is king these days?"

"There is no king," I reply, amused. "We have a president."

"England has no king?" he asks, astonished.

"Well, England does have a queen, but we're not in England!"

"Where are we?" he asks, even more shocked.

"US of A."

I WISH FOR YOU

"And where is that?"

"You know, across the ocean."

"The New World?" he asks, nonplussed.

"Yes, the New World," I reply with a smile. This guy is so much fun.

"You are living in the colonies?"

"We're not much of a colony anymore."

"This explains the lack of style, of elegance…"

"Hey, snobbish British you. The United States is the most powerful country in the world, even more than your precious little England!"

"Well, power does not add any sophistication to it," he replies. "Besides, what can you expect from a land artificially populated with the scum of society, outcasts, and criminals? Basically a horde of barbarians."

"Hey, no need to offend. And how does it feel to have had your butt kicked back to Mother England by low-class scum and outcasts?"

"Everybody thought it was a temporary setback."

"Well, it wasn't." I decide to put an end to the discussion. "We should get going. We need to do some serious shopping."

"Shopping?"

"Yes, I need a new wardrobe."

"Why?"

"I am at war."

"At war, milady? Why, and with whom?"

"A she-wolf." It's my turn to be mysterious.

"And new clothes would help?"

"A lot, believe me. And you…" I say, and eye his attire, which hasn't changed since last night. "We'd better update your gear as well. You need to change before we go out."

As I enjoy a sip of my hot coffee, he raises his brows questioningly.

"I mean, you don't *have* to dress in that absurd lord costume, right?" I add. "It isn't some kind of genie uniform?"

"This is no costume! All my garments follow the latest fashion in London."

"No doubt they were good two hundred years ago, but if you go around dressed like this in this century, everybody will think you are a freak. Can you change?"

"Yes, I can. You just have to provide me some new garments of your liking, milady."

I still don't understand if this milady thing is a mockery, or if he is serious. I'll give him the benefit of the doubt.

"I imagine the most convenient choice would be to have a tailor come to the house and take my measurements. Are there any good tailors on this side of the world?" he asks, slightly wrinkling his nose.

"No time for your personal tailor come to the house," I reply, not sure he will catch the irony in my answer. "Can't you magically change into new clothes?"

"No."

"So you can create a food feast, produce the finest porcelain set I've ever seen... but you can't make your own clothes. Why?"

"Allow me to remind you that I did not set the rules. And for the one who did, she was a woman whom I cannot presume to praise. She probably regarded food as a necessity, but did not feel similarly toward garments."

So this curser person was a woman after all. I bet she had red hair.

"Well, I don't have any male clothing in the house," I say without pointing out the information he has just given up.

"I most certainly will not wear female ones," he protests.

"Then you'll have to stay invisible while I go shopping, and I'll buy you something."

"I was much anticipating the feeling of the sun on my skin after so long, but what it is another day of waiting compared to centuries?"

I WISH FOR YOU

Can anybody be any more passive-aggressive than this? He has succeeded in making me feel guilty.

Let me see... he could perhaps keep the shirt, get rid of the tailcoat, the tie, the vest, and all the accessories... hat, gloves, and cane. The buckskin pants will make some heads turn, but he is European, so he is allowed a certain degree of eccentricity. The only real problem here is the boots with the golden tassels. Nothing could make them pass for normal or fashionably acceptable.

He can make me feel as guilty as he wants, but considering the circumstances, there's really nothing I can do. Unless... Do I want to go there? I don't think I'm ready. No, no way. He'll have to sit this one out. Oh, he's giving me the puppy dog eyes. I can't leave him at home. Damn, I need to learn how to say no.

"Come with me," I say, defeated. "Maybe there's something we can do."

If he had a tail, he would be madly wiggling it right now.

I drag a chair next to my closet, mentally preparing myself for the task ahead. I climb up onto the chair and begin emptying the top shelf, passing a myriad of linens, comforters, and towels to the genie. Finally, I reach the most secluded spot on the shelf where a nice lilac box has remained hidden and untouched for over a year. I take it down, refusing to pass it to the genie and keeping it close to my body instead.

I carefully lay it on the bed, lifting the cover with trembling hands. Inside I can see all the gifts James ever gave me, plus some small things he left in my apartment after breaking up with me. I rummage inside to do a quick inventory until I see a stupid teddy bear wearing a blue T-shirt with the name James printed across it, the kind you buy for newborns. He gave it to me one time when he was on a business trip for a week, saying it was so I would not miss him. I touch it and smile sadly. This was a bad idea. I'm not ready for this. I quickly grab James's old flip-flops and seal the box and its contents out of sight, afraid I might start crying otherwise.

For the record, as far as family and friends know, I've thrown away all the gifts he gave me and the things that he left at my apartment. But I could never bring myself to actually do it. I am glad at least there were no pictures; *that* would've been too much. Luckily, they're all safely stored in a faraway cyber cloud.

It's weird to give the genie things that belonged to James, but there's no other option at the moment. These are literally the only shoes in the house that will fit him.

"We'll keep your pants as I don't have any."

"Is this particular, hmm... footwear fashionable these days?" he asks, examining the flip-flops skeptically.

"Absolutely," I lie.

"May I inquire whose shoes these are?"

"No."

"Very well. Are they at least clean?"

"Wear them or stay at home. I don't care," I say, exiting the room.

I need some more java after this ordeal of memories.

BANG!

While I'm pouring myself a nice cup of steaming coffee, the genie goes and makes that stupid magic noise again. It startles me so much that I throw both mug and jug in the air, splashing myself, the entire kitchen, and part of the living room with black coffee.

"Are you nuts?"

"I apologise. I did not intend to startle you, milady, I was just trying to oblige your plea."

"Did you really need to make all this fuss just to change your shoes?"

"I beg your forgiveness once again. Have I at least pleased you?" he replies, outlining his frame with his hands.

His whole gentleman's attire complemented by flip-flops is hilarious.

"Not yet," I say, suppressing a smirk. "Please remove everything else except your pants and the shirt."

"Everything?"

"Yep."

"Gentlemen do not carry a cane or a hat? No gloves?"

"Gentleman may still wear them, but I'm afraid the problem is that there aren't many left. Come on, go ahead," I urge him. "Without any bang, please," I quickly add.

"There will be no more bangs for the lady," he replies, smirking.

Did he mean...? Is he messing with me, or am I imagining it? No, I am sure it was an innocent reply. They surely didn't use "bang" to say *that* in the 1700s.

POOF!

This time, a soft poof accompanies his magic.

"What say you now?" he challenges.

I only see his top half from the kitchen, and he's really handsome without all those distracting frills and only a simple white shirt on. I remain quite impressed until I turn the bar corner and take in his full figure. The shirt with the riding pants and the blue flip-flops are an atrocious ensemble.

"Not bad for an old fossil like you," I tease, smiling. I don't want him to be self-conscious; he most likely doesn't have a clue that he'll still be perceived as a total weirdo.

"Not bad, indeed," he replies with a dashing smile.

I don't know what got him into trouble all those years ago, but I am beginning to form an opinion.

"Can you do something about all this mess?" I ask, pointing at the coffee stains adorning my entire house.

Another soft POOF and my favorite mug is back in one piece on the countertop, steaming with the hot liquid inside. Every trace of the previous disaster is completely erased.

Seven

Shopping Fever

I would usually take the metro to get to Michigan Avenue, but since I am filthy rich now, the time of taxis has come. I even decide to call one instead of waiting for a random cab downstairs. It may not seem like much, but believe me, for someone who has lived on a budget for a long time it *is* a big deal.

"How does this money thing work?" I ask the genie in the elevator on our way down.

"It is complicated magic. However, since last night a number of bank accounts have been opened in your name."

"Is it legal? I will not get indicted or anything, right?"

"Do not trouble yourself, milady. As I said, it is complicated magic. Your money will keep investing itself—you will sustain profits and losses, but the profits will always exceed by far your losses, and your wealth will keep building itself perfectly legally."

"Cool! How do I access all this new richness?"

"Your purse should be filled with whatever method of payment is current these days."

When I open my wallet, I find four new shining credit cards plus a wad of cash.

When we exit my building the cab is already there waiting. I jump in and beckon the genie to follow me. I give the destination to the driver, and as soon as the car speeds away, the genie grabs onto the seat and holds on for dear life.

"This carriage is moving extremely fast," he observes, stupefied. "How is it possible? I did not see any horses attached to it."

"I know, right?" the driver says. "It's just a hybrid, but it still has eighty horsepower."

I WISH FOR YOU

"Eighty horses!" the genie exclaims, shocked. "But I did not—"

I kick him in the ankle to cut him off. Luckily we're not alone, so the freezing-when-I-touch-him rule does not apply. "Wonderful car," I say to the driver. "Good for the environment, too."

"Saves me a ton on gas," he replies cheerfully.

"Genie," I whisper. "We are in a *car*, not a carriage, and the horsepower is in the engine."

"They hid eighty horses inside this *car* thing?" he asks, nonplussed.

"No," I shoot back, amused. "An engine is a machine that has the power of eighty horses, but there are no horses anywhere."

"And how does this engine work?"

"What do I know? I am not an engineer! Listen, we'd better buy some books for you. History, engineering, informatics, etc...."

"What is it informatics?"

"See what I mean?"

When we arrive, I tip the driver a humongous sum and exit the cab, anticipating the most outrageous squandering of money I've ever had.

The day is clear and warm. The sky is a deep shade of blue; without even the smallest cloud, and the sun is shining, its reflection bouncing off the tall glass buildings. Chicago in late spring is incredible. The genie seems a bit overwhelmed. He is walking slowly, staring upward in awe. It must be the first time he sees a skyscraper. He also seems mistrustful of concrete, and a bit frightened by the cars zooming past us.

"These buildings," he comments with his nose still up in the air, "are pretty magnificent."

"Are you liking modern architecture?"

"Very much, very much indeed."

He also appears to be enjoying the amount of limbs on display on this fine day. Let me just say that even I, who am used to modern customs, find some of the shorts and skirts we encounter today to be quite scandalous. It must be some sort of retaliation against the harshness of the cold season; in winter girls must cover up so much that they most likely feel the need to compensate in warmer times.

Usually, on a day like this, I would love to simply walk up and down the Magnificent Mile, indulging lazily in window shopping and enjoying the hot weather. To be honest, most of the time window shopping would've been the only option available for my finances. Ah, but today is special. Today, besides the means, I have a purpose. So I need to be smart and efficient. There'll be plenty of time for leisure shopping in the future.

I decide that the best solution is a luxury department store; this way I'll have many brands of clothes, accessories, and shoes all in one place. I opt for Barneys New York, which I had always drooled over in my poverty days. When we reach it, I pause in front of the entrance, bursting with anticipation. I take a deep breath and then push the heavy revolving doors, thrusting my way into a world of luxury long forbidden to me. No wonder we are in the Gold Coast. Everything in this store seems to shine with a golden sparkle. Even the air smells expensive.

As soon as I step into the women's department, a friendly sales assistant approaches me.

"Good morning, welcome to Barneys New York," she says, smiling. "Can I help you with anything?"

I like to do my shopping on my own without pushy clerks around, but having some help today could be a winning idea.

"Mmm... actually, would it be possible to hire a personal shopper?" I try to sound self-assured like this is something I do every day.

I WISH FOR YOU

"Did you book an appointment with us?" she asks, with only a trace of condescension audible in her voice.

"Hmm, no. I didn't." Stupid, of course, you take an appointment if you want a personal shopper.

"Let me see what I can do for you, may I have your name, please?"

"Ally Johnson."

"Nice to meet you. Please give me a moment to check our schedule."

She turns on her heel and goes back to her station, where she picks up a phone, talks into it for about two minutes, and then heads back toward us.

"Brittany will be able to assist you, Miss Johnson," she announces, satisfied. "Please wait here. She will be down in just a minute."

"Thank you."

I do as I'm told and stay rooted to the spot. Less than a minute later, a short, blonde girl walks over to me.

"Hello, I'm Brittany," she says. "I'll be helping you out today."

"Hi, I am Ally, and this is my friend th—"

"Arthur!" He steps in, cutting me off.

Hmm, good point. I shouldn't call him "genie" in public.

"And what are we looking for today?" she asks, eyeing my attire suspiciously. "Anything specific?"

Well, I guess I don't exactly look like the average Barneys' customer. My clothes are pretty cheap, and the genie's must be quite a sight. Brittany here is probably thinking she has been given a raw deal, but she is in for a big surprise.

"I need a total wardrobe makeover: clothes, shoes, and accessories," I reply smugly.

"And what kind of budget are we looking at?" she inquires even more skeptically.

"I don't have a budget." Never would I have believed it possible to utter such fabulous words. "You can go crazy," I add, beaming at her.

***

And crazy we went. I spent a couple of years' salary in a single session of shopping. In fact, after styling myself with new outfits for every possible occasion, I informed a by-then ecstatic Brittany that we would be needing some complete outfits for Arthur as well because he'd just arrived from London and his luggage had been lost on the plane.

Once the shopping was over, we had a late brunch on the rooftop, and afterward, we shopped for books. When he's done reading, the genie will have an encyclopedic knowledge of modern civilization. We covered all the basics, from history to technology to politics. At least, I hope the important stuff is included because the volumes weren't cheap!

After the bookstore, we returned to my apartment with too many shopping bags to carry and ready for a quiet night in. So, right now, the genie is immersed in his new books and I need to do some serious strategizing.

I glance down at my pad to recap what I've written so far:

New body, ok!
New wardrobe, ok!
Strategy????!!!!!

Not very helpful!

Ok, the first thing I need is more facts. Find out how long James and Vanessa have been together and how serious they are. I hope not very long and not very serious. Did they have sex already? Oh, my... I want to gag. My heart is back to one hundred and fifty beats per minute. *Focus Ally, you need to focus.*

I WISH FOR YOU

Okay, okay. I *am* focused. So, the key to winning a war is to collect the right information. But how to get it? I could ask the bitch directly, maybe using an indifferent conversational tone. Who am I kidding? She'd bust me in two seconds. Do I care? If it gets what I want, no. I bet she will enjoy providing me the sordid details of her new (I hope), perfect (I hope not) relationship with my ex.

Ok, and once I have the info? Well, it depends on how bad-slash-good it is. One thing I should probably do, regardless, is to introduce the "new me" to James. Excluding Friday, when I didn't exactly look very charming and I'm still praying he didn't see me at all, we haven't seen each other in over a year.

After I had one... okay, a couple... let's just say *some* embarrassing episodes of drunk texting/calling/stalking him, I came to the decision of utterly avoiding him at any cost. I made all of his usual hangout spots taboo, even if some of them were my favorites too. I changed gyms, not that I went that often anyway, and even renounced deep dish pizza completely.

Maybe seeing me in such good shape could stir something for him, or I could finally man up and ask him why the hell he dumped me, which remains one of life's greatest mysteries.

"Who is Vanessa?" the genie asks, startling me. He came up behind me without me noticing, and he's peeking at my notes.

"None of your business. And please, would you mind not spying on me?"

"And who is James?" he presses on as if I hadn't said anything.

"None of your business either."

"I see."

"And what is it exactly you see?"

"Have you ever wondered why the coffer chose you?"

"Do you always respond to a question with another question?"

"Do you?"

"What do you mean, the box chose me?"

"It is not a fortuity that you came into its possession." He finally breaks the questions game and gives me a straight answer. "It was driven to you."

"Driven to me by what?" I ask, irritated.

"By your pain."

Ouch! Genie-1, Ally-0.

"The coffer can only be opened by women," he continues. "Did I already tell you?"

"No, you didn't tell me *anything*!" I lash out.

"You see, the coffer was made with a dual purpose." He says, ignoring my confrontational tone completely. "The first was to punish me..."

"Punish you for what?"

"We are not talking about me right now."

"And why should I open up with you if you won't tell me a damn thing about yourself?"

"Because you can still be helped, whereas *I* am beyond redemption," he hisses, enraged.

"You know, talking things through is useful by itself. You'd feel much better afterward," I reply quietly, reacting to his anger with sudden calmness.

He raises a perplexed eyebrow at first and then smiles victoriously. Right, I guess I just argued against myself.

"As I was saying," he continues, "the coffer was also made to help its possessors. It picks only women suffering for love, and in particular women facing a rival."

"Why?"

"The why is not important."

"It would help me to better understand." Will he buy it?

He is silent for a long while before he says, "The coffer was created by a woman in a similar situation."

This woman again. What did he do to her?

"What did you do to her? Was she a witch?"

"Not relevant." He brushes my first question off. "And yes, she was," he adds heatedly.

"You said witches didn't exist!" I exclaim, outraged.

"They do not, at least not anymore," he states in a curt tone that doesn't allow any more retorts.

This is all I am going to get for tonight, but still... I am making progress. My turn to share something.

"James is my ex-boyfriend."

"You mean you were betrothed?"

"Hmm, not exactly."

"Did you dishonour yourself with this man?" he asks seriously.

"Meaning?"

"Did you have physical intercourse with him?" he elaborates.

"You mean sex? Duh! We were together for three years—of course, we had sex."

"So he had your reputation ruined," he concludes gloomily.

"Hardly so," I comment, suppressing a grin.

"How is it possible? If you were not married, I do not understand."

"Let's say relationships are a bit more flexible these days."

"What do you mean?"

"That having a man asking to marry you is almost impossible," I reply, exasperated. "First, you date, and finding someone you actually like to date, is per se extremely difficult. If you're lucky and find this guy, he has to like you back. If he does, doesn't have a Peter Pan complex, and he's not too jealous of his man cave, you may be asked after some years of togetherness to move in with him. Finally, if you are even luckier, after some other years of cohabitation the guy, at last, proposes to you."

"Are you saying that women live together with men *before* they are rightfully married?" the genie asks in astonishment.

"Precisely."

"And this is socially accepted?"

"Come on, don't be such a prude. This is the twenty-first century."

"This is the most contemptible thing I have ever heard. It is something beyond common civility, and as for understanding it, I am surely incapable."

"It is not so weird after all." I try to better explain emancipation. "Women are independent nowadays. Many have important jobs; they can be rich, powerful, have key roles in politics…"

"Women can *vote*?" he asks, shocked.

"Yes. It's universal adult suffrage these days."

"And you do work?"

"Yes."

"I am truly sorry. I never realised you were in such a state of abjection. Is your family too poor to provide for you? No wonder you were looking for financial security."

"No, I have a job because it's normal. It's what people do today."

"Even women?" he asks, growing more perturbed by the minute.

"Yes."

"And what do you do? Are you a maid, a nurse, perhaps?"

"No, I am a marketing associate for a company that makes food bars."

He gives me a blank stare.

I suppose that both marketing and food bars are alien concepts to him as is the emancipation of women for that matter.

After some other politically incorrect questions, we resume talking about my love triangle. The genie, idiot that he is, keeps maintaining that I should have at least an inkling why James left me. He keeps arguing that truly-in-love people don't just leave each other for no reason. I keep telling him that it is exactly what happened and that before the day we broke up

I WISH FOR YOU

there were no omens whatsoever of the approaching catastrophe.

The discussion goes on for a while, making me increasingly angry and him increasingly skeptical. It gets quite late, and with no productive outcome, I become too tired to keep arguing. I take my leave with a weary "Good night" and retire to my room. All his pompous talking is getting into my head.

Before getting into bed, I lay out my outfit for tomorrow: a black Armani suit with slim fitting pants, and a jacket to die for that screams sophisticated.

Once I'm tucked into bed, it's hard to actually sleep. I have too many thoughts swirling inside my head. What will happen tomorrow? Feeling the need to still do something, I take out my notepad and browse to the "Rules" page to add a couple of things to the footnote before I forget them.

Note to self: investigate Genie's curse, age...
Red hair? Punishment? Two women? Witches!!?!

Finally, I run through my strategy list one last time. It is not much, but I particularly approve of the last point.

New body, Ok!
New wardrobe, Ok!
Strategy????!!!!!
Extort info from Vanessa casually
Accidentally on purpose bump into James
Make the bitch FAT!!!

Eight
Monday

I would be so late if I were regular me; luckily enough, I am supernatural me, so I might get to work just in time. One of the perks of having superpowers is that I don't need to apply makeup anymore. I only need to imagine a style, and bibbidi-bobbidi-boo it's on my face, impeccably done, magazine perfect.

Minus twenty minutes.

Plus, having added taxis to a new list of affordable commodities, I can now skip the usual hustle and bustle of running to the subway station just in time to see the train leave, waiting for the next train, making the actual journey packed like a sardine in a box (with the same delightful smell), squeezing my way out of said sardine box, and jogging desperately toward the office.

Minus thirty minutes.

Appraising my total delay time at about forty-five minutes, I will still be able to arrive at the office five minutes in advance.

"Remember," I tell the genie for the millionth time. "Today you stay invisible, inaudible, and entirely imperceptible."

"Yes, sir," he replies mockingly. "Or, rather, madam."

He doesn't understand. I already don't exactly shine in the eyes of my boss, and the last thing I need is to be seen with a lunatic only capable of uttering outrageously politically incorrect statements.

Can you guess who my boss's favorite is? Yeah, right! Dear old Vanessa. Why should I care what my boss thinks, anyway? I'll keep working there only to fake normality for a while and fish for information. I could buy the company with all the money I have now. Yeah, I should buy the company and fire him—and Vanessa, too. This, unfortunately, would not prove to be a great strike for her, as she belongs to some rich snob family, the true high society of Chicago. My boss, on the other hand, would lose it.

The genie passes his first test of invisibility as we cab to work. The driver seems to be oblivious to his presence. Yesterday I bought one of those Bluetooth devices so that if I need to talk to him while he's invisible, I can do it without people thinking I'm hearing voices in my head or talking to an imaginary friend. I've already instructed him about the deception, but I want to test it before we get to the office.

"Um, hello, Arthur. How are you?" I say into the tiny microphone.

"Me? Oh, it is very considerate of you to be calling me by my proper name," he replies sarcastically.

"Hmm, right," I say, annoyed by his constant bantering. It's an important day for me! He should be more serious about it. "I just wanted to check our communications for today. I'll talk to you later. Bye."

"Always at your service, milady," he says, smirking.

I don't say anything and scowl at him for the rest of the journey.

As predicted, the taxi ride is much shorter than my usual commute, and we reach my office's building, which is right in the center of the famous Chicago Loop, in fifteen minutes. Unfortunately, as soon as I am out of the cab, I run into a coworker. Sally is a fortyish-year-old accountant with a bulging figure, oily hair, and absolutely no taste for clothes.

Despite her lack of fashion sense, I really like her. She is always cheery, kind, and collaborative with everybody—except for Vanessa, who thinks overweight people should be banned from Earth and, when presented with Sally's abundance, can't maintain her usual angelic façade. She always teases Sally one way or another about how being fat is a choice, and how only weak people... how did she say it? Ah, yes. *"Only weak people would voluntarily desecrate the temple of their body in such a disgusting way."* Let's see what she does after she has joined the ranks!

Vanessa is so mean, and from the day she's been transferred to our floor three years ago, poor Sally has tried every possible diet cited in every book or magazine with no visible results. She must have some real metabolism problems. I should help her. I could use my new abilities to do some good.

"Hi, Ally." Sally stares at the taxi in surprise. "Did you cab to work?"

I need to be more careful; I don't want to blow my normality cover. Next time, because I am never taking the metro again, I'll have the taxi driver drop me one or two blocks away. Or I could just buy a car. Actually, that would be a good idea.

"Yeah," I say. "I was so late that Kyle would have killed me this time." Our boss's name is Kyle.

We go inside together, and while we're in the elevator, I imagine her five pounds lighter.

She shrieks at once in a high-pitched voice.

"Everything all right?" I ask, suppressing a tiny smile. I know the funny sensation she just experienced.

"Yes," she answers, still a bit shocked. "I just felt a weird prickle all over."

"It must have been electrostatic air," I state confidently. "It can give you small electric shocks." This way she'll assume she's having a random electrostatic reaction every time I make her lose weight. And it'll take a while, as I can't make her drop fifty pounds all at once. At least, not without freaking her out.

Bing!

A metallic sound announces that we've reached our floor. I leave Sally at her desk and move forward to mine with a quick, nervous pace. I settle down while the genie explores the surroundings.

"So, this is your place of work?" he asks.

I nod imperceptibly.

"And what do you do, precisely?"

I WISH FOR YOU

"Sorry, I can't talk right now," I say, and then pointedly remove my ear gadget so he gets the message.

"Hi, Ally."

Oh, great. Here comes the harpy to prey on me.

"Good morning, Vanessa," I say.

She is eyeing me suspiciously in silence. Circling the quarry before the kill?

"Can I help you with anything?" I ask, standing.

"Did you change something?" she asks, with a hint of disappointment in her voice. I bet she expected me to be a wreck, which of course I would have been if it wasn't for the genie.

"New haircut," I offer casually. Ally-1, Harpy-0.

"Wait, is that Armani?" she exclaims, even more aghast, pointing at my new suit.

"Yep." It's all I deign to give her. Ally-2, Harpy-0.

"Well, I just wanted to check if we were good, you know?" she announces with that honeyed tone of hers, but I can hear the malice sneaking underneath.

"You mean for the Dover project?" I feign ignorance.

"No, I meant regarding James."

I am sure that if she were offering me a poisoned chalice, she'd use the same sweet, nonchalant tone.

"It was a bit awkward the other day," she continues. "I spotted you running away when you saw us together…" She leaves the sentence hanging in midair.

"I wasn't running away," I lie. "I had forgotten something in the office and had to go back." Lame excuse. She won't believe it, but I don't care.

"Oh good," she says viciously, "because I know you guys had a fling some time ago blah, blah, blah…"

I don't hear a thing she says after the word fling. A fling? A *fling*? We were in a serious relationship for three years! He is the love of my life, and this arrogant, obnoxious bitch is discarding our history together as *a fling?*

I'm concentrating on my face to stop it from going red—a typical reaction for me when I am angry, embarrassed, or extremely drunk.

"No worries," I say, keeping my eyes fixed on the papers on my desk. "We broke up over a year ago." I sound false even to myself.

"I am sooo glad," she says with her most fabricated voice.

"Hmm, are you guys serious?" I throw in oh-so-casually while browsing through my files.

"Actually—" She breathes for suspense. "We're engaged."

I shoot my head up and stare at her, astonished.

"You are not wearing a ring." It's all I can manage to say.

My voice comes out hoarse and throttled, at the same time I am strenuously trying to control the sobs forming in my throat to prevent them from coming out. I will not give her the satisfaction of crying in front of her. As for the rest of my body, my heart is pounding faster than two hundred beats per minute. A sucker punch in the stomach from Mike Tyson would have been less painful than knowing James is engaged to someone else, to *her*.

"Ah yes," she says, finally appearing satisfied with herself and visibly enjoying my dismay. "My fingers are so slim that I had to drop it at Tiffany's to have it sized."

Tiffany's?

Ally-2, Harpy-2000.

***

I barely manage to excuse myself politely before running away, aiming for the safety of the female restrooms, where I'll be able to give free course to my agony. I storm into the bathroom and check each stall to see if there is somebody else inside before I speak, like in the best movies.

"Can you magically lock that door?" I shout desperately at the genie who has followed me in here.

I WISH FOR YOU

As soon as he complies, I sit on a toilet—gross, I know—and open the dam of my tears to let them flow freely. Frantic sobs make my entire body shake. My shoulders bounce up and down in time with the sobs, and I am not able to stop. I am shivering. My stomach is so contracted with cramps and twinges that it aches. I spread my arms wide, resting my open palms on both sides of the tiny stall. The cold metal is somewhat soothing. I concentrate on the cool sensation to try to calm myself.

"Um, are you well, milady?" the genie asks tentatively.

"Does it look like I'm well?" I yell back, still crying uncontrollably.

"You should try to remain calm, milady, and not distress yourself this much. Please tell me, what has happened to trouble you so?" He is muttering apologetically, undoubtedly taken aback by my shouting.

"They are engaged!" I wail. "The love of my life is marrying someone else." By this point, I am howling like a wounded wolf.

"I thought you said men did not get married in this time."

I grab the nearest thing I find, a toilet paper roll, and throw it at him with ferocity. It hits him right in the face. Correction—it would have hit him in the face if he were substantial. In this case, the roll passes right through him, bounces off the mirror, and drops in the sink. What the hell?

"There is no need to resort to violence," he says, affronted.

"Then try not to be such a jerk."

"No need to be offensive, either."

I grab a second paper roll and hurl it at him. I know there's no point, but throwing things is making me feel much better.

"I want her dead. *Dead*," I hiss, homicidal.

"Cannot do."

If a stare could kill, mine would have pulverized him right away.

"Can you make her disappear?" A sudden illumination on my part.

"I am afraid that is against the rules as well."

"You worthless..." A third roll is making its way to the sink.

"Would you st—"

Fourth roll landing.

"My fingers are so slim I had to have it re-sized," I mimic Vanessa. "Did you hear her?"

"You should try to recover yourself and reflect." The genie is trying to reason with me, but I am beyond reasoning. "I am going to ask this one last time," he adds. "Are you still sure that this James is the love of your life, considering he is marrying someone else?"

Boom. A fifth roll just crashed on the soap dispenser as my reply. Paper roll throwing: the newest pain relief therapy by Ally Johnson!

After throwing all the rolls at my disposal, I detach myself from the toilet and begin to pace up and down the empty room. By now the genie is being as inconspicuous as he can, in order to avoid another bombing, I suppose.

This doesn't make any sense. James and I—yes, me, the fling—have talked many times about marriage, he always said it was the most important decision he could make in his life and that he would never rush into it. That you have to know the other person as much as possible before committing for the long run. He wanted to live together with a person for at least a couple of years before tying the knot because living together was the real deal breaker for a couple, and if you could survive that you could overcome anything.

Now, assuming he never cheated on me—which I am almost sure of—he dumped me in early January a year and a half ago. This means that even if he started dating Vanessa right away, they certainly haven't lived together for two years! Oh, do they live together now? Do they go to sleep together every night? Do they have sex every night?

I WISH FOR YOU

Ouch, here comes the nausea again. My head spins so much I have to steady myself, grabbing the sink. I open the tap and let fresh water flow on my wrists for a while before rinsing my face and continuing with my reasoning. Even if they don't live together, if they are engaged, they must have done the deed. Is she better than I am? I bet not. I can't stand the idea of her hands on him, on my James. *My* James.

I don't understand how he could change his mind so radically in just over a year. Or he was just feeding me a bunch of BS because he was playing around with me and didn't want to get serious. Maybe I really was a fling for him. Could it be that for three years I lived in my happy bubble alone, and never truly understood anything about us? So much so that, the night he broke up with me, I was expecting him to ask me to move in together.

I resume my nervous pacing, pondering my past with James intensively, anxiety building up in my tummy. I'll probably develop an ulcer or something by the end of this. The sound of somebody trying the door and giving up after a few attempts rattles me even further. I have to go back outside; I can't hide in here all morning. *Retaliation*! I need to retaliate. I won't let her push me around like that.

She'll have him over my dead body.

Nine

A Little Revenge

"Genie!" I get another inspiration. "I am thinking hard about inflating her stupid left hand. Is it working?"

"Um... no," he answers, with a note of worry in his voice.

"Why?" I sibilate like an attacking cobra.

"When I said you needed to be in the proximity of a person to perform any magic on him or her, I actually meant that you need to have eye contact with them. Not necessarily eye to eye, but you have to be able to see them," he explains, a bit subdued.

"Genie, I am sorry," I apologize, regaining some of my humanity; he has been the sole target of my fury for the past fifteen minutes. "I am not mad at you. But please stop saying James is not the one, okay?"

"But—"

"No buts." I silence him with a raised finger.

"By all means, you heard the last of it. I promise." He seems sincere.

"Ok, am I forgiven?" I ask.

"Nothing to forgive, milady."

I examine my reflection in the mirror. Not good! I look like a scarecrow. My eyes are bloodshot and puffed up from all the crying, my hair is scattered in all directions and tangled, plus my magic makeup is smeared all over my face. I guess they didn't get the message to use waterproof mascara for their enchanted maquillage, whoever they might be. How did I accomplish so much disrepair in such a short time? I stare in the mirror and concentrate hard on my appearance of this morning *before* coming to work.

SWISH.

I am back to a presentable status. These superpowers are truly coming in handy; I've no idea how I would have survived

I WISH FOR YOU

without them. Probably I wouldn't have. Thank you coffer and thank you Genie.

"Let's go take the bitch down, then," I blurt out, determinedly exiting the bathroom like a soldier marching to war.

***

I sit down at my desk, sleek as a cat preparing for the attack. My positioning is perfect. From my cubicle, I can see Vanessa well enough, but the right panel shelters me from being seen.

The genie looks at me with a concerned expression.

"I should warn you," he speaks up in his lecture tone, "that to harm someone can always rebound on you. Look at me. I am the clearest example—"

I raise a hand to stop his sermon. "Sorry, I am not in the mood for a 'what goes around comes around' speech." I'm too vindictive.

And I've already thought of a solution. To avoid compromising my karma too badly, I've decided that for every evil I perform on Vanessa, I'll bestow the same amount of godsend on Sally. You know, to even everything out.

She will never be able to wear that engagement ring if it is the last thing I do. I'll keep inflating her hand until it explodes.

I lean back in my chair furtively to observe the enemy. She's busy typing on her keyboard. I fix my gaze on her left hand, staring at it and imagining it slightly swollen. The moment I do that, she stops typing, scratches her hand, and then resumes her inputting.

Aha, it worked! I do a mini triumph dance, hidden behind my panel walls and under the disapproving scrutiny of the genie. For about ten minutes, I lie quietly. But I can't contain myself. I draw back again and carefully examine an unsuspecting Vanessa.

She looks extremely beautiful, as usual. She has long voluminous dark hair, piercing blue eyes, a small straight nose, voluptuous pink lips, and a fair complexion with flawless skin. Basically, she's Megan Fox's secret twin sister. Today she's wearing a sleeveless sheath dress, which is bright blue with black seaming and trim. A size zero, or even a double zero. The dress is as tight as it gets, and she complemented it with an expensive-looking pair of black patent leather strappy sandals with four-inch stiletto heels.

Even with all my improvements, I'm not swimming in her league yet. To be honest, I never will. But it doesn't matter. She is mean, obnoxious, and full of herself, whereas I am nice, kind (to most people at least), and easy-going.

How does James even bear it? I mean, I understand that a man could get sidetracked by the physical attraction at first, and get an infatuation, but after hearing her talk for more than ten minutes he should've come to his senses, right? Even if she fakes it big time after a while it's impossible not to notice the evilness underneath.

Maybe it's impossible only if you're a woman. Kyle, our boss, is leaning over her cubicle right now, asking her for some documentation she had to prepare. She is saying she hasn't done it yet and that she won't be able to finish it by today, but the sugarcoat she puts on her words by flirting, batting her long lashes, and leaning some cleavage forward must conceal the actual meaning of her speech to her male audience. In fact, Kyle leaves as happy as a puppy that has just been cuddled. If it had been me delivering those lines, I would have gotten an entirely different response.

She makes me so mad! Time to get some other action. I focus on Vanessa's tiny figure, ready to gift her five pounds.

SWISH.

She emits a little surprised cry and jumps in her seat.

I WISH FOR YOU

Sally, who is just now passing in front of Vanessa's desk headed to the photocopying machine, notices her little screech and stops.

"Did you get an allover prickle?" Sally asks, smiling.

"Yes," Vanessa replies curtly while tugging at her dress. Evidently, cajoling is reserved for the male species.

"I had it before, too. It's electrostatic air. Did you know?" Sally continues, ignoring Vanessa's rudeness.

Ah, Sally, I love her. I'll shed another five pounds from her.

SWISH.

She squeaks. "See, it just happened again." She giggles, moving on to go copy her files.

I scrutinize Vanessa a while longer. She's twenty pounds underweight, so an additional five pounds will not make her fat. If anything she'll seem less anorexic, but with the dress she is sporting today, she must feel like a squeezed sausage at the moment. In fact, I watch her as she undoes the tiny black belt on her waist and changes holes to give her compressed stomach more room.

I do an evil laugh in my head while the genie keeps scowling at me, shaking his head in a gesture of disapproval. I dismiss him with an innocent shrug and decide to give Vanessa's hair a bit of a frizz, drop a few zits on her flawless skin, and chip a couple of perfectly manicured nails. To protect my aura, I make Sally's hair and skin less oily.

Ah, I'm better already.

***

Unfortunately, the happy sensation vanishes almost at once, and shortly after my little pranks are over, sadness invades me again. The enormity of the situation is beginning to dawn on me. My main reaction so far has been rage, but now that the adrenaline has left my body, I feel... I don't know. I'm confused.

The truth is that I could make Vanessa as ugly as I want, but knowing James, he would never be with someone merely for looks. He wouldn't marry someone just because she is beautiful. My heart skips a beat as the thought that he may actually love her crosses my mind for the first time since I've seen them together. Here comes the tachycardia again.

I try to calm down and rationalize a bit. I don't know. My instinct tells me something isn't right here, that things don't add up the way they should, but I can't put my finger on what's amiss. I've always trusted my sixth sense, and my intuition has never failed me. Well, with the one exception of James, but that doesn't count. It's all part of the same scheme.

I need to see eye to eye on this. I'm too involved to see straight. The situation calls for some consultation, and there's only one person's opinion I'll trust on this. Namely, my best friend Brooke.

By now they all must be back from their romantic getaway since it's a work-day. It's weird that I haven't heard from her yet. We usually text each other at least a couple of times per day.

I grab my phone and text her right away.

> Hey sweetheart, how was the WE? Did u miss me too much?

> I need to talk to u ASAP!

> Can u meet me for cocktails at 6.30?

> xo

I WISH FOR YOU

Brooke and I have been friends forever. We lived in the same neighborhood growing up and she's like a sister to me. She's always been there for me when I needed her. In fact, I get her reply immediately.

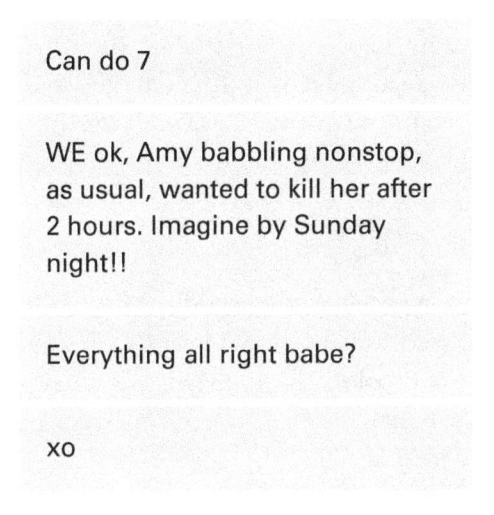

> Can do 7
>
> WE ok, Amy babbling nonstop, as usual, wanted to kill her after 2 hours. Imagine by Sunday night!!
>
> Everything all right babe?
>
> xo

In our group besides me, there are Brooke and Dave, her college sweetheart, Megan and John, and Amy and Luke. Brooke and I met Megan in college, then Brooke and Meg found a job in the same company as head hunters and Amy works with them. I am not very close to Amy; she's not my favorite, but she isn't too bad, and she throws the best house parties ever. As I've said, I'm the only single one.

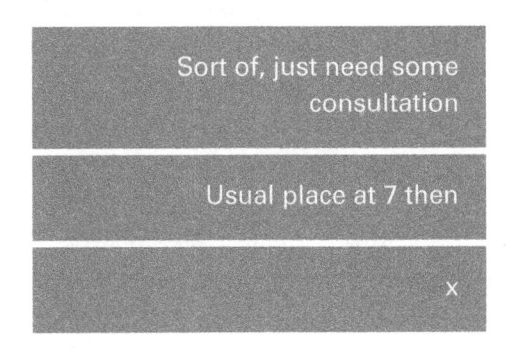

> Sort of, just need some consultation
>
> Usual place at 7 then
>
> x

I've been forbidden to even utter James's name for a while now; my friends think it's the best strategy for me to move on. That, or they couldn't stand my self-pitying whining anymore. Maybe a bit of both. But for an ex-boyfriend engagement to a long-loathed colleague, Brooke will make an exception.

That's also why I want to see her alone. She's my oldest friend, and I'll be more comfortable if it'll be only the two of us. She never judges and always listens patiently to all my rambling.

***

At six-thirty I grab my new black leather Miu Miu bag and leave the office.

"Do you want to meet Brooke?" I ask invisible Genie in the elevator. "She's my best friend."

"Do you want me to meet her?"

"Do we always have to play this game?"

He eyes me with a mischievous expression.

"You have ten seconds to decide and appear." I give him an ultimatum. "Once these doors open, you stay in whatever form you're in."

He doesn't respond, just smiles smugly. I understand he is visible purely from his reflection appearing on the shiny metal of the elevator.

"I see you're up for some sociability," I comment matter-of-factly. "Here's our story. You're from London, we met there during..." I stop mid-track.

We are walking down the street, and he keeps looking around wide-eyed, not paying attention to what I am saying.

"Are you listening to me?" I ask, annoyed.

"Most certainly, Miss Johnson." He snaps into focus.

"Another thing—none of this miss-milady crap." Maybe it wasn't a good idea to have him visible. "Today I'm just Ally, and everybody else is just their first name. No Miss, no Mister, and no milady."

"Yes, mi... Ally," he stutters clumsily.

I glare at him for a few seconds to make it clear this is important for me.

"I will try my best," he says, raising his hands defensively.

"And please try to sound as modern as you can manage."

He nods, probably too scared to speak.

"As I was saying," I resume where I left off, "you are English, from London. We met there during my semester abroad. We haven't been in touch for a long time, but you were transferred to Chicago to work... hmm... as a consultant on a project in finance. Keep it vague and you should be fine—nobody wants to hear about boring financial stuff. Everything clear up to now?"

"Yes," he says, repeating the story to memorize it.

"Okay," I continue once he's done. "Now comes the difficult part for you. You remembered that I was in Chicago and you tracked me down on Facebook."

He looks confused.

"Did you read any of the books we bought yesterday?" I ask.

"Yes, all of them."

"All of them?" I ask skeptically.

"Yes."

"And when exactly did you do that?"

"Last night. I was striving to keep myself occupied."

"You read twenty-something tomes in one night?"

"My magic was of assistance in the process," he says apologetically.

"Okay," I answer, still unconvinced. "So you're up to date on social networks?"

"Ah, yes. I am."

"Good. If Brooke asks you where you are staying, say you are at the Whitehall Hotel." I keep building up a bulletproof story. "You are there temporarily because you are searching for an apartment to rent as you don't know how long your job will keep you here."

"Do you foresee it is going to be a long time?" he asks keenly.

"Depends on how well you behave." I smile at him teasingly. "We'll have to give you a Facebook profile tonight, just to make the lie more believable," I add. "Anyway, to conclude our fake story, we were really good friends for the six months I was in England, you arrived here Saturday and didn't know anybody in the city, so we've been catching up during the weekend. We went shopping because they lost your luggage and I told you everything about James."

"Have you told me everything?" he asks, interested.

"All you need to know," I reply curtly.

"We were supposed to meet for drinks tonight as well, but I called you to tell you there was a James emergency and that my friend Brooke would be joining us, okay?"

"Yes."

"If she asks you some random questions, you'll have to improvise. Do you think you can do it?"

"Yes, madam."

"Good, 'cause we are here," I say, pushing my way through the heavy glass and metal doors of my favorite cocktail bar.

Ten

Brooke

The atmosphere inside is dark and sophisticated, the only brightness coming from the occasional blaze of the burning gas fireplace. Lounge music is playing in the background, and that's why we love this place; it has such a cozy atmosphere, and it's perfect to talk without having to shout.

I spot Brooke at once. She's perched on a stool at our favorite table, and she has already ordered a cosmopolitan for herself and a lemon drop martini for me. I love her! She's a tiny brunette, with an impossibly sleek bob, thin, on the shorter side, and she has huge breasts that she's very conscious of.

She always tries to cover them up as much as possible. In fact, today she is wearing her summer uniform—a black turtleneck dress. The only thing differing from the winter uniform is the lack of sleeves. She allows herself plenty of variability with colors, but the neckline is pretty much set in stone. Nobody knows how many turtlenecks she has. It's classified. That's why I thought about demoting her to a C cup. I was being a real friend.

"Hi, honey," I say.

"Hi." She looks at me with a weird expression. Is she surprised to see me accompanied by an unknown man? "You look great!"

"Thanks," I reply curtly. I don't want to get into discussing my makeover now. "This is Arthur." I introduce him and feed Brooke the made-up story I fabricated on the way here.

I don't jump right away into telling her about James. We do some small talking first, mainly because of Arthur. Brooke seems to become more relaxed with every passing minute. It's as if she was happy that Arthur is here, which is weird. It almost looks like she doesn't want to be alone with me, something that has never happened before. Or maybe I'm just being paranoid.

Once introductions and civilities are over, I'm more than ready for my revelation. I sip my cocktail and launch into my speech. "I need to talk to you. It's serious—you have to cut me some slack and make an exception. We need to talk about James."

She shots me a pitiful glance—the same she'd throw at an abandoned puppy dog in a pet refuge that she can't take home—and then lowers her eyes and whispers, "Yeah, sure."

"Brooke, what's wrong?" All the gauges on my mental control panel simultaneously go way off scale, swinging back and forward like crazy, sending all sorts of alarms blipping and flashing in my brain.

"Nothing, nothing," she mutters uncertainly.

"So why are you looking at me like that?" I ask, unconvinced.

"Nothing," she repeats. "I'm sorry, it's just... we, uh... got back late last night and I'm really tired. Please, go on."

I am not buying it one bit, but I have more pressing matters to discuss so I'll let it pass.

"As I said, it's about James." She gives me the sad eyes again, but I choose to ignore it. "Well, there is no easy way to say it. I've just found out he's engaged."

She looks at me, mortified, and doesn't say anything. I would have expected a bigger reaction to a bomb of this size, but she doesn't seem surprised... that's when the penny drops.

"Huh," I inhale sharply, bringing my hand to my mouth, comprehension dawning on me. "You knew!" I accuse her, pointing my index finger at her chest. "Admit it!"

"Yes," she confirms, barely audible. "I knew already, but—"

"How long have you known?" I hiss while angrily narrowing my eyes, something I always do when truly enraged. It's my evil stare.

"A couple of days. We found out—"

I WISH FOR YOU

"We?" I cut her off. "Who's *we*?"

"Well, everybody else," she stutters, embarrassed. "We found out at the cabin—"

"Let me get this straight," I interrupt her again, my anger mounting. "All my friends knew that my ex-boyfriend, who I still love, is engaged, and *nobody* bothered to tell *me*?"

"You should refrain from—" the genie tries to say something.

"Stay out of it." I freeze him before he has a chance to add something weird.

I stare at Brooke expectantly.

"Look, we've just found out—" she starts explaining.

"How?"

"John," she stammers uncertainly.

John, Megan's boyfriend, was James's roommate in college and I introduced him to Megan. Well, at least the two of them are working out, I think bitterly.

"But he and James don't hang out that much anymore." Mostly for my sake, I have to concede.

"No, they don't, but of course they're still friends on Facebook. John was browsing through his newsfeed on Sunday and saw that James had changed his relationship status to engaged."

"When?" I ask glacially.

"Saturday night." Brooke's whole body screams *awkward*.

He proposed this weekend! They weren't engaged when I saw them. Not that it matters.

"And why didn't you tell me right away?" I press her angrily.

"We thought it would be bad to tell you while none of us was there… to support you."

"Ah yes, of course! Poor Ally, she can't take it on her own." I am almost crying. "You just thought that talking behind my back from your romantic couples' retreat was a better idea."

"It's not like that."

"No, Brooke," I say adamantly, "at this point I don't know anything. I'm out of here." I get up, fumble in my purse furiously, throw a twenty-dollar bill on the table, and storm away toward the entrance doors.

I run out of the bar, rushing into the street. She won't be able to follow me right away. She still has to ask for the bill, so it will take her a good ten minutes to sort it all out, and by then, I'll be long gone.

I hail a taxi, ready to make my escape complete. Except the genie hasn't caught up with me yet... he's still trailing behind me a bit distraught, and definitely too slowly.

"Are you coming or not?" I prompt more than ask him.

"Are you sure you want to leave in this fashion?" he asks, a hint of reproach audible in his voice.

"I am going. Either get in the car or stay here. I don't care," I state sharply, slamming the cab door shut behind me.

The genie comes in from the other side while I am giving my address to the driver who promptly takes the hint and speeds away as soon as the genie shuts his door. The guy is smart enough to drive without asking questions and makes himself as inconspicuous as possible.

"Your behaviour was a jot harsh." The genie, on the other hand, doesn't seem to understand that talking to me right now might be dangerous. "Do you not agree?"

"I don't want to talk about it," I mutter, crossing my arms over my chest and keeping my gaze fixed outside the window, away from him.

"May I just point out that—?"

"Shut. Up." I stress each word, fuming. "Have I not made myself clear?"

He finally falls silent and sits still on his side of the cab. The driver eyes me disapprovingly from the rearview mirror. He's probably labeling me as a bitch and definitely getting a lousy tip for this ride.

I WISH FOR YOU

As the tall, familiar buildings of Chicago sweep by rapidly, I can't help but feel so completely betrayed and humiliated by the persons I trusted the most. The thought of my entire group of friends gathered around the fireplace while on their expensive, only-for-perfect-couples little vacation, pitying me, talking behind my back, thinking I was too fragile to handle the news, makes me sad.

I could have expected it from Amy, maybe Megan, but not from my best friend! Not from Brooke! *They* are the cowards, not me. The mere thought of the pity in her eyes makes me sick, along with all the lame excuses she blabbed.

The hell she wanted to tell me! I texted her today, she didn't text me. What was she waiting for? If she wanted to tell me so badly, she would have reached out to me somehow. That's why I haven't heard from her since Saturday night; it wasn't just today. Before, I hadn't noticed that the radio silence had started Saturday, but it all makes perfect sense now.

I'm not sure exactly why the knowledge that everybody else knew is so upsetting. It must be the same as finding out your husband or boyfriend was cheating on you, and after a while, discovering that you were the only one oblivious to the fact. It makes you feel like a fool, a complete idiot! It makes you feel cheated twice.

I sulk in my thoughts all the way home, not uttering a single word. The genie keeps unnerving me by sending preoccupied side-glances in my direction. I pretend not to see; maybe he also thinks I am too fragile, a damsel in distress!

Once in my apartment, I strip off my new suit and toss it on the bed in disarray. I decide to wear my comfort clothes: a pair of old, saggy sweatpants paired with an even more ancient baggy T-shirt. Comforted on the outside and discomforted on the inside, I move to the living room, grab a packet of m&m's, my all-time favorite candy and preferred substitute of breakup ice cream, and sag ungraciously on an armchair, ready for an evening of self-pity.

"Am I allowed to speak now?" the genie asks, circling around the apartment like a lion in a cage.

"Suit yourself," I respond, scowling.

"I believe your reaction was exaggerated." He launches into one of his sermons. "Brooke seemed truly sorry. I did not detect any malice in her."

"She wasn't sorry," I hiss bitterly. "She pitied me. It's different! I don't need anybody's commiseration, thank you very much!"

"It appears to me she was just being a sensitive and empathetic friend to you."

"Yeah, sure," I blurt. "Did you hear all the crap she said? I wanted to tell you, but you were alone, blah, blah, blah... she should have said 'unattended.' That's what she meant. As if I was some emotional wreck who can't cope on her own."

"Maybe she wanted you to have the support of your friends in a moment of need before revealing such troubling information to you." The lecture continues, "It is nothing to be ashamed of. We all have to lean on someone else at one point or another in life."

"So why didn't she tell me today, then, huh?" I practically shout. "I asked her to go out, not the other way around! What do you have to say about that?"

"Probably she knew she was about to break your heart, and she could not bring herself to do so because she deeply cares about you."

"Did she hire you as her lawyer?"

"No, I am just trying to make you see reason. What I mean is, would it have been so effortless for you to break her heart if the roles were reversed? Even if you knew it was the right thing to do?"

The answer, of course, is no, but I am not giving him the satisfaction of saying it aloud. I keep glowering at him from under my frown, stuffing my mouth with delicious chocolate-

I WISH FOR YOU

coated peanuts. He stares back unflinchingly, knowing he just scored a point.

We prolong the silent stare-war for some minutes until the buzzer rings in the background, distracting us. What now? Who is it?

I get up reluctantly to check who's out there.

"Yes," I say in the intercom.

"Hi Ally, it's me." Brooke's voice comes with a metallic distortion from the little plastic box.

"Brooke, I don't want to see you right now," I say, sighing. "I want to be alone tonight!"

"I brought sushi," she replies, hopeful.

"Brooke, you're not bribing yourself out of this with sushi!" I reproach her, only half convinced.

"I also got cookies and cream from Ghirardelli as dessert," she adds.

Ah, true breakup ice cream.

A long silence follows. I don't want to cave in, but she knows how to get to me. Sneaky Brooke, this is too much even for the most resolute person. I am totally bought.

"Did you bring chocolate cones?" I ask, somewhat mollified.

"Mm-hmm."

"Come on up," I say, pressing the door release button as an involuntary smile spreads on my lips.

Eleven
Sushi 'n' Cream

"You," I whisper to the genie. "Go to invisible mode. She can't see you here or she'll get suspicious."

I've just finished saying this when a light knock comes from the door. I open it and let Brooke in. She's carrying a gazillion little plastic bags.

"Uh, comfy clothes!" she exclaims, giving me the once-over. "I am in serious trouble, then."

"Let's eat," I say vaguely. I want her to bring up the subject this time.

I lay the table while she opens all the mini sushi boxes and places their contents on different platters. She knows her way around my kitchen better than I do. I admire all the serving plates covered in mini colored rolls, my favorite nigiri, and a vast selection of sashimi. She must've spent a fortune on this. I almost feel sorry for her. *Almost.*

We start eating in silence. The only noise is Sugar purring under the table. It's one of his techniques to get food; he purrs in advance to make you feel obliged to share. He's brushing against Brooke's legs insistently.

"Don't be nice to her," I tell Sugar only half-jokingly. "She's been bad."

"Listen, Ally, I'm sorry." Brooke finally cracks. "I should have told you right away, but there was no point in telling you over the phone and completely ruining your weekend when you were here alone."

"You could've said something *today*," I retort icily. "What if I hadn't texted you—would you have called me?"

The harshness in my voice takes even me by surprise. The genie, who's been leaning against the fridge listening intently to every word we say, gives me a reproachful scowl.

I WISH FOR YOU

"I... I..." She squirms guiltily in her chair, not able to catch my eye. "I'm not sure," she finally confesses.

I just raise my eyebrows, surprised.

"I should've called you first thing this morning, but I kept putting it off with one excuse or the other," she continues. "I've been fidgeting with my phone all day long, picking it up and putting it down."

"But why? Is it so difficult to talk to me?"

"No, honey, I simply couldn't just call you and break your heart," she admits. "I know how you feel about James, even if we never talk about it, and that deep down you still think of him as the love of your life. I wanted to spare you the pain—you're my best friend!"

The genie is giving me a smug I-told-you-so look.

"Didn't you think I'd find out anyway?"

"Ally, I'm sorry. I wasn't being rational. I just wanted to protect you."

"Well, I can assure you that having Vanessa Van Horn flaunt it in my face this morning wasn't the best of protections."

"Vanessa? He's engaged to *Vanessa*?" She's as shocked as I was. I've been bitching about Vanessa with her since we started working together.

"Yep." I feel a familiar choking sensation in my throat.

"I don't know what to say. I had no idea he was engaged to *her*. I can only apologize again. I wanted to protect you, and instead, I ended up hurting you even more."

She's on the verge of tears. Her sincere apology moves me, so I get up, go around the table, and hug her tightly.

"I am forgiving you only because you brought sushi," I whisper, near tears myself.

She looks at me, relief spreading all over her face.

"Just promise to tell me everything from now on, no matter how bad it is," I add, to mark my point.

"No more secrets, I promise," she agrees.

The word "secrets" makes me flinch, considering that right

now I am the one keeping a huge, invisible one. But hey, I have no say in the matter.

Once the sushi is devoured, I grab two huge bowls, fill them with ice cream, and bring them to the living room where Brooke and Sugar are already sitting on the couch.

"Do you want to talk about it?" she asks tentatively.

I open up and tell her everything: my casual encounter with the happy couple on Friday night, my weekend passed in tribulation, and the final stroke of this morning. I carefully leave any reference to the genie out of my tale.

"Vanessa, huh? Not really James's type," Brooke comments. "I mean, of course, she's beautiful, but James didn't strike me as the superficial kind."

"That's what I thought—this whole thing doesn't make any sense," I say passionately. "He can't love someone like her; not after loving me! You all think I'm crazy, but I still hope that he will come back to me one day."

"Ally," she says in a tone that you would use to explain to a three-year-old why he has to brush his teeth every night, "it's been over a year and he's engaged to another woman."

"But even that doesn't make sense," I insist. "Remember how he always said he wanted to move in with somebody before getting married?"

"Yeah—"

"I know what you're about to say," I interrupt her.

"No, you don't."

"So you're not about to tell me that it could have been a way to avoid getting serious with me?"

"No."

"Oh."

"I was going to tell you that even John was surprised by the news. He said the same about the living-together-before-getting-married thing."

"Do you think they live together?" I ask, alarmed.

"No, they don't."

I WISH FOR YOU

"How can you be so sure?"

"Well, this morning while avoiding calling you I did some digging," she replies shyly. "Remember when James was looking for a cleaning lady, and he asked me if I knew someone available since we live in the same neighborhood?"

"Yes, but what does this have to do with—"

She halts me with a raised hand.

"I gave him Linda's reference," she continues, excited. "I called her this morning and, well, it turns out she's still working for him. So I questioned her—I asked her if James had moved out, and she said no. Then I asked her if someone else had moved in, a female someone, and she said no again. She assured me that in his apartment there's no trace of a female roommate."

"Brooke, you're the best!" I exclaim, excited. "You're totally forgiven."

"At least I helped somehow. Again, I'm sorry for not telling you right aw—"

"Stop, no need to apologize again," I reassure her. "You just made my day! I needed a piece of good news, and that proves something is definitely off."

"Ally," she says pensively. "It's true that when James left you it came as a shock. We all thought he was in love with you." It's the first time she's admitted as much to me.

"See... see? I am not crazy," I cry.

"Yeah, this engagement thing seems too quick," she continues.

I sense a "but" coming.

"But, baby—" Here it is. "It happens all the time... people meet their missing half and throw any previous belief out the window."

"Don't say that," I wail. "She's not his missing half. *I am*."

"I'm sorry, babe, but I'm not very naïve about luurve," she says matter-of-factly. "I always try to see things for what they are. If a boyfriend leaves you, cheats on you, or gets engaged to somebody else, it's not because of a cosmic conspiracy. People do what they want to do."

"No exceptions?" I ask, hopeful.

"I haven't seen one yet."

"I know it seems absurd," I admit. "But I'm telling you, there's something wrong here. I simply can't put my finger on what it is—*yet*."

We keep obsessing about James for another hour or so. We don't reach any conclusion except for the one that it's time to go to bed.

"Are you planning on being a contestant on *Who Wants to Be a Millionaire?*" Brooke asks me as she gets up to leave.

"Why?" I ask, puzzled.

"Why else would you read all of this?" she asks, pointing at the scattered array of manuals adorning my living room.

"Oh, these, you mean," I stutter, trying to find a plausible excuse for their presence in my apartment. "No, they are... um... just some old books, um... my mom gave me to fill the cabinet. She always complains this place still looks as if I'd just moved in."

"Really?" she asks, perplexed. "They all look brand new to me." She picks up *Submarines Explained*.

"Well, Mom always keeps everything in a perfect state."

"Why was she reading about submarines, anyway?"

"That, uh..." Will the third degree ever be over? "It must've been my dad's. He loves war stuff." I take the book from her and gently shoving her toward the door.

Meanwhile, the genie is eyeing me from his comfortable position on my armchair, his facial expression growing increasingly amused by the second.

"Good night, babe," she says, hugging me.

"Night."

"Have you lost weight?" She detaches herself from me to check me out.

"Just a few pounds. It must've been the stress..."

"By the way, you look fantastic. I've never seen you this, well—your hair, your skin... did you do something?"

"Um, yes. Actually, um, I gave myself a spa day Saturday. Mani-pedi, haircut, and a Brazilian hair reconstruction. I didn't want to go to work looking too scruffy today and give the bitch too much satisfaction." Lie upon lie. I'll need to prepare my excuses in advance next time. I'm not very good at deceiving.

"Well, you're fabulous, girl. Speaking of good looks, what about that Arthur friend of yours?"

"What about him?" I ask, taken aback, worrying she might've found our story unbelievable.

"He seemed pretty handsome to me. Is he single?"

"Uh, oh. Yes, he's single." This is even worse. I know where she's going...

"So have you two ever...?"

"Shh, Brooke." My face is burning scarlet. "We're just friends."

"Why are you shushing me? It's not like he's around," she mocks me. If only she knew. "You should give it a thought. Besides being gorgeous, he behaved like a true gentleman."

"Please, Brooke, don't be absurd! We are just friends, and he lives in England. Plus, my heart is already taken."

"Okay, okay. I'm just saying," she says teasingly. "But we're going out Friday. Ask him along, will you? Good night."

"Okay, I will," I confirm, rolling my eyes. "Night."

She finally leaves, shutting the door behind her with a loud thud. I lean my forehead against it for a few seconds, relieved. I thought the questions would never end. Eventually, I turn around to the sight of the genie beaming with self-satisfaction.

"Gorgeous and a true gentleman," he repeats contentedly, standing in the center of the living room. "Not bad for an old fossil like me. Not bad at all."

"Come here, Mr. Attractive," I call sarcastically, moving into my room. "We have to give you a Facebook profile. She'll search you as soon as she gets home."

"Whatever you wish, milady," he replies complacently.

"Pick up a chair from the kitchen," I say, sitting at my desk and turning on my laptop.

"I will be fine standing."

"Okay. Let's see... First, we need to give you an email. Ah yes, and a cell phone. Remind me of that tomorrow—if you meet people they will ask for this kind of stuff."

"Life was easier in the eighteenth century," he observes dryly.

"Let's start." I ignore his comment. "Name: Arthur. Family name?"

"I would rather not say."

"Still being secretive, huh? Can you at least tell me the first letter?"

"P."

"You'll have to invent a surname if you don't want to say your real one," I clarify. "P. Let me see what I can do with that."

After some trials with different email providers, I finally find one with a free username coming only from the combination of Arthur and P.

"Date of birth?"

"Twenty-ninth of March."

"How old were you when you were, uh…" I hesitate a little. "Imprisoned in the box?"

"I was twenty," he answers in an indecipherable tone.

"But you look way older than that!"

"And I am indeed. However, I am afraid ageing occurred more hastily in my time." He doesn't seem offended by my age remark. Good thing the genie is not a woman.

"I can't put twenty. You have to be at least twenty-six or seven. Better twenty-eight, my age."

"You are twenty-eight and you are not married?" he asks, genuinely surprised.

"Rub it in, won't you?"

"Is it difficult to find potential good suitors at your *age*?"

I don't like the inflection he puts on the word "age."

"Don't worry. Nowadays the official spinsterhood age is thirty-something, or even forty."

"How interesting," he comments, genuinely perplexed.

"Back to your profile." I decide to drop the subject of age-appropriate singleness. "You are twenty-eight—remember this."

"Indeed, it feels good to drop several hundreds of years at once."

"Gender is male... password?"

"What do you mean?"

"A unique combination of letters and numbers only you know, so that only you can access your profile. Tell it to me, I'll type it in."

********** appears on the screen as I push the different keyboard buttons.

"It asks for a backup address. I'm putting in mine and..." I pause for suspense. "Congratulations, you have an email. Now Facebook."

I input all the basic information again and click the sign in button.

"Now we should add some pictures and some basic information to make it believable," I say, grabbing my phone. "Stay against that wall. I am going to take a picture of you. Cheese."

"I beg your pardon?"

"Smile." I roll my eyes.

He smiles charmingly as I take a couple of shots of him. I quickly email myself the photos so that I can open them on the laptop.

"Wait a minute!" I exclaim, opening the attachments. "You're not in the pictures—you're completely invisible!"

"I am afraid I cannot help you, milady—photography was not properly invented when I was last returned to the coffer."

"Let me try again." I touch the screen hopefully and check the result. "Nope, completely invisible. You'll be one of those snobs without personal pictures."

"Suits me perfectly." He smirks.

"Apparently."

I open some pictures from my London gallery for him to choose some.

"Is this London?" he asks, astonished.

"Yep."

"I do not recognise it in the least." Longing surfaces in his voice, along with wonderment.

"It has changed a lot in two hundred years, what did you expect?"

"Not this." I don't know if he's more scandalized or sorry.

"Some of the old parts are still there, though," I say, searching for some historical buildings. "This is the Parliament."

"This?" He sounds even more baffled.

"Wasn't this how it looked like in your time?"

"No."

"Hm, the Tower Bridge?" I ask hopefully.

"I am pretty sure it was not there," he comments, disdained.

"Ok, um…" I search desperately for something old-looking. "How about St. Paul's Cathedral? Was it there?"

"Yes, it was," he whispers, losing himself in the picture.

After that, I hit two other successes: the Tower of London and Buckingham Palace. But mostly modern London appears foreign to him.

At last, he selects a photo of the lion statues in Trafalgar Square with Big Ben in the background as his profile picture. Talk about a snob! As a cover pic, we put a nice night shot of the Tower Bridge that I took from a rooftop bar. We then add some plausible personal information, make everything as private as possible, and his profile is complete.

Twelve
Wrong Direction

I am about to close his page when an old urge pulls at me after being dormant for a long time. I slowly move the mouse pointer to the search box... it would be so easy.

"Upon my word, I have only witnessed guilty people wearing that expression," The genie cuts into my dilemma. "What are you doing?"

"Nothing." I sounded so insincere that I could've just admitted I was up to something.

"No point in denying it. I might as well have caught you red-handed from the countenance you are displaying. However, it is not my intention to accuse you of any wrongdoing. I am simply trying to resolve your nature as a function of my curiosity." He eyes me knowingly from his standing position next to me. "Let the cat out of the bag," he orders.

"Okay, okay. Guilty as charged," I admit and spill the beans. "I wanted to spy on James's profile. I blocked him so I wouldn't be tempted, but from your account, I can see his. He has no privacy settings."

"I don't quite grasp the meaning of all of this," he replies, a bit puzzled. "The only question I have is: do you find it a good idea?"

"Genie, I've already decided I must confront him," I argue. "I don't think viewing a picture or two will make much difference."

My last uncertainty dissipated, I type his name in the search box and press return. I guess I'll have to throw away my J.A.A.—James Avery Anonymous—token after this.

He left me in January last year. We've been apart for a year and a half, and I haven't looked at his profile for a long time. In fact, nothing on his page looks familiar anymore. My heart jolts in my chest the moment his smiling, tanned face appears on the screen. At least he doesn't have a happy couple shot as his profile picture, I console myself.

My eyes quickly flicker to his last relationship status update. I read the word "engaged" on the screen, and my heart drops into my stomach. Somehow seeing it in writing makes it more real. I decide to prolong my agony and scroll down one alien image after the other. My chest tightens at the thought of how little I know about his current life.

Of course, I come across the occasional picture with Vanessa, which makes me sick to my stomach. Fortunately, they seem more catalog shots than a portrait of two people madly in love with each other. Or maybe I'm only kidding myself, and Brooke's cynical version is the real one: love simply can end, and James has moved on.

As I keep sliding his profile further and further into the past, a bolt of lightning suddenly hits me. There on the screen staring back at me is a picture of our very last happy night together!

We were at Amy's New Year's party. The image shows me sitting on James's lap with one arm around his neck. I am wearing a bright red dress. I have one of those stupid glittering party hats on my head and a matching silver foil horn in my other hand. James is wearing black pants, a white shirt, and a ridiculous red bow tie that I'd bought him to match my dress. The picture must've been taken right at the stroke of midnight because there is silver confetti falling everywhere around us. The photographer caught that perfect moment of suspension before a kiss when the lips are about to touch but they haven't quite yet. He captured me staring deeply into James's eyes, smiling, radiating with happiness, and James staring back at me with the same intensity, his hands wrapped around the small of my back and pulling me toward him.

James broke up with me just four days after posting this picture. I am frozen to the spot, speechless, unable to move.

"Are you ill, milady?" the genie asks. "You look like you are about to faint."

His voice brings me back to present. I raise my gaze only to stare at him blankly, my head spinning with dizziness.

"Trust me, I can tell when a lady is about to collapse," he states seriously, and then magically levitates me onto the bed. "You should drink some hot tea with plenty of sugar."

English! Of course, they would solve everything with hot tea. As annoying as the genie can be, he probably just saved me from passing out. I'm shocked by my reaction. I mean, not even seeing James in the flesh, and with Vanessa nonetheless, caused me such an internal turmoil.

Maybe because seeing him in person didn't remind me so vividly of the sensations of that night. The feelings of pure love and of untainted happiness. The sense of belonging, of fulfillment, and the security of having one person there for you always. After seeing that picture, it's like I've survived life this past year instead of living it. I can't go on like this. I need to get to the bottom of this story and either win James back or get closure.

"Was that gentleman the famous James?" the genie asks, handing me a steaming cup of hot herbal tea. "Or, should I say, infamous?"

"Please don't joke about him," I murmur, still shaken.

"I apologise, milady. I will try to hold my tongue. You seem truly affected."

"I am," I whisper. "I wasn't prepared for what I felt."

"You never told me your story. How did you two meet?"

He's trying to keep my mind busy by changing the subject, and I am glad for it. I'd rather talk about how we started than how we ended.

"It was very romantic—a stroke of destiny, you might say." I gratefully sip my heavily sugared tea before launching into my narration. "It was a rainy day in September. I had just found my first job... well, my only job, since I'm still in it, and it was time for me to move out of the apartment I was sharing with Brooke.

"Upon graduating from college, we decided to split the rent for a nice condo in Wicker Park. But after just a couple of months of cohabitation, it became clear for the both of us that living together wasn't good for our friendship, as we kept arguing about almost everything. Plus, she was getting quite serious with Dave, and I sensed they were just waiting for me to move out so he could move in.

"So, I started searching for a place to live on my own where the rent wouldn't cut too deep into my entry-level salary. After four years of hideous college roommates and the not-so-good experience with my best friend, I'd decided I was going to live alone, no matter the financial stress. If it hadn't worked with Brooke, it would've never worked with anybody else, and I wanted to be free for once. Free to shower at any weird time of the day or night, to clean when I wanted to, and not when it was 'my turn', to watch whatever the hell I wanted on TV, and I was tired of having to wash every single dish the second I'd finished using it."

"Is it not a custom to have maids attending to these mundane tasks?" the genie asks without a trace of irony.

"Not if you're young and broke. Anyway, back to that day. I was heading home from work, and of course, I'd forgotten my umbrella. Soaking wet and in a hurry to reach the subway, I had my leather bag suspended over my head in a vain attempt at salvaging my hair from the pouring water, achieving only a reduction of my field of vision by half.

"Partly blinded by the rain and by my outstretched arms, I jumped on the first stair leading to my station without paying much attention to the track, and I gladly leaped on the arriving train. Inside, I found a seat right across from James and one of his friends.

"I was immediately fascinated by his dirty blond hair and warm, mocha brown eyes. He smiled at me, made a funny comment about the weather, and started a conversation. We chatted comfortably for a while until I heard the train's speaker announcing the next stop. I asked no one in particular about what direction we were heading, and James confirmed that I had taken the train in the opposite direction to Wicker Park. At that point, I jumped up from my seat, eager to get off as soon as possible, but with my usual clumsiness, I sent my bag flying in the air, spilling its contents all over the floor.

"I quickly managed to collect everything in time to get off, and I was looking around to check if anything was missing when James handed me a book I had just started reading that had fallen under his seat. He had a dashing smile stamped on his lips, and I remember disembarking the train feeling sorry I would never see his charming face again."

"But if you left, how did you find him afterward?" the genie asks.

"Be patient, I am getting to it," I say, carrying on with my story. "The very next day I found this apartment. I know it may not seem like much to you, but for me, a one bedroom with a decent size living room, one and a half baths, in a nice neighborhood, and at an affordable price was all I could hope for. Having five hundred and twenty square feet solely to myself was a humongous improvement at the time, and more than enough for my first bachelorette pad. Anyway, that weekend I packed all my belongings, including the novel I was reading, and I was ready to move.

"As you may have noticed by now, I am not the tidiest person in the world. In fact, it took me a couple of months to sort through all the boxes, and it wasn't until then that I rescued the famous book from lying forgotten at the bottom of one of them. I remember it as if it were just yesterday. It was a freezing Saturday afternoon in November—going out was out of the question due to the weather, so I decided to spend the afternoon cozily reading at home.

When I reached about halfway through the book, a white business card fell out of it. I recall being equally puzzled and excited by the discovery, even more so when my brain did the math and I understood it was the card of the attractive guy I'd met on the train. He must've slipped it in before returning the book to me.

"I kept flipping it in my hands for a very long time, undecided whether to call or not. I mean, I had met him two months previously—for all I knew, he could have a girlfriend by then, or he could be mad at me for not calling him sooner. In the end, I decided to give it a go. Whatever, I thought. Nothing to lose here. So I called him.

"At first I was a bit embarrassed, and I rambled a bit until he connected the dots and asked me if I was the soaked girl from the train. I said yes, and he joked that I was the slowest reader he knew. Then he asked me on a date, to which I said yes again. And, well, the rest is history."

"Your story is indeed charming," the genie says. "I fail to see what could have possibly happened to bring you to your present situation. It must have been something terribly wrong."

By now I'm calm enough to throw a furtive glance at my laptop. I look at the New Year's picture one more time and shake my head.

"I wish I could tell you, Genie, but I genuinely don't know. We were madly in love for three years. Everything was going well—no, not well, perfect. But after that night..." I point at the screen, "I don't know. The next morning James left my apartment, saying he had to see his mother to wish her happy new year. He was acting completely normal. I would even go as far as to say he was happy, excited. He told me to cancel everything for the following Saturday because he had something special planned. I thought he wanted to ask me to move in with him or something. But after he left, I didn't hear from him for the rest of that day or the two following. He wasn't picking up his phone, and he barely responded to my texts.

"Then Saturday came. I wasn't sure if we were still supposed to go out or not, so I stayed in waiting for him. He came here very late. It was January and freezing, but he didn't want to come up. He insisted that I met him in the street, so I put on a heavy coat and went downstairs.

"He was wearing only a shirt, no jacket, no coat, but he didn't seem to be feeling the cold. I assumed he was drunk since he reeked of vodka. He looked like a crazed man; he had bloodshot eyes, disheveled hair, and he hadn't shaved for at least a few days. I asked him what was wrong, and he told me it was over.

"We talked—actually, it was more me pleading desperately and crying while he stood there silently. He didn't give me any explanation, and when I tried to touch him, he pushed me away. I remember him shouting that he didn't love me and that he didn't want to see me ever again. To me, his eyes were saying the opposite of his mouth. I don't know how to explain it. He was crying, too. After that, he turned on his heel and ran away."

"I tried to contact him afterward, but he shut me out completely and my friends made me promise I wouldn't try to reach him again. So, after a month or two of utter rejection, I gave up."

"And you have not had an occasion to talk to him since then?"

"No. I tried to ambush him a couple of times since he wouldn't pick up his phone, but only succeeded in embarrassing myself further." I sigh. "So you tell me what happened, Genie, because I still have no clue."

Thirteen

Storm Winds

The next few weeks pass by without anything notable taking place. I spend most of my nights at home with the genie and Sugar watching TV or discussing the last two centuries' art, history, wars, and society.

It's interesting to hear the point of view of an authentic eighteenth-century gentleman. To witness his genuine indignation at the promiscuity, as he calls it, of this era, his passion in discussing his country (he was a bit shocked that the British Empire doesn't exist anymore), and his wonderment at the works of Monet, Van Gogh, Picasso, and many others. We even visited the Art Institute of Chicago so that he could see some of those paintings in real life.

We go out a lot with my friends, too, and everybody likes him. I have to say I am surprised at how well he gets along with everyone, considering that he is so old and all. I also like having someone by my side, even if it's only the genie. It feels good to be an even number again. I don't have to sit at the head of the table being the odd one among pairs anymore. It might seem like a trivial thing, but believe me, it's not so easy to go out with your friends when they're all involved in serious relationships and you're heartbroken.

I hated always being a solo witness to their constant PDAs. At least now when they start I can talk to the genie. I'm not jealous of them in a mean way; it's just that it's hard to be around happy people when you're not. Before the genie came into my life, I was beginning to retire into isolation and saying no more often than yes to their invitations to hang out, like the weekend at the lake. Yeah, I'm still single, and that having the genie doesn't really change anything, but it makes me feel less

I WISH FOR YOU

alone. I am a bit sad at the thought that I'll have to say goodbye to him sooner or later.

Anyway, for almost a month I basically go on with my normal life... well, with a bit more free spending and a lot less beauty torment. My recent list of acquisitions includes my apartment, a brand new car, and more clothes and accessories that I could ever wear. I've also grown my hair another inch and a half so that it's well below shoulder-length.

I go in to work regularly, except now I drive there every morning in my white Tesla. Yes, I could have splurged a lot more on the car, but I didn't want to attract too much attention toward my recently acquired wealth, and I like being "green."

Unfortunately, sticking to my semi-regular routine means that I have to face the bitch every day. But at least I get the satisfaction of constantly noticing her ring finger remaining inexorably ring free. I'm also keeping up my good work of equally improving Sally's appearance and damaging Vanessa's.

In short, my attitude could be referred to as burying my head in the sand, hoping that everything will fall into place naturally. In other words, James dumping Vanessa and marrying me instead. It's stupid, but since the next item on my list is confronting James, I'm scared to death, and going into hiding doesn't seem such a bad alternative.

What am I scared of? Learning the truth for once. Truth can be harsh, and it crushes hopes. I need hope. *You need to move on,* says a nasty little voice in my head. Ok, she's right, whatever "moving on" means. I can't live in a limbo forever, but what if I see him and the love is gone from his eyes? What if he's completely changed? What if he's not my James anymore? And what about me? Will I be able to keep my cool, or will I cause the mother of all scenes and have to live in shame for the rest of my days?

The ocean, however, can't remain calm for long, as the storm winds are always hiding below the horizon, ready to suddenly swell and bring gale. My storm punctually arrives on a Monday morning in the form of a call from Megan.

"Hi, baby," I say. "What's up?"

"Hi Ally, um…" She sounds awkward. "I was wondering if you were free for lunch today."

"Yeah, sure. Is something wrong?" I ask, worried.

"Um, we need to talk about it, um… in person."

"Can you at least give me a heads-up?"

"No, babe, I'm sorry. I have to go. See you at the Protein Bar on Adams Street at noon. Bye." She hangs up before I can add anything.

I don't try to call her back as it'd be pointless. Meg is very stubborn; once she decides how something should be done, there's no changing her mind. Noon, noon. It's only nine o'clock now! How can she leave me agonizing for three whole hours?

I spend the morning looking at my computer's clock every minute, not able to accomplish anything. Of course, when you wish time to speed up it begins to drag lethargically, one minute slowly turning into the next. It's driving me crazy! My mind is flying in all directions. I analyze all the possibilities and conclude that the big secret has to be about James, and if she wants to tell me in person, it can't be anything good.

At eleven-thirty, I can't stand it any longer. I grab my new Balenciaga and head to the elevator. Since the place is only ten minutes away from my office, I try to pace as slowly as I can, but arrive fifteen minutes early, anyway. At least I'm not caged inside, and I can distract myself by compulsively walking in circles around the block.

Finally, at five to twelve I spot Megan hurrying toward the bar. She has a weird expression on her face. A strong gust of wind prompts me forward and my third eye envisions rising waves looming in the distance.

I WISH FOR YOU

"Hi, babe," Meg says. "Sorry for keeping you in the dark all morning, but I didn't want you to break down in front of the bitch." She's being very direct. No sugar coating for me today.

We both order a Bar-rito and sit at the farthest table at the back of the bar to try to have some privacy.

"So what is it?" I ask, not sure I want to know.

"Ally, there's no circling around it," she replies grimly. "John has received the invitation to James's wedding." She fumbles briefly in her purse to retrieve an ivory envelope that she promptly hands to me. "I thought you would've wanted to see it," she adds.

"Sure. Thanks," I mutter, turning over the *thing* in my trembling hands.

Inside is my death sentence, written in black and white.

The paper feels soft under my fingertips; it must be expensive. The front of the envelope has two letters in bas-relief, J and V, which intersect nicely in the middle with the lower part of the J over the higher part of the V. James and Vanessa.

I open it.

Mr. and Mrs. Adam Van Horn
Request the honor of your presence at the marriage of their daughter
Vanessa Elaine
to
James Douglass Avery
Saturday, the fifth of September
At half past three in the afternoon
Van Horn Mansion
R.S.V.P.

Of course, she has a mansion.

The fifth of September. What? Is this the shortest engagement in history? What's the rush?

I imagined they would get married next year, or two years from now, even. Instead, I only have two months to stop this wedding. Even seeing it in writing doesn't make it seem real.

But *it is*. The ugly truth is staring back at me, nicely inscribed in fancy golden ink.

"I'm not going," Megan announces. "John has to since he's the best man, but I refuse to be there."

"Is he ok with it?"

"No, he's mad at me! Whatever... he'll get over it."

"Meg, you don't have to—"

"I know I don't have to," she interrupts me. "But I want to."

"Thank you, honey," I murmur.

Her gesture of loyalty is the last straw; two fat tears escape my lids, running down my cheeks. I quickly wipe them away with the back of my hand, but it's too late. Megan has already seen them.

"Come here, baby." She comes around the small table and hugs me tightly. "Can I do anything for you?"

"No thanks, I'm ok. It's just a moment, it will pass," I reassure her. "Thank you for telling me right away and for not going to the... *thing*." I don't think I can say the *w*-word right now. "How is everything with you and John, besides this?" I say, waving toward the invitation, trying to change the subject.

"Same old, except Amanda called him a few days ago."

"Amanda, as in his college sweetheart?"

"Yep, the one and only!"

"And what did she want?"

"Honestly, I think she was drunk-calling him."

"You're joking. Perfect Amanda, drunk? What did you do?"

"I sure as hell listened to the whole thing. Then I went a bit cuckoo for about twenty minutes raging about it, but he assured me it was a one-off and that he's neither in touch with her nor

I WISH FOR YOU

interested in being in contact. He said that he took the call only out of politeness. We concluded the argument with extremely passionate make-up sex."

"Aw, you guys. So you are cool about the whole thing?"

"Hmm, I don't know. It unsettled me a little," she admits. "I mean, he was with her way longer than he's been with me, but they broke up for a reason. It was her calling him, not the other way around, so yes, I guess I'm ok. Especially because she lives a thousand miles away." She winks.

We spend the rest of the lunch bitching about Amanda and spying on her Facebook profile, which keeps me distracted enough from my own problems.

However, once I say goodbye to Megan, the enormity of her revelation hits me full frontal and leaves me drifting back to work like a castaway struggling in the sea of my sorrow.

***

In the elevator ride up to my office, I decide to maintain a positive attitude. I need to come out from under the comforter and do whatever I can to stop this wedding, fire all my weapons, and if it doesn't work, at least I'll have no regrets.

The genie hasn't said a single word to me all morning, and I am thankful for it. He seems to have good empathy levels. He understands when I need to be left alone.

No more excuses, I say to myself while sitting at my desk. I need to set up a casual encounter with James. What should I do? I used to know the places he liked, but since I made it my life's mission to completely avoid setting foot in any of them for the past year, I'm not sure if he still goes there or not. The only way to find out is to try them out one after the other until I hit a winner. If this doesn't work, I'll regroup and think of something else.

I'm trying with difficulty not to think about the invitation, but its image keeps randomly flashing into my mind. I can't help myself, so I count the days I have left before the dreadful event. Sixty-one, including today.

Vanessa's proximity is not helping in keeping my mind off the topic. My awful mood gains her a few more pounds, and as I watch her squirm when my magic hits her, I notice with satisfaction that it has started to show.

Over the last couple of weeks, she has quit wearing uber-tight outfits, leaning more toward loose silky tunics that better complement her new form, so that an unaware eye could not note the difference. Unfortunately for her, I know she has fifteen more pounds to carry around.

Instinctively, I look at the other side of the office to where Sally's desk is. She, on the contrary, has her clothes hanging loosely around her a size too big. I shed her another five.

When both Vanessa and Sally screech in a matter of minutes, the genie raises a suspicious eyebrow at me. He still disapproves of my methods, but today I am mutinous. I'm a mess. Thinking about her perfect invitation, to her perfect wedding, in her perfect mansion, with *my* perfect man is giving me hot flashes.

I don't try to accomplish something workwise. It would be pointless in these conditions. Who cares if they fire me! That way I won't have to bear the bitch's presence next to me every day. Instead, I browse the Internet to check if the bars I intend to scout Thursday are still in business, have changed names, or something like that.

I say Thursday because I wouldn't stand a chance before then; James never goes out earlier in the week. When we were together, Thursdays were his reserved nights to hang out with his buddies. I'm hoping the same rules apply to his new relationship. Seeing him with Vanessa would be a no-no situation for me.

While I'm immersed in these reflections, I spot Vanessa furiously typing on her iPhone. She seems angry, and she keeps shaking her head, annoyed. If only I could snoop what she was

I WISH FOR YOU

texting, and with whom! Wait a second, there could be a way. I frantically grab a notepad from my desk and scribble on it as fast as I can.

Go spy who she's texting with and about what.

I then discreetly attract the genie's attention, tapping my pencil casually but noisily on the pad for him to read my message. He sees it and obediently moves over to Vanessa's desk, towering behind her, his neck stretched forward to peek at her bright phone's screen.

As soon as she stops texting, he comes back. I don't give him the time to reach me, but shoot up from my chair and head for the office restrooms. He follows me, used to the fact that the bathroom is the only safe place where we can talk without people thinking I'm hearing voices in my head.

I do my usual stall check to verify that we're alone and then start my interrogation.

"Was it James?"

"Yes."

"Were they having an argument?"

"Yes."

"Well, tell me more, don't just say yes," I cry out, impatient.

"He was saying he couldn't accompany her to some sort of event on Thursday because he was going out with his friend Bruce." The genie launches into his report. "She wrote it was really important for her that he went, he replied that she knew Thursdays were off limits and something else about alone time I don't remember. Then she asked him if he planned on keeping Thursdays for himself even when they were going to be married and have a family, and he answered he didn't see anything wrong in having one day of the week for himself. She did not text back."

"She's already suffocating him," I comment, delighted. "I bet he doesn't like it one bit. Did he say where he's meeting Bruce?"

"A place starting with H, and with a number afterward."

"Hub 51?"

"Yes, that could be it."

"Perfect! Genie, you're the best," I exclaim.

This is it. Thursday is my opportunity. James will be out, I know where to find him, and best of all, he's going to be Vanessa-free.

Now all I have to do is decide what to wear and, most of all, what to say to him. Ah, easier said than done. How will I get him to open up to me? Will I have the guts to ask him all the questions that have been swirling around in my head unspoken for eighteen months and twelve days? Not that I'm counting.

I also need to keep Bruce occupied while I'm talking to James, otherwise, he could easily dismiss me with a polite greeting and go back to his friend, but I'm already planning a decoy to make sure it doesn't happen.

I eye the genie maliciously. I don't think he's going to like it.

Fourteen
Hub 51

I'm at home in front of my mirrored closet, admiring the results of Brittany's efforts of these past two days. She has become my official personal shopper. I have her number, she has mine, and whenever I am in need of her services, I text her half an hour in advance and she's promptly available for me.

I'm undoubtedly her best client, and she's jubilant every time she sees me. It doesn't have much to do with my charming personality, but more with the commissions she gets on all my purchases. I must've given her income quite a boost.

Brittany, who by now knows my tastes and magically improved body-type to perfection, selected a ton of different outfits for me to try on. After two three-hour try-on sessions, I finally chose an outfit for tonight.

I'm wearing a black strapless jumpsuit with a gorgeous peplum detail. I went for it because it clings to my body flawlessly, giving me the sexy-but-classy look that I was going for. Looking at myself now, I'm confident I made the right decision.

To complete my styling, I've opted for an essential makeup style that will enhance my "natural" beauty and loose hair arranged in soft, voluminous waves, all magically obtained. To add some sassiness, I am pairing the suit with an outstanding pair of black leather Louboutins with an elegant T-strap, a peep toe, killer stiletto heels, and—my favorite—a petite bow detail at the top of the strap.

I put the shoes on and practice a few tentative steps. Uh... maybe an almost five-inch heel wasn't the best of ideas; I am not used to such heights. I hope I'll be able to walk in them without tumbling.

"What would you like to wear?" I turn toward the genie holding a magnificent dress in each hand.

"Nothing of the like," he says, eyeing the garments in my hands, disgusted.

It's clear that he doesn't have an eye for fashion because I'm offering him a choice between two statement pieces. The first is a sleeveless silk tunic in magenta with a loose drape fit. The second is a long-sleeved, lace sheath dress by Nina Ricci in a pale shade of blush with a jeweled neckline, ruched lace seams, and an asymmetric tulle hem. I bought them along with my jumpsuit; they're from last year's collection, so I got them at half price, but I'm not sure I can call it a bargain since the Nina Ricci alone was still worth a month's salary.

"Well, you have to choose one. I need you to be my wing-woman tonight," I explain.

"I beg your pardon?"

"My wing-woman," I repeat, enjoying the expression of pure shock on his face. "Your job is to keep Bruce entertained while I talk to James."

"And why should I wear a woman's dress? I would appear ridiculous."

"Not if you are a hot chick."

"A what?" he asks, shocked.

"A beautiful woman! *Capisce*?" I say, exasperated. I need to add *Urban Dictionary* to his book collection.

Horror appears on his face as comprehension finally dawns on him.

"You would not ask such a humiliating thing of me," he says with disdain.

"Yes, I would, and I am," I say firmly. "So which one is it going to be?" I ask, shaking the hangers with the two fabulous and very short dresses dangling from them.

He assumes the brow of a sulky child refusing to speak. He's so handsomely boyish when he does that.

I WISH FOR YOU

"Okay, I am choosing for you," I say, putting the lacy dress back in the closet. "Now—Bruce has a thing for blondes if I remember right."

"You are not seriously expecting me to go around wearing that pink rag," he protests.

"First, this is not a rag, but a very expensive dress, and second, yes, I do expect you to wear it. You said that when we were in public together, you could be any person I needed you to be. Well, tonight I need you to be a sexy blonde."

"Could I at least have the mercy of wearing something more covering?" he asks, desperate.

"No, that would be counterproductive," I reply ruthlessly. "Here, you should aim for something like this," I say, handing him a magazine. "You should be at least five-feet-eight because I'm giving you low heels." Not just any heels, in fact; a beautiful pair of silver metallic-leather Prada ankle-strap sandals.

"Anything else I can do for you, milady?" he asks, vitriolic.

"No thanks. Here are your outfit and underwear," I say, pulling a pair of plain, no-show Victoria Secret hiphuggers out of a drawer. "You can change in the bathroom if you need some privacy."

Lingerie is the last straw; he storms away, slamming the bathroom door loudly. I don't care if he throws a tantrum. I wouldn't have asked if I didn't really need his help.

While I wait for him, I check my reflection in the mirror one last time before I declare myself totally hot and ready to rock.

"Are you done?" I shout at the genie, who hasn't emerged from the bathroom yet.

"Are you sure you want to go through with this farce?" he asks pleadingly from behind the closed door. "Is it absolutely necessary?"

"Yes. Come on, don't be shy."

He finally comes out, presenting me with a ridiculous sight. He's wearing the pink dress, but he still looks like himself.

There is chest hair emerging from the neckline that is impossibly stretched over his broad chest and shoulders; his hairy arms and legs appear bizarre coming out of the silk dress, and his masculine feet are bursting out of the sandals like stuffed sausages.

"I thought I made myself clear when I said I needed you to be a W-O-M-A-N."

"Everybody else will see me as a woman—everyone but you," he hisses with nothing less than cold wrath. He then grabs the pochette I prepared for him and heads straight for the door and into the elevator.

I follow him, and from the look of admiration he receives from my neighbor in the hallway, I really have to believe that he looks like a hot chick to others. I barely manage not to giggle in the elevator as it'd be too much for him.

"So, Bruce likes to talk a lot. All you'll have to do is to pretend to be interested in what he's saying." I instruct him/her. "Just get him started on his job and you're good."

He nods without raising his gaze from the elevator floor.

"We should prepare a basic background story and pick a name."

He snorts loudly.

"I see I can't expect collaboration from you." I give him a mean side-glance.

I ponder a little while before telling the genie a brief credible tale to use with Bruce. I'm getting better at this kind of stuff. I choose Melissa for his name, informing him that I am going to call him Mel.

He doesn't comment and gives me the silent treatment for the entire taxi ride, but the closer we get to the bar, the less I care about his hurt feelings, and the more I worry about mine. As usual, the first victim of my emotional status is my stomach, which is becoming more clenched by the minute. It's a bit like before an important exam; my palms are sweaty and sticky, and

I WISH FOR YOU

I keep rubbing them against my tights in a vain attempt to dry them.

I am already regretting my decision. I wish I were in my apartment comfortably nestled on the couch in front of the TV, watching something funny. Except that if I were home, I probably wouldn't be paying attention to the TV; I would be obsessing over James and Vanessa. So, better find out whatever there is to find out and rest in peace. I have to be brave and confront him face to face.

"It's twenty dollars, miss," the taxi driver informs me when we arrive. I pay him with trembling hands and step on the curb in front of the entrance door.

I stumble awkwardly across the curb in my heels and anxiously push my way into the bar. "Melissa" comes in right behind me.

Inside, loud music is playing, giving me some rhythmic courage. I take in the scene and scan every table to locate James. My stomach does a tribal dance when I spot Bruce instead. He's tall and beefy just as I remembered him. He's holding a beer in his left hand while talking drunkenly to... James.

I can only see his back, but I'd recognize that nape anywhere. For a moment everything goes silent, and there's only him and me. My body is refusing to obey my brain. I want to step forward, but I am rooted to the spot, paralyzed, and I am just looking at his back from forty feet away! How will I manage to talk to him if just seeing his backside, and not even the best part, affects me so badly?

The spell is broken by a bulky guy bumping into me and almost knocking me down.

"Hey, watch out!" I yell, while struggling to remain on my feet. The Louboutins aren't helping.

"I'm sorry, babe. H-h-eeey, you're hot, wanna drink sumthing?"

He's clearly had too much already. I push him aside, disgusted, refocusing my attention on James.

Two girls are freeing a table right behind him. It's time to act. I grasp Mel's hand and drag her/him with me. This is the first time I touch the genie. Luckily for me, we're not alone, and I won't freeze to death.

I pick a stool and position myself shoulder to shoulder with James. Our backs are so close they're almost touching.

"The noise in here is atrocious," the genie complains. He seems pretty distraught by this whole evening.

"Shh. We're not here for the musical entertainment." I shout-whisper to him. "Now it's your turn." I pause a moment for emphasis. "You must stare at Bruce intently, batting your long lashes while smiling seductively."

"What?" he cries out, incensed.

"Shhh. You're acting weird—you need to be natural and in your element. You have to lure Bruce over here so that James will follow and I'll be able to talk to him. Please, Genie, please."

"It is not enough that I had to dress in this repugnant tatter that you call a dress—now you are whoring me out like a common tart. Never in my life!" he states, crossing his arms over his chest and pouting.

Of all the genies of the world, I had to get one too full of himself and with no self-irony. I have a feeling forcing him won't work, so I resort to pleading.

"Genie, please, I'm not whoring you out. I'm asking you to do me a favor as a friend. I'm begging you. All you have to do is look pretty, bat your eyelashes, and make some conversation." I do my Puss-in-Boots supplicating eyes.

"So be it, I will do as I am bid," he replies, serious but mollified.

I mouth a silent "thank you" and sit back to enjoy the show. Given the fact that I see him as a six-foot-two man dressed in a pink tunic, it is hard to keep a straight face while he's smiling coquettishly at Bruce.

"Is he looking at you?" I ask him eagerly.

"Yes."

"Good. Now you have to smile at him and then ignore him."

"Is this how courtship works nowadays?"

"Precisely."

His smile comes out more like a suffering grimace, but I'm hoping it appears better on his female face.

"Do you see what they're doing? Don't stare at them too directly," I add quickly. "Just do a quick peek," I instruct, glad to spot a server arriving with our cocktails. I take a long sip of my martini. Some Dutch courage may help as well.

It's funny to watch the genie go undercover. He's so obvious, but I hope Bruce will think that "she" is really into him.

"So?" I ask, impatient.

"Bruce is talking to James, and James is shaking his head. Bruce is shrugging and..." He stops, aghast. "He is coming here. What do I do?"

"Perfect. Remember, stay calm, smile, and ask him questions about himself. You're hot, you'll be fine."

"Hi. I'm Bruce." He throws a quick glance at me and then directs all his attention to "Melissa."

I don't think he has recognized me... good.

The genie seems a bit reticent, but I am sure they'll be just fine. "Mel" will probably pass for a hot but shy girl. So cute!

So far my plan is working. Bruce has taken the bait, just as expected... will James?

Fifteen
The Third Wish

I turn slightly to my left to check if James is following Bruce to our table, and he *is*. In the background that song from the nineties, "Sexy Boy", is playing. Is somebody being ironic? I watch him coming toward me as if in slow motion. He hasn't spotted me yet, but when his eyes meet mine, I feel an electric shock run through my body. He stops, standing rigidly by my side, looking at me as if I were a headless ghost.

We stare at each other in silence for a long moment. Then the song finishes and a trashy hip-hop one replaces it, breaking the spell.

"H-hi, it's nice to see you," I manage to stutter, choked by emotions.

"Uh... nice to see you too." He's more awkward than I am. I can't believe this is the same man that used to... well, you know.

"I hear congratulations are in order." Crap, did I really just say that?

A flash of rage passes in his eyes at my comment.

"Ally, I'm so sorry." If possible, he seems even more embarrassed than before. "I wanted to tell you in person. I asked V not to tell you until I had spoken to you."

Oh, but the bitch couldn't wait to rub it in my face. Does he really call her V? I hated the familiarity in his voice when he said it.

"Well, we haven't exactly been on talking terms lately. I haven't heard from you since..." I look him straight in the eyes, trying to find the courage to say what I've come to say. "Since the night you left me," I add in a low whisper.

"Yeah, right." He sighs, staring at the floor.

I WISH FOR YOU

I'm trying to read his body language, but it's impossible. He seems upset, but I don't understand if it is out of regret or if he's annoyed he has to listen to his ex-girlfriend giving him grief.

"Ally, listen." He suddenly raises his head and looks me straight in the eyes. "You're the most wonderful person I've ever met. I wish things had happened differently between us. I'm sorry if I've hurt you—it wasn't my intention."

As soon as he's finished talking, somebody shoves him from behind and his hand ends up on my bare shoulder. He removes it immediately, but even the slightest touch is enough to make my skin burn while a million questions pop into my head.

What do you mean I am the most wonderful person? What about Vanessa? Why are you marrying her and not me, then? How did you wish things had happened between us? Why did you hurt me so badly if you didn't want to?

"What do... about... marrying... didn't want to?" is what I say instead. Unfortunately, my brain appears to be going into overload as I try to voice all the questions at once.

"Yeah, nobody thought I'd get married so soon." I'm not exactly sure what question he thinks he's answering.

I try to regain my cool before speaking again. I need to be ballistic if I want to get something out of him. Let's play a little mind game.

"Well, when you meet the right person," I offer.

"Yeah, Vanessa is the right one," he says while scratching his nose. "I'm glad you're cool about it." Another scratch.

He's lying! All he just said is a big fat lie. He always scratches his nose when he lies. It used to drive him mad when we were arguing as I could always tell when he was lying and he never understood how.

"As long as you're happy, I'm happy for you," I push.

"Yeah, I'm happy." Scratch. "Truly happy." Scratch.

This is BS! I don't understand. If she doesn't make him happy, why is he marrying her? And why is he lying to me about it? And above all, why is he looking at me as if I was the forbidden fruit? He's the one who dumped me without a second thought.

It doesn't make sense. He's not telling the truth. If I keep asking questions, he'll just keep lying. How can I find out what's going on?

At that moment, a light bulb appears above my head! I know what I need to do...

"Can I borrow Mel for a few minutes?" I ask, turning to an overenthusiastic Bruce. It's understandable since in real life it'd be impossible for him to have a go at such a beautiful girl. If he knew what's underneath, I bet he wouldn't be so pleased with himself.

"You're stealing the light away from me," Bruce says, slurring his words in a disgustingly drunken fashion.

"I'll bring her back ASAP, I promise," I say, grabbing the genie by the hand to drag him toward the restrooms, our favorite conversational ambient.

He suddenly squeezes my hand forcefully while squealing.

"Ow, you're hurting me. What's up?" I protest, trying to free myself from his tight grip.

"I will let you know exactly what is going on. That troglodyte you call a man just now slapped my buttocks," he announces, indignant.

"Who, Bruce? Yeah, he's a pig," I say dismissively, and pull him down the stairs toward the ladies' room.

"This farce has to end," the genie says furiously. "I will not stand a second more of this humiliation. My lineage will not allow it."

"Genie, please, we're almost there. I need only another ten minutes," I say, entering the dark restroom. There is no line, but every stall is occupied.

"I will not stand another second of it." He's going berserk.

"Yes, you will, because I need you to." I'm becoming angry myself. "I don't have time for your whining right now. Can't

I WISH FOR YOU

you see how important this is to me?" All the emotions of the evening are coming out, infusing my words with passion.

As soon as I'm done speaking, a stall frees, and I push the genie inside, closing the door behind us and taking away any chance he has to reply.

"What are you doing?" he asks, scandalized. "It is not decent to be seen together in such a place. Where is your sense of propriety?"

"It's perfectly normal," I say crossly. "And I don't have time for etiquette lessons either. I want to express my third wish."

"What? Here? You certainly cannot!"

"Why? Is there another stupid rule against expressing wishes in improper surroundings?" I retort, irritated.

"First of all, you are befuddled by alcohol, and secondly—"

"First of all, you need to lower your voice." I interrupt him, whispering angrily. "And second of all, I am perfectly sober, and I most definitely don't need your advice. I want to know what James is hiding from me, and I need to find out now. I want to read his mind. Can I wish for it?"

"You are insane," he blurts, shocked. "That would have terrible consequences. You would never trust anyone again. People's thoughts are private for a reason. Trust me, I've seen it happen before. Mind reading will lead you to paranoia."

"I. Don't. Care. Can I do it or not?" I am adamant.

"Yes, but I beg you to reconsider. Think it through, wait until tomorrow."

"I can't wait until tomorrow. James is here *now*. For better or for worse, I need to know."

"I implore you not to go through with this. You will regret it."

"Why? I won't be reading people's thoughts all the time—only when I need to."

"The temptation will be too powerful to resist. You'll never be able to see people for what they really are—you'll get lost in the labyrinths of their psyche."

"I can handle myself."

"Everybody does. Only a few really are able to."

"It's a risk I am willing to take. Now, do I follow the usual procedure?"

He simply nods, his crumpled forehead clearly expressing his deep concern.

I admit it's a little difficult for me to take him seriously, given the fact that I still see him as a hairy dude in a pink dress. And he always worries too much.

I take a deep breath and cast my spell.

"I wish to be able to read people's minds—or not read them," I add, taking into account the genie's warning. "Whenever I want, forever. Avra Kehdabra."

This time there is no sound to confirm that everything went through all right, and I don't perceive any changes in myself.

"Is it done?" I ask the genie, uncertain.

"Unfortunately for you, yes," he replies gloomily.

"Great! So how does it work? How do I do it?"

"As always, you need to be able to see the person you want to read," he explains. "Again, it is not necessary to have eye to eye contact. However, as the eyes truly are the window to the soul, if you do, you'll have a much more powerful connection, and their intellects will be more open and available to you."

"So I just fix on somebody, decide I want to read this person's thoughts, and I'll have access to them?"

"More or less—however, mental objects aren't always clear text to be read. You could receive emotions, images, memories, and other unpredictable things. Please always remember what you're doing and never underestimate it."

"Okay."

"One last thing. Please keep in mind that not everything you see will necessarily be real—you could get figures that are just the products of people's imagination. The brain is able to conjure the most horrible things, but it doesn't mean a person will automatically act on what he or she is thinking…"

I WISH FOR YOU

Oh no! Another sermon that will last forever. I wonder what *he* would think if he could read *my* mind. I just want to go get some answers.

I try to interrupt but without success.

"Please let me finish." He stops my attempt to free us from this cramped stall. "It is very important you understand that even if you are re-living a memory of something that happened in reality, it doesn't mean that the way you are seeing it develop is what actually took place. The subconscious could be filtering the memory, making it different from what it really was, changing the facts, turning one's perspectives into truth."

"I'll be careful, Genie, I promise. Stop worrying so much—I swear I'll keep a critical approach to all that I see or hear," I reassure him. "Now let's get out of here."

Before going back upstairs, I want to test my new gift. I pretend to wash my hands to select my target. There is a cute girl standing next to me applying pink gloss on her lips. Let's see if I can really penetrate inside her inner self. I side-glance at her, concentrating on my intent.

Maybe I should be at home studying... Dad will cut my funds if I get another B... Whatever. I'm already too drunk to study anything, and Kevin's so cute...

I did it! It's amazing! I want to try it another time just to make sure I master the process. I turn toward a woman on my other side and focus.

Did he believe I was twenty-nine? I'm too old to be going around bars picking up boys... I'm thirty-five years old... I want to be married, I want kids, I want a house and a dog... I hate you, Marshall! You ruined my life! I hate you I hate you I hate you...

Whoa... back off, lady. Not only I could hear her thoughts loud and clear, but she also transmitted a strong wave of hatred so forceful that it scared me. And no... no chance in hell she'll pass for a twenty-nine-year-old.

I'm beginning to better understand the genie's admonitions. This gift is definitely not something to play with.

"Everything all right?" he asks me in a low voice.

"Yes," I whisper back. "Just dealing with other people's feelings."

He raises an eyebrow, and I don't need to read his mind to know he's thinking "I told you so."

I run up the stairs, unable to contain myself. I stop abruptly at the top when I see Bruce standing alone at our table looking pissed for some reason. I concentrate on him to understand what's going on.

I can't believe he left me here... first, he begs me to go out with him to avoid a boring dinner thingy with his stupid fiancée... then when I have something good going on for me, he ditches me because he's scared of his ex... bastard... Vanessa is ten times hotter than that Ally... what's he complaining about? I hope Melissa is the easy type...

After that, I receive a clear vision of what Bruce hopes to do with "Melissa" later tonight. Eew. I'm not sure if I feel more revolted by Bruce, or disappointed that James took off. I feel like crying. He literally ran away from me. *Again!*

My lower lip begins to wobble. I bite it, resolute. I'll see him again and get my chance at the truth another time; I just need to be a little more patient.

"Come on, we have to get out of here without Bruce seeing us," I inform the genie.

"Why? What happened? What about your quest for truth?"

"I'll explain later. I want to go home."

"Thank goodness tonight is over," the genie sighs in relief behind me.

Sixteen
The Help

Finally, it's the weekend. It's Saturday morning and I am optimistic. Vanessa didn't show up for work yesterday, so I didn't have a chance to pry into her mind to check how her little row with James is proceeding, or if he has told her about seeing me on Thursday. Instead, I've developed a plan to peek in her home—or her daddy's mansion, to be precise.

Mom has invited me to lunch today, and since my parents live in Lake Forest, forty-five minutes north of Chicago, I've decided to do a tiny detour on my way back to the city and make a brief stop to check out the Van Horn palace... at least from the outside.

Megan has sent me a scanned copy of the wedding invitation with the address, and I've input it into three separate electronic devices to be sure not to lose it.

"Do you want to taste an original homemade American meal?" I ask the genie.

"I would love to," he replies, enthusiastic.

"There's a catch, though."

"As always in life. Pray, tell me what it is."

"You'll have to be a girl again. I wouldn't hear the end of it if I brought home a man," I explain. "Plus, I wouldn't want my parents to get the wrong idea, have any false hopes... you know?"

He fiercely protests for half an hour, but when he sees that I am immovable, his curiosity for the world gets the best of him.

"Would you have me wear that hideous pink rag again?" he finally asks, resigned.

"Oh no," I reassure him. "You can choose whatever clothes you like from my wardrobe, and you can be as covered up as you can bear in this sultry weather."

He browses through my closet unwillingly, his expression becoming grimmer and grimmer with every passing item. In the end, after having scrutinized every possible article, he settles for a pair of beige, loose linen pants, white sneakers, and a white T-shirt, and goes resentfully into the bathroom to put them on. When he reemerges changed, I don't have the slightest idea how he looks, as I keep seeing him like a man dressed in feminine clothes.

Having him come along simplifies my plan a great deal. I texted Mom saying I was bringing a friend over and that we planned to go to the beach in Evanston afterward, which is a perfect excuse to leave early and get a head start on my spying mission.

The lunch goes smoothly. Mom prepared one of her famous pasta salads, tasty but refreshing; in short, the perfect meal for this weather. We all enjoy it while sitting in the shadows in my parents' garden among one of the vastest flower displays I have ever seen.

In one corner loaded with vases, I spot the little rack Mom bought at the flea market and find myself wondering what would have happened without it. Was I really destined to find the coffer? Or was that day a mere coincidence? It's impossible to say. What I do know is that without the magic help of my little coffer, I'd be lost.

Melissa, the genie's female alter ego, now has a strong background story. It's been embellished and enriched since the basic one we gave Bruce, and I am pleased to say my parents like "her" very much.

"You can tell she's European," my mom comments at one point while we're alone in the kitchen. "Such good manners."

"Yeah," I agree. "She almost seems to be from another time," I add, suppressing a smile.

***

I WISH FOR YOU

At two-thirty, lunch has been over for a while and I am impatient to go, so I use my ready-made beach excuse to leave without opposition. We say our goodbyes and speed away in my new car, which, by the way, impressed my parents a lot. Of course, I had to lie about it. I told them that I've been promoted at work and decided to reward myself with it, which gave their parental pride an extra boost.

I follow the driving directions the built-in navigator is kindly providing me, and twenty minutes later I'm pulling up in front of the Van Horn mansion. I decide to park after a bend in the road, in a small parking lot out of sight from the house.

"Where are we?" the genie asks, perplexed as we stop.

"Vanessa's parents' house."

"And why exactly are we here?"

"I'm curious," I answer. "I want to have a look at it."

"What are you doing?" he asks, shocked, staring at my nose as it pops about half an inch forward.

"Camouflage. I can't risk being recognized; I'd be ashamed for the rest of my life."

I make my hair a light reddish blonde color, change my haircut to a short bob with bangs, turn my eyes green, cover my face in cute little freckles, and shape my nose thinner and more pointed, sort of like Jenna Dewan before and after. I check my reflection in the rearview mirror, satisfied. Nobody should be able to recognize me.

"Is the house open to visitors?"

"Not that I know of."

"What is your plan, then, if I may ask?"

"Just to walk past the main gate and see if we can get a peek at the house."

"It seems a waste of time to me. What shall we do afterward?"

"Nothing, we go home. I just want to see what it looks like."

We walk along the side of the fenced garden to try to find an opening. Unfortunately, a dense hedge, impenetrable to the eye, lines the whole perimeter. Once we arrive at the gate, the situation doesn't improve much. All we can see is a long driveway lined with tall cypress trees whose end gets lost in the horizon. I try to walk a bit forward along the perimeter, but I can't see anything apart from impeccably pruned shrubberies. I head back to the gate, linger there a little longer, and finally, pronounce myself defeated and ready to go home with nothing accomplished. I'm already moving away when I hear someone calling rather desperately.

"Hey, young lady. Where do you think you're going?"

I turn back to see a rather plump lady dismounting an electric golf cart driven by a young man wearing a uniform.

"Me?" I ask, surprised.

"Yes, you and you," she confirms, pointing at the genie and me. "You're already late—what were you doing walking up and down? Enjoying the nice weather?"

"Late?"

"Yes, almost two hours. I was beginning to lose hope," she says, panting, apparently from the effort of sitting in the cart.

I have no clue what she's talking about, so I enter her thoughts to get an idea.

This is the last time I call Monique's agency. Joe keeps insisting I help her, but she's so unprofessional and disorganized... I don't care if she's his sister! I hope these two can do a decent job... Mrs. Van Horn is so fussy about the house help.

She thinks we are substitute maids or something. We could play along and see the actual house from the inside! This is great!

"I'm sorry," I say. "Monique gave us the wrong directions, and we got lost."

Typical, damn Monique. And damn you, Joe.

"Well, come in," she says instead, "we don't have any more time to waste."

I WISH FOR YOU

The genie is eyeing me, astonished, but has the good sense not to say anything. He follows me silently as I get in the cart.

I hope that sorry excuse of a sister-in-law didn't send them over without the uniforms again so that they can steal some others from here... the cheap vixen.

This lady is a wonderful source of information.

"I am sorry, madam. Monique didn't give us any uniforms—she said you would provide them."

"Of course." From her polite reply, you'd never guess the stream of insults flowing through her head.

The ride on the golf cart takes at least ten minutes. On the way, we pass a large pond with a nearby gazebo, some of the most amazing flowerbeds and shrub sculptures I've ever seen, a couple of tennis courts, an Olympic-sized pool, and a riding area with adjoined stables. This place is a castle! When we finally reach the house, I am surprised we don't find a moat and a drawbridge.

The building is a classic Victorian style with heavy stone walls, turrets, round towers with cone-shaped roofs, stone archways, and windows popping out from every direction. We are shown in from a side door, directly into what must be the servants' quarters.

"Here are your uniforms. Change quickly and remember to return them before you leave." Plump Lady retrieves two perfectly folded black and white bundles from a cupboard. "You can use the service toilette to change."

The uniform consists of a simple black dress with a white collar, a knee length skirt, three-quarter sleeves with white cuffs, a white apron, and a maid's hatband. Very old-fashioned.

"Do you care to enlighten me on what is happening?" the genie whispers angrily as soon as he shuts the bathroom door.

"We've just been hired as replacement house help," I explain nonchalantly.

"Now you want me to be *a servant*?" he asks, affronted.

"You've already played the whore," I tease. "Being a maid won't be much worse."

"I will not do it."

"Oh, come on. We are completely incognito. This is the perfect opportunity to see the house."

"Again, I fail to see why."

"For the hell of it," I reply curtly. I'm fed up with his constant complaining. He's too full of himself and has no sense of humor. "And you have to do as I say, like it or not. So shut up and get changed."

When he's done, he storms out of the little bathroom with his usual frown, and I follow. Plump Lady is waiting for us exactly where we left her. She eyes us thoroughly, raising an inquisitive eyebrow, and finally gives us an almost imperceptible nod of approval.

"Mr. and Mrs. Van Horn will be arriving at six o'clock sharp." She proceeds to give us our instructions for the night. She speaks like a military general giving his orders to his field troops before a battle. "We expect Miss Van Horn and her fiancé, Mr. Avery, to arrive shortly afterward."

Vanessa is coming here! And James too! My stomach does a double flip. What if they recognize me? No, it's impossible. My own mother wouldn't recognize me in my current disguise. Oh no, this is bad. Or good? I'm not sure. I'll have a chance to study them closely without anyone knowing, which is good. But I'll also have to endure their togetherness for a whole evening, which is bad. I guess that at this point there's no going back... I hope they're not too PDA-y. It would be too painful.

"By then their four bedrooms and en-suites must be prepared and cleaned to perfection," Plump Lady continues.

Four bedrooms? Ah, ah. Vanessa's parents must be really antiquated... I love them. At least Private Displays of Affection are ruled out.

"You," she says bossily, pointing at the genie. "You will be in charge of Mr. and Mrs. Van Horn's suites. And you," she adds, pointing at me, "will be in charge of the guest rooms. I'll give you freshly laundered sheets and bedspreads. Mrs. Van Horn needs an extra comforter because she's always cold. Mr. Van Horn, on the contrary, doesn't want any blankets but requires extra pillows for his back. The floors need to be vacuumed and mopped. Dust thoroughly everywhere and open a window to let fresh air circulate. You'll have to bring up a cold bottle of water in its glacette and a crystal glass to be placed on each nightstand. The gardener will provide you with a bouquet of fresh flowers for each room..." She goes on detailing every petty element of the homemaking we have to do. After she's done with the rooms, she goes on and on and on about the baths, halls, and whatever other parts of the house the owners might be using.

While she's talking, I zone out completely. Who cares if Vanessa gets the wrong scent of soap? The only information I register is that we will be serving dinner as well. Plump Lady kindly informs us that this means the cleaning chores will have to be completed by five in order to give us enough time to arrange the dining room for dinner.

It all sounds like so much fun!

Seventeen
The Van Horns

This visit is going beyond my wildest dreams. Not only do I get a full tour of the house, but I'll also be able to spy on its unsuspecting inhabitants. I can't wait for dinner to start. I'll hear every conversation, study mutual behaviors, and, of course, read everybody's mind—all at the same time. I am positive that I'll finally discover what James is really up to.

"Follow me," says Plump Lady, interrupting my musings and brusquely shoving in our hands a ton of cleaning supplies she retrieved from a storeroom.

Unfortunately, dinner will not be for another two hours, so, for now, I just have to be patient and concentrate on the house profiling. We follow Plump Lady into what I assume must be the grand hall. I can't avoid gaping open-mouthed at its grandeur. The stairs here have at least a hundred steps.

This foyer is as big as my apartment, or more like mine plus the ones of the tenants up and downstairs since it's a three-story atrium. I knew Vanessa was rich, but I didn't think her family was this loaded. The luxury of this house is overwhelming.

Getting up the stairs appears to be the ultimate effort for Plump Lady. It takes us a lot longer than necessary to reach the upper level. Once there, she shows us the rooms we have to clean, and from the quick glance I get before we move on to the guest baths, I happily realize that by being assigned Vanessa's room, I was gifted an additional opportunity to poke my nose into her privacy. In fact, where James has been assigned to a plain guest room devoid of any character, Vanessa is sleeping in her old bedroom that is still decorated with all her teenage memorabilia.

As soon as Plump Lady leaves us, I decide to begin my work there. Going inside is like entering into Barbie World. If you

I WISH FOR YOU

could use a room to describe the stereotype of a girly girl, this would be it. Pink in many shades is the dominant color. There's so much it gets offensive to the eye.

I look around the shelves to see many trophies and pictures of an adolescent Vanessa. There's several of her in a cheerleader uniform, one where she's kissing a football player, and another where she's being crowned prom queen... Bah, can it get any cheesier than that?

Her wardrobe is full of out-of-style clothes. I scan the tags to confirm that every single one is designer. The en-suite bath, mostly made of pink marble, is stocked with the most expensive lotions and beauty products.

On impulse, I grab her toothbrush and dip it in the toilet, but I regret the move almost at once, so I throw it in the trash and replace it with a new one. Plump Lady gave us each a bagful of toiletries. This house feels more like a hotel; it doesn't have that warm, homey feeling. I escape the crime scene and decide to concentrate on the vintage contents of the walk-in closet.

Once I'm done scrutinizing every possible space, I open the French doors and walk outside on the balcony where I am presented with the most beautiful view of the lake. This must be the estate's private beach. I wonder what it was like to grow up amidst all of this.

It takes me about one hour to do the cleaning. I've never been good at house chores, so I'm not sure what the outcome is, but I suspect it would not rise up to Plump Lady's standards. My only hope is that the stairs represent too much of an obstacle for her to come up again and check.

My last chore is to get the freshly cut flowers and the water. As I jog downstairs to get them, I'm struck by a sudden inspiration, and before running up again I grab a small sample of my favorite perfume from my bag. Back upstairs, I spray a generous quantity of it on James's pillows, hoping he will dream of me tonight.

***

"Maid apparel suits you, you know?" I tease the genie while we set the table.

"Not funny."

Oh, he wouldn't say that if he could see himself with the maid hat, complete with its white frills, beautifully perched on his masculine head.

I look perplexed at the flatware. There's more spoons, forks, and knives than the Titanic.

"What do we do with all of this?" I ask, confused.

"It seems pretty basic dinnerware to me."

"Oh yeah? What is this then?" I challenge him, picking up a random piece.

"Fish fork."

"And this?"

"Salad knife."

"And what's the difference with this?" I ask, lifting an almost identical knife.

"That is clearly a bread knife." He then proceeds to show me the correct order for the entire cutlery set, the glasses, and the correct placement of the bread plate and napkin.

"Finally, a proper dinner table," he comments once we're done positioning everything.

Argh, I hate it when he plays the lord.

"Let me see what you two have done," Plump Lady chimes in, and carefully scrutinizes the table. When she can't find anything out of place, she seems more annoyed than relieved. "Come with me," she snaps curtly. "We have to await the owners on the front porch."

Seriously? Is this an episode of Downton Abbey?

Lined up with us in front of the house is the butler, the cook and her assistant, three gardeners, the stableman, two drivers, and of course Plump Lady. Twelve people in total, rigorously aligned according to service hierarchy. I find it classist and

I WISH FOR YOU

tacky. The genie, on the other hand, seems to appreciate it very much.

While we wait, I try to calculate how much they must spend to maintain this lifestyle. The running of this estate must be comparable to a small country's GDP. Luckily, our vigil isn't long as Mr. and Mrs. Van Horn arrive in a black Bentley at precisely six o'clock.

Vanessa's dad is a tall, stylish man with short white hair and piercing blue eyes. Her mother could be described as an emaciated blonde who looks ten to fifteen years younger than what her real age must be, and she has the snootiest facial expression I've ever seen. She literally sticks her nose up in the air, slightly wrinkled, as if she was constantly smelling something disgusting.

"Miranda," Mrs. Van Horn says to Plump Lady, stopping on the entrance stairs and eyeing the genie and me with the same offended expression. "Who are these?"

"Replacement help, Mrs. Van Horn."

"What happened to Betsy?"

"She wasn't able to find anyone to look after her kids, so she was forced to remain at home."

"It's the third time she's taken unauthorized leave this month. Unacceptable. I want her fired." Her tone is glacial while she pronounces the sentence.

"Yes, madam." Plump Lady—well, Miranda—says, subdued. She seems mortified.

"Adam, would you believe this," Vanessa's mother adds, turning to her husband. "It is becoming increasingly difficult to find reliable housemaids, and they talk about rising unemployment rates! If people simply showed up to work…" Her voice trails off, and I'm not able to hear the end of her disheartened speech.

She just left a single mother with who knows how many kids jobless, but hey, life is hard. What about her suffering for lack of proper servants? She's even meaner than her daughter.

"Come on, you two, there's still work to do in the kitchen. We don't have time to waste." Miranda recalls us to our duty, her voice still wobbly.

"How many kids does Betsy have?" I ask tentatively.

Three. If it weren't for Mr. Van Horn, I would have quit the job a long time ago. That wife of his is pure evil.

"None of your business, Miss," she says harshly. She's playing tough on the outside, not letting her internal disappointment show. "Now let's make sure dinner goes by without any accidents tonight," she adds in a business-like voice.

We're busy with the last preparations when a male voice interrupts us. "Excuse me, ladies."

"Mr. Van Horn, what are you doing back here? Is something wrong?" Miranda frets.

"I wanted to give you this," he replies, handing her a white envelope. "It's a severance check for Betsy. She should be good for some months."

At least there's someone decent in the family.

"Thank you, Mr. Van Horn." Miranda is practically tearful.

"It's nothing," he says curtly. "Excuse me again, I have to go. I think my daughter has just arrived."

Is James here as well?

I have to wait another half an hour before I can find out as we're not allowed out of the kitchen again before dinner starts and Miranda the Plump sends us out to serve soup and salad. The genie got the soup and I'm glad for it; I'm sure I would've splashed it somewhere, somehow.

"I hope this is worth it," he whispers to me.

"Sure is," I say, grabbing the silver tray with the four tiny salad plates.

The atmosphere at dinner is serious and awkward. The formal setting, and the fact that they are four at a table for at least twenty people, aren't helping. The Van Horns are sitting at

I WISH FOR YOU

the opposite extremes of the table while Vanessa and James are in the middle on opposite sides. Nobody is talking.

I decide to quickly scan everybody's mind while I serve the salad. I start with Cruella Senior.

I have a fat daughter.

Her day isn't getting any better.

I move on to Vanessa.

Mom is probably thinking that I'm fat.

You betcha.

"How is your mother, James?" Vanessa's father says, breaking the silence.

"Very well, thank you, Mr. Van Horn."

I hope this is over quickly, he mentally adds.

James is definitely not enjoying himself. Good!

We give them fifteen minutes to finish the salad before we clear the plates and bring out the appetizers. This time, the genie is in charge of the plates and I'm in charge of the wine and water. This way I get to stay in the room the whole time. Perfect!

I start a refill round, beginning again with Vanessa's mother and continuing in the same order as before. Of course, I keep reading everybody's mind as well.

And what's with the acne?

That would be me! I smirk inwardly.

We'll have to hire some makeup expert for the wedding. The wedding! I hope she'll fit in her dress after I've spent twenty thousand dollars on it.

This woman is obsessed with her daughter's weight.

Mom will kill me if I don't fit into my dress, Vanessa thinks.

Never have the words "like mother, like daughter" been more right. Their minds are perfectly tuned.

"James, tell us... have you decided where you will go for your honeymoon?" Mrs. Van Horn asks.

Yikes! I never thought of the honeymoon; surely because I never thought about the wedding actually taking place. At least, not if I have my way.

"I have it all planned, but I can't say anything, Mrs. Van Horn. I want it to be a surprise for Vanessa."

Really? Does he mean it? I focus on him for a moment.

I have to stop thinking about Ally. She's in the past. I'm losing my mind. Even this maid reminds me of her, her smell...

I actually sense the aroma of my perfume as he thinks about it. Whoa, he recognized me! And he's thinking about me! But why does he want to stop? And why is he organizing a romantic trip for Vanessa if he's thinking about me?

I want to know more, but Mrs. Van Horn engages him in conversation, not leaving any room for him to think about anything, least of all *me*. Bitch! I resign myself to move on to Vanessa's father, filling his glass with red wine.

I know you don't love my daughter, but I sure hope you'll make her happy, or I'll strangle you and your harpy of a mother myself. I swear!

"That will be enough, thank you," Mr. Van Horn says to me, and I suddenly notice I've filled his glass to the point that the ruby liquid is about to overflow. I was so taken by his thoughts that I wasn't paying attention to what I was doing.

"Oh, I-I'm sorry, sir," I stammer, still shocked by the implication of his brain streaming and by the strength of his spite for James and his mother.

I quickly fill James's glass and resume my position in a corner of the room, concentrating entirely on Vanessa's dad.

I need to make some changes to the Hudson contract... the assignment clause needs to be stronger...

What? How can he switch topics like that? Go back to your daughter's future, will you?

Liquidated damages are too low... I don't trust those bastards...

I WISH FOR YOU

I desperately read his mind on every possible occasion, but his thoughts stay resolutely on legal matters, and everybody else's thinking is worthless crap. Tonight, instead of providing answers, has generated an entirely new stream of doubts.

Eighteen

Sleeping Arrangements

Date: Mon, July 13 at 6:07 AM
From: HRManagement@CrispyKoob.com
To: Undisclosed Recipient
Subject: Corporate Retreat 25th and 26th of July

Dear Employees,
Crispy Koob Corporation is glad to announce the upcoming yearly Corporate Retreat. As we are celebrating our fiftieth year in business, we are happy to announce that this year we will be hosting a special two-day event at the Hilton Chicago Indian Lakes Resort. All full-time staff members and their families are invited.

This special weekend will be a unique opportunity to unwind after our busiest year so far and enjoy the company of fellow employees outside the office blah, blah, blah…

Participation, albeit not compulsory, is strongly recommended for all employees.

Dress code is semiformal for Saturday and Sunday morning, sportswear for Saturday afternoon, and formal for Saturday night's Gala.

Schedule

The first business session begins promptly at 9:00 a.m. on Saturday with a continental breakfast available beforehand. The program ends at 5:00 p.m. on Sunday.

I WISH FOR YOU

Registration

You can register directly blah, blah, blah.
Online registration will close on Monday, July 22.

Meals and Lodging

Blah, blah, blah...

Directions

The Resort is located approximately half an hour's drive west of Chicago. Follow I-290 W to Bloomingdale, then take exit 7...

The email continues with a list of directions I won't need, as per the Tesla built-in navigator.

 The Corporate Retreat. I completely forgot it was coming up. Will Vanessa come with James? If she does, I'll be in the same place as James for two whole days. I didn't expect it so soon, but what better occasion to find out what he's hiding?

 On the other hand, I hope they're not too cute and cuddly when Vanessa's parents are not there. I don't think I could stand it! It could be either the perfect opportunity or a recipe for disaster.

 I need to clear my head. I'm still wrecked from the weekend. Housekeeping is an exhausting job; last night we didn't get home until after ten. In fact, after serving dinner on Saturday evening we discovered that the maid job was a two-day engagement. We were lodged in the servants' quarters (not joking) for the night and had to attend to the pretty family for Sunday brunch. Unfortunately, nobody had anything interesting to think about for the whole time, and they all left as soon as the meal was over.

 We weren't so lucky. Miranda the Plump didn't let us go until the whole house was pristine and every little piece of flatware, glass, and linen was perfectly clean and back in its rightful cupboard or closet. After that, once we got finally home, I spent half of the night mulling over Saturday's dinner, wondering if James still loves me and why Mr. Van Horn is so sure that he doesn't love his daughter.

I've never been so tired in my entire life; the only hope lies in coffee. I'm glad my company fully understands the link between good coffee and employees' performance, ensuring staff members never lack their needed dose of caffeine by offering complimentary Starbucks in the office kitchenette, which is where I am headed right now.

Pouring the dark, hot liquid and inhaling its rich scent makes me feel better already. I lean against the countertop and relish the strong taste of my get-up-and-go elixir, closing my eyes. Mmm, I needed five minutes of peace.

"Excited about the retreat?" Vanessa's voice snaps me out of my little serenity corner.

She startles me so much that I spill the precious beverage all over the place, luckily missing my body, or I'd be in for third-degree burns by now.

"Um, yeah, sure," I reply distractedly while wiping the mess I created—or should I say that *she* created—with a paper napkin. Did she follow me here? I turn around, decided to find out immediately.

I wonder how she will cope with two days of seeing James and me together.

That answers my question; she came here on purpose and to brag. Is she the only one who didn't notice something is terribly wrong in her so-called love story with *my* James?

"Will you bring someone?" she asks casually.

I bet she'll come alone, single and pathetic.

All the sympathy I may have had for her after meeting her mother vaporizes faster than a vampire who has met the sun, along with any idea I had of losing her a few of the pounds I've given her. Nope, she's keeping all fifteen of them.

"Yeah, I'll bring my boyfriend." The lie escapes my lips before I can think about what I'm saying.

I WISH FOR YOU

A boyfriend? She just made it up. Even more pathetic.

"I didn't know you were seeing somebody. What is the lucky gentlemen's name?" she asks instead.

"Arthur." Again, words seem to be coming out of my mouth of their own volition. But the look on the genie's face is priceless; he's here but invisible, still coming to work with me every day and following me around.

"Arthur what?" she asks rather rudely.

"Uh, hmm... P... Pemberley." Did I just name the genie after Mr. Darcy's house? I was never good at thinking on my feet, and I guess the only British name my brain could associate with the letter P was Pemberley. I'm going to strangle him for not telling me his real surname.

"Pemberley? It sounds familiar; where have I heard it before?"

Only in Jane Austen's most famous novel, you ignorant cow.

"Well, enjoy your coffee," she adds. "I can't wait to meet this Arthur beau of yours." *If he exists.* "Ciao."

Needless to say, my quiet, relaxed moment is irremediably disrupted.

"May I inquire what came—" The genie tries to ask me something, probably an explanation for the recent turn of events.

"No." I cut him short. "I need to think." I don't have any explanations to give; I need to form some of my own first.

What now? There's no going back. I sit at my desk, follow the registration link on the email, and fill out the registration form for two guests. I will not give Vanessa the satisfaction of turning up alone. The genie will have to come with me to the retreat as my boyfriend; at least he won't have to be a girl this time.

Right, I need to cook up a romantic version of our usual story. I'll keep it basic. The best way to go undercover is to stick to reality as much as possible. I've watched my fair share of spy flicks.

Past history: we met in England all those years ago.

Recent history: he moved to Chicago a few months ago, and we fell madly in love.

Yes, it will do; by now we know each other well enough to sustain a two-day farce. I'll just have to pinpoint some details. This could actually be a great idea. Good job, brain! I'm going to make sure he's the most attractive man at the party. Vanessa will drool over him if it is the last thing I do, and James will be sick with jealousy.

"Let's go," I mouth as soon as the clock strikes five p.m.

"And where is it we are going?" he asks once we are on the street.

"To buy you some expensive trinkets."

"Who am I to complain?" he enthuses. "May I ask why?"

"If we're going to do this, I need to bling you up," I reply, pushing my way into Tourneau.

***

It's the day before the retreat. I've kept a low profile in the past two weeks and nothing relevant has happened. I've bought loads of expensive clothes and accessories to transform the genie into the perfect, rich, and absolutely enviable boyfriend, planning the weekend's outfits to the last detail. Our bags are packed, and I only have one final test before I declare us ready for the retreat.

"Read it and memorize it," I tell the genie, handing him a piece of paper and interrupting his newspaper-reading session.

"What is this?" he asks, reluctantly putting down the *Chicago Tribune*.

"A list of basic stuff a boyfriend should know about me."

"I am pretty sure no one is going to ask me your favourite brand of tampons," he comments after quickly scanning the list.

I WISH FOR YOU

"You never know, we'd better be thorough. Tomorrow you'll have to play your part to perfection. You should get started on it. Let me know when you feel confident enough."

While he's studying, my phone blips, and I quickly look at it.

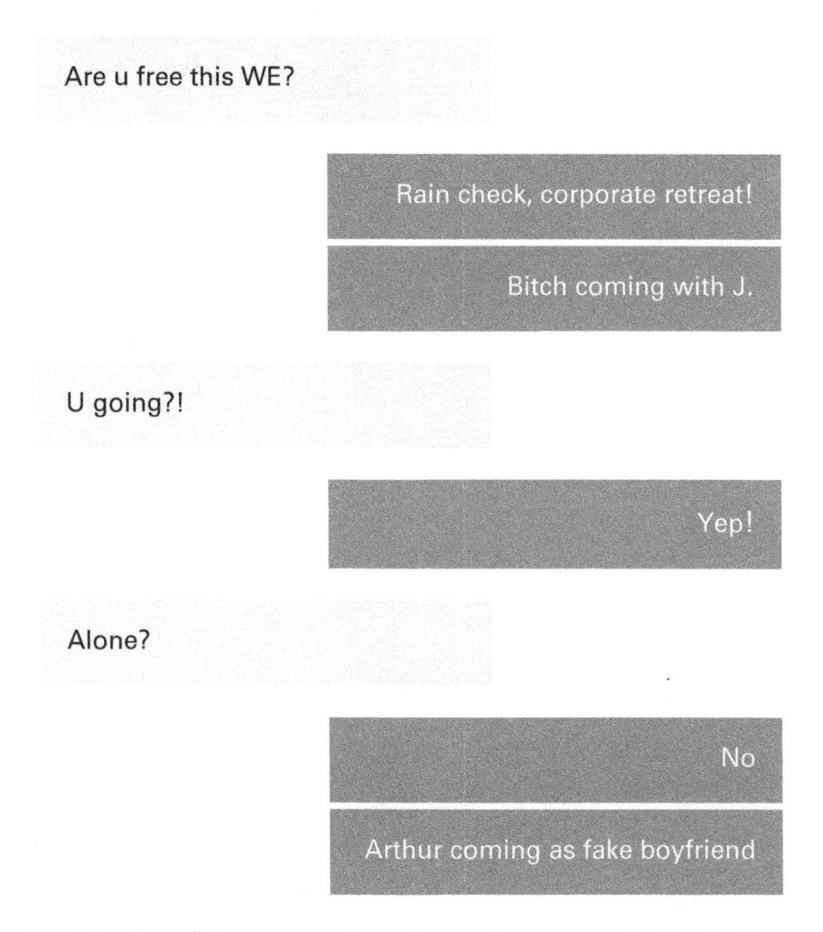

Are u free this WE?

> Rain check, corporate retreat!

> Bitch coming with J.

U going?!

> Yep!

Alone?

> No

> Arthur coming as fake boyfriend

We chat in quick sequence, but after my latest text, the "typing" icon appears by her name and then disappears, only to come back a few moments later. I guess she wrote something, then changed her mind and decided to go with something different.

> Fake?

> U sure?

>> 100%

>> He's only doing me a favor

> Sleeping arrangements?

I'm not dignifying that question.

"I pretty much have it," the genie says as I press send.

"Just a second." I hold up a finger to silence him and finish my chat.

Brooke texts to call her as soon as I get back. I promise to, say bye, and focus on the genie.

"You've already memorized all of it?" I ask. "In only thirty minutes. Are you sure?"

"I am," he replies, confident.

"Okay, let's test you, then." I smile devilishly, snatching the sheet of paper from his hands. "What is my middle name?"

"Rose."

"When was I born?"

"November 22."

"Where is my hometown?"

"Lake Forest, Illinois."

"What are my allergies?"

"Anthony Johnson," he says on autopilot. "Wait, you changed the order," he adds, realizing his mistake.

I WISH FOR YOU

"You can't simply memorize the list in its precise order. You need to be able to randomly access all the information in here," I say, tapping the paper lightly.

"You are allergic to bees."

He's challenging me. Very well, game on.

"Father's name?"

"Anthony Johnson."

"Mother's name?"

"Lily Cooper."

"Siblings?"

"No."

"How many kids do I want?"

"Three. Two boys and a girl."

"Favorite movie?"

"How to Lose a Guy in Ten Days."

"Favorite food?"

"Breakfast food in general, croissants, and pizza."

"Favorite ice cream flavors?"

"Pistachio and yoghurt."

"Favorite drink?"

"Lemon drop martini."

"Favorite perfume?"

"Light Blue, Dolce and Gabbana."

I shoot one question after the other, but there is no tricking him. He gets correct my job, college, all the names of my friends and of a few cousins, my dream vacation destination (Italy), favorite pet (Sugar, that was easy), and favorite TV shows, songs, and books (I don't have an absolute number one). I have only two questions left.

"What was my nickname in high school?"

"Ally Jelly."

I wait a while to see if he'll ask me why.

"But we do not talk about it," he adds, reciting my side annotation.

"Good," I comment. "And finally, what are my lingerie sizes?"

"A small for panties," he says, blushing slightly, "and a thirty-four B for bras." His cheeks turn a deeper shade of scarlet.

"Good job, Genie! We're ready." I exclaim, getting up from the couch to go to bed.

"Should you not learn the same things about me?" he asks, not moving from his position on the armchair.

"I made up all the lies about your life. I'm sure I have it under control."

"We had better be thorough. After all, tomorrow you will have to play your part to perfection as well." He annoyingly mirrors my speech word for word.

"Okay," I concede, flipping the paper to write on the other side and sagging back on the couch. "I'll ask you the same questions." This could turn out as a good opportunity to finally gain some information about him.

"Do you have a middle name?" I start.

"No."

"I know your birthday is the twenty-ninth of March, we say my same year, and you were born in London."

"No, I wasn't."

"Oh," I say, surprised. "Where then?"

"Nantes."

"You are French?"

"By part of Mother."

"What was her name?"

"Konstanza."

"Beautiful," I comment. "Surname?" I ask, uncertain.

"Invent one."

"I don't know any French surnames, you tell me."

"Breizh."

"Doesn't sound that French. Father's name?"

"Geoffrey."

I WISH FOR YOU

"The surname is going to be Pemberley as yours, of course. Siblings?"

"I had three sisters, but they all passed a long time ago. You would not want to include them in your report."

"I'm sorry, Genie."

"Don't be. I've had centuries to overcome my grief."

"Allergies? Phobias?" I try to continue as neutrally as possible. I write everything down nonetheless for a thorough follow-up Google search.

"No."

"How do you like coffee?"

"I prefer tea. I take it with lemon, no milk, no sugar."

"Ah, there. You are English after all," I comment, still writing.

"Favorite drink?"

"Scotch."

"Ewww. Favorite food?"

"Steak."

"How manly of you."

We reuse the information we already fabricated for studies and work, and choose some believable items for books, music, and motion pictures.

"Genie, one last thing," I suddenly worry.

"Yes?"

"Do you have any documents?"

"What kind of documents?"

"Like identification papers—they will ask for them tomorrow at the hotel."

"I should have my calling cards in my coat."

Calling cards?

"Um, no," I say, mildly amused. "We'll need something more official, like a passport."

"I am afraid I do not possess such a thing."

"But can you make a fake one?"

"I believe so if you show me how it looks."

153

ID forgery, what's next?

Half an hour later we have a complete set of forged papers: British passport, Illinois driving license, and a green card. You know, just in case.

Nineteen
Faking It

As soon as we arrive at the hotel on Saturday morning, we collect our identification badges from a big table placed right at the lobby entrance. Then we proceed to the check-in desk to get the key to our room.

"Good morning, are you here with the Crispy Koob corporate event?" a pretty brunette receptionist asks me.

"Yes," I confirm, annoyed. As if she needed to ask after taking a good look at the badge pinned on my chest.

"May I have your name, please?"

"Ally Johnson."

"Thank you." She starts typing on her computer.

How long will it take? What is she typing, anyway? It's taking her ages. I'm nervous; I don't want to run into them right away. I'm fidgeting, but we are pretty early and if I know James they will get here just in time, if not late.

"You are booked in a standard double room, is that correct?" the receptionist asks after an impossibly long amount of time.

"Yep," I reply, not looking at her and still scrutinizing the surroundings.

"Are you looking for something? May I help you?" she asks.

This must be the nosiest employee of the year.

"No, just checking for the arrival of colleagues," I reply, devoting my full attention to her and catching a nasty comment inside her head.

She thinks I'm having an affair with one of my colleagues. Well, miss, you are wrong. If anything, I'm interested in the *fiancé* of one of my colleagues.

"Do you have any allergies?"

What kind of question is this? Is she going to give me a full medical background check?

"Bee stings, why?"

"We proudly offer allergy-friendly rooms, which feature improved air quality and significantly reduced irritants. Everything is sanitized, and special air purifiers are installed in each room to provide—"

"That won't be necessary, thank you." I interrupt her, doing my best not to roll my eyes. "Can we speed this up a bit? I would really like to have some time before the conference begins."

"Certainly, madam. Are you a speaker?"

Madam who? My grandma is a madam, not me.

"Uh, no."

She's definitely having an affair in the office then. I wonder why... with such a boyfriend why could she possibly want more?

"Very well, just a few more questions," she says, throwing a furtive look at the genie.

Good, I want Vanessa to have the same awed reaction.

"Is a king bed fine, or would you prefer two queen beds?"

"Two queens please," I answer without hesitation.

He must be lousy in bed. He doesn't look the type, though, she thinks while typing some more.

No, he doesn't, I silently agree with her.

"Non-smoking is fine?"

"Absolutely," I spit out, irritated.

"Two keys?"

"Yes."

"You are in room 5216. The elevators are right behind you. I hope you will enjoy your stay."

"Thank you." I grasp the key quickly and rush away.

"Did you know her?" the genie asks while we wait for the elevator.

"No, why?"

"She seemed like a nice young lady, but you were quite impolite to her."

I WISH FOR YOU

"Oh please, she was being slow on purpose because she thought I had an affair with a colleague and hoped I was caught between my boyfriend," I point at him, just in case, "and my lover."

"She was simply doing her job..."

"She also referred to you as an allegedly lousy lover."

"I thus declare that she has thoroughly earned all your rudeness," he proclaims with mock outrage.

I smile and enter the elevator.

Our room is spacious, with big windows and a nice view of the lake that I am too frantic to fully appreciate. I have to get dressed. I didn't put on my outfit for today at home because I didn't want it to get wrinkled during the drive; unfortunately, my magical powers don't extend to clothes. Plus, I'm still undecided between two options.

First: a little black dress, very simple but very classy. A "less is more" kind of thing.

Second: a trendy suit, in total white with skinny pants, a cool vest jacket, and a simple white tank top underneath.

After several trials and a large extent of second-guessing, I end up choosing the white silk suit. It's more summery and, I don't know, it just feels better.

Footwear: I leave my perpetually manicured feet almost bare in a pair of flat Sergio Rossi pink gold sandals. Lunch is going to be outside, and I don't want to wear heels while walking in the grass.

We get changed and go back to the lobby where I regretfully watch the genie head to the dining room while a man in uniform ushers me toward the conference hall instead.

As I enter the room, my emotions sway between tranquility and impatience. On one hand, I am relaxed as I am sure I will not bump into James here; on the other hand, I am a bit restless, as three hours before I can see him. I choose my seat comfortably in the back on the left side and as close as it gets to the wall-wide windows where I can ignore the whole conference without being spotted, and where I have a vantage point to see what's going on outside.

Another perk of sitting in the back is that I get to see Vanessa sneak in with a thunderous expression half an hour after the first speech has begun. I adore being right. They probably argued all the way here. After that, I zone out completely. It takes a couple of hours for the guest of honor to be finally presented.

"...please welcome Henry Georges," somebody is announcing in the microphone, "CEO of Crispy Koob Corporation World." Round of applause.

Last year, I muse, if such a speaker was present at the corporate annual event, I would have been eagerly sitting in the first row, notepad in hand, ready to suck in any precious word of wisdom I could absorb from the mighty figure. I would have recorded the whole speech on my phone to go over it again later, making sure I didn't miss any fundamental bits, and I would have studied days, maybe weeks, to come up with an intelligent, cutting-edge question to pose for the Q&A session.

This year I couldn't care less about the company vision; my sole focus for the last couple of hours has been to alternately scan the outside in hope of spotting either James or the genie and to compulsively check the time on my phone. I don't think I've missed a single minute.

I can't wait for these boring speeches to be over; being stuck here the whole morning is pure torture. I want to show off the genie and see the expression on Vanessa's face, but mostly I am nervous about seeing James. Surprise, surprise. I feel like the only thing keeping me away from the truth is this stupid round of motivational talks!

***

When I finally get out, I spot the genie first. He's leisurely leaning against a giant tree, his gaze lost on the horizon past the

I WISH FOR YOU

lake. I have to admit that he looks dashing in his carefully selected casual clothes. After a morning spent in an artificial sixty-degree climate, I rush toward him, relishing the warm sensation of the sun on my skin and the fresh air.

Luckily, the weather has cleared out. When we arrived here it was cold, the sky overcast and threatening to storm. But now the clouds are gone, and the sky is an immaculate expanse of blue. It's so bright out here that I put on my new sunglasses.

"Hey you, how was the morning? Did you miss me?" I ask, approaching him from behind.

"Dearly so," he says, turning toward me, "although I was kept company by Mrs. Reynolds and Mrs. Pitt... most generous women," he says, smiling.

"So you had fun?" I ask skeptically, as from the surnames they must've been the wives of our chief accountant and his vice. Not the funniest people in the world.

"My patience was badly abused," he confirms, still smiling.

"Let's check out the buffet, I'm starving." I take his hand and we walk arm in arm toward the food station. "Have you perhaps seen James?" I ask casually.

"Indeed, I've spoken to him briefly."

"What?" I stop mid-step, letting go of his arm. "And you weren't going to say anything?"

"You did not ask."

"Sometimes you are impossible. Come on, tell me everything. Be as detailed as possible," I urge him.

"I will try my best. Let us see... I was in the refreshments area and I was trying to select a flavour of tea to go with the lemon biscuits. I was undecided between a white tea blend and..."

"I meant be precise about what James said, not about what stupid tea you were choosing." I swear he's doing this on purpose.

"Right, let us get straight to the point then. While I was sipping my delicious tea—an Earl Gray, in case you were wondering…"

I roll my eyes, cross my arms in front of me, and stare at him with my most powerful evil stare.

"I assume you were not," he comments, smirking. "Well, to be concise, I found myself standing next to him and I politely said hello. He said hello back."

"And what else?"

"Nothing, it was a very civil greeting. That was all."

"Are you joking? That's not it, is it?" I ask furiously.

"In fact, I am… you should soften a little. It is never a good thing to meet an ex-lover in such a distressed state."

"The only thing stressing me right now is *you*! Can we move on to what James said?"

"We made some small talk, establishing we were here with our respective girlfriends, and then he proceeded to copiously compl—"

"Wait; did he say, girlfriend or fiancée?"

"Does it matter?"

"Yes, it does."

"I do not recall precisely, but I believe he did not use the word fiancée specifically."

"Good, go on."

"As I was saying, he complained profusely about being dragged to such an event when he could have been doing something productive instead."

"Yeah, I know, he hates this kind of thing. I only ever managed to bring him to a Christmas party, and we broke up two weeks later, so I'm surprised she managed to get him here for a whole weekend. Could she have him under some sort of spell?"

"I hardly believe so. However, to confirm what you just said, he as well told me that his ex-girlfriend was great as she never forced him to accompany her, except if it was a real party with free... boos?"

"Booze. He meant alcoholic beverages. Is 'great' the actual word he used to describe me?"

"Yes, he said great."

"So I am great. I wonder what Vanessa is. Anything else?"

"Yes, he added that both his ex-girlfriend and new girlfriend were here today and that he hoped to avoid a... let me quote... 'cat fight'?"

"Did he say that? Arrogant bastard, what does he think? That I'm spending all my time pining after him?"

"Are you not?"

"Of course I am, but he's not entitled to think so. I bet he'll have a bit of a shock when I introduce him to my handsome, exotic boyfriend."

"Exotic?"

"Everything European is considered exotic over here."

"Oh my, the world has turned upside-down. In my time it was the other way around. I will keep handsome, though," he says with a mischievous look.

"Don't flatter yourself. It's mostly due to my makeover," I mock him.

"If you say so," he replies, giving me a wink that causes my stomach to do an unintentional little flip.

He really must've been a lady-killer in his time. For the first time, I find myself thinking that the freezing-upon-contact rule isn't so stupid after all, or it's just my abstinence talking. I haven't been with a man for how long? Awk, since James! I'm probably regrowing my virginity by now. At the thought, a furious blush spreads over my cheeks.

"Are you well, milady?" the genie asks, noticing my sudden coloring. "You seem flustered."

"I'm fine, and how many times do I have to tell you not to call me milady?" I hiss, glad that I am the one who can read minds and not him. "Let's go eat."

Twenty
Don't You Remember?

My company spared no expenses to organize this event. I assume Kyle really wanted to impress the big boss, and he went out of his way, and possibly budget, to do so. He must've spent every last penny for recreational activities on this. In all likelihood we're not going to have a Christmas party this year; that is if I'm still with the company by then.

I've been mulling the question of what to do next for a while now. I want to find something that will make me happy, something that will give me purpose. The only reason I'm staying is "keep your friends close and your enemies closer."

Being able to spy on Vanessa is definitely a plus for my mission, but by Christmas they will either be married or not, meaning that I'll no longer need to spy on her. Whatever happens, a change of scenery will be good for me. I foresee that being in Vanessa's proximity will become impossible either way.

But let's get back to the present. The buffet tables have been set outside in the garden and offer a magnificent display of sophisticated finger food. Under normal circumstances, I would be overexcited at the prospect of splurging on such a feast without having to worry about my waistline, but today my stomach is on shutdown and I barely nibble on a couple of canapés to avoid fainting due to low blood sugar.

"You have barely touched anything," The genie echoes my thoughts.

"I know, but I'm too nervous. Do you see them?"

"No, I have seen neither of them since breakfast. Let me get you a glass of Champagne. It will help your nerves a little."

"You sure know how to treat a lady. I'll wait here."

I WISH FOR YOU

I decide I'd better eat something else if I want to survive until the next meal. According to the event program, we'll have team building activities and games until four-thirty, and dinner will be at six-thirty.

"So, where is the secret boyfriend?"

Vanessa's voice makes me almost choke on half a cheese puff and squeeze the other half in my left hand.

"Hi... chwk... Vanessa. He... hwk... went to get me something to drink."

"Same for James," she says. "I expect he'll be here any minute."

And with that, my insides lock for good. I quit any attempt at eating anything else and throw the remaining crippled half of the cheese pastry in a trash can. I am trying to cleanse the squishy mash on my left hand when Vanessa very unceremoniously grabs my wrist.

"Is this a Rolex?" she asks in disbelief.

Okay, while boosting the genie's accessories collection, I bought a little extra bling for me as well.

"Mmm, yes," I answer her very impolite question. Mrs. Van Horn should worry a little less about her precious daughter's weight, and a little more about her manners, if you ask me.

"It's very expensive," she remarks, probably implying I can't afford it. Even ruder!

"Oh, I know." I've come prepared. "It was a present from Arthur."

"Who?"

"My boyfriend, remember? Who else?"

"What does he do?"

"He works in finance."

That shuts her up.

To avoid any further unpleasant conversation, I pretend to be busy selecting my next tidbit while fixing my gaze on the bar instead. I see James coming in our direction the moment he detaches himself from the drinks line. He's stunningly handsome in a simple white shirt, military green chinos, and white sneakers.

I turn around, pretending to be completely absorbed by the pending choice of the next delicacy to eat. I still have my back to Vanessa when I hear him arrive.

"Hey babe, here's your drink."

"Is this water?" she spits meanly.

See? No "thank you." She should definitely take that etiquette class.

"Yeah, the line for the booze was infinite," James answers.

"Hello," I say, turning around when I can no longer feign interest in the buffet.

"Hwk... hi." It's James's turn to choke on his water.

I wave my hand once in an awkward response.

"Ally is waiting for her boyfriend to bring back drinks as well," Vanessa kindly explains.

James raises his eyebrows in what seems a mix between surprise and interrogation; I don't know what to say in front of Vanessa, so I simply keep my mouth shut while I briefly infiltrate James's subconscious.

I don't pick up any words, just a mix of contrasting emotions: shock, bewilderment, anger, jealousy, and melancholy. But what astonishes me the most is that he also feels a deep pain, exactly like mine when I think about him with Vanessa, but mingled with something different... a sense of resignation and hopeless defeat.

I am sure that dumping me and seeing me with another man must be two very different things, but I don't understand; he's feeling desperate at the thought of having lost me for good! It doesn't make any sense. I so wish Vanessa wasn't here so that I could talk to him alone.

Finally, the long, embarrassing silence is interrupted by the genie coming back with our drinks.

"Your Champagne, darling," he says, offering me a tall glass filled with the sparkling liquid.

I WISH FOR YOU

"I thought the line for the wine was impossible," snaps Vanessa again, eyeing James reproachfully.

"Indeed it was, but I have my ways," the genie replies, showing off all his charm. "Arthur Pemberley, and who do I have the pleasure to be speaking to?" His Queen's English accent sounds so posh.

"Vanessa Van Horne, nice to meet you," she says, extending her hand.

"Enchanté," he replies, kissing her hand in the French style instead of shaking it.

"May I introduce my *fiancé* James?" she says, giggling, visibly impressed by the genie's gallantry but still stressing the word fiancé. For my sole benefit, I am sure.

"I believe we briefly met over breakfast. Nice to meet you properly. Arthur Pemberley." He gives James a manly handshake.

"James Avery." *Is that a real surname? Good-looking and strong handshake, but I can't believe Ally could fall for such a moron.*

James is right. I dressed Arthur more to Vanessa's taste than my own. He's wearing a pale beige linen suit, something James would never wear, but the trick is working. It's making both of them jealous, only in different ways.

"So what do you do, Arthur?" Vanessa asks.

"I work in finance. I was just recently relocated to the United States from London."

Finance... what? She hates bankers! James's brain chimes in.

I don't *hate* bankers.

This encounter is driving James and Vanessa crazy. Yep, exactly as planned. Muahahah!

"So you just met," Vanessa affirms, saying it as if it was the only possible explanation for our being together.

"Oh no, we go way back," I chip in. "We met when I was in London many years ago. And when Arthur moved here, well, it was… it just happened," I say in a dreamy voice, sticking to my act.

The small talk goes on a little longer; I don't intercept any more comments from James's mind, just a strong wave of aversion toward the genie. And the best thing is that he is jealous of me and not of his fiancée, who is openly flirting with Arthur!

Luckily, soon enough a speaker interrupts us, announcing the beginning of the afternoon's activities, inviting everybody to go change into sportswear. I'm grateful for the intrusion in our conversation. Watching Vanessa try to simultaneously mark her territory with my ex-boyfriend and seduce my fake boyfriend was too much. I hope I'll find a way to get James alone later…

It doesn't happen.

The afternoon passes in a whirl of ball games, boat races, and role games. They didn't leave us a free second; I was either busy running away or toward a ball, depending on the game, paddling, or strategizing. Overall, it was a fun afternoon. The genie was a good sport, and we had so much fun during the boat race, even if we qualified second to last.

Admittedly, it wasn't entirely our fault since we were in a team with Sally and her husband Josh, who has the bulkiness of an Atlantic whale, and even if I shredded him twenty pounds upon sight he still conserves the weight of a small elephant. Getting him in the boat was an accomplishment by itself, and by the end, I was grateful we arrived without tipping over into the lake.

Anyway, he and Sally are really nice, down-to-earth people, plus Josh has as much liveliness as body fat, and it was a blast to ride with them. I kept chuckling and couldn't be bothered to row that much. I let the genie do all the puffing.

On the other hand, Vanessa is very competitive. She and James ended up on the podium.

I WISH FOR YOU

***

"What do you think?" I ask, twirling into the room in my new gown for the evening.

I am wearing a silver silk Marchesa evening dress, embellished with lace and some see-through details.

"I could not imagine anything nearer to perfect beauty."

"Thank you," I smile, doing a little curtsy. "I want James with his mouth open, gaping like a fish."

I admire my reflection in the wardrobe's giant mirror. It's great to have a model's body. Clothes fit me to perfection, and I never wear a bra anymore as everything stays exactly where it should. Unfortunately, there's no magic that could spare me the discomfort of wearing high heels, I muse, putting on a pair of metallic-leather Jimmy Choo sandals in silver.

I mean, I could have elongated myself a bit, but it would've been too obvious a change. I can have more hair, flawless skin, and no cellulite. On the other hand, nobody would believe I've suddenly grown two inches overnight.

"You are not so bad yourself," I concede, eying the genie approvingly.

He's gorgeous in his black tuxedo, white shirt, black bow tie (impeccably tied), and black leather shoes.

"I feel more comfortable in this kind of attire," he comments. "I still wish I could wear a hat and bring my cane."

"No hat for you, I'm sorry. But you can give me your arm and escort me downstairs."

"Gladly so, but I suggest we wait until we are outside." He smiles.

"Oh, right." I'd been having physical contact with him all afternoon during the games. I had almost forgotten about the freezing rule.

To find our seats, we check a huge board standing at the entrance of the dining room. The moment I find our names, I search for James and Vanessa's, but it's no good. Their table is on the opposite side of the room.

So far this day has been a huge disappointment, James-wise. I got half an hour of interrupted small talking with him and that was it. If I don't talk with him tonight, this whole weekend will be a total waste. My time is running out. At least we are at a table with Sally and Josh; if useless, at least dinner will not be boring.

And it isn't. I'm enjoying myself so much that between the amazing food, the good wine, the great company, and the genie who is a true charmer, I almost forget about James. *Almost*.

But as soon as the speaker takes the microphone to announce a round of karaoke, the heaviness of the situation comes back to me immediately and my feeble exterior cheeriness fades away quickly, leaving me in a gloomy mood.

There is a sign-up sheet being passed among tables for people to book a spot onstage. How tacky! I would never sing in public. I'm not a showoff. Hm, truth be told, I could never strike an on-tune note for the life of me; I am as off-key as it gets.

I am surprised to see how many people show the confidence to do it and sign-up on the list, Sally and Josh included. I must be openly staring at them because they feel the need to justify themselves and tell me they're doing a little duet they always like to do on such occasions.

"What about you?"

"Oh, no, no. Not for me," I say, passing the sheet of paper along as fast as I can.

After half an hour of amateur karaoke, we had some good singers, some mediocre ones, and one terrible performance from a girl in human resources who probably doesn't have a clue how bad she is. I'm becoming restless. I keep shifting in my seat and I'm bored out of my mind.

"I'll go get some air," I tell the genie.

"Do you want me to accompany you?"

I WISH FOR YOU

"No, I'm good, thank you," I reply, getting up.

"Next on stage we have... Ally Johnson from Marketing!" the guy in charge of the karaoke announces.

Did he just call my name? I stare up at the stage in confusion. If I were still sitting, I could try to hide until they call the next name, but I'm already up and everyone is looking at me. They think I am about to sing!

I'm frozen to the spot. I feel cold drops of sweat trickle down my back. I'm vaguely aware of some people cheering and encouraging me to take the stage. How the hell did this happen? I look around, still confused, searching for an answer. The genie is looking at me, perplexed, Josh and Sally are giving me the thumbs-up, and everyone else seems to be getting impatient at my indecision. I scrutinize all the surrounding faces that are quickly passing from a benevolent, encouraging smile to a more of a what-is-she-waiting-for annoyed expression until my eyes stop on Vanessa's. She, contrarily to everybody else, has an amused expression with a devilish smile barely surfacing her lips.

They're all going to laugh at you, Ally Johnson... you're so going to make a fool of yourself.

Then, I get a clear mental image of her writing my name on the karaoke list.

Oooh. The bitch! She did this to me!

"Come on, Ally," the audience cries from every direction. "Go, girl."

Crap, there's no way out. I'm done for, ruined. I'm going to sound worse than Cameron Diaz in *My Best Friend's Wedding* singing "I Just Don't Know What To Do With Myself!"

Should I go for the same song? The title is appropriate enough, and I could try to cute-out the public as she did, making them forget how badly I suck. Or...

"Get up," I hiss to the genie, signaling him to come toward me. "Come here, hug me."

He does as I say, and while he's holding me close I whisper in his ear the only hope I have for salvation.

The crowd is applauding and cheering us on. "Kiss the girl," someone shouts. I'm about to shush the howler when the genie surprises me and presses his lips onto mine in response to the challenge. My knees become a little weak, but I don't even have the time to register what's going on because he's already releasing me and giving me a gentle push toward the stage, smiling at my affronted scowl.

He gives me that little wink again, and my stomach promptly responds with a tiny flip. No, I'm sure it's just stage fright. I stride toward the stage, dread mixing sheer excitement. Will it work?

I confabulate briefly with the band to choose my song.

"Are you sure?" the guitar player asks me. "It's a very tough song, you know?"

"I've never been surer of anything in my entire life," I answer, grabbing the microphone and positioning myself in the middle of the spotlight, ready to sing Adele's "Don't You Remember."

Not many people in the room are paying me attention; they're still busy chattering at their tables, but the moment I open my mouth to sing the first few lines, the whole room falls silent and every single face turns toward me.

My voice surprises even me when I hear it as I've never heard it like this before. It's dark and heavy, full and bright, but soft and airy at the same time. I've no idea what I'm doing, so I trust completely in my vocal cords that seem to have a mind of their own as they spiral from one note to the next.

Vanessa's mouth is hanging open in utter disbelief. I want to look at James, but I wait until the chorus to lock my eyes onto his and sing the words I've been wanting to say to him since he left me. Asking him again and again if he remembers me, our story, our love...

I WISH FOR YOU

I pitch the higher notes of the song, piercing the silence of the room, baring my soul and making it one with the words, finishing in a soft whisper infused with all my love and pain.

When I finish, the crowd stays still for a few seconds, awestruck, enchanted by my spell. The applause that follows is equally thunderous to the outright silence preceding it, and it goes on forever. I make a small bow and almost run out of the room, overwhelmed by my own emotions.

How did I do it? I cheated. I used my fourth wish to ask for the best singing voice the world has ever heard. It might seem foolish to use a wish like this, but any doubt I might've had, dissipated the moment I started singing. I've never felt more free or powerful than tonight onstage.

From the hall, I decide to go outside. Some fresh air will be good to cool down the rollercoaster of emotions I've just been through. Once in the garden, I head toward the lake and stop on a covered deck over the water where the night air gently brushes my skin. I lean against the deck wooden railing and stare at the moon glowing in the night sky. I breathe in the scent of the water and feel liberated.

Twenty-one
Truth

As I stare at the glassy surface of the lake, I hear muffled footsteps in the grass behind me.

"Did you see how great it..." I turn around expecting to see the genie but find James standing beside me instead.

I cling to the railing for support.

"I never knew you could sing like that," he says in an admiring tone.

"Before tonight, I didn't know it myself," I admit sincerely, pondering about telling him the part his nice fiancée played, but deciding against it since her little scheme already totally backfired on her.

"I didn't know you had a boyfriend, either."

Ah. There it is. He's jealous.

"Up until a little while ago, I didn't know you had a fiancée, either," I can't help but retort childishly. "And it's not exactly like we kept in touch," I say harshly, betraying my emotions. "If I remember correctly, last time we saw each other you left without even saying goodbye."

"I'm sorry. I had an early morning the next day. I had to go," he lies.

"Sure, you did," I comment sarcastically.

A long, heavy silence follows.

"Ally, I..."

"Yes?"

He doesn't reply; he simply stares at the ground as if scouring it for answers. He lifts his head and looks at me with an anguished expression, still mute, so I search his eyes to discover what it is that he's not able to put into words.

Suddenly I find myself propelled into a different reality; I am seeing the world through James's eyes as he's talking on the phone in his apartment. I am inside one of James's memories! I'm not sure how long ago this happened, but it couldn't be so long ago as James doesn't look much younger.

He's holding an envelope in his hands while he's speaking into the microphone of his white headphones. "...I've just received the invitation to the Fall Charity Ball," he says in a casual tone. "I saw it's only for one person. I was wondering if I could bring Ally along."

"James, dear," his mother replies, "I hoped you'd be my date. Otherwise, I'll have to go alone. Please spare me the embarrassment."

He flips the invitation in his hands; I peek at the date printed on it and see that I'm in a memory from the October before we broke up.

"Mom, you are a widow. There's nothing embarrassing about going to a ball on your own."

I can feel his annoyance at the situation. The discussion continues for a while until James's home disappears into a vortex and I find myself in a majestic room dancing with... Vanessa!

Is that ball where they met? Did he cheat on me with her? I try to explore James's sensations while he's dancing with her, but he doesn't seem particularly happy about it. Even better, he's thinking she's pathetic for throwing herself at him so openly after he's already told her he has a girlfriend. Ah! Me!

The room swirls again, and I find myself standing in my office. *What?* The office is bursting with decorations, and hanging from the ceiling, there is a huge banner saying "Merry Christmas." Of course, we are at my office's Christmas party. The one and only we attended together.

I see myself, a little tipsy, approaching and kissing me. I mean James. That was weird! He hugs me and ruffles my hair affectionately. I jokingly protest for him to stop, and after looking at me intensely for a couple of seconds, he kisses my forehead, whispering, "I love you." And he does mean it with every cell of his body; I can sense it in him.

He then spots Vanessa talking with Kyle, and he decides to try to avoid her for the rest of the evening. In fact, he asks me right away if I am ready to leave, and when I say yes, the room starts spinning around once more.

I am now entering James's Victorian family house; it's clearly winter because the outside of the house is covered in a thick coat of dusty snow. The entrance hall looks familiar, except it appears a lot darker and gloomier than what I remembered it to be. It's as if his brain has filtered its real appearance with a veil of bleakness, which is weird because as I close the door behind me, I mean as he does, he feels happy and excited. He moves a few steps inside and calls out for his mom.

"Here, in the dining room." Her voice comes faint, almost spectral from the left. The atmosphere, if possible, becomes even grimmer.

"Hi, Mom. Happy New Year," he says merrily, kissing her on the cheek.

His mother is sitting in a rigid posture at the head of an interminable mahogany dining table. "Hello, James." She barely looks at him when she greets him. Her face is very pale, and she seems worried.

"Mom, I have some great news," he announces, smiling, oblivious to his mother's anguished state. "I want to propose to Ally."

My heart stops. Propose to me? But this was only one or two days before he broke up with me! I was right; he wanted to bring our relationship to the next level, except he didn't simply want me to move in… He wanted to ask me to marry him! My heart starts beating faster. Why didn't he propose to me? What happened? I decide to try to concentrate on the rest of the conversation as I'm pretty sure I will find my answers there.

"Didn't you want to live with a person before marrying her?" his mother asks, taken aback. "Not that I am suggesting it as the right path."

"Yeah, but with Ally, I just know. She's the one," he affirms convinced. "Mom, what's wrong? Aren't you happy?" he adds, finally noticing her stony expression.

"Oh James, I don't think this is a good time to start a family," she says in a shaking voice.

Dread and worry clamp my throat. I'm not sure if I'm feeling it or James is, as his next question comes out choked.

"What do you mean?"

"James." She pauses, shakes her head, and then drops it in her hands.

"Mom, what's wrong?" he asks, concerned.

"James, we're broke, or soon to be," she says, raising her head and looking him straight in the eyes. "In less than a year all of this," she waves her thin knotty hand around feebly, "will be gone. This house, the company... everything."

"Mom, I know the West Lake Project has been a hit, but the company's finances are solid. We can take the loss. I just have to dismiss some equipment leasing—"

"Your father," she interrupts him, raising her hand.

"What about Dad?" he asks, with mounting anguish in his voice.

"The crisis... it hit us harder than he could ever imagine. You were still in college and were not involved in the company. To push through that year and the following one, your father had to take a loan, a substantial one..."

"Mom, the company has little debt—"

"James, please let me finish." His constant interruptions and reassurances seem to be draining her of any remaining strength. "He didn't want to scare the other investors away," she continues, "as things were already bad as they were, so he took the loan using his personal assets as collateral without making it appear in the company's books. That's why this house is in it as well. He calculated that he could repay the loan completely in nine years if nothing else went wrong. The interest rate was absurdly high, as nobody was lending money at the time, but he had faith in the company so he decided to take it anyway. It was his only hope to avoid bankruptcy."

"How bad it is?" This time James's voice is harder.

"Bad. Without the West Lake Project income we can't pay," she whispers.

"Are you sure?" he asks, shocked. "In the company's books, there's nothing about this." Worry is mounting inside him. He pulls out a chair and sits beside his mother.

"Because your father hid it," she repeats, close to tears.

"How?" James asks, serious.

"It's complicated. I didn't understand everything, but he made it look like he was renting equipment. Instead, he was repaying the debt to a shell company he created, but that has the actual debt with the bank. You should talk to Doug—he knows the mechanics. But James… those contracts you said you needed to dismiss? I don't think you can."

If I remember correctly, Doug was his father's most trusted collaborator.

"Doug knew about this?"

"He's the one who told me."

"Mom, is this even legal?"

"I am not sure," she admits. "Ask him."

"Even if it was illegal, he had to do it so that we could remain strong in the eyes of our partners," James reasons bitterly. "Otherwise, they would have squeezed us out."

There's a long, pregnant pause.

"How long have you known?" James asks his mother.

"Almost a year."

"And why didn't you tell me right away?" he shouts angrily.

"Because until the last few months we were fine," she says, shaking her head.

"You mean until West Lake was canceled."

"Yes."

"How much do we still owe the bank? What bank is it?"

"The bank is P.C.N., and James, we owe them millions."

"Damn!" He pushes his hands through his hair, anguished. He gets up and starts pacing frantically while thinking hard. "How much is the next payment?"

"James, we only have enough for the next one—at least, that's what Doug told me."

"But, Mom." He stops pacing suddenly. "What does all of this have to do with Ally and me? I'm sure it wouldn't matter to her."

No. It wouldn't have!

"Ah, James, you are a dreamer."

You old hag! Where is she going with this? Is she calling me a gold digger?

"Don't you dare tell me she's with me just for the money," James defends me, "because I can assure you—"

"Oh, I'm sure she's not. She seems like a perfectly nice girl. But that's beside the point."

"Mom, I'm not following," he says, exasperated.

Yeah, me neither. At this point, I'm as confused as he is. If she didn't think I was with him just for the money, I would like to understand what the company's imminent bankruptcy had to do with us. I'm finally convinced that this family crisis is somehow the reason why he broke up with me.

"Think, James, think. What kind of life could you offer her? If we go belly up, we will have to sell the company, this house, and every other asset we have to repay the debt. You will be penniless and jobless. Nobody is hiring in real estate now, and definitely not in managerial positions. What would you do?"

"Mom, I'm sure it would be hard at first, but I could find another job. Anyway, I'm not convinced that the company is beyond saving."

"It is James, believe me. I know how Adam Van Horn does business in this city, and he doesn't offer discounts to anyone."

Vanessa's dad?

"Van Horn? Why is the name familiar?" James asks.

"You met his daughter. She has a pretty bad crush on you."

Thu-thump. Thu-thump. Thu-thump. My heart is threatening to jump out of my chest.

"Who?" He pulls a puzzled face.

"The beautiful young lady you danced with at the Autumn Gala," his mother explains.

"The one that works with Ally, you mean?"

"They work together? I didn't know," she says.

"And how do you know she likes me? We barely talked once! And why should I care?"

"I do some charity work with her mother, who brought her up to be a very spoiled, but at the same time very insecure young lady. Your polite denial of attention was enough to make you the object of her affection."

"Mom, what does all of this have to do with anything?" he asks, impatient.

Yeah, I want to know as well, even if an unpleasant idea is taking shape in my mind.

"Nothing, nothing. I shouldn't have said anything."

Oh, but she did.

"Mom, what is it that you're suggesting? That I dump Ally and marry Vanessa Van Horn instead so that her daddy could bail us out?"

"No, James, of course, that's not what I meant. But I don't know, you could try to talk to this girl. Maybe she could ask her father to help us."

"And why would she do this?"

"Because she thinks she's in love you."

"Mom, there has to be another way. I would never..." He says not sure of what his mother is asking him to do.

She stays silent and keeps looking at the floor with a disparaged expression, successfully managing to make him feel guilty.

I WISH FOR YOU

"I can't do this Mom, not if I'm with Ally!" he insists.

"Then maybe you shouldn't," she replies in a whisper.

"You think I would let go of the woman I love? Never! I'd rather lose everything else."

"And how do you think you'd feel ten years from now when you look back at this moment and she's the reason why you lost everything?" she challenges him, rising from her chair. "James, I know you. If you were to lose the company, you would get bitter. And bitter is never a good ingredient in a marriage," she adds somewhat more softly. "You love that company—it's part of you, it's in your blood. When you were a kid, instead of wanting to play video games you wanted to go with your dad to building sites. James, your father put everything he had in it, even his life, and I know you're just the same. If you were to let it go to ruins, you'd never forgive yourself."

This is a low blow, and it cuts a deep wound into James's heart. I knew his father had a heart attack while working. James was the one who found him still struggling on the office floor, clasping a bad quarterly review in his hand, but until now James hadn't realized how connected the two things were. He gapes at his mother, dumbstruck, opening his mouth to say something and then closing it again, unable to speak.

"James, life is made of hard choices. Love comes and goes, but family stays forever. You have a responsibility not only to this family and yourself but also to the people who work for you. They have families as well."

"Please, Mother, spare me the fake altruism. You only care about yourself," he says bitterly, but inside him, a heavy stone settles. She might not care about the workers' families, but he does. And she just made sure he remembers that he's responsible for them.

She doesn't deny his accusation, and they face each other in silence for a long time.

"I will never go along with your little scheme!" he finally says, pointing his index finger on the table and glaring at her. "I'll find another way."

The scene whirls away again, only this time James's brain leafs in quick succession through the next couple of days. At first, he's arguing animatedly with an older guy in his office. The man must be Doug. Afterward, he's in a bank office where he is speaking to a manager who's shaking his head irrevocably. Then his mind quickly shuffles to the offices of at least ten other different banks, with as many managers all shaking their heads and saying they can't help him.

Finally, I see him at home, searching for a solution he can't find. He drinks a full bottle of vodka, caught in his own desperation, rummaging around random sheets of paper scattered all around his apartment's floor like a mad person. His eyes are bloodshot, he has deep black-blue circles under them, and he's crying, thinking about his father's last words before he died. "I did all I could, son. Now you must be the man of the family."

I feel his pain as he struggles to choose between his father's ghost and me. Tears prick my eyes as I understand it was a battle I could have never won. I watch him wrestle with his emotions some more, cry, scream in frustration at no one in particular, and finally, come to a decision.

Next, he's standing drunk in front of my apartment, pushing my buzzer and asking me to come down to talk. He's speaking in a hoarse, strained voice that I remember only too well; it chills me to the bone. I don't want to relive what comes next. I can't experience it twice, so I blink, pulling myself out of the vision and back to present.

"Is everything okay?" James asks me in a soft voice.

"Yeah, why?" I manage to stumble, my heart still racing. I feel like I was gone forever, but it must have taken me just a few seconds to surf across James's flashbacks.

I WISH FOR YOU

"You have your hand on your mouth—you look like something scared you to death," James points out.

"No, I'm fine," I lie, forcing my hand away.

"Ally, I..." he repeats.

"Yes?" I ask again, knowing everything he wants to tell me this time. I witness his internal struggle once more from the movements of his forehead, which creases deeper and deeper with every passing second.

"Nothing. I just wanted to say you were great tonight." He lowers his head in a gesture of final defeat. I can perceive his shame at his own cowardice.

I want to say something, but I am at a loss for words, and the silence between us becomes unbearable.

"I thought you might have been cold out here." The genie's deep voice makes me jolt. "I have brought you a jacket."

"Thank you," I say to him. Turning to James, I add, "We should get back inside. Good night, James."

"Good night, Ally," he replies, strangled.

We leave him alone on the deck and head back toward the hotel in silence.

Twenty-two
Arthur

"You have not said a word for quite a while."

"I am thinking."

"Would you like to pick my brain as well?"

"It's James."

"That much I could tell on my own."

We're back in the hotel room, and we're lying on opposite sides of the bed. I don't know how long we have been in this position; it could be a minute or an hour.

"I've finally found out the truth, and it's shocking," I say, on the verge of tears, and seek his contact as comfort. The moment I reach for him, he jerks away as quick as a cat.

"I would hold you in my arms and lull you to sleep, my dear—unfortunately, that would only make your situation far worse, as you would be frozen. But I can provide you the comfort of hot chocolate," he adds, conjuring my favorite mug filled with the dense, soothing drink. He passes it to me and then repositions himself on an armchair opposite to the bed at a safe distance.

"Thank you," I say, savoring the strong flavor of the cocoa mix.

The genie lets me finish the hot chocolate before resuming his interrogation. "Do you want to tell me what happened?"

"I had a long vision. It must have been a stream of memories. James was doing a mental recap of the events that led to the end of our story..." I launch into the narration of what I just witnessed, and the genie listens to me without interrupting. After I am finished, we stay in silence for a long moment.

I crack first. "Aren't you going to say anything?"

"I am sorry. It must have been a hard truth to become

I WISH FOR YOU

acquainted with," he remarks. "At least now you know, and you can leave him in your past."

"Leave him in my past?" I repeat, thrown, the tone of my voice rising. "Have you been listening to what I said?"

"It seems to me that you have not been paying attention to your own words." He is getting as worked up as I am; we both get up from our respective positions, facing each other in the middle of the room. "From what I gather, you are pining after a greedy man who did not think twice before tossing you away to preserve his wealth."

"It wasn't like that," I snarl, barely able to contain myself. "It was his mother—she made him believe he had to do it to honor his dead father's memory and to save the people who work for him."

"How old is he that he has to do his mother's bidding?" the genie sneers. "If he loved you, he would have stayed with you."

"I was up against a ghost, can't you see that?" I hiss, simmering. "And he does love me! I felt it, but he feels guilty. He feels responsible for his employees, and he thinks he owes it to his dead father to save the company as if he had some sort of debt of honor to repay. I thought you would have understood that."

"Honour? You talk to me about honour? Pray tell me, where is the honour in abandoning the woman you claim to love to string another poor maiden along, marrying her solely for her family name?"

"Vanessa is anything *but* an innocent maiden. And he does love me!"

"Not enough, apparently."

"What do you know about love? Your last lover cursed you for eternity," I snap, enraged.

His blue eyes light up with anger.

"Never dare say I do not know love!" he roars. "I had loved... and nothing, not family nor honour, could have kept me from her." His every word sizzles with cold wrath.

As he finishes talking, his teeth clench with anger. His whole face transfigures into a mask of pure rage; his cheeks turn blazing red with passion, his lines harden like iron wires, and his thick eyebrows meet over his nose in a deep scowl. But his eyes scare me the most; not for the rage in them, but for the pain flaring behind. And it's that look of agony that makes my own anger evaporate in a second.

"I'm sorry, Genie, I shouldn't have said that. I shouldn't talk about things I don't know."

"No, I am the one who should apologise, milady," he says, regaining some humanity. "My temper got the best of me." He sounds a lot calmer.

"Genie?"

"Yes?"

"What happened to you?" I ask simply.

"Maybe the time has come for me to tell you my story…"

I do not respond, afraid he may change his mind, as he looks like he is still pondering whether to go ahead or not. I simply reposition myself comfortably on the bed, ready to listen to his tale. He sinks back down onto the armchair, gazing at the ceiling as if it was a gate to another time, and he begins to talk.

"I was a man of great fortune—fate had been kind to me. I am the son of Geoffrey Plantagenet, fourth son of Henry II and of Konstanza, Duchess of Brittany. I was Duke of Brittany and Earl of Richmond. Richard the Lionheart himself had named me as his heir. After him, I was first in line for the succession to the throne of England.

"I never knew my father. He died during a joust before I was born, but his Plantagenet blood runs strong in my veins, and my mother's love was more than enough while I grew up. She raised me to be a king, and I became the man of the house very quickly, even for those times.

"I had lands, castles, servants, and an army at my command. I had everything a man could desire. I was rich and powerful, young and arrogant, strong and handsome. The world lay at my feet, and I thought everything was mine for the taking, be it a horse, a country, or a woman. I could do all that it pleased me, as I was above the law, and hell seemed too far a threat to actually preoccupy me.

"I lived a reckless life, constantly on the edge. I spent my days drinking, fighting, and conquering both lands and hearts. Many were the women I ensnared—I did not care if they were innocent, married, prostitutes, or simply naïve enough to fall for my deceptions. I would use all my powers of seduction to lure them into my bed, promising the world at dusk, and unfailingly disappearing at the first light of dawn, leaving behind me a trail of broken hearts and ruined lives, not once caring about the consequences of my deeds. I am not proud of what I did—I was selfish, and I brought pain to too many souls. I deeply regret my actions to this day. Mind you, I never took anyone by force, but I understand now that a false promise can be more hurtful than an act of violence in many different ways.

"At the time my story really began, I was sojourning at my mother's castle in Brittany. I had been there for quite a long time, and I occupied my days as usual with futile activities. It was during those lazy times that I first noticed a peasant girl. She was a servant in the town's tavern—she was beautiful in a compelling way. She had red lips the tint of blood, fair skin underlined by a deathly pallor not of this world, eyes as green as venom, and flaming hair of such a vivid colour they appeared to have flames from hell-fire itself blazing in them.

"I should have known better and kept my distance from that infernal creature, but I was young and stupid, and she was too much of a tempting prize for me to let go, especially after she adamantly refused my first overconfident advances. I pursued her day after day... she became an obsession. I was consumed by her sortilege. I didn't sleep at night, brooding over her, and when I finally collapsed into unconsciousness, exhausted, she visited me in my dreams, turning them into nightmares of unfulfilled desire. I couldn't see any other woman; she was the only one.

"I used all my charms on her, never imagining that I was the prey and not the hunter, and when she finally gave way we were devoured by an unyielding passion. I was with her every night, and when we weren't together all my thoughts would go to her anyhow. I lost myself in her without reservation. I believed I was truly in love. My friends warned me—they told me that I was not myself anymore, that I seemed hypnotised. But I wouldn't listen to anyone, not even to my mother.

"It wasn't until the outside world collapsed that I awakened. It was the time when my Uncle Richard, the King of England, was suppressing a revolt in Limoges. The chronicles of the times report that he, I quote, 'devastated the land with fire and sword.' However, it was during that rebellion that he met his downfall by an archer's arrow.

"It was only by chance that when the news of Richard's death reached my mother and me, my other uncle, John Lackland, was staying with us as well. Being the son of an elder brother, I should have inherited the crown by right of succession, but John was not too keen on leaving it to me without a fight. He left immediately for Chinon Castle to put his hands on the royal treasury that was housed there. At that point, the leading barons of England betrayed me and declared their loyalty to John. They feared that, given my upbringing across the English Channel, I was too close to our French enemy.

"It is true that at the time I barely spoke the language of my subjects, but my heart was English. However, on my side were the Breton Lords, the nobles of Maine and Anjou, and Philip II of France. To claim my seat on the throne of England, I had to raise an army and descend into battle, beginning a fratricidal war. Not even Morgene's sorcery could have kept me from fighting for my birthright."

"The girl's name was Morgan?" I can't refrain myself from interrupting; he pronounced it in a different way, but the name was definitely Morgan. "Like in the legends of Camelot?" I ask, bewildered.

"Every legend springs from a seed of truth," he replies calmly.

"Sorry, I didn't mean to interrupt. Please go on," I plead.

"I had to leave my mother's castle in haste. I bade my farewell to Morgene, assuring her of my undying love, and promising to come back to her as soon as I would be able to, and for once I truly believed my words.

"I marched with my troops relentlessly for two days. The farther away I got from her, the more my senses seemed to regain capacity, as I was out of reach of her spell. She, our passion, were quickly becoming a distant memory that I regarded as a dreamlike blur out of reality. I never knew if she bewitched me on purpose, or if it was just a consequence of her being what she was and of her own obsession for me.

"However, during my campaign across the Loire, I met Héloise. She was the only daughter of a local lord whose manor we were stationed at. She was everything Morgene was not. Her beauty was pure, delicate, and untainted. She had long, dark brown hair, amber eyes, and porcelain skin. Whereas Morgene's skin was pale as death itself, Héloise's had been equally fair, but as lively as the rosy blush that would so often surface on her cheeks.

"Then I understood what love really was. The love I felt for Héloise freed me of the last vestiges of Morgene's enchantment, setting me free once and for all.

"My attachment to Héloise became evident almost immediately, and unfortunately not only to us. Her father was scheming to keep her away from me—he had secret plans to send her to a Carthusians convent in Provence. However, one of my most trusted men intercepted one of his messengers and informed us of the plot. I married Héloise in secret the following night. The full moon served as our sole witness as a young priest consecrated our union before God and mankind. In that warm spring night, we were pronounced as one for eternity.

"Of course, given my standing, I was already betrothed to another. She was Marie of France, the daughter of the King of France and his disputed third wife Agnes, and her father was, without doubt, my most powerful ally.

"As you can imagine, with a war raging I had enemies everywhere and John had many spies following my every move. It didn't take long for him to come to know of my secret nuptials. He didn't waste any time, and informed Philip II right way, depriving me of his support. In fact, that same year they signed a treaty in Le Goulet that recognised John as the legitimate heir.

"I was left defeated and without allies, but I had never been so utterly elated. I had Héloise at my side, and the entire realm of England didn't seem too much of a price to pay for her. We were together for two years, away from the court ploys and manoeuvres. It was just us and our love... we were content." His voice cracks a little at this point. "My mother... if not wearing a crown, saw me happy before she died in childbirth."

"That's horrible." The comment escapes my lips before I can catch it.

"It was very common at the time," he says matter-of-factly, "and at least she was serene. I am glad for it. She never had to witness what was to come. Because, in a twist of fate, John fell into my same trap, and it was once again love, and not reason, to decide the course of the war for the throne.

"He fell deeply in love with Isabella of Angoulême and decided to marry her. Some said he had fallen for her beauty and youth, while others maligned that the union was merely a means to get a hold of the Angoumois lands that came in dowry with Isabella. Those territories were vital to John, as they would guarantee him a strategic land passage between Poitou, where he held the title of Count, and Gascony, significantly strengthening his grip on Aquitaine.

"In his schemings to marry Isabella, John cheated and offended many and lost the support of his French vassals. Some appealed their case to Philip of France, John's own feudal lord as Count of Pitou. But when John was summoned before Philip to answer for his actions, he refused to suffer such a humiliation and weakened his authority in western France even further. His French vassals did not like that he thought himself above their customs. And Philip, at his stubborn refusal, declared a breach of the treaty of Le Goulet, and in the aftermath of this squabble I was pardoned and all of John's lands subjugated to the French Crown were reassigned to me. Philip had begun a fresh war against John. It was my time to act—I had to gain control of Normandy immediately.

"I summoned an army of rebels and marched toward the Castle of Mirebeau to besiege my formidable grandmother, Eleanor of Aquitaine, an implacable supporter of her son, my uncle John.

"As soon as John received the message that my forces were threatening his mother, he swayed his mercenary army rapidly to the south to protect her, flanked by his seneschal in Anjou, William de Roches, and took us by surprise.

"The Castle of Mirebeau rested in a clearing surrounded by green hills. It was shortly after dawn when a cloud of cold mist descended over us from the hilltop. It made its way toward our camp, drifting through the air with uneven swells, curling on itself as it advanced. In its race toward us, the fog seemed to transform from its natural greyish colour to a hellish green. It came at us sinuous like a snake, inexorable, dense enough to turn the day back into night. It clung to our bodies with its clamminess, stalling our every movement.

"And then we saw them, and the enemy was upon us. John's cavalry had surrounded us. The horses, their eyes ablaze like those of demons, were galloping in the mud sending gushes of dirt flying everywhere, their breath reeking of death.

"In a matter of minutes we were overcome, and I was taken prisoner."

Twenty-three
The Curse

"It was about the same time of the year as now, mid-summer," the genie continues. "John had managed to cover with his entire army the eighty miles from Le Mans to Mirebeau in just two days. Nobody would have thought it possible. They had ridden hidden in the malefic mist, leaving our rearguard and scouts oblivious to their descent. We did not see or hear them until they had us surrounded. It was a massacre—half of my forces were slain, the other half, taken captive. I was imprisoned at the fortress of Falaise in Normandy, where Hugh de Burgh, John's chamberlain, was appointed as my warder.

"With my mother and me gone, my elder sister Eleanor was left defenceless, and she was abducted by John. With my capture, which might as well have been a death sentence, she was the legitimate heir to the lands of England, Anjou, Aquitaine, and Brittany. You see, in those realms, the law barring the ascension of females to the throne did not apply, therefore she posed a potential threat to our Uncle John's claim. And after his death, equally to his successor. I learned later on that she spent most of her life incarcerated—her captivity became the longest one for a member of an English royal family. She went down in history as the Fair Maid of Brittany."

"How old was she when they took her?" I ask sadly.

"She was eighteen."

"And she spent her entire life in prison?"

"She was more of a guest with limited freedom. Don't imagine her shackled to a wall in a cell. That treatment was reserved for me."

"Oh, I'm sorry. Did they torture you?" I ask, horrified.

"Not in the general sense of the term, but spending your days in the dark, famished and filthy, is enough to make a man crazy. I did not have any news from the outside world. I was sure that John wanted me dead, even if he could not openly execute me. But what troubled me the most during those long days spent in a dim dungeon was Héloise. I was more afraid of what could happen to her than of dying. I tried to keep count of the days by keeping track of the meals I would get, but they didn't come regularly, and after a while, I was simply lost in a vortex of obscurity and frenzied insanity.

"Every once in a while the lifeless body of one of my comrades would be brought outside. John kept us in such awful conditions that twenty-two of my fellow rebel leaders died of privation in those cells. I survived only because Hugh de Burgh took a personal interest in me; as loyal as he was to John, he didn't want to be responsible for the death of a pretender to the throne.

"After I don't know how many months, I was transferred from Falaise to Rouen, and William de Roches became my warden. The only information I could gather from my gaolers' conversations was that John's victory at Mirebeau had considerably strengthened his position in France, but that his treatment of the prisoners had quickly undermined these gains.

"John had also dealt with his allies with contempt and disrespect, as usual, causing more and more defections to his cause among his French territories. The quick degeneration of his situation convinced him that he had to get rid of me once and for all.

"The legend has it that when he finally ordered my murder, both his lords and my jailers refused to slay a member of the royal family in cold blood. The myth narrates that one night John, after drinking considerably, descended in my cell and, intoxicated with alcohol, slaughtered me himself, making my lifeless body disappear by tying it to a heavy stone and dumping it into the Seine. My corpse was allegedly found by a fisherman who dragged it ashore in his net—he is said to have identified the cadaver as the lost prince and to have buried it in secret for fear of the tyrant John.

"My disappearance still is, as of today, one of the greatest mysteries in mediaeval history. However, no living soul could have guessed what truly became of me that ill-fated night.

"I was in my dungeon—I assumed it was night only because the prison guard had been snoring loudly for a while. That remained the only audible sound for some long hours until I heard the noise of muffled footsteps approaching my cell. A hooded figure opened the door, entering the chamber. It was almost completely dark, and the only source of light was the faraway blaze of a torch in the crypt corridor.

"My eyes rapidly adjusted to the newfound glow, and for a split second, I thought that Héloise was standing in front of me. That was until the figure removed the hood, and the flames in her hair hovered above us, illuminating the dungeon with a sinister red glare. Her face remained mostly in the dark, but her green eyes flared in the night—they were two incandescent pits filled with hatred.

"At that moment, John with a longsword in hand would have been a much more welcome sight.

"We stared at each other for a long instant before she broke the silence, 'Well, well, look what we have here, a king on a throne of disgrace.' Her lustrous voice chilled me to the bones.

"'Morgene, what are you doing here? How did you get in?' I asked her.

"'Now, is that the way to greet an old friend? Tell me, Arthur, has imprisonment made you forget your good manners?'

"'Go away... I don't want to see you.' I thought I was talking to a hallucination—my mind could not come to terms with her being there, but she was real.

"'You don't? Oh dear, what an awkward situation... and to think that the last time we were together you were professing your undying love for me. Imagine my surprise when I heard that Prince Arthur was to be king no more because he had married a fair maiden. I really felt quite distressed, considering I thought the prince to be in love with *me*.'

"'I never was in love with you. You had me under your sortilege. You are a witch!' At my mention of the word, her eyes sparkled with cold fury.

"'That,' she continued in the same calm, unnerving tone, 'will come to an end soon, I am afraid. See, Arthur, my kind is not supposed to fall in love. It is dangerous for us... a broken heart lets the magic bleed away and mine is almost completely gone. I have to admit, I used a big chunk to ensure your current accommodation.' She waved her arm in half a circle, indicating the dungeon.

"'The mist... it was you. *You monster...*' I screamed, launching myself at her, but my chains held me back close to the wall.

"She sneered at my attempted attack with a soulless laugh, a sound so hellish that it was not apt to come through human lips. Her voice rang through the room, bringing its despair along—it reverberated on the walls and on the low ceiling, leaving my heart hollow of any hope.

"'How did you think it possible that an army of thousands of soldiers descended on you unheard and unseen?' she asked rhetorically once she'd finished jeering at me. 'Of course, it was me!' she hissed maliciously, before regaining her composure. 'See, I find your Uncle John to be quite a reasonable man, contrary to you. We made ourselves a little arrangement—he got the kingdom, and I got, well...*you*. I admit his side of the bargain took some reminding on my part, but finally, here we are. Reunited at last.'

"'You are delusional—I am never going to be yours. I never was,' I sibilated with scorn.

"'Now, now. I believe myself to be quite a practical woman, and to show I bear you no ill will, I am ready to condone your actions and welcome you back.' With these words, she aimed her sorcery at me, trying to entice me once more. But to no avail.

"Héloise's love was my armour against her incantations—her magic could no longer breach its shield to enter my heart. I was safe, or at least I thought I was.

"My rejection lashed at Morgene with force, sending her recoiling in a corner.

"'I see there is no persuading you,' she said, massaging her arm where her own spell had backfired. 'Very well, I shall put the last of my power to a better use. Brace yourself for me, dear prince, and for all the powers of darkness!'

She chanted my sentence in a soft, forlorn voice:
'A coffer of gold shall thee enslave,
The ones thee once hurt, thee must now save.
For eternity shall thee strive,
Granting wishes in the number of five.
Now fare with the curse in dire farewell,
Round Prince Arthur cast my spell!'

"The moment the echo of her words subsided, I felt a powerful otherworldly force latching onto me, bringing me to another dimension, and since then I have been cursed."

I look at him, at a loss for words. I've been enraptured by his story for the better part of the night. He brought me to a world of dames and knights, of castles and wars, of love and despair. And he seems still lost in his memories.

"Do you know why five wishes?" I finally break the silence.

"Equal to the moons we spent together, I suppose."

"Moons?"

"Months, lunar phases. There is more power to the moon than to govern the tide."

"Oh. What happened to Héloise?"

"To this day I do not know." The agony behind his eyes seems to be as recent and alive as if it all happened just yesterday. "I was summoned for the first time thirty-something years later in Rome. I was at the service of my first charge, a noblewoman from Florence named Caterina. She helped me search for Héloise, but those were different times. There were no proper registries, and people could disappear without leaving a trace. The only way to search for someone was to travel around and ask questions. Yet travelling was a slow and risky endeavour, especially for an unaccompanied woman, even with all the powers of the universe on her side.

"However, Caterina was brave and strong and decided to risk the journey to France anyway. We tried my castle first—we gathered only some conflicting tales of the lady of the chateau escaping to a thousand different supposed destinations. Life was shorter in the thirteenth century—diseases, plagues, and malnutrition had many dying young. The majority of people that were alive and old enough to remember when I was lord of the manor were dead already.

"Afterward, we tried her father's castle, but it was another dead end. Nobody had heard of the princess since she had left the house—nobody could even talk about Héloise! Her father considered every memory of her as an offence to the family's honour. We collected these few bits of information from her old wet nurse, the only one who truly loved and missed Héloise. She risked her life to follow us after we left the town and tell us what little she knew.

"After that, my last remote hope was to search the convent her father had destined her for safe keeping. But she was not there and never had been. I didn't know where else to look, and I relinquished my quest."

"I'm so sorry. I can't begin to imagine how painful it must have been for you," I say with empathy.

"I console myself thinking that having her, being loved by her, even for such a brief time was the greatest blessing I could ever ask for."

"I really don't know what to say. I've been complaining to you for weeks, not once worrying about you. I'm sorry, Arthur."

"You have called me by my real name."

"It's the least you deserve. I feel like all my problems seem so small now compared to what you've been through."

"Do not worry about me. I had a long time to come to terms with what happened to me and Héloise and accept it. My curse could have been a lot worse. I am fortunate enough to at least help others find the happiness I once had."

"But you said the curse could be broken somehow," I chip in, optimistic.

"Every piece of magic has a counter spell, but the old knowledge was lost a long time ago. There is no hope for me. Magic has left this world—"

"It hasn't," I interrupt him. "You are here, the coffer is here, and it found me! There is still magic in this world, and there is hope," I conclude.

"However," he says without acknowledging anything I've just said, "the purpose of me telling you my story was to make you understand what true love is. Do you still believe James to be the love of your life?"

"Ah, that is a whole different matter," I say, defensive. "I can see your point now, but I still think that James deserves the benefit of the doubt. You were right when you said those were different times. Things are different today, less heroic, less extreme. And, forgive me for saying this, but he truly had a special bond with his father, and given that you never knew yours I am not sure you can really understand."

He tries to object, but I don't let him.

"Anyway," I continue, raising my hands to stop his protests, "I have a plan. I want to free James of his obligations and see what he does. With your help, I am sure we can succeed. What do you say?"

"I still believe he is not worthy of you. But of course, you have all my support."

I WISH FOR YOU

"Thank you, Arthur. Now we should try to sleep," I say, setting the alarm on my phone for five a.m. "I want to get out of here before anyone wakes up."

"You don't want to see him tomorrow?"

"No, everything is still too raw. And I need to plan my actions carefully. Plus, we need some extra time to work on your curse."

"Then it is good night, milady," he says, shaking his head at my stubbornness, but still with an affectionate smile surfacing on his lips. "Can I only ask you one thing?"

"Sure, fire."

"What is this grand plan of yours?"

"I want to buy myself a bank," I answer, with an even bigger smile spreading on my face.

Twenty-four
Mumbo Jumbo

When my phone's alarm goes off the next morning, I'm already wide awake, my eyes open and staring at the ceiling. Actually, I never got to sleep; after yesterday's discoveries about James and the genie... scratch that, Arthur, my brain was overloaded with new information, and I spent the remainder of the night trying to process it.

"Ready to go?" I call out, jumping off the bed.

"Absolutely, milady." He is already fully dressed.

I guess he didn't catch much sleep either. That is if he ever does.

"Arthur—" He smiles slightly when he hears me calling him by his real name again. "Can you please call me just Ally?"

He nods in agreement.

I change from my pajamas into a pair of jeans and a dark gray T-shirt and only need a quick stop to the bathroom before we can leave.

"Let's get out of here," I say as soon as I am ready.

On the way home, we stop at a Starbucks to have breakfast.

"You should really give coffee a chance, you know?" I say to Arthur, handing him his cup of hot tea. "But considering that you're partially French, I thought you could appreciate a butter croissant."

"Indeed, you are most kind." He thanks me, and takes his drink and food.

"How are you?" I ask, worried. After talking about Héloise and the curse, a new veil of sadness seems to have wrapped itself around him.

"Fairly good, maybe a jot on the melancholic side. But it will pass—it always does."

I WISH FOR YOU

"Good! We need all your positive energies because today we are in the business of breaking curses," I announce with enthusiasm, trying to stay on the positive side of things.

He doesn't say anything; he simply rolls his eyes while sipping from his paper cup.

While enjoying my breakfast, I open up a Google search on my phone and type in "how to break a curse". I know I probably won't find anything useful, but trying won't hurt anyone either, so why not?

The first website has a long introduction before telling me I could learn everything about curse breaking in their next seminar at the convenient cost of one hundred fifty bucks. No thanks.

After opening most of the search results, I decide on a few that seem to descend from some old magical beliefs or traditions. Hey, I know it sounds crazy, but if a while ago someone had spoken to me about magic and curses I would have called an asylum, so I'm keeping an open mind on the subject.

Some of the rituals require a waning moon, I read, claiming that the moon while disappearing can bring along any bad influence. These rituals are out of the picture since, by checking again on Google, I find out that the moon is now on the opposite phase, and considering what Arthur said about its power, I don't want to mess with it.

Luckily enough, some other incantations require a waxing moon, as it will help grow the power of the person performing the spell. We're good for those, and for the ones that don't say anything specific about lunar phases. We just need to do a little shopping before we can get started.

***

A few hours later, back at my apartment, I decide that our first attempts should be the ones we can easily try in the kitchen. Victim number one is a lemon.

"You have to purify the fruit first—here, use this," I say, passing a more-skeptical-by-the-second Arthur an aromatic stick of incense.

"May I express my doubts about this entire process?"

"Hush—we need faith for it to work."

He takes the stick and passes it under the lemon multiple times.

"What now?" he asks, voice still loaded with skepticism.

"You have to cut it in two perfect halves and say:
'Forthwith I crush this acid lemon
Freeing myself of the malefic venom
Hither I let thee rotten
Let my curse be forgotten.'"

"Could you repeat the magic formula one more time?" he requests, deadly serious with his arms crossed on his chest and the knife in one hand. "I am not sure I remember all of it."

I begin to repeat it when a smirk escapes his lips; he tries to hide it and regain his original composure, but it is too late. I saw it.

"You had it the first time," I say with feigned outrage. "Go on."

He laughs, openly this time, before proceeding with the killing of the poor lemon. He pronounces the words with great solemnity. Another mockery, I suspect.

"What shall we do with the corpse?" he asks teasingly.

"Leave it there—it has to rot for the night," I answer, reading the instructions on my phone. "Tomorrow we'll have to throw it away, far from the house."

"Perfect," he says, putting the small plate with the crushed fruit next to the window. "What is next on our list?" he asks, maintaining his pretended gravity.

I WISH FOR YOU

"We have to pass the curse on to an egg," I reply, trying to keep a straight face.

After the egg, we proceed to brew a disgusting concoction of curry, ginger, and vervain that he has to chug at once. We write his and Morgene's names on a piece of paper with black ink and burn it to break the bond between them. We do a ritual with crystals, and Arthur bathes in hot salted water mixed with lavender and juniper within a circle of thirteen white candles. He had a bathing suit on, in case you were wondering.

Sugar happily participates in all our rituals, mostly playing with the ingredients, stealing them, or trying to eat them.

"Are we finished, milady?" Arthur asks, dabbing his wet body with one of my towels.

"Hm…" I am momentarily distracted by his muscular chest and toned abs. It really has been too long since I've been with a man… "We only have one thing left that we can try," I say, shaking the image of his naked, damp body out of my head.

I move back into the living room to prepare everything for our last ceremony, a cleansing ritual with sage. We must burn a dried stick of it and wave the smoke around Arthur in circles to purify him.

"Stay put," I tell him when he joins me from the bathroom and reaches the center of the room.

He raises both eyebrows, but stops as instructed, watching me in silence while I light the little twig.

"Don't move. I am going to circle around you," I say, flapping the stick in the air surrounding him.

I am about halfway through the process when suddenly the smoke sensor goes crazy.

"No, no, no," I shout, trying to put out the stick. "Open the windows," I yell to Arthur while, pushing the entrance door ajar.

I try to wave the smoke out of the apartment with my hands while madly stretching upward to push the security button on the detector, which is definitely too high and out of my reach.

I'm brushing it with the tip of my finger, but it's too late... the security sprinklers go off, and suddenly it's raining in my house.

The fire alarm of the whole building picks up and adds its awful noise to the general confusion. The doorman is on my floor in a matter of seconds, and he stares aghast at the ruins of my apartment through the open door.

"Miss Johnson, what happened here?" he asks me, panting hard. Poor guy, he must have run the five flights of stairs to my apartment because he thought there was a fire going on, and you are not supposed to use elevators during fire emergencies.

"Here, uh... I am so sorry, Fred. Nothing happened—it was a mistake." In that moment I follow his gaze that moves from my face to my general bosom area. Oh no, with my T-shirt wet and stuck to my body, my nipples must be showing. I concentrate deeply on bringing them back to order while still trying to say something reasonable to Fred, inwardly thankful that my T-shirt is not white. "I... umm... think these smoke detectors are a little too sensitive," I continue, embarrassed.

"There is no fire then?" he asks, still gasping for breath. Given the roundness of his belly, this is probably the first time he has taken the stairs in his entire life.

"No, Fred, no fire," I confirm.

"I'd better let the other occupants know or the panic will spread." With this, he turns on his heel and takes long, worried strides down the hall. "No. False alarm, nothing to worry about. It's only apartment 5B—she was burning some sort of medical herbs," I hear him reassure one of my neighbors. Ouch, perfect! Just what I needed... the entire building hating me and thinking I am cuckoo-crazy.

Unfortunately, my ordeal is not as easily over as I have to explain myself also to an angry fireman. Apparently, my building's alarm system is directly connected to the closest fire station.

I WISH FOR YOU

"And why were you burning herbs in your apartment? Don't you know that it's dangerous?" the fireman asks after hearing my story.

I can't come up with anything better than the truth, so I go with it. "It was a cleansing ritual for spiritual purification. I didn't think..." I try to justify myself, keeping my eyes on the floor and wringing my hands like a five-year-old.

The fireman's astonished gaze passes quickly from me to Arthur, who hasn't moved from his position in the center of the living room. I have to admit he is quite a sight. Even though the sprinklers are now off, he's soaking wet and has water trickling from his hair into his face and dripping from his clothes on the floor. His expression is mutinous at best. Sugar is sitting at his feet, equally drenched and indignant.

The fireman takes in the scene and sends Arthur a look of manly sympathy mixed with utter pity. He too must be thinking that I am looney-tunes, and he's empathizing with Arthur for having a wacky-into-new-age girlfriend. After a long sermon on fire prevention and security, he finally lets me off the hook. I wait patiently until he's finished, apologize one more time, and gladly shut the door behind him, blocking out the external world.

"Hm..." I clear my throat. "Could you possibly do something about this?" I ask in a small voice.

Arthur stares at me from under the damp hair clumping on his forehead and says nothing.

"Please?" I add with my most innocent expression.

He snaps his finger without further comment, and my apartment, Sugar, and our clothes are magically back to normal.

"So how are you feeling?" I ask, sagging on the couch. "Any less cursed?"

"I am afraid not. But I thank you for the effort." His features finally relax in an amused smile. "It was a rather interesting afternoon."

"Sure was," I agree, smiling back. "We will have to come up with something more effective tomorrow because the last bullet points on my research list are to summon the dead and exorcism. Speaking of research," I continue, "I need to do some of my own. Will you be fine here by yourself?"

"Completely. I have two centuries of literature to catch up with," he reassures me.

Since he discovered my eReader I have had trouble using it; he reads one novel after the other. I should buy another one.

As I step away toward my room, I call out for Sugar, but he gives me a defiant stare and jumps on Arthur's knees instead, the little traitor.

Once in my room, I switch on my laptop, recently upgraded to a top-of-the-line model, and Google the following:

How to buy a bank
Prime Capital National Bank assets
Adam Van Horn
M&A banks in Chicago
M&A banks in Chicago -jobs -career
Vanessa Van Horn
Vanessa Van Horn James Avery
James Avery
Cheney Smythe M&A Chicago appointment
How to evaluate your net worth
Vanessa Van Horn James Avery wedding
P.C.N. Stoke Exchange Value
Barneys' latest fashion

Some searches prove to be more profitable than others, but I manage to find a phone number to call first thing tomorrow to get an appointment with a Wall Street animal. At least, I'm hoping I'll get a ruthless financial beast; apparently, bank acquisitions require a little longer than a month to be achieved, but according to all sources Cheney Smythe is the best. It's the most aggressive you can get, so I'm hoping they will live up to their reputation and get me what I want in time.

I WISH FOR YOU

The tiny clock on my screen tells me that it's not very late, but after a sleepless night, I feel completely exhausted. I stroll into the next room. Arthur hasn't moved from his reading station on my favorite armchair, and Sugar is still comfortably nestled on his lap, producing a constant purring sound as Arthur strokes his fur absentmindedly. The little deserter has definitely been spending more time with Arthur than me! This is weird; with James, he always used to hiss and claw at him any opportunity he got.

"What are you reading?" I ask to make my presence known.

"*Dracula*, Bram Stoker," Arthur replies without lifting his head.

"Uh, scary!"

"Count D. makes Morgene look like an amateur," he comments, looking at me for a brief moment before returning his gaze to the book.

"Glad you can joke about it. Hey, I'm going to bed," I add, yawning. "You should go too. Tomorrow we have to go into shark mode, and that book is going to give you nightmares," I tease.

"I am not a little boy," he states, too engrossed in the story to look at me again, so I bid them both good night and go back to my room. I gladly peel off my clothes, trading them for the soft comfort of my pajamas, and jump into bed.

Today has been a nice distraction from the James drama. I needed to give my brain a bit of a rest. An image of the shocked expression on Arthur's face when the sprinklers started spraying water on him is my last thought before I doze off with a soft smile stamped on my lips.

Twenty-five
Bear Hug

"Cheney Smythe M&A Division," an efficient receptionist says. "Good morning, how can I help you?"

"Um, good morning." Once again I am up super early and I am on the phone already. "I need a consultation for an acquisition deal—I would like to schedule an appointment for this afternoon." I'm trying to sound as professional as I can.

"Very well, is your company already a client with us?" the receptionist asks matter-of-factly.

"Uh, no. I mean, I don't have a company. I am... mmm... a private investor."

"Very well." She doesn't sound "very well" she sounds "very skeptical." "Can I have your name, please?"

"Ally Johnson." This is the first question I know how to answer properly.

"And what kind of acquisition were you interested in?"

"What do you mean?" I'm once again in the fog.

"What kind of business sector are you interested in?"

"Ah, ok. I want to buy a bank."

"A bank? You are a private investor and you want to buy a bank? Excuse me? Is this a prank?"

"I can assure you I'm very serious. If your M&A department is not able to assist me, I can easily ask one of your competitors—"

"I'm sorry madam, I didn't mean to be rude. It's just that your request is quite—" She pauses a second or two, probably to select the right word. "Unconventional. Please hold."

Scaring people always works.

I have to listen to some classical symphony for fifteen minutes before she gets back on the line. My request must have rattled their procedures.

"Thank you for waiting, Miss Johnson. At what time will you be available today?"

"Six p.m. would be fine."

"Okay. I have you down for six p.m. at our downtown office—one of our senior VPs will take care of you. I just need to ask you a few more questions and we'll be all set." She then proceeds to interrogate me in absolute detail about my generalities, social security number included, apparently so that they can perform a background check on my finances. I bet they are in for a huge surprise.

"Arthur," I say as soon as I put down the phone. "You should wear one of your sharpest suits today. You're going to play my assistant."

"I presume to say it would not be much of an act," he comments.

"You're right," I say absentmindedly, browsing through my wardrobe to select my most down-to-business-looking suit.

***

When I enter the office a little later I am saluted by a round of applause and a mini standing ovation. Everybody is eager to compliment me on my vocal exhibition of Saturday night. As flattered as I may be by all the attention, I need to do a million other things this morning, so I brush my nice colleagues off and hide away behind my cubicle, but not before noticing the evil eye Vanessa is giving me. I quickly scan her mind just in case there's something new I need to know. Hmm. I detune immediately, as I only get a strong wave of utter jealousy coming my way. Good!

I need to get some more information on banks, acquisitions, price valuation, and loans management. I want to perform a little better than I did on the phone. But most of all, I want to see if I can get a clearer idea of how much money I have since they are background checking me right now.

I turn on my PC and quickly enter my access password. I decide to have a look at my regular bank account first and... Meh! It is plump and healthy, but nothing spectacular. I switch to my little investment fund. After five years of hard work, I managed to save something close to ten thousand dollars; at least it was as much in the B.C. (Before Coffer) era. I type in my client number and pin code and... Oh! I am loaded. But not I-could-buy-all-the-clothes-in-the-world loaded, more like I-could-buy-an-island-with-spare-change loaded.

I lie back, staring at the number in front of me in shock. I mean, I'm not in Bill Gates's league yet, but I'm getting there fast. I should really leave this job and do something more inspiring with my life, but what?

Unfortunately, I don't have a clear dream or goal in life, at least workwise. My wildest dream has always been to have a family of my own, and I am afraid that is the one thing money—or wishes in my case—can't buy.

Anyway, I occupy the rest of the day alternately surfing the Internet to acquire new financial knowledge and to find inspirations for my future dream job. I even end up subscribing to a career counselling service, filling out an infinite questionnaire about my hobbies, my lifestyle, and myself in general. They'll send me a detailed ideal-job-profile within a few weeks, along with all the required steps for me to sway my career in the right direction.

***

At five-thirty I'm already in the street, walking briskly toward Cheney Smythe's offices with Arthur in tow. I'm glad I'm wearing pants, as their office is located in the opposite direction of the lake, and today the Windy City is living up to its name.

Their building is one of those polished glass-steel tall ones, sleek and sharp; I hope this is a good indication of their attitude as well. The entrance hall is, well, in one word: grand. The space is ample and modern, a little intimidating, to be honest. To reach the reception desk, I have to walk the entire length of the room, my heels breaking the religious silence with loud clicking sounds.

The receptionist looks like she belongs in a fashion magazine doing bikini commercials more than in a corporate office, and she's equally intimidating. However, when I talk to her, she's very kind to me and, after taking my name, she directs me to suite number twenty-two.

The secretary upstairs is less friendly and eyes me suspiciously; she must be the same one from this morning. Nonetheless, she shows me into a posh meeting room with a crystal, boat-shaped table surrounded by black leather chairs.

Before leaving me alone, she offers me high-end refreshments, which I gladly accept. I choose one of the chairs at the head of the table and nibble my premium macadamia nut cookie. Arthur too seems to be enjoying himself.

After only a few minutes, a tall man dressed in an impeccable dark suit with shiny black shoes joins us. He's your stereotypical banker. He looks pale and taut, with a hint of dark circles around his eyes. I can't help but wonder if he ever sees the light of day; this is what a vampire must look like. Exactly what I needed: a bloodsucking creature that lives in the office.

I browse his thoughts quickly to see what I can expect.

Damn Brent, he dumped this on me...

Next, I get a mental image of another suited guy being sucker punched, assumedly Brent. Okay, so I am up against a little bit of prejudice. Nothing I can't overcome, I'm sure.

"Welcome to Cheney Smythe." He sits next to me, opposite from Arthur, and quickly verifies the name on the folder. "Miss Johnson, I am Nathan Murphy, senior VP. What can I do for you today?" he asks, producing a dashing smile.

Good, he's a salesman.

"Nice to meet you, Mr. Murphy—"

"Please call me Nathan."

"Nice to meet you, Nathan. This is my assistant, Arthur Pemberley." They exchange a nod of acknowledgment. "We are here today because I am interested in the acquisition of a local bank."

I haven't had the time to read her file. A bank? Is she crazy? Does she know how much it costs?

"I'm aware this may sound like an unusual request, but I assure you that I'm a serious investor, as I'm confident you had time to verify," I continue, staring knowingly at the folder in his hands.

He takes the hint and flips a couple of pages nonchalantly, probably searching for my financial profile. When he finds it, his eyes widen involuntarily.

You have my attention, girl. Faux pas Brent, this could backfire on you... I bet you didn't check the numbers before assigning me the client...

"I see from your file you haven't specified a name. Are you after any bank or a specific one?" he asks, pretending that was the information he was looking for in my dossier.

"A specific one. Prime Capital National Bank," I announce.

"Ah, that could be tricky, Miss Johnson. Mr. Van Horn is the majority shareholder of P.C.N., and we know for sure that he's not interested in selling."

Never mind, she's crazy. She wants to go after the most powerful man in Chicago.

"Oh, I know, but you see, that's a conspicuous cause of interest on my part."

"Miss Johnson, Adam Van Horn has a strong control share in P.C.N. An acquisition was attempted only last year, which he adamantly refused. We were actually involved in the deal as mediators, but he created the bank himself forty years ago. It was his first entrepreneurial breakthrough. It's his baby—he would never part from it."

Unless you forced his hand, he adds to himself.

"As you well know, there are ways to push this kind of thing into happening..." I pause, mostly because I have no idea how this could happen. I need to fish for it in his brain. Luckily enough, he promptly delivers me the answer.

The only way is to bear hug the entire company.

I have no idea what "bear hug" means, but once again Nathan's clever mind provides me with an explanation, and from the sound of it, something directly out of a textbook.

Bear Hug: An offer made to buy a company at a much higher per-share price than effective market value. Technique used when in doubt of the willingness to sell of the management of the targeted company, which is forced to accept the overgenerous offer due to its legal obligation to look out for the best interests of its shareholders.

Mmm, interesting.

"Is Adam Van Horn the only shareholder?" I resume my speech after my fruitful little pause.

"No, but he has the majority share."

"Is he also CEO?"

"Yes."

Where is she going with this?

"So tell me, Nathan, assuming the economics weren't a problem, could I bear hug P.C.N. out of him?"

Whoa, girl, I definitely underestimated you. You may look like a kitten, but you do have claws.

I admit I am tempted to meow aloud, but that would give away too much of my game.

"That would be technically possible," he concedes. "However, if you do not have a serious strategic reason to buy the company, these kind of acquisition rarely proves to be profitable."

Plus, you and I would be making an enemy for life, and a powerful one... but the commission on such a deal... I would bring in millions out of nowhere... I could steal the promotion from right under his nose...

He's very ambitious. Perfect. He would risk being on the wrong side of Vanessa's daddy if it meant an advancement in his career. I just have to play him a little.

"Humor me, please. Moneywise, how much would it take to 'hug' P.C.N.?"

He does a mental calculation to which I listen carefully.

Last year they made about fifty million in profit. I will have to analyze their debt and equity ratio, but a fair multiplier would be around fifteen... to pull off a bear hug that number would at least need to be at twenty, which is... One billion. Yep, one big guy should cut it...

"Miss Johnson, let's not throw numbers. I would need to do a proper evaluation before I can be confident enough to give you the right figure." *And bill you for the hours it takes me to do it.* "But judging from your financial profile, a hostile acquisition would be within your means."

"Again, humor me, Nathan. Do you reckon a multiple of twenty would be sufficient? You think that one big guy would cut me a deal?" I steal his thoughts to add credibility to my financier character.

She knows her math as well...

"Yes, that would be a good rough estimate," he answers. "But as I said, I would need to examine all the numbers properly first to give an accurate number. But Miss Johnson, I'm not certain that Cheney Smythe is willing to perform a hostile acquisition against Adam Van Horn."

"What is your commission on this kind of deal, Nathan?"

One percent.

"One point five percent," he says instead. Sneaky old Nathan.

"What if I doubled that? Would that be enough to ensure your support?"

Thirty million out of nowhere? Yeah, girl!

I WISH FOR YOU

"Welcome to Cheney Smythe, Miss Johnson." A wolfish smile spreads on his lips. "I'm confident P.C.N. will be under your control by the end of the year."

"Ah, no." I quench his enthusiasm. "I need it by the end of next month. Is it possible?"

I watch his expression switch to one of controlled panic.

I would have to work my team and myself to exhaustion... a month... a month with no sleep in it... if we reuse the due diligence we already made and update it... we would barely make it... it would be a nightmare... but thirty million, plus all the billable hours...

"We are the best M&A division in the world, Miss Johnson. Anything is possible with us." His answer is far more confident than his actual thoughts.

"Very good." I smile. "One last thing."

What now?

"I need to remain an anonymous buyer. My name can't be linked to the deal in any way."

"We can make it happen. Would that be all?" he asks, hopeful.

"Yes, thank you very much for your time," I say, getting up and stretching my arm forward to shake his hand.

"It has been a pleasure." He has a strong, dry grip; I like it.

I'm about to leave the room when he calls me back.

"Miss Johnson."

I stop and turn toward him. I can tell he's hesitant about what he's about to say next.

"May I ask you why you want to buy P.C.N. so badly?"

"You may ask." I pause for more effect. "But I may not answer."

And with that last comment, I leave the room highly satisfied.

Twenty-six
Deal or No Deal

I'm staring at my silent phone, filled with anxiety, wondering what is going on a few blocks away downtown. Today is the day; three and half weeks after my first encounter with Nathan, they are signing the papers that officially pass the possession of P.C.N. Bank over to me... or, should I say, to a private investment fund of which I am the covert owner.

I can almost picture all the parties involved sitting in the posh meeting room on the twenty-second floor at Cheney Smythe's offices. Vanessa's dad barely suppressing cold fury, Nathan as much incapable of containing his triumph, and Brent sulking in the background, green with envy. He has been assigned to the project *under* Nathan's direction.

My phone bleeps with a text from Nathan.

> It's done

I observe the two little words on the display with mixed feelings: excitement, hope, anxiety, and a bit of remorse. I look over at Vanessa; she appears preoccupied, and she is nervously nibbling one of her perfectly manicured nails while staring at her screen with a lost expression.

> Good
>
> See you at your office in a few hours

I WISH FOR YOU

Over the past month, I've been in contact with Nathan twenty-four hours a day, seven days a week. He has been working nonstop on the acquisition, and today we snatch our victory from the jaws of defeat. Adam Van Horn is no easy man to take down. He has fought the takeover with everything he had; at one point he tried to buy back the minority shares of the bank from other shareholders at market price, but Nathan was quicker in submitting our offer to the board. In the end, the old lion had no other choice than to surrender.

I tune on Vanessa's channel to see what's going on.

I wonder if he's okay... I've never seen Daddy so tense, and he has never been dismissive, not with me! I hope it's not about James again. I know he doesn't like him, but it's my decision.

Yep, exactly what I thought. I feel a stab of guilt. I mean, Vanessa's dad didn't do anything to me, and I am stripping his first company away from him. But, on the other hand, I'm showering him with money, not to mention that I'm saving his daughter from a loveless marriage... something he wants, but doesn't have the attributes to do himself. So, everything considered, I am almost doing him a favor.

I get distracted by my inbox flashing; it's my career test result. Wow, I had almost forgotten about that. Today it seems everything is falling into place. In fact, regardless of what the result of the test is, today may very well be my last day at Crispy Koob. Let's be honest, Corporate America is not my life. It doesn't inspire me, and the wedding is in a little over two weeks. I don't need to spy on Vanessa anymore, and frankly, I don't want to have to see her every day either.

Now that P.C.N. is officially mine, I plan to free James of his obligations immediately. After that, if he still wants to go through with the wedding, there's nothing I can do and I was wrong all along. Before I can second-guess myself, I forward the unopened email to my personal account, shut my computer down, and march straight into Kyle's office.

***

Forty-five minutes later I'm standing on the large curb in front of my office's building holding a cardboard box filled with all my personal belongings, and I'm feeling both exhilarated and melancholic.

When I announced my sudden departure, my colleagues—Vanessa included—were shocked. I couldn't tell if she was happy or not that I was going, and I didn't bother to read her mind to find out. Instead, I decided that I was truly sorry for her because, as mean and wicked as she could be, at this point one of two fates awaits her: either she's going to marry a man who doesn't love her, or she's going to be left at the altar. And I wouldn't wish either of the two on my worst enemy.

So, just before leaving I decided to restore her figure. I shredded fifteen of the twenty pounds I gave her (after the karaoke incident I had given her another five that I've left on her for health reasons), and I put her hair and skin back to normal.

In a way, letting go of my anger toward her has lifted a big weight from my stomach. Arthur was right in saying that nothing of this was her fault, even if she made a pass at my boyfriend knowing he was with me and afterward enjoyed rubbing their relationship in my face at every possible occasion. She wasn't my friend, and she didn't owe me anything. James did. Maybe I shouldn't have taken it out on her, but I'm not going to admit it to Arthur. It was too much fun, anyway.

Getting out of the office took me a little longer than expected, as everybody was eager to say goodbye in person, and they all kept asking me why I was quitting. I lied, saying I got a better offer from another undisclosed company. Everyone appeared legitimately sad I was going, and for a moment, I was shaken by the fact that I would no longer see many of the faces I've got used to looking at every morning for the past five years. They'll not be there tomorrow. Bam... a big chunk of my life is gone in an instant. It's a weird sensation; I am even being sentimental over my stupid cubicle.

I drop the cardboard box off in my car. Cheney Smythe's offices are just a few blocks away, and I shake the sad thoughts away with a liberating, full-body shrug. I blink away the tears that were menacing to form in my eyes and decide to concentrate on what's ahead of me, so I start walking in that direction.

"Are you feeling all right?" Arthur asks me as we walk.

"Absolutely," I reply sincerely. "A bit nostalgic, but great."

"So, what shall you do now?"

"The bank is mine. I just need to ease the terms of James's loan and—"

"I meant besides that," he interrupts me, a little annoyed. I have a feeling he doesn't like James very much; he gets hostile every time I talk about him. He's just being overprotective like a big brother would. "What are you going to do with your life?" he clarifies his previous question.

"Hmm, we're on for easy questions, huh?" I mock his seriousness. "I haven't decided yet. We'll see." Abruptly realizing where we are, I halt right before turning the corner of Cheney Smythe. I grab Arthur's jacket to stop him, too.

"I should check with Nathan before we go upstairs," I explain, while texting simultaneously. "I don't want to risk bumping into Mr. Van Horn by mistake."

Nathan's answer arrives immediately after.

> All clear

By now the receptionist knows us well enough; she doesn't ask anything and simply waves us toward the elevators.

On the twenty-second floor, Nathan, his boss, and the rest of the team that has worked on the project meet us with jubilant applause. I have to shake countless hands before I can get to

Nathan, who is smiling brightly at me; all the fatigue and apprehension of the last month have been brushed away by today's success.

It takes me a while before I can speak to him alone as we are the center of attention and everyone wants to congratulate us. After a bottle of Dom Pérignon is opened, and a toast is made, I spot my chance. Clinking my flute of champagne into Nathan's, I murmur in a low voice, "I need to talk to you."

He gets the hint, and after a few minutes ushers me away to his office after exchanging a knowing nod with his boss.

"Miss Johnson,"

"Please call me Ally, you've earned it after today," I say, leaning against one of his office's cabinets. "So tell me, how was it?"

"To be honest, it was tense. Mr. Van Horn was livid. I bet this was a first for him."

"A first?"

"Let's say I don't think he's used to losing."

"He'll get over it. But that's not why I asked to see you."

"What else can I do for you?"

"Actually, it's quite simple. You see, now that I have a bank, I will need someone to manage it. I can't certainly expect Adam Van Horn to keep his place as CEO."

I take a sip of champagne as an excuse to pause and check if Nathan is following my lead.

What is she getting at?

He's not there yet, so I continue. "I would need someone with previous banking experience, someone ambitious but trustworthy at the same time." I look him intently in the eyes.

Is she offering me the job?

"So Nathan, would you happen to know of somebody with such characteristics?"

A rapacious smile spreads on his lips.

"I have just the man for you," he replies, enthusiastic.

"Very well," I nod. "Take tomorrow off and celebrate. I expect you to start on Monday. When you get to the office, please send me all the files on private loans between one and twenty million that requested a modification of conditions in the past three years and were denied it. I need to review them, and I'll be making some adjustments. Other than that, I'll give you carte blanche on the management strategy. Welcome aboard!" I conclude, outstretching my hand.

He shakes it with his usual vigor, giving me the sensation of having chosen the right person to administer my new business. I bet his boss wasn't expecting this; he had probably unleashed Nathan to make me a permanent account at Cheney Smythe, not to lose one of his brightest talents.

I like being a business shark. I am curious to see what my ideal career appraisal says.

***

Once at home, I kick off my shoes and leave them scattered on the floor of my little entrance hall. Sugar sniffs them inquisitively before rubbing his little body on my legs and bare feet, purring loudly. I deposit the box with my personal effects on the kitchen peninsula while Sugar jumps on it, eager for attention.

"Dinner is coming," I say, scratching his head affectionately, and while I'm busy filling his bowl, he gets some extra cuddling from Arthur. As usual, as soon as the meal is served we are both forgotten.

While Arthur assumes his usual position on the living room chair and starts reading, I sit at the table and turn on my laptop, ready to discover what's in my future.

I log into my email account and get a last pang of nostalgia when I see my former work email address staring back at me in bold font: Ally.Johnson@CrispyKoob.com. I push away any wistful thoughts and am about to open the career center message when Nathan's name flashes in my inbox. I consider for a brief moment what email I'm more curious about, and decide to open Nathan's first, as I have no idea what it could be about. I click on it and start reading.

Date: Thu, August 20 at 6:47 PM
From: nathan.murphy@gmail.com
To: ally.johnson@aol.com
Subject: Small Businesses Loans

Hi Boss,
I know you told me to take the rest of the week off, but I couldn't resist the temptation of checking out my new offices, and since they were just a few blocks away I went right after resigning.

I hope you don't mind, but since it seemed important to you I took the liberty of checking out the loan files you requested. Here's a list attached; there are twenty-one in total.

See you on Monday.

Nathan

He's a real genius! I scroll the attachment list, and even if I'm expecting it, my stomach flips when I spot the name of James's company: Avery Constructions LLC. I quickly print everything and leaf through the rejected requests.

It takes me about an hour to instinctively select six other petitions to grant. I base my decision on no financial variables, as they already projected, and it would make no sense to adjust the loan terms. I simply follow my intuition on the various businesses and whether I like them or not.

I click the reply button and write back to Nathan.

I WISH FOR YOU

Date: Thu, August 20 at 7:03 PM
From: ally.johnson@aol.com
To: nathan.murphy@gmail.com
Subject: Re: Small Businesses Loans

Thank you, Nathan,
That was actually really helpful. Please see attached list of files. I'll be authorizing the modification on these seven accounts.

Please convene all the interested parties for Monday afternoon at the downtown office starting at two-thirty p.m., intervals of half an hour between each appointment should be ok. I'll be sending down two of my people to deliver the news.

Relax now and do nothing work-related!

Ally

Of course, I plan to be the one who does the talking, only with a little disguise on, and I suppose Arthur will want to tag along as well. My plan seems to be right on track.

I stretch back in my chair; I have no excuse left not to go over the results of my job-counseling test. I'm delaying looking at it because I am scared it will tell me that marketing is the only thing I can do, even if I'm hoping otherwise since I marked the "radical change" tick-box.

I brace myself, literally, as I wrap both my arms around my body in a final stretching position and click on the dreaded email.

I skip-read through the introductory part:

Date: Thu, August 20 at 11:22 AM
From: Ally.Johnson@CrispyKoob.com
To: ally.jhonson@aol.com
Subject: FWD: Your Future Career Awaits You

The purpose of this test is purely intended as self-discovery… blah, blah, blah…

The user assumes sole responsibility for any actions or decisions that are made as a result of undertaking this test blah, blah, blah…

Personality profile blah, blah…

Skill profile blah, blah…

Attitudes and interests' blah, blah…

Ideal job…

"Uhh!" I inhale sharply.
"Is something bothering you?" Arthur asks from behind me.
"No, I'm just… surprised."
"About? If I may enquire…"
"I just discovered what my ideal job should be!"
"And?"
"It says I should become a vet."
"As in a veterinarian?"
"Yes."
"And what do you think?"
"It's… it's brilliant!" I exclaim. "I could have my own pet rescue, open an animal clinic. I'd be around animals all day, it would be wonderful."
"Meeeoww," Sugar protests, jumping on the laptop and pressing some random keys.
"Don't worry, baby, you'll always be my favorite," I reassure him, patting him gently.

I WISH FOR YOU

"Don't you have to study in order to be a veterinarian?"

"Yep, I should go to grad school first," I confirm. "Here it gives me a complete list of the best programs in the country. Madison is in the top five and it's only three hours away. I could go there, or I could move somewhere completely different, depending on how things go." My imagination is flying miles ahead.

"Things?" Arthur asks rhetorically.

"If James marries *her*, I don't think I'll want to stick around here," I reply, as if he had asked me an actual question.

"I do not think it wise to base decisions of this magnitude on what James does or does not do."

He sounds like my mother!

"Please don't give me an 'independent woman' speech," I say, rolling my eyes. "But if you want to be helpful, there's something else you could do for me..."

"Whatever you require."

"Do you think you could make me win the lottery?"

"The lottery?" he asks, perplexed. "Don't you already have all the money you need?"

"Yes, but now that I'm jobless and want to go back to school, I'll need to justify my financial stability with my friends and family."

"I see. It would not be a problem. How much do you want to win?"

"Oh, nothing crazy. Make it in between ten and twenty million." Ha, as if. Three months ago, "between ten and twenty million" would have been crazy.

"At your orders." He flips his fingers, and immediately a shiny golden ticket floats in front of me.

Sugar tries to catch it with an outstretched paw, but I snatch it away before he can turn it into confetti.

Twenty-seven
Revelations

Now that I am officially a jobless millionairess, I need to break the news to my friends and family. I've decided to start with the girls, so I've invited them out today for an early drink. We're at the Elle on the River, a posh bar on the riverwalk. If I have to announce to the world my newfound wealthy status, I might as well do it with style! The weather is perfect for this place; it's a warm Saturday afternoon, we're sitting outside in the sun, and there is a gentle breeze coming in from the lake that makes it cool enough to sit outdoors.

A model-looking hostess with impossibly long legs showed us to our table two minutes ago, and everybody is already busy checking out the cocktail menu to decide what to order. I scroll the menu; not that I really need to. I always order the same, but I like to browse the list anyway. I've invited Amy as well; she's not really a close friend, but she's part of the gang, so it would have been awkward not to involve her.

Arthur, to his utter disappointment, had to sit this one out, as for once I wanted to be truly alone with the girls. He didn't want to stay home, so we came downtown together and did some errands. When the time came for me to meet the girls, I left him to wander around the city alone, but not without equipping him with a conspicuous wad of cash for emergencies first. I hope nothing bad happens to him. How motherly of me to worry.

"So what is it this big announcement?"

Meg's voice brings me back to here and now. Ah, Megan, ever the impatient. We are barely seated, and she's already asking questions.

I WISH FOR YOU

I wait until the waiter has gone away with our orders before replying. "Girls, this may come as a bit of a shock, but recently something big has happened in my life. I—"

"I knew it," Brooke blurts, interrupting me.

"You knew what?" I ask, taken aback. She can't possibly know.

"Oh, just say it, we've all been suspecting it!"

"You have?" I ask, looking around the table, even more crestfallen as they all nod. "How?"

"Oh Ally, we're so happy for you, and he's such a nice guy," Amy chimes in.

"Who?" I'm getting more confused by the minute. "Who's such a nice guy?"

"Um, your new boyfriend?" Amy offers tentatively.

"My what? Am I missing something?"

"So you're not about to announce you have a boyfriend?" Brooke asks, blushing visibly.

I laugh loudly. "And who would this new boyfriend be, in your opinion?"

They stay silent, so I try to pick up their mental vibes, and I am surprised to find that they are perfectly tuned, all three of them.

"We thought you had a thing going with Arthur," Megan announces, the only one with the guts to say it.

I bite my lip, inwardly thankful that I've banned him from this meeting.

"Oh please, he's just a friend," I protest, and before I can help it, I voice the next thought that comes into my mind. "I could never have a thing with him. I'm still in love with…" And there I catch myself, as it has been a while since I discussed James so openly with the group.

"With we-know-who." Amy finishes the phrase for me.

"You can say his name out loud, Amy. It's James!" I snap. "He's not freaking Voldemort!"

After my little outburst, there's an awkward moment of silence, during which they exchange preoccupied gazes. So far this get-together isn't going too well. I wanted this to be the perfect afternoon with my friends. I've planned everything to the last detail, and now somehow Amy has managed to upset me. It must show on my face because Brooke speaks next.

"We're sorry, babe. We didn't mean to upset you," she says softly. "It's just that in the last month you've practically disappeared, and we thought..."

"I've been busy," I defend myself, which is absolutely true. Buying a bank is a demanding business!

"So there's nothing going on between you and Arthur?" she insists.

"Nope."

"You haven't thought about it, even in the slightest?" This time the interrogation comes from Megan.

"No."

"But why? He's such a nice guy, and so good-looking." Brooke again.

Because he doesn't really exist, and I know him only because a witch cursed him a thousand years ago... and we're not really friends. In fact, he's my own personal slave who I've summoned from an enchanted coffer to fulfill all my wishes. And I've been lying to all of you for all this time because if I utter a single word of truth, he will vanish immediately and all my powers with him. Ah yes, and if I as much as tried to touch him when we're alone, I'd freeze to death.

Of course, I can't say any of this, so I go for: "He's really nice, I agree, but we are just friends. I love James. There, I've said it," I say, half upset, half exasperated by all their questions.

"You do realize he's getting married in two weeks." Megan is never one to hide behind pretense, but her voice is soft and understanding without any trace of pity or condescension, so I forgive her.

"Speaking of which," I say, "did you already RSVP?"

I WISH FOR YOU

"No, John has been nagging me to change my mind nonstop. Why?"

"I want you to go," I declare.

"What? Why?" she asks, astonished.

"I want somebody on the inside."

Brooke doesn't say anything; she simply raises an eyebrow inquisitively.

"What do you mean?" Megan asks.

"If he goes through with it, I simply want to know in real time."

"You think he might not?" Amy asks sheepishly.

"You never know," I reply mysteriously.

I want to change the subject before they start bombarding me with a lot of questions I can't possibly answer, so I deliver a little speech to stop the boy talk.

"Listen, girls, one way or another it'll be clear in two weeks, and I'd rather find out as soon as possible. So if you," I say, waving my hands toward Meg, "are there, I'll know the moment he says I do." My logic is impregnable. "If he marries her, I will have all the answers I need, and I'll move on. Which—" I pause for suspense. "—in my new situation could be a lot easier," I add, steering the conversation in the direction I want it to take.

"What new situation?" Megan follows my lead immediately.

"If you three sillies had let me talk, you'd already know." By now, I have their undivided attention. "It'll sound crazy, but it's true... I. Won. The. Lottery."

After my announcement, they all speak at the same time.

"Seriously?" Brooke.

"How much?" Meg.

"This explains the clothes." Amy.

"Yeah, seriously. Just above fifteen million." I answer the questions.

They're still too excited to speak one at the time, so after some exclamations of surprise, they keep doing it simultaneously.

"What will you do now?" Brooke.

"How will you spend it?" Meg.

"And the car, and the watch..." Amy.

I tell them about quitting my job and taking the career survey, and that I'm thinking about going back to school next year. In the meantime, I'll take a sabbatical, traveling the world and preparing my applications.

We spend the rest of the afternoon discussing the best ways to spend my money, the must-haves of fashion that I can't lack as a rich woman, and all the places I will travel to in the near future. Luckily, James could not be any further from their minds at this moment.

We're discussing jewelry when I decide this is the perfect moment to have my surprise brought out. I catch the eye of a waiter and nod imperceptibly. Minutes later, he comes toward our table with three huge, impeccably wrapped packages in his hands. He distributes them among my three stunned and finally silent friends according to color as I had instructed him before.

I did some shopping earlier today and bought a few presents for the girls, then came here ahead of time to set this up with the staff. Now that I can openly display my wealth, I'm not going to be stingy.

"You shouldn't have," says Brooke.

"Oi, she so should have," says Megan.

"How nice," says Amy.

"Come on, open them," I encourage, and as soon as the words leave my lips, it's as if I've said ready, set, go!

They start racing one another in ripping the expensive paper, exclaiming in unison once they find the treasure within—three identical top-handle Prada bags in saffiano leather. Red for Brooke, black for Megan, and baby-pink for Amy. A chorus of thanks and wows goes around the table.

I WISH FOR YOU

"Ally, thank you! This is too much," Brooke gushes.

"Oh, wait until you see inside before you say it's too much." I beam at their dazed faces as they dig inside the bags to find three tiny light blue boxes.

I've bought us Tiffany key pendants. They're platinum with some diamonds here and there, but in different shapes: a vintage oval for me, a crown for Brooke, a knot for Megan, and a heart for Amy. I take mine from my bag and open the little box together with them. Again, it is ooohs and aaaahs all around. We all put them on and clink our glasses soundly in celebration of my luck, because, after all, it was good fortune that led me to the coffer. Like winning the lottery, only better.

***

"Rich girl," Brooke teases me just as we're about to leave. "Would you mind giving me a lift home?"

I nod. She smiles.

She seems a bit nervous; actually, she's been slightly off all afternoon. Nothing too obvious, but I know her too well. I hope this is not an excuse to give me a pep talk about my being helplessly-romantic-detached-from-reality-desperately-in-love-with-the-wrong-man.

The beginning of the ride home passes in utter silence. I don't dare say anything, just in case of an upcoming lecture, and she seems very busy looking out the window. When I'm about to make a turn for her street, she stops me and says, "Can we go to your place instead?"

"Mmm-hmm," I mumble, eyeing her sideways and waiting for the rest. Once it's clear she's not going to say anything else, I prompt her. "Why?"

"David is probably there."

David? What happened to Dave? Ouch, maybe this one is not about me after all.

"And why don't we want him around?" I could read her mind, but as good as I am at multitasking, I prefer not to try to look at her, concentrate on her thoughts, and drive all at the same time.

"Can we wait until we are at your house?"

"Sure."

In the elevator, I text Arthur not to come home too early, or to come back invisible because of Brooke. I don't want her to get any more weird ideas in her head. Him showing up here *as if* he lived here is definitely the last thing I need. In the meantime, I try to remember how many of his things are scattered around my apartment, and how to hide them as quickly as possible before Brooke notices them.

Unsetstood

I am retrieving my keys from my bag when his answer pops up on the screen. I mentally translate it to *understood*. He's not too familiar with touchscreens yet. Inside my apartment, Sugar is loyally waiting behind the door. Brooke picks him up and sits at the dining table, holding him close and cuddling him. He is the picture of animal bliss; she is the image of human misery.

I quickly scan the living room for any Arthur-presence-giveaway things, breathing a sigh of relief when I can't spot anything too obvious, and then join them at the table.

"What's going on?" I ask Brooke.

"I might be pregnant."

I'm going to be an aunt, is my first thought.

"Are you sure?" I ask instead.

"No, that's why I'm here. I bought a test earlier, but I don't want to do it at home with Dave there." She sounds in between mournful and hysterical.

"Mmm, okay," I say, encouraging. "Do you want to talk about it or do the test first?"

"Talk," she says. "But you ask the questions. I'm not very mentally organized right now."

"A drink first?" I ask, opening the freezer.

"I don't think... know, if..."

"Argh, you're right, sorry!" Did I just offer vodka to a presumed mother to be? "I thought that pink blob you were drinking today was suspicious," I add jokingly.

"Yep, it was a virgin flamingo," she confirms.

"Milk and cookies, then." It was our favorite childhood treat, which admittedly is a bit more possible-pregnancy friendly.

I fill two big glasses of milk and put heaps of organic chocolate bear cookies on a plate. Halfway through my second bear, I ask my first question. "How did it, if... I mean, I thought you were on the pill." *Not so smooth, Ally—keep it together. You are not the almost pregnant one.*

"I skipped one, but I basically forget one in every pack since I've started."

"How many days late?"

"A week."

"Has it ever happened before?"

"Twice."

"And?"

"It was nothing."

"So why are you so worried this time?"

"It feels different."

"Mmm." I have to phrase the next question right. "And would you be happy if..."

"I would." She answers with a tone that's the opposite of joy.

"But?" I offer.

"Dave."

"You think he wouldn't be happy?" I ask, shocked. He strikes me as the daddy type.

"No, he would be thrilled."

"So?"

"So, that way I will never know." She starts to pour it all out without any need for further questioning on my part. "He would do the right thing—ask me to marry him right away and be the perfect father and husband. But if he does, I will never know if he did it only because of the baby, or because it's what he really wants. We've been together for what? Nine years now. We have lived together for almost five, and he hasn't proposed yet. What if he doesn't want to... ever? We've barely discussed the whole marriage thing, and he wasn't the most enthusiastic of men. So... I'm worried this whole thing could be bigger than me, bigger than us."

Ah! What do you say to that? Mmm...

"Oh, baby!" Really? Did my useless brain just choose *this* of all pet names? "Um, honey." I start again. "You know men. Sometimes if they don't do something right away, it doesn't necessarily mean they don't intend to. Dave is just a guy being a guy. He probably hasn't realized he's thirty yet—he must think of himself as a twenty-two-year-old who just graduated from college and started working. Plus, he adores you. Totally, completely adores you. I'm sure he wants to marry you, maybe not next month, but eventually... I'm sure." I try to be as positive as I can, and I will most certainly do a complete scan of Dave's mind to make sure everything I just said is *actually* true.

"You think?" Hope is rising in her voice.

"I'm positive."

A shy smile appears on her lips.

"Should we find out then?" I ask.

She nods and we head to the bathroom together.

Twenty-eight
Boys Will Be Boys

"Is Brooke still here?" Arthur's voice makes me jolt in the armchair where I'm comfortably nestled.

When Brooke left I had the house all to myself for the first time in, well, forever... and for once I got to sit in my favorite spot in the living room without Arthur usurping me. Sugar is once again curled up on my lap. My cat, apparently, is more loyal to furniture than he is to me.

"How many times do I have to tell you not to creep on me like this?" I snap. "One day you'll give me a real heart attack."

"You also told me to come back invisible in case Brooke was still here," he says, nonplussed by my rebuke, "and that is exactly how I proceeded."

"Whatever." My favorite reply when I don't know what to say, especially when "sorry" or "you're right" would be much more appropriate responses.

He seems somehow aware of this particular trait of mine, and he smiles, accepting my unoffered apology. Ah, months of cohabitation can do wonders for a relationship. As the thought crosses my mind, I feel flustered at the idea that Arthur is the first, *and only*, guy I've actually lived with.

Ah! Admittedly, not the most typical guy-roommate, considering that when he sleeps he evaporates into a jewelry case, that he only takes up the coat wardrobe as personal space, that he always does the dishes (magically so, but still), and that he always makes me breakfast.

Yep, since that first morning when he transformed the house into a culinary display that would have made breakfast at the Peninsula Hotel look like a casual arrangement. I told him he could tone it down a notch, and that a simple cappuccino-croissant combination would be perfect for me. From that day, on each morning I am presented with exactly that. I'm still not sure if he supernaturally conjures the food or if he buys it every morning before I wake up from the Starbucks across the street because the taste is exactly the same.

He really is a nice guy. At least, he is now. I wonder how bad he was before Héloise, with all those other women he told me about, and especially with Morgene. She must have really hated him to doom him to this half-life for eternity, or truly loved him, or both. The force of the respective sentiments is proportional, especially after a breakup, although I don't hate James. I never did. But I still have hope for us, for James and I, and I suppose hate arrives when the last bit of hope is lost.

I also worry I will not be able to help Arthur out of his curse. We tried a couple of other tricks with the same poor results, and I've leafed through all possible sources, from ancient legends to myths and superstitions. Nothing helpful came out.

"Was everything all right with your friends?" he asks, probably noticing my worried expression and assuming it has something to do with Brooke coming over.

"Yeah, I was just thinking about Brooke," I lie and then proceed to give him a full account of the afternoon.

"So is she with child?" he asks.

Ah, Arthur. I smile at his choice of words; his old-fashionedness used to bother me, but it has grown on me. I almost find it compelling now.

"I've no idea. I'm waiting for the news myself."

"I thought you said she did some sort of test here."

"I did." I skipped the mechanics, having a feeling that openly referring to the act of peeing on a stick would have made his nose wrinkle. "But then she changed her mind at the last minute," I explain. "She sealed the test and ran off to her apartment to discover the result with Dave. She realized that, one way or the other, it was a moment she wanted to share with him."

"What do you think it will say?"

I WISH FOR YOU

"They'll be fine whatever it says," I reply, convinced. "If ever two people were made for each other, it's them. Of course, I hope we'll be having a little soft baby in our lives soon." I regret my words the moment they escape my lips.

Arthur seems deeply perturbed by my baby talking. A thought suddenly strikes me. "Did you ever… I mean, were you…"

"No." He answers the question I was trying to pose. "At least not that I know of," he adds, pain clearly audible in his voice. "It is my deepest regret, never to have known the joy of being a father."

At that moment the phone rings. It's Brooke, so I have to pick up. I throw one last guilty, sideways glance at Arthur before summoning all my cheerfulness and beaming "Hello" into the phone. "How did it go?"

"Ally, you were totally right, men are dumbasses!"

"Oh," I say, worried things didn't go the way I predicted. "Tell me everything," I encourage, eager to know what happened.

"You're going to laugh so hard by the end of this." She sounds cheerful and ecstatic, so I relax and listen to her story.

She basically went home to find Dave as a living picture of immaturity: he was sitting on the floor with his back leaning on the couch, intently killing a bunch of monsters with the PS4, wearing basketball shorts and a Red Hawks tank top. "In that moment," she tells me, "I couldn't help but think I'll have to raise two babies, not one."

After a brief moment of indecision, she told him everything with a big lump in her throat, her sitting on the couch, him still on the floor with his arms wrapped around her legs, sort of like a loyal dog. She told him she thought she might be pregnant, but wasn't sure, that she wanted to get married and have the baby, but that she understood if he didn't want to, and that she didn't want him to marry her because he had to, or because it was the right thing to do.

"What did he say?" I can't help asking.

"He just got up, ruffled my hair with a weird expression, and went into the bedroom."

"Oh."

"Ally, I swear I thought I was going to pass out."

"So?"

"He was back in the living room in about two minutes." I can hear the excitement growing in her voice. "And he..." She's choking with emotion now. "He... went down on his knee and gave me the most beautiful ring I've ever seen."

"He proposed?" I squeal, excited.

"Yes, right there in our living room, with Dragon Age in the background, wearing shorts and a tank top, and he had put on this stupid black bow tie. Ally, I felt my heart explode with love!"

"Brooke!" I am at a loss for words. This is so romantic. "I want to cry. I'm crying." I gush, smiling and sniffling at the same time.

"I know."

"Wait, this means he had already bought you a ring! When?" I ask, recovering my composure.

"The moron bought it eight months ago," she says affectionately.

"Eight months? What was he waiting for?"

"I don't know. He doesn't know. He muttered something about a special occasion—well, I guess nothing could be more special than today." She has a different note in her voice, suddenly making me remember where all of this started.

"So are you...?" I ask tentatively.

"I am."

"I'm so happy for you guys! I'm going to be an aunt!"

"Mm-hmm."

"Did you find out before or after he proposed?"

"After," she says, and I can tell she's glowing with happiness even if we are on the phone. "He said it didn't matter

I WISH FOR YOU

what the test said, that he wanted to spend the rest of his life with me. The plus sign was the icing on the cake. Oh, Ally, I'm so happy! I didn't think I could contain all this joy!"

"You dummy, you should have seen your face two hours ago," I tease her. "Put that daft fiancé of yours on the phone. I want to congratulate him as well."

"Hey, Ally." His voice is spurting with glee.

"Hey daddy-Dave, congratulations! I am so thrilled for you."

"We're so happy too. It's the best day of my life."

"We'll have to celebrate soon," I say.

"Yep, Ally, gotta go, my mom is calling on the other line for the second time since I told her. She's going nuts. Talktoyousoonbye."

"Bye."

"Mary is going crazy." Brooke's back on the line. Mary is her soon-to-be mother-in-law. "Not even my mom went ballistic like that."

"Uh-huh. Well, with a wedding and a baby on the way, I can understand. Have you talked any specifics yet?"

"No, not yet."

"Do you know when the baby is due?"

"Around the end of April."

"Are you going to have a shotgun wedding?" I ask jokingly.

"I'd rather think of it as a winter wedding, probably mid-November. What do you think?"

"I luurve the winter theme. We have serious work to do, buy some magazines, look for dresses, venues… wow, you must be over the moon!"

"I am," she says simply.

Then she tells me she has a million other calls to make, that she loves me, and that she can't wait to hug me. I tell her that I love her too, that I'll buy some crazy stack of magazines and stop by their place tomorrow before I go to see my parents. I then ask for a picture of the ring, she promises to send it immediately, and we hang up.

Sure enough after just a few seconds my phone bleeps and I stare at a photo of Brooke's hand adorned with the most beautiful ring. The diamond is a princess cut, and the band is made of two hand-braided wires covered with a pavè of tiny brilliants. It's classic and original at the same time.

I stare at the image with mixed feelings. I'm happy for them, I am. But seeing them take such a big step forward, actually, *two* big ones, makes me wonder where I stand and where I'm going. *Stuck in the past and nowhere*, I can't help thinking. I feel so alone.

"You are not alone." Arthur chips into my thoughts.

"Hey," I say, faking offense. "I thought *I* was the one doing the mind reading around here."

"It did not take a genius, or a genie," he jokes, "to interpret the dismayed expression on your face."

I smile.

"Would you like to talk about it?"

"No." It's too depressing. "Can we just watch TV and eat comfort food?"

"Absolutely," he says, arranging a tray of my favorite junk food and sinking onto the couch, leaving the armchair and the soothing ball of fur that goes with it for me, I notice.

I'm so glad he's here; I would have sunk into utter depression without him tonight.

***

By morning my bad mood has evaporated, and I truly enjoy leafing through a gazillion magazines with Brooke, making wedding plans. I might say that I managed to be only twenty percent jealous and eighty percent happy for her. Okay, thirty-seventy.

Now it's almost lunchtime and I have to go tell my parents about my new life plan. From Brooke's apartment, I head straight to their house in Lake Forest. I go bearing gifts, hoping they won't freak out about my joblessness and new life-changing, carpe-diem attitude.

Arthur has been with me all morning, invisible. I gave him a choice between coming as Melissa or unseen, and this time he said he would rather much disappear than impersonate a woman again. We had a repeat of the discussion where I tried to convey the concept that as a single twenty-eight-year-old daughter of an impossibly-keenly aspiring grandmother, I simply couldn't bring home an eligible bachelor to meet my parents without ever hearing the end of it. Although, thinking about it, it could've been a good tactic to distract them from the main purpose of my visit.

"Baaabyy." The moment I park the car in my parent's driveway and exit it, my mom is already hugging me desperately.

"Mom, it's ok. What's up?" This is unusual behavior.

"You tell me," she frets. "Are you okay, honey? Is it your health?"

"No, Mom, I'm fine."

"You're not sick?" she asks, breaking the hug.

"Nope."

"Then why do you go around scaring your mother to death?" she howls.

"Did I? I'm so sorry, Mom. I didn't mean to."

"So what was it that you couldn't tell us on the phone?"

"If you let me get inside, I'll tell you and Dad." I put an arm around her waist and usher her inside.

At first, they think I'm joking, then they get worried when I tell them I quit my job, excited when I inform them of my future career plans, and finally hysterical when I tell them I've booked them on a ninety-day world cruise.

I'm glad they took it so well; they were extremely supportive of my decision. They even went as far as telling me that they never thought I was right for an office job, but they never said anything because they didn't want to pressure me in any way. Before I "won the lottery", I guess that the financial security involved in a desk job was also a substantial variable taken into account in their discretion.

When I leave them, my mom is leafing through every travel magazine she has in the house, getting excited about all the places they will visit, and my dad is getting a Ph.D. on veterinary schools' ranking in the country. I expect a full report before I get back home; he's always been efficient and methodic like that. I leave their house filled with a sense of peaceful contentment. It felt good that it was me doing something for them for a change.

The peace of mind, however, is short-lived, because now that the weekend is almost over I want to go home and prepare myself for tomorrow. Monday is coming, and I have to put the last piece of the puzzle, my plan to win James back, in its place.

Twenty-nine
Minus Twelve

I check my reflection in the hallway mirror one last time... *perfect*! It's almost noon on Monday, and we are about to leave the house to go inform a few lucky P.C.N. customers of the change in their loan terms.

Arthur and I have transmuted into my stereotype of what a successful banker type should look like. Arthur got to keep his fit body and imposing height, but I gave his facial features a total makeover and I changed his hair: lighter color, shorter cut, and curlier texture. I, on the other hand, am a taller version of myself, and I have platinum blonde hair cut in a classic long bob, sleek and barely layered at the tips. My eyes are blue, and my face is a mash between Claudia Schiffer and Rebecca Romijn. A bit over the top, but I couldn't resist.

We are wearing expensive tailored suits; his black, mine a silvery gray, and we both have fancy Italian leather shoes. Let me tell you, being an out-of-this-world-five-foot-nine-plus-heels top-model is fun I bet Nathan will be impressed with "my people."

Yesterday I had an early night; after visiting my parents I came back straight home, did a mental recap of today's schedule, watched some TV with Arthur and Sugar, and dove into bed super early. I wanted to be well rested for today, but it did me no good. I didn't sleep at all. I was too agitated.

In just a few hours I will inform James that his original loan extension request has been accepted, and the idea of seeing him again is making me a helpless bundle of nerves. But I have to do it as I want to see and study his reaction firsthand.

Analyzing his file earlier today, I was able to get a better idea of what his marriage to Vanessa is supposed to achieve for his company. For the first time since my decision of going to college, I was glad to have majored in business and happy to finally be able to exhume and apply some of the knowledge painfully acquired in the ECON 20000 classes.

But back to James. Mr. Van Horn basically extended his loan while keeping him on a very short leash. They agreed on a ten-year-extension with slightly higher interest rates but considerably lower installments, with the contingency of a quarterly reevaluation by P.C.N. with absolutely no obligation for the bank to maintain the new, improved terms. I suppose that Vanessa's dad was trying to ensure the continued well-being of his daughter by keeping her husband-to-be under constant blackmail. That family is really dysfunctional!

I find myself pitying Vanessa more with every passing day. I mean, think of a normal father who was aware of the situation; he would have simply told Vanessa the true reasons behind James's hasty proposal. But from what I gathered when I was at their home, he still sees Vanessa as a five-year-old who must be sheltered from the cruelties of this world, he must really believe that he's sparing her unnecessary pain. He mustn't be the romantic type, or he would never doom his own daughter to such a fate. Well, seeing his wife, he probably has no idea of what love is in the first place. However, he no longer has a say in the matter. Now it's in my hands. Well, James's, actually.

***

We arrive at the bank, my bank—I own a bank, ha, ha—at two-thirty sharp. Nathan welcomes us and shows us into a posh meeting room where we'll inform our customers of the big change in their good fortunes. I'm glad to see that he arranged coffee supplies for us.

As expected, I can tell Nathan is impressed with us when he informs us that our first appointment is already waiting and that if we're ready, he could send them in. I nod in agreement and sit at the meeting table rehearsing the speech I've prepared one last time.

James is scheduled to be the fifth appointment, which means my stomach will stay churned longer, but I'll be more practiced by the time I have to speak with him. He'll be here at… four-thirty, exactly two hours from now.

***

Luckily, in those two hours, I don't have much time to fret over James, as each meeting takes up the majority of the planned time. Each one of them goes pretty much the same; the person or persons coming in look utterly terrified. They all think we will irreparably crash their business's line of credit, and even more so after they take a good look at us.

Then, after I begin to talk, they become guarded, suspicious, and incredulous. In the end, when they finally realize that I'm not joking and that they will actually get improved terms, they all start going out of their way to thank us with profuse words of appreciation for the bank.

I'm not sure about the logic of my decisions from a business perspective, but it feels great to do some good for these people; everyone struck me as the hardworking, I-am-trying-to-get-my-business-back-on-track kind.

However, the moment James crosses the threshold of the room, all my cheeriness disappears and the nerves are back. I try to maintain a straight face as I deliver my first line.

"Good afternoon, Mr—" I pause to pretend I have to read his last name on the folder. "Avery. Please have a seat. I'm Amber Lewis, and this is my colleague, Robert Benson. Nice to meet you."

I outstretch my hand for him to shake it. He does. It is the first prolonged physical contact we've had in twenty months! His strong, dry grip sends little electrical tingles all the way up from my fingertips, to my hand, to my upper arm. I wish I could hug him, jump on his lap and kiss him, run my hands through his hair, and nuzzle his neck while taking in his clean scent, my favorite smell in the entire world.

He lets go. I feel hollow inside.

He moves on to shake Arthur's hand, thinking that I am hot. Should be flattered or jealous?

Once the introductions are over, I continue with my script. "Mr. Avery, I don't know if you are aware that recently P.C.N. has undergone a change in ownership and management." I pause to check if he's following me, but he just stares back blankly. "With this change," I continue, waiting for the penny to drop in his head, "there have also been some modifications in regard to the approach the bank has toward our lines of credit, and in particular for our small and medium-sized businesses customers. We are—"

"You mean that Adam Van Horn has a new board?"

Ding, ding.

"No, I mean that Adam Van Horn is no longer CEO, nor a shareholder in this bank. There has been a takeover," I reply patiently.

Shock emerges in his eyes as his brain does the math.

"Who's the new owner?" he asks.

He's taking time while forming a pitch for his case in his head; he is beyond worried now. I'd better let him off the hook as soon as possible. Can somebody have a heart attack before forty?

"The hedge fund we work for," I answer curtly, wanting to get to the good part quickly. "Anyhow, as I said before we brought you here to discuss the new management strategy for SME Businesses. We—"

"I can assure you both that my company will be solvent—we simply hit a bump in the road and needed some extra time to recover." He interrupts me and goes on the defensive like his predecessors. People really don't trust banks these days, do they? "But our finances are good," he continues. "Our partners trust us and we have been in business for more than—"

"Mr. Avery." I raise my hand to stop his rambling and put him out of his misery. "If you had let me finish, I would have told you that the new approach P.C.N. wants to adopt is more of a conciliatory one."

"What do you mean?" he asks, still guarded.

"We went over rejected demands for a credit extension on SME business loans and reevaluated every request, case by case. I am happy to inform you that your original proposal, the one you submitted on—" I again pretend to have to check the date in his folder. "The second of January last year, is that correct, Mr. Avery?"

"Correct." The hint of a smile appears on his lips.

"Has been accepted in full," I conclude.

He stares at me open-mouthed, saying nothing.

At this point, Arthur takes the stage with his part of the recital. I had him memorize an article on how important it is for banks and businesses to recover reciprocal trust.

"Mr. Avery, the new team at Prime Capital National Bank firmly believes in maintaining a healthy and trustful relationship with our customers, especially so to medium-sized businesses like yours, which for centuries have constituted the backbone of the economy in our country blah, blah, blah…"

While Arthur is talking, I look at James, who appears utterly shocked, to check what's going on inside his head. It is pure mayhem!

He feels freed, surprised, elated, confused, undecided, shocked, scared. He instantly thinks he's getting married to Vanessa in twelve days, and a boa constrictor of fear wraps himself around his chest. I can feel it because he passes the sensation on to me.

Immediately after his brain spins in a whirlwind of memories; at first, things go in the same order as at the retreat, but soon enough they become intertwined with memories of our relationship and, to my utter horror, also of his relationship with Vanessa.

It's like he's comparing and matching up the two of us. He's reliving our first encounter on the train, and a moment later he is at the autumn gala where he met Vanessa; only this time the atmosphere, instead of being ghastly and dark, is warm and luminous. I get a flash of Vanessa telling him how embarrassed she was that day, of how she fell for him at their very first dance, and how miserable she was when he ignored her. She's sweet and adorable, and I have a deep affection for her. I mean, James does. Uhh. Is it love? I don't have time to muse about it because the next second the vision is over and his mind is back to us.

Me. It's summer and we're sailing on Lake Michigan in his boat, the *Sunrise*. James is pulling the sheet to stretch the mainsail, and when he's done, he calls me to take control of the helm. As I grab the huge wheel, he positions himself behind me, our bodies touching, his hands firmly placed on mine. He then proceeds to give me sailing instructions that I remember were impossible to follow because, while talking, he was occasionally brushing his lips on my neck, turning my whole body into jelly. Needless to say, we anchored the ship shortly afterward and ended the day below deck.

Vanessa. James is sliding down a skiing slope at an atrocious speed. Vanessa reaches him from behind, shouting something playfully, and speeds up in front of him; they are racing each other and he is having a lot of fun! I don't know how to ski. He wanted me to try it, but I thought I was too old to learn, and, not liking the cold too much, I was just lazy. But now, living his elation and sense of freedom while he dashes forward pumping the muscles in his legs, I wish I had tried it. I hope their day didn't finish as ours on the boat.

I'm trying to decide who wins this round when he switches to us again.

I WISH FOR YOU

Me. We are at Amy's New Year party, the one before the breakup, our last night together. He's having a blast; we are drinking and doing stupid dance moves to the notes of Pharrell Williams's "Happy", and we are, well... happy. Then the night sort of fast forwards as we do a stupid drinking game until midnight when suddenly everybody is shouting the countdown. *Ten, nine...* he grabs me by the hips from his chair. *Seven, six...* I sit on his lap, leaning forward. *Four, three...* I look into his eyes. *One...* Midnight strikes and we are kissing passionately, both unaware of the noises and chaos around us.

Vanessa. I can tell it's winter because it's cold, and, of course, Vanessa is wearing an expensive-looking white fur coat. James is slightly mad. They're going to some sort of exclusive high society event. There's a banner; it's New Year's Eve again. This is truly a one-on-one match between her and me. They leave their coats at the reception desk and enter an elegant room filled with a crowd of mostly middle-aged people sipping champagne from fancy crystal glasses. A live orchestra is playing soft, classical music in the background. Vanessa's parents are there, as well as James's mother. James sighs inwardly while preparing himself for a night of fake smiles and absolute boredom. At midnight, he and Vanessa exchange a polite and composed peck on the lips, and he starts eyeing his watch, wondering when it would be considered polite to leave.

I'm pretty sure I scored this one. Go, Ally.

Me. We are at his apartment. From my hairstyle, I can tell it must have been about six months after we started dating. And judging from the dress I'm wearing... mmm, I remember that night. It was one hell of a passionate one, and he has sharp memories of it too. I feel myself blushing as his mind brings me back on his bed, half-naked as his hands explore my body. This time, not only do I have my own memories of how I felt, but I'm also feeling all of his excitement. Mmm... I have difficulty keeping my eyes open, and I have to bite my lower lip not to moan aloud.

Abruptly I receive an image of Vanessa in a nightgown approaching me tantalizingly, boobs forward, lips puckered. Oh no! My brain clicks on what's about to happen, and I stop looking at James just in time not to witness him and Vanessa have sex.

I refuse to call it making love, and I don't want to know who wins this one.

They had sex. *What did you expect? She's attractive and he's, well... a man!*

"Yuck," I say aloud against my own will, recoiling in my chair.

Arthur stops talking and they both look at me.

"Is everything all right?" they ask at the same time.

"Yeah, sorry. I took a sip of coffee and it was cold," I lie, glad James wasn't looking at me, but pretending to pay attention to what Arthur was saying. "Disgusting," I finish for more emphasis.

Arthur looks at me raising both eyebrows and I shrug. Luckily, at that moment an assistant politely knocks on the door and informs us that our five p.m. appointment is waiting outside. I look at my watch and see that it's five fifteen already. I thank her and quickly dismiss James, telling him he just has some papers to sign before he can go.

I watch him leave the room mesmerized, my head as full of doubt as his. I wish I didn't have to talk to two other persons, and that I could go straight home to analyze what I've just experienced.

Thirty

W-Day

I spend the following days madly obsessing over James and his memories. The thing that bugs me the most is having discovered that he's actually fond of Vanessa. Love? I honestly don't know. It's undeniable that there is some affection between them, and more compatibility than I thought possible. More than even James expected in the first place.

This scares me, but, on the other hand, it's a relief. I mean, at least he's not a total scavenger marrying someone solely for money or social status. I haven't admitted this to anyone; well, I haven't confessed it to Arthur, since he's the only one fully aware of the situation. But I thought he had a point when he was trashing James's honor so vehemently, father's ghost or not.

Which, anyway, leaves me to the main topic to examine: James cares about Vanessa! Do you leave a person you care about at the altar? I don't know! The notion of his feelings for her, whatever they may be, doesn't help in the least. It only serves to raise a million other questions.

Do you marry a person you don't love? Does he love her? Does he love *me*? Yes, this one I know. Can you love two people at the same time? I'm afraid the answer is also yes. Who does he love more, her or me? Can he break the heart of someone he loves or cares about? This is the third yes.

He was head over heels in love with me and he left me anyway. So I know that he is capable of hurting people he loves, which doesn't necessarily sound like a good thing, but since it helps my preferred outcome I will list it among the pros.

My line of questioning is getting longer by the hour. Is breaking up a relationship the same as canceling a wedding? In the scale of hurt, what would be the difference? Do men even reason in these terms? I doubt so. They just do what they feel like doing, or... they don't do anything at all, simply because it's easier. And this is my bottom line... He knows he will have a good life with Vanessa, and canceling the wedding now would be a mess.

Plus, he has some doubts about me. I know because I glimpsed a flash of insecurity in his subconscious at P.C.N. offices. While he was thinking about our story, Arthur's face flickered into his mind briefly, along with an ominous thought. He wasn't sure if I still loved him, and my "new relationship" made him wonder if I've moved on or not, or if he could convince me to go back to him. Ha, ha, ha, as if I needed any convincing. Maybe my fake boyfriend idea wasn't so great after all.

This is pretty much how I spend every minute of every day: wondering, hoping, and waiting for something, anything, to happen. My brain is a broken disk where the same questions are repeated over and over again in an endless loop.

I compulsively search the Internet for any hint of a scandal in the Van Horn family, like a canceled wedding. I refrain myself and manage to ask Meg only once a day if anything has changed if she and John have received any formal communication about a cancellation. I even phone Sally to ask her how everyone at work has been since I left, dropping the casual inquiry about Vanessa. When Sally tells me Vanessa's been even more obnoxious than usual, as she's boasting nonstop about her dream wedding, I want to die.

Eleven days pass this way. Eleven sleepless, restless days. Eleven days during which James knows he doesn't have to marry Vanessa to save his family, and he doesn't do anything about it. Eleven days of agony that I live in a haze of hysteria anticipating today, because yes, today is finally the day. W-day.

My ultimate hope is that he gets a last-minute case of cold feet. It's now or never; he would have to somehow opt out at the very last second, breaking Vanessa's heart in the worst possible way and generating a huge scandal, since I've heard that basically all of Chicago has been invited to the ceremony.

As these thoughts keep bouncing around in my head, I might just go crazy. The ceremony is at four p.m. and I've been sitting at home all morning, alternately nibbling at my nails and regrowing them after the carnage.

Arthur has been parked in the living room's armchair, reading, since I came out of my room. He's pretending today is no special day, which is definitely an annoying attitude. He must know that I need to talk about it! Even if we already examined all the possible alternatives and scenarios! What is he playing at? I have a distinct feeling he hopes James will marry Vanessa, which is utterly disloyal.

"You cannot read me," he says suddenly. "If you want to know what I am thinking, you simply have to ask."

"Uh... what? I wasn't... uh..." Busted, I so was.

"You have been looking at me and squeezing your eyes for the past twenty minutes."

"And how do you know? You've been staring at that stupid book all day!" Attack is the best defense.

He finally lifts his head and locks those penetrating blue eyes of his right into mine. "As a soldier," he explains, "you have to learn the virtue of exploiting your whole field of vision, as it could save your life in battle. I have quite an experience at seeing things I am not looking at." He tilts his head expectantly; he will not answer a question that I haven't posed. Sooo annoying.

"So what is it that you're thinking?" I give up as curiosity and the need for a distraction have the best of me.

"Ah." And from the tone of it, I already know I will not like what will ensue. "As I told you before," he continues, "the past is the past and there is no way to go back there. I am sorry to say that if you try, you will just end up disappointed."

Hear, hear.

"And how come you're so sure, Mr. Know-it-all?"

"Have you ever been to the same place twice, but in two different moments of your life?" he asks. "Not somewhere nearby where you can always go; it must be some other city or a faraway country where you have to expressly travel to."

New York. I've been there three times altogether. "Yes," I say.

"And was it the same?"

"Yes." Ah, gotcha.

He raises one eyebrow at me. "The surroundings, maybe, but did it *feel* the same?"

Uh, no! I think back and realize that each trip has been unique. The first time I visited was as a kid with my parents. The Big Apple at Christmas was a wintery fairy tale. I remember the music pervading the whole city, the ginormous toyshops, the decorations…

The second time was with Brooke, to celebrate our twenty-first birthdays. We were staying in a rented house in Brooklyn and exploring the cool neighborhoods of the Meatpacking District, Soho, Tribeca… spending all of our long-saved money in a shopping frenzy and experimenting with legal public drinking for the first time. We tried a different club every night and ate breakfast no sooner than at two in the afternoon. It was the best trip ever; we will never forget it.

The third and final time was with James, and it was more of a daytime experience. We used to take long walks in Central Park, do some cultural excursions to the Met and the Guggenheim, places loathed during my first visit and carefully avoided on the second one, and then reward ourselves with a lot of fancy eating. I remember we would try to find secret and secluded bistros, less known to the public, going for a different ethnicity every evening, always drinking red wine and making love at the end of the night as if there were no tomorrow. It was the most romantic week of my life.

I WISH FOR YOU

Arthur takes my silence as an acknowledgment of his point and seizes the opportunity to jump into one of his philosophical lectures.

"It has happened to me countless times. Over the centuries I have visited many cities more than once. No matter when, on each stay, they were alike and yet somewhat different, whether a year or a hundred since I was there last. Every time I would find things linking those places to my previous sojourns, but they never felt quite equal. They would give me different vibrations, or their vibrations were unchanged, and I was the different one. It is the same with places, food, or..." He pauses briefly. "Ah, people."

I'm about to go berserk with my answer when my phone trills, and I stop dead to read it. It's Megan.

> Baby, we are about to leave for the W.

> So far no changes in the schedule...

I can't tell if my heart is beating super fast, or not beating at all.

> Ok, keep me posted

At this point, any hope I might have had is really low. It's time to begin taking advantage of the make-your-own-lemon-drop-martini kit I bought yesterday. Vodka—the most expensive I could find—triple sec liquor, cane sugar, lemons, electric cocktail shaker, and cocktail measuring tool. I jump up from the couch and move into the kitchen.

I'm busy mixing and measuring all the ingredients when my conscience's official voice speaks beside me.

"Do you find it wise to take on drinking at this early an hour?" Arthur is examining my creative process carefully. "You barely had anything to eat all day."

"It's the best idea I've ever had," I retort nastily. "And it's certainly better than listening to your negativity."

"Do as best befits you," he says in a neutral tone.

I've noticed that he's especially polite when he's trying to give me venom.

I taste the mixed drink to perfect the sugar level and bring my first glass back into the living room, where I sip it while nestled on the couch, staring sulkily at the black screen of my TV. I say my first because I'm assuming many more will follow if the day keeps going like this. And the TV is off because I've already tried having it on as a distraction, but on every movie, TV show, or talk show there seemed to be a wedding involved. Even freaking teenage vampires were getting married!

Mmm, this martini is delicious. I wish I could enjoy it. For now, I'll settle for its oblivion-bringing properties.

My phone pings again.

> We r here

> And?!

> Just having Champagne in the garden

> How Nice!

> You asked!

I WISH FOR YOU

I drain the glass and help myself to a second one. I have a full pitcher in the fridge awaiting me. Right on track, girl.

> A fat woman is asking all the guests to sit down
>
> John is taking his place at the altar

Ah, that must be Miranda the Plump.

> Is James there?

As I type the question, anxiety grips me.

> Arriving now...
>
> He's at the altar waiting

He's there! No cold feet after all. I chug a third glass. I am so pathetic, getting drunk alone in my living room. I know I'm not technically alone, but Arthur doesn't count.

> How does he look?

> In a tux

For the first time since I've known her, Meg is trying to be sensitive and spare me the worst... he must be dashing. I should probably give up, but I decide I want to hurt myself even further instead.

> Pic?

Looooong pause. Typing appears and disappears in the upper part of my phone's screen many times in a row until finally, she sets her mind.

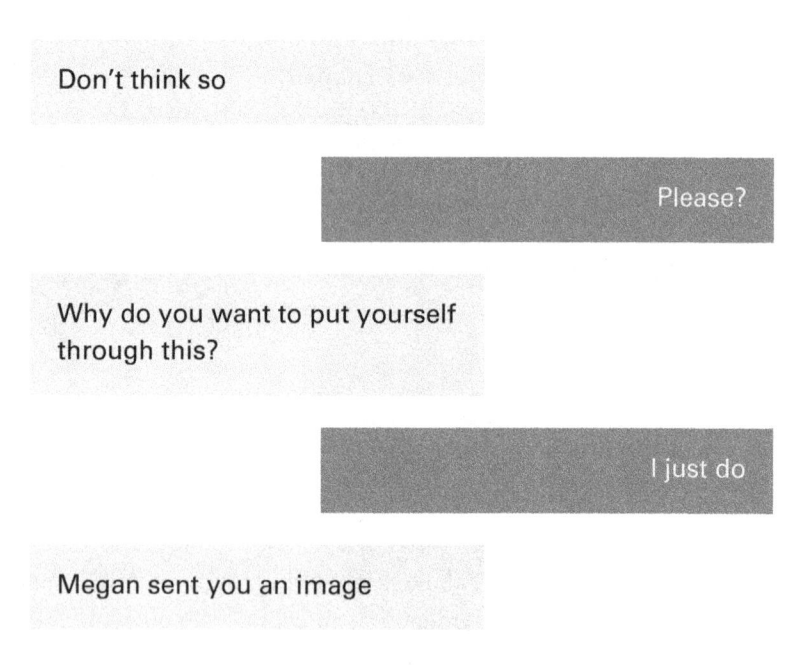

Don't think so

> Please?

Why do you want to put yourself through this?

> I just do

Megan sent you an image

I tap on it with trembling hands, holding my breath while it's downloading.
Oh.
I'd never seen James in a tux, and now I wish I hadn't. The picture is from far away and a bit unfocused so that his features are not clearly distinguishable, but one thing is clear; he's absurdly handsome. He's standing under a gazebo adorned with white roses, his body turned three-quarters toward the camera. It's the end of the summer so his tanned skin stands out against

I WISH FOR YOU

the pristine white of his shirt, and his hair is a sun-bleached, lighter shade that makes him even more attractive.

I feel tears welling up in my eyes. There he is, the man of my dreams ready to marry another woman. *What did you think? That he would pull a no-show?* Yes. *So stupid. He's there, and he's going to go through with it.*

The next text I get is from Brooke.

> Any news?

I don't know what to reply, so I just send her the picture.

> Want me to come over?

> No, thx

> Have to sit this one on my own

> Ok

> If you change your mind, I'm here at any hour

> Love you

My fourth martini is on his way to my empty stomach. I'm probably going to be sick, but I don't care. I don't care about anything anymore. That's when Megan texts again.

> Nuptial march on, bride arriving

> Want me to ditch here and come over there?

I'm tempted to ask for a picture of the bride as well, but this time I know better. Anyhow, I'm sure I'll see her gracing the cover of some local, possibly national, magazines, resplendent in her gown. Fifth martini gone.

> No, thx

> Text me if something happens, or when it's over...

> Will do

> Love u

I close my eyes and wait. I don't move, I almost don't breathe and keep waiting. I wait for the trill that will put an end to all of my dreams. I lose the sense of time; I simply stay on the couch hugging my legs, resting my head on my knees, waiting.
PING.
There. It's over. All is lost.

Thirty-one
Ally

I don't even look at the phone. Screen downward, I clench it in my hand. I don't want to see it. I don't want to know. I wish I wasn't here. I wish I wasn't anywhere. I just want to forget everything, to stop the pain. I consider using my last wish to ask just for that, to erase James from my mind. But the thought of losing Arthur as well is somewhat unbearable; I don't want to lose the love of my life and my best friend all in one day.

Plus, we're made of our experiences. Knowing James, losing him *twice* has made me what I am today and I wouldn't want to be any different. I will cherish our time together forever; the memories we created are mine, and no one could ever take them away from me. I've been cheated out of a life with him, but no one can steal away our past.

I console myself thinking that today, right now, it's the hardest. This is as bad as it gets. From here on I can only recover. I wish I didn't have to go through it all over again, but unfortunately fast forward is not an option. Not even for me, apparently.

PING. PI-PING. PING. PI-PI-PING. PING.

My phone is exploding with messages. I turn it around in my hand as a flicker of hope rises inside me.

All the texts are from Megan.

> He said your NAME!!!

It's the first text she sent five minutes ago, which I didn't read because I was too busy commiserating myself. Why didn't I read it? He said my name? My head is spinning. I quickly scroll through the other messages.

> He said I take thee ALLY
>
> Like Ross in Friends!
>
> This is crazy... madness!
>
> The bride is fainting
>
> The father of the bride just punched James right in the face
>
> They are both down now
>
> Groom and bride, I mean
>
> I can't see anything anymore because everyone is rushing to the front to see
>
> Ally ARE U THERE?!?!?

Am I here? Yes, I am. Yes! Yes! Yes!

I shoot up from the couch, pacing around nervously. My energy suddenly comes back as an adrenalin rush pumps through my veins.

What do I do?

> What's happening?!?!

I WISH FOR YOU

Oh, forget it! I can't wait for an answer. I am calling her. The phone rings barely once before she picks up.

"Ally, WOW!"

"Don't WOW me! What's happening? What's happening?" I ask hysterically.

"I don't know. I have like a million other people in front of me."

"Are they going through with it?" I squeal.

"From what I saw last, the bride and the groom both seemed unconscious. I don't think they could go through with it even if they wanted to."

"Meg, give me something more. Where's John?"

"I can try to reach him, but I have to push my way into a mob. Stay on the line."

"Okay."

I keep pacing furiously around the room, my heart in my throat.

"Everything all right?" Arthur's voice surprises me from behind. I had forgotten he was here.

"I'll explain later."

He pulls a face, but I'm far too busy to pay attention to him. I listen to some more scuffling sounds coming from the phone until Megan gets to where John is. I can overhear them talking.

"Baby," he says.

"What's going on?" she asks.

"No idea. It's absolutely crazy."

"Where are they?"

"They all went inside the house. Vanessa's father seemed like a madman. After he punched James, he kept repeating 'this is my fault, this is my fault.' He acted like a lunatic."

"What? Why should it be his fault?" Meg asks, surprised.

"Like I know." I can practically see John shrugging. "They brought Vanessa inside. She was still half out. And James ran after them."

"He did?"

"Yes."

"I'll be back in a sec. I love you."

"Love you too."

I hear some more scraping until she's back with me.

"Ally?"

"Yep."

"Did you hear?"

"Yes. What do you think?" I ask, worried. I don't like that he ran after her.

"Hard to call, baby. He was running after Vanessa. I don't know if it's a good sign." Megan confirms my fears. "And what about her father? I honestly have no idea what's going on here."

I do.

"Mm-hmm," I mumble to avoid the question, not that she expects me to answer it. What now?

"It's killing me not knowing what's going on," I tell her.

"I can only imagine. Let's do this." As usual, she takes control of the situation with a rational approach. "For now, nobody has said anything about the ceremony being canceled, but at this point, I honestly don't think it's going to happen today, or ever."

"You don't?" I'm hopeful.

"No, I don't see how they could after what happened, but we have to wait and see. Nobody told us to leave just yet—if that's what's going to happen, someone will have to come out and say it, eventually. We'll stick around for a bit longer and I'll let you know if something happens."

"Ok, thanks. Tell me everything, even the smallest thing. You promise?" I press her.

"Don't worry, I'm on it."

"Thank you so much. I love you."

"Ally, I should apologize to you. I've been giving you crap about James for two years, but today, when he said your name—I felt I've been wrong all this time."

I WISH FOR YOU

"Oh shut up, Meg. It doesn't matter. You were doing what you thought was best for me. Just tell me what's going on over there. It's all I care about right now."

"Ok, I'll go stick my nose around then. Talk to you later."

"Ok, bye."

I spend the rest of the afternoon living and breathing for the next text from Meg. I get twenty-two in total.

> There are penguin waiters coming out now with drinks and refreshments to keep the guests going

> So far no announcements...

> I'm trying to mingle with different crowds to see if anybody has an idea of what's going on

> Most people have no idea!

> Some didn't even notice that he said the wrong name. Half the people here probably don't know the bride's first name

> Random theories going around... like the dress was too tight and the bride should sue Vera Wang...

Or the father of the bride is suffering from emotional detachment stress disorder... Does it even exist?!?!

I've tried to sneak into the house...

But only immediate family members are admitted

I'm not joking, there are two huge bulky bodyguards at the doors wearing earpieces! They won't let anyone "unauthorized" in

Ok. The wedding planner, I assume, said an announcement would be made shortly

A young guy in a black suit is taking the "stage"

He has introduced himself as Mr. Van Horn's chief assistant. How many does he have? O.o

He's saying there will be no wedding today...

I WISH FOR YOU

> Ally, they're calling it off! It's over. Done. Finito. Caput

> He's saying it's off due to a sudden illness of the bride...

> Nothing alarming, but the family prefers to be cautious blah, blah, blah...

> All the guests are invited to stay for dinner and enjoy the party, blah, blah, blah...

> John has been trying to reach James for hours, but his phone always goes straight to voicemail

> I don't know if there's much left we can do here. John wants to leave

> You want us to stay? How are you coping?
> Want me to come over there and have a full postmortem?

I need to think.

> No, go home and relax.

> I'm ok
>
> Need some alone time
>
> Thx again for today
>
> Love u

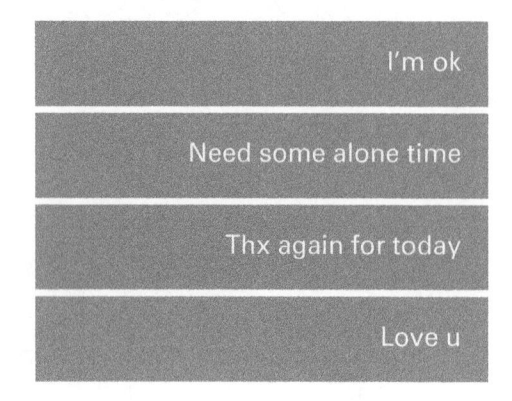

I press send and turn off the phone.

The good thing about alone time these days is that mine has a personal counselor in it... Arthur.

"The wedding is off," I tell him.

"I applaud your success."

Is he being sarcastic?

"Are you being sarcastic?"

"Well, I simply do not find it tasteful to rejoice in someone else's unhappiness."

"Oh puleease, spare me your do-goodism."

"What is next then, a happy reunion?" he asks acidly.

"Are you in a mood or something?"

"Are you?"

"You can be the most annoying person I know."

I wait a couple of seconds for a retort that doesn't arrive.

"Whatever," I say, shrugging. "I'm having another drink." I am so on edge that I need to relax.

"You did not have anything to eat all day."

"Oh, are you worrying about me now? I thought you were too busy being obnoxious."

"Ally Johnson, sometimes you make me want to snap your neck."

"Death threats, really?"

I chug my sixth or seventh martini—I've lost count—and go to my room, slamming the door shut. I jump on the bed, ready to reflect on the events of the day. Being truly alone sometimes is actually better.

"Mao?" As if reading my mind Sugar seems to be asking permission to join me.

"Don't worry, baby, you are always welcome," I reassure him, patting the empty space on the bed next to me.

He jumps on it and starts purring loudly as soon as I begin scratching him behind the ears.

***

Where am I? *In your bed.* What time is it? *Late, it's dark outside.* What happened? *James, the wedding...*

After going to my room, I got lost in thoughts while cuddling Sugar and I must've dozed off. My head is throbbing. *You had a pitcher of martinis.* Why am I awake? I want to sleep! *Something woke you.* What? *A distant sound.*

As I remember the sound, I regain proper consciousness and look around me, searching for the source of the noise without finding it. I'm almost ready to get back to sleep when I hear it again, only this time it's loud and clear. Someone is knocking on my door.

I launch myself out of the bed and run into the living room as if Jack the Ripper was chasing me, all the while ignoring the fact that my apartment seems to be spinning around me. In four quick strides, I reach the door and peer through the peephole.

I almost die. It's James!

"You," I hiss to Arthur. "Beat it."

"Pardon me?"

"It's James at the door," I whisper furiously. "I don't want you here."

"So things worked out exactly the way you wanted," he says flatly, his jaw tightening slightly.

"Do not cheer too loudly," I retort, sarcastic. "Off you go."

"I will make myself invisible immediately."

"No, no. No, no, no. Not invisible, I want you to *go away*, like wherever it is you go when you're not here." I press him when there is yet another knock at the door.

"I'm coming," I shout toward the hallway as if I was in another room. "I don't want you here, it's James. I want to be alone with him. *Really* alone," I add, murmuring.

"Ally, you are making a mistake," Arthur says, still very here and still very visible.

I'm losing my patience.

"Arthur, I need you to *go*," I hiss, trying to keep my tone low. "We can discuss your philosophical views another time."

"Another time may be too late. Listen, there is something I need to tell you…"

"I don't care right now, and you can tell me tomorrow. Would you just go away now, please?"

"No, I will not," he states stubbornly, his tone rising.

"Shhhhhh. Why of all moments now, why?" I plead. If I could touch him, I'd be shoving him away, but I can't.

"Because tomorrow it could be too late," Arthur repeats gravely.

"Too late for what? Please don't start throwing riddles around, not now."

As the fourth knock resounds in the room, I resort to threats. "Arthur, go away or I'll make you go."

"You promised never to."

"So just go."

"No. Ally, please—what I have to say is very important."

Fifth knock.

"I'm sorry, Arthur," I say in a whisper, soft this time. "I order you back into the coffer."

As he begins to dissolve in front of me, I barely have the time to take in the look of utter betrayal on his face and glimpse his eyes filling with hurt just as he looks away from me.

I WISH FOR YOU

For a second there I am breathless. What have I done? But he was being impossible! And in what could be the most important moment of my life. I'll make it up to him later.

I catch my reflection in the hallway mirror and it's horrible! I quickly give myself a magical restyling, take a deep breath, and open the door.

Thirty-two

Awakening

I blink twice in the darkness. Did last night really happen? A faint, irregular snoring beside me and the unbearable weight of a heavy arm casually tossed across my chest, confirm that yes, it happened!

Oh my! I feel as if I was crushed underneath a mountain of ice. I'm cold, and I can't move. This must be what claustrophobia feels like. There, my pulse is accelerating; if I don't do something quickly, I'm going to have a full-blown panic attack. I need to get out of here! If I move I'll wake him, and I don't want to face him just yet. But if I stay still, I'm going to relive last night over and over again in my head, and experiencing it once was more than enough.

Actually, I don't have a crystal clear picture of what happened; it's all a bit fuzzy. Maybe drinking so many martinis on an empty stomach wasn't such a good idea after all. But no matter how blurred the memory is, I'm sure of one thing: it wasn't good.

I remember opening the door with a beating heart to find James leaning on my doorframe, admittedly a little disheveled. His bow tie was hanging loose on both sides of his collar, his shirt with two or three unfastened buttons, and his face sporting a bluish shade around the left eye, but desperately handsome all the same.

We talked for a while, drank some more, and he professed his undying love for me and told me that the last two years of his life had been a huge mistake. Somewhere along the line, I said I loved him too, half crying, half laughing, I'm not sure, and then we shared the most passionate kiss of all time, at which point I let him drag me into the bedroom.

But after James pulled me in here all the chemistry went to hell. We fumbled awkwardly around each other for a while, our bodies refusing to get along. I would bend my head on the right to kiss him and he would do the same, so we would just end up clumsily bumping our noses. When I tried to remove his shirt, I painfully stumbled on his foot, and he jerked his leg up, hitting my hip with a knee. His hands on me were clammy and sticky; it was as if he didn't know me at all as if we had never made love before. And this was merely the physical aspect of it!

Being able to read his mind, I occasionally peeked inside and didn't like what I found one bit. I should've known better. It was like nothing I had experienced before, probably because he was so drunk and confused himself. It was as if his mind was literally being split in two; one side wanted to be with me, the other with Vanessa, and everything was swirling in a vortex of memories, regrets, and mostly utter misery.

Anyway, by the point we got onto the bed, I was desperately thinking of a way to get out of the situation. I was considering smothering him with a pillow to get him off me when luckily providence took over and solved the problem for me. He had been on top of me for a mere five seconds when he suddenly collapsed on me, *asleep*!

That definitely put a stop to any romantic or physical development the evening could've had. He was still dressed in his wedding suit and he hasn't moved since. I wanted to go sleep on the couch, but I was so exhausted and drunk that all I could do was to wriggle away from underneath him and then pass out beside him.

In retrospect, the only positive note about last night is that we didn't have sex. I'm glad for it. But why? James has been the center of my life for the past five years, two of which I've spent obsessing over getting him back, and now that he's finally here by my side, telling me he wants me back in his life, instead of feeling utterly elated I just feel... well, like shit!

I try to reason that it's only a physical condition. I've had nothing proper to eat since yesterday at breakfast, and I'd had a lot to drink even before James arrived here. Add to it the stress of these last few weeks... and boom, there you have it. My indisposition has a perfect clinical explanation.

But deep down I know it's not it. Something is wrong here, very wrong. I just can't put my finger on it. My stomach grumbles loudly. Right, I should probably give my brain some food before I ask any deep exertion of it.

Mmm, breakfast seems like a good start. I picture a butter croissant and a steaming cappuccino. I wonder if Arthur has already prepared them. Unfortunately, thinking about Arthur triggers the reminiscence of his facial expression when I banned him to the coffer. Even shrouded by the fumes of alcohol as the memory is, I'll never be able to forget it. Something tells me I will not get my usual breakfast treat this morning.

Why does everything I think about today have to upset me?

My best option right now is to wriggle out of the bed, trying not to wake James in the process, get something to eat, and collect myself a little before I have to talk to him. To say *what*? Oh, I so don't know. Here comes the cabin fever again. I need to get out of here.

I tentatively drop my left foot to the ground, sliding my whole body sideways to slip away from under James's arm. I move very slowly, careful not to wake him. It takes me five good minutes and a lot of effort before I can finally squat on the floor beside the bed. I wait there, curled up for a few seconds to make sure I made it safely, and that there is no sign of life from the bed. I get up and try for the door, but the moment I do so I sense, more than see, a movement. I freeze, hoping he's just stirring in his sleep, but a loud yawn immediately crushes my hopes.

"Myyaww, good morning," he says in a thick voice. "Gosh, my head is pounding. I need some coffee. Would you make some, babe?" he asks, stretching on the bed like a starfish.

Babe? Coffee? I just stay there frozen to the spot, a cold fury mounting inside me.

At this moment, an old saying from an immigrant who came to the US in the nineteenth century comes to mind: I came to America because I heard the streets were paved with gold.

I WISH FOR YOU

When I got here, I found out three things: First, the streets weren't paved with gold; second, they weren't paved at all; and third, I was expected to pave them.

I'm making my three personal discoveries today: first, I will not get my favorite breakfast; second, I will not get any breakfast at all; and third, I am expected to prepare it, at least the coffee part of it.

I march into the kitchen, taking out my anger on my dishes and appliances. After a couple of minutes, James joins me, sitting at his usual spot at the bar; well, what used to be his usual spot, waiting for his coffee. I fill a mug and practically smash it on the countertop, sending the hot liquid spilling in all directions and making it overflow from the mug's rim in angry waves that splash all over.

"Whoa, what's wrong with you?" James shouts, jerking back in his stool to avoid being hit by the flying droplets.

"What's wrong with me?" I yell back. "What's wrong with *you*?"

"Why are you being such a bitch?"

"Oh, well, James, did you expect a homecoming party? I'm sorry I've disappointed you." I'm seething with suppressed rage.

"You didn't seem so unhappy to see me last night!"

I snort at that.

"Are you this mad because I passed out?" he asks bewildered.

"No," I grunt. "Why are you here, anyway?"

"I told you why I'm here. I want to fix things between us."

"Really? Do you really want to?"

"Why, don't you?"

"I don't know," I wail. "What did you think—that I just spent the last two years waiting around for you?" *I so did.*

"Well, it wasn't me going around singing 'Don't You Remember.' It was as if the song was written for us."

Ouch, a blow below the belt.

"That wasn't for you," I lie. "It was just a song I like. And I have a boyfriend, remember him?"

"Phew, that jerk. Last night you didn't seem to care much about him. Please, Ally, don't tell me you really like *him*."

"What's not to like?"

"He's just not you."

"Not me? What do you know about me?"

"You're right! I don't even recognize you anymore. I don't know what to say, you are not making any sense."

"Oh, you don't? *I* don't know what to say." I'm hysterical at this point. "You come here drunk one night and break my heart for no apparent reason. One day we are perfectly happy together, and the next you tell me you don't love me anymore and go get engaged to another woman. Then, you come back two years later, still drunk, on your wedding day, *no less*, and give me a load of bullshit about how you never stopped loving me, about how we are meant to be, and whatever. And *I* am the one not making any sense? What, did you expect to just snap your fingers and instantly get back to where we left?"

The moment the words leave my lips I realize precisely two things: first, I had expected exactly that; and second, it's just impossible. You can't go back. Arthur was right.

James seems about to give me some heated retort when I suddenly witness the fight break away from him. He sinks on the couch, resting his head on both hands, and hunches his shoulders forward in defeat.

"You're right," he says, and lifts his head. "I haven't been honest with you. I need to tell you everything."

And he does. I sit next to him like a confessor, listening to the sad story I already know. And for once he's completely candid, he doesn't leave anything out. He gives me every shameful detail... New Year's, his mother, and the debt. He tells me about Vanessa, her crush on him, and her father owning the bank he was indebted to. He swears that at first, it was all pretense with Vanessa, that he was heartbroken over me, but that after a while as he began to settle into his new life he would think about me less and less while opening up to

Vanessa more and more every day, beginning to feel something real for her.

So everything was good for a while, but after bumping into me at Hub 51 his mind filled with doubts all over again, and he couldn't stop thinking about me for one second. He says that I had always been at the back of his mind like an unsolved riddle, an unanswered question, but that seeing me triggered an emotional rollercoaster.

He finishes by saying that when the bank lifted his obligations, his confusion grew even bigger. He immediately thought that he was finally free to leave Vanessa, but having the option to do so, he wasn't sure what he really wanted anymore. So he just let the days pass without doing anything. Then yesterday when he said my name instead of Vanessa's, he thought that his subconscious had made the decision for him.

"So after the wedding fiasco you just came here?" I ask softly.

"No, I stole a bottle of champagne and went on the *Sunrise*," he says, shaking his head.

"You got that drunk with just one bottle?"

"It was a Magnum. Plus your martinis are no lightweights," he jokes.

"Ah."

"I wanted to clear my mind a little, but I ended up messing with it even more. Coming here seemed like the right thing to do so that we could finally have the future we wanted before all of this happened. But now that I'm here it just feels, I mean, it's just..."

"Different." We say it at the same time.

"Do you hate me?" He looks at me, searching for absolution, and I decide to give it to him.

"No, I don't hate you. You just made a mistake—well, a lot of them, but we're human. Nobody's perfect. You just did what you thought best at the time."

"You forgive me?"

"Yes, I do," I say sincerely. Never had I thought that I would say these three words to him in such a circumstance.

"But you don't love me anymore." It's more of a statement than a question.

"Do you?"

We look at each other and neither of us knows what to say. This is the man I've loved with all my heart for so long, and now that he's here right in front of me, I feel… nothing. And I can tell it's the same for him. It's too late for us. What we had, whatever it was, is gone forever.

"James?"

"Yes?"

"Do you love her?"

I feel his answer before hearing it.

"I do."

"So don't make the same mistake twice. Go fight for her." Am I really saying this? "It's not too late for the two of you."

"Ally, you weren't there yesterday. It was pretty horrible."

"How was she? I mean… after," I ask tentatively.

"I don't know."

"What do you mean you don't know?"

"They wouldn't let me talk to her. Her father told her everything, about the bank and my debt. He came down after talking to her and told me I had to leave and never come back, that Vanessa didn't want anything to do with me. She must've been disgusted by me."

"So you haven't talked to her at all?"

"Nope."

"Then you don't know what she thinks!" I exclaim. "Listen, she's very gullible, especially when it comes to her father. He probably didn't even give her a chance to think about the whole thing. You need to explain yourself to her, pour your heart out. Maybe there's still a chance."

"Really?" His whole face lights up with hope.

I nod.

"You're the best."

He gives me a bone-crushing hug.

I WISH FOR YOU

"Ally?" he asks when he finally lets go of me.

"Mm-hmm?"

"Can we still be friends?"

Ah. The friends question.

"James, I'll always care for you. And if you pull your neck, and you're lying on the floor unable to move, and nobody else can help, feel free to call me. But let's be honest—we were never friends, and we could never be. Plus, I don't imagine Vanessa would approve."

"Ah, no, you're right. Maybe it's for the best." He looks at me intensely with those warm chocolate eyes before asking, "So, is this goodbye?"

I am only able to nod, afraid I won't be able to fight back the tears if I speak.

"Goodbye, Ally, take care."

"I will," I murmur. "Bye."

Have a nice life seemed a bit over the top.

He hugs me one last time for what simultaneously seems like forever and no time at all. When we pull apart, he gives me a soft peck on the lips and exits my apartment—and my life—forever.

The moment the door closes behind him, an immense sense of emptiness washes over me. It's not pain; the time for that was two years ago. It's just this overwhelming hollowness that seems to have taken the place of my heart in my chest. I have no purpose, no direction. I have nothing. I'm numb.

All my wishes, all my abilities, are useless... nothing can buy me happiness, not even all the money and power in the world.

Thirty-three
The Breakfast Club

After James leaves, I lean my forehead on the door, feeling pitiful. I'm not sure what to do next. My stomach grumbles loudly in protest. Okay, maybe I don't need to be making life-changing decisions right at this moment. I can start with baby steps, like eating for the first time in twenty-four hours.

"Did you sleep well, milady?" Arthur's sudden question startles me.

Admittedly, it sounds more like an accusation than a question. And the long-gone milady appellative is back. So it *was* scornful. Or, if it wasn't, it certainly is now.

"Do you have a problem?" I turn around on the defensive.

He doesn't reply, just mumbles something behind gritted teeth that disturbingly sounds like "harlotry."

"Are you calling me a slut?" I yell.

"If this is the word that goes by nowadays," he answers infuriatingly, casually waving his left hand dismissively.

"I didn't sleep with him." I try to defend myself.

"I thought he was in the room with you this morning."

How does he know? Was he spying on us? Is he able to see me even when he's in the coffer?

"Yes, but—"

"So, strictly speaking, you *did* sleep together."

"*Yes*, but we didn't do anything *besides* sleeping."

"And why is that?" His blue eyes x-ray me.

I'm not sure what to answer. If James hadn't fallen asleep, would we have done the deed? *No*, but I really don't need to explain myself to Arthur.

I observe him as he stares into space while sitting in the living room's armchair as usual. I take in his appearance, and note that it's more disturbing than his attitude! I can hardly recognize him. His face is kind of bloated and, underneath the dark shadow of his day's worth of stubble, mottled with red irregular patches of irritated skin.

I narrow my eyes and get closer to him; he reeks of whiskey. The stink of the heavy liquor is so strong that it makes me recoil. This explains the face. Why does every man in my life have to be drunk?

"Are you drunk?"

"Very much so," he spits back defiantly.

He's angry with me for sending him away, I get it. Okay, it was wrong, but his reaction seems a bit exaggerated.

"Okay, about last night. I'm sorry. I shouldn't have sent you away the way I did, but I wasn't thinking straight, and you weren't helping either."

"There is no need to apologise, milady. You did not do anything wrong. I am your slave and it is your right to dispose of me as you see fit."

"Arthur, stop it. It's not like that. You're not my slave. We're friends."

"Are we?"

"Arthur, I'm trying to say I'm sorry, okay? Can't you forgive me?"

"As I said, nothing to forgive." He's cold and distant.

"Why are you so mad at me? What can I do more than to say that I'm sorry?"

"If you have not figured it out yet, you are even more foolish than I thought."

"What does that even mean? You're having a serious case of alcohol poisoning."

"Do not worry. It takes more than a bottle of whiskey to cut me down."

"Oh Arthur, why are you being so difficult?" I sag on the couch, exhausted. "I need some support now, not more drama."

"Well, you can call dear old James for that."

"James is gone," I say, and for the first time, I'm not upset.

"Nevertheless, I assume he will be back pretty soon. Well, I will not wait around," Arthur says while getting up from the chair, unsteady as a drunkard, stumbling forward a couple of steps. "I will open my second bottle instead. Milady, if you will excuse me." He performs a mocking bow and then disappears into thin air.

"AAARRRRGHHHH!" I scream in frustration, grabbing a vase and throwing it in his general direction. But he's gone, and the vase smashes on the wall, breaking into a thousand pieces.

Why is the argument with him more upsetting than the whole James thing?

I could summon him back. He has to come if I call, but right now I don't see the point. What I need now is a huge breakfast and a sober person to talk to, and I know exactly who will be beyond any possible doubt.

***

I have arranged to meet with Brooke at a Starbucks halfway between our two apartments. I grab my car keys, my bag, and open the door, ready to exit.

As I do so, I'm in for a big surprise. The *Psycho* violin screech, the *Kill Bill* iron-side siren sound, and the scary theme from *The Shark* all start to play loud and clear in my head at the same time! Because standing on my doorstep is the scariest thing of all—Vanessa in the flesh, arm raised in midair, ready to knock on my door.

"Where is he?" She pushes me aside without greetings and barges into my living room.

"Uh, who?" I might as well play dumb. What is Frank up to these days that he lets everyone in without giving me the heads-up?

"You know *who*, Ally." She glares at me with such hatred that I'm actually scared. "He wasn't at his apartment this morning, so he must be here!"

"No one is here," I retort innocently.

"Fine, you won't tell me! I'll find him on my own," she threatens, and then proceeds with a thorough search of my apartment.

I try to stop her a couple of times, especially when she turns my walk-in closet into a war zone, but she's a madwoman and there is no stopping her.

When she doesn't have anywhere left to look and is definitely satisfied that James is not here, she sinks on the couch, depleted of all energies and purpose. She's sitting in the same exact spot James was occupying half an hour ago, in the same position. The irony of it isn't lost on me.

I stare at her for a moment, unsure what to do. I decide to enter her mind to check what's going on in there. I concentrate on her, and from the first vibe I get back, I am appalled by the bubbling cauldron of pain and confusion that I find.

She's in love with James but loathes him at the same time for what he did. She's furious with her dad because he knew everything and beaten by the fact that her own father thought the only way for her to keep a man was if he was blackmailing him with his money. She's overwhelmed by pain, and she hates me.

Hmm, it's worse than I thought.

"Um, Vanessa?" I ask tentatively.

"Don't you patronize me."

"I wasn't going to. Have you perhaps considered the possibility that, ah... James—" She hasn't spoken the name since she arrived, so I'll be the one to put it out there. "That he could be looking for you at your apartment right as we speak, and that's probably why he wasn't at home this morning?"

"So he never came here?"

"No."

If I tell her the truth, she will never forgive him, and I've damaged their relationship enough as it is.

"But you knew we didn't get married yesterday."

"Yes."

"You know he said your name?" she asks without looking me in the eyes.

"Yes," I murmur softly.

"And how did you know if he wasn't here?"

"It's the era of cell phones, Vanessa. John's girlfriend is a friend of mine. She told me."

"So you had your spies inside, I see," she comments bitterly.

"Hmm, can I offer you something? Coffee, maybe?" I ask, pretending not to have heard.

"Why are you being so nice to me?" she asks, suspicious.

Because I'm the one who gave you acne and twenty pounds before your wedding so that you would not fit into your dress. Because I'm lying to you about James never being here, and because it's entirely my fault if your wedding was a complete disaster.

I go with, "You seem to have enough on your plate without the need to add a catfight to the list. Plus, I really don't see the point in arguing with you."

"So you know he said your name, and you don't care?" she asks, skeptical.

"No, James is my past. I've been over him for a long time." A whole twenty minutes.

She eyes me for a long time before speaking again. "So you are not after him," she concludes.

"Oh no, I'm extremely happy with my boyfriend." *If only.*

"Yeah, he did seem like a great guy."

"He is." Uh, finally something exits my mouth that is not a lie; well, at least it wasn't up until this morning.

"I'm sorry I came here throwing accusations at you. It's just that after yesterday, I've lost it. I was so sure he had run right back to you. I'm being paranoid."

"Probably it's the stress," I reassure her, feeling lucky I didn't oversleep or she would have found us still in bed, even if innocently so. "Um, I was actually going out to see a friend. I

I WISH FOR YOU

don't mean to be rude, but I really need to leave if you don't mind."

"Of course, I'll be off immediately. Sorry again, Ally. Lately, I've been a bitch to you. But it's normal not to like your boyfriend's exes."

She sounds sincere, so I will not point out that she was a total bitch way before James was in the picture, and that she just ransacked my apartment without offering any help to clean it up. She probably thinks we all have maids. I am simply glad she's getting off my couch and moving toward the door.

"Don't worry and please say hi to everyone at the office for me."

"I will," she says while exiting my apartment. "You know what?" She stops halfway through the door. "We could have been friends in a different situation."

Ah, that's taking it a bit too far, but I smile politely nonetheless, relishing the newfound emptiness of my apartment once she's gone. I rejoice in it only for a couple of seconds before I think of alerting James; if he tells her that he was here, he'll lose every chance he might still have. So I text him quickly and finally get out of the house, hoping I will not be very late.

***

Unbelievably, I manage to arrive at Starbucks first. Brooke from time to time has the nasty tendency of being outrageously late. In fact, before she arrives, I manage to order, be served, and am already halfway through my second croissant when she finally joins me.

I also got glazed donuts, and for drinks a skinny-caramel-macchiato for me and a green tea for her, since I am not sure if pregnant women are supposed to drink coffee or not. When she arrives, she takes in the cemetery of empty pink pastry bags plus the ones still full and immediately gets the gist of the situation.

"That bad, huh?" she asks, pulling over a chair and sitting next to me.

"I'm fforry," I answer with my mouth still half-full, unable to stop eating. "I haven't featen anyphing solid in ptwenty-four mhours. I'm starffing."

"Are you ok?" she asks, worried.

I stopped texting her yesterday more or less at the same time as Meg. I forwarded her all the messages, so she's up to date on the canceled wedding, but she still doesn't know what happened last night.

I am only able to nod since I've just stuffed the remaining half of the croissant in my mouth.

"I tried to call you last night, but your phone was off," she adds.

I make an effort to swallow, take a sip of coffee, and am finally ready to talk. I tell her the whole story, relieved that at last, I'm free to reveal all the details I had to hide before. She listens patiently to everything and doesn't interrupt me once; one of the traits I love about her.

"So." I inhale deeply once I've finished my narration, feeling as if I haven't breathed once since I started talking. "What do you think?"

She looks at me, raising both eyebrows, at a loss for words.

"Really? Nothing? I thought my story was at least a bit interesting."

"It's not that. Oh, Ally, I have so many questions I don't know where to start."

"Fire all of them at the same time and I'll decide what to answer first," I suggest.

"Okay, ready?"

"Yes!"

"First, are you sure you're okay you and James broke up again? Do you really not love him anymore after all this time?

I WISH FOR YOU

After all the time you've waited, it's over? Just like that? Nada? No more the love of your life? And you forgave him anyway? I still can't believe he left you for money—it's beyond me. And I'm sorry I didn't believe you, there really was a cosmic conspiracy going on. I'm kind of relieved you're over him, though, and that he's not going to be this baby's uncle," she adds, patting her belly affectionately.

"I know you think he did it for his father, but honestly? And do you think he really loves Vanessa, or is she just his last option? Did she really have the guts to show up at your place? I don't know how you handled it, with a hangover and on an empty stomach. The fact that you helped them get back together leaves me speechless."

Believe me, she is everything *but* speechless right now.

"And are you moving far away now? Are you looking for schools anywhere but here? When are we going to see each other? Please don't make me give birth alone, I need you there. If I poop on the table I don't want Dave to be there—it has to be you. Sorry, I am being selfish, I guess the only big question here is how are you feeling? What now?"

It's time for her to catch her breath.

"Whoa, those really were a lot of questions." I smile and take a moment to put my thoughts in order. "Let me see. About James: I know it sounds crazy, but it's like when you don't like a kind of food for many years, and then once you try it again boom, you love it." I steal Arthur's analogy. "Only I guess the other way around. For me, it was zucchini—have you ever had one of those?"

"Liver, I guess."

"And you like it now?" I ask, making a face.

"Oh yeah, if you make a pâté it's delicious."

"Blech, you already have weird pregnant woman tastes."

"I'll make it for you once without telling you what it is. You'll see."

I have my doubts, but I let it pass. "So, James. I was so focused on getting him back, especially after learning about Vanessa, and I was so sure we were made for each other that I never stopped once to analyze what I really felt—that is, until this morning."

We chuckle together, both thinking about the swift account I gave her of my awakening.

"And you should know," I continue, "that he would have made a great uncle."

She rolls her eyes exaggeratedly but doesn't retort.

"And yes," I continue, "he really loves Vanessa. Before we talked, I was the forbidden fruit in his life. I was over there on the pedestal, the sad heroine of a romance, the unanswered question... and when I suddenly became available to him, he was just so confused. He was so busy regretting our lost love that he didn't realize he was actually developing a new one, a real one. And if you had seen Vanessa this morning, you would have done exactly the same—she was desperate. I felt so bad for her, even if she did come on to my boyfriend knowingly. I mean, in the end, she was another victim of the scheming. Up until yesterday, she thought James had chosen her freely, and now that he really has I just hope she finds it in her to forgive him."

"You are very noble," Brooke comments, impressed.

I blush, I feel this way mostly because Vanessa's wedding fiasco was basically my doing.

"About schools," I carry on, "I don't know. A change of scenery could be good for me..."

She makes such a sad, involuntary expression that I rush in, reassuring her.

"Honey, don't worry—I'll always be there for you. And I can fly back and forth as much as I want. I am a wealthy woman now." I manage to make a little smile appear on her dubious face. "And about how I feel? To tell you the truth, just empty, purposeless. My sole objective lately has been to win

I WISH FOR YOU

James back, and now that the goal has faded away, I don't know what to do. It's horrible!"

"Can I say something?" she asks almost shyly.

"Sure, fire away."

"What about Arthur?"

I snort so loudly that she's taken aback.

"What?"

"Oh Brooke, he was such a jerk to me that I'm not sure I want to see him again."

"Why? What happened?" she asks, shocked.

I tell her about the verbal abuse, making it sound as if it all happened over the phone. I change some of the dynamics here and there, like instead of saying that I banned him to a magic coffer I just say that I hung up on him, but it gives her the essence of Arthur's behavior all the same.

"So you have no idea what he wanted to say to you?" she asks, as if she did.

"Nope. And he hung up on me when I tried to say I was sorry this morning. What a jerk!"

I expect her to join me in my bashing of his actions, but she shakes her head and smiling softly, saying only. "Oh Ally, sometimes you are so clueless."

Thirty-four
Clueless

"What do you mean I am so clueless?" I ask, offended.

"Oh Ally, don't you see?" Brooke says. "The guy is smitten with you! He's probably having a major jealousy crisis."

"Arthur? Please, don't be absurd!" I laugh it off. "He's still totally hung up on, um... his ex." I can't say long-dead wife, right?

"No, he's not. If only you saw the way he looks at you, the way he treats you."

"Brooke, he's British—they're different. They're just over polite and more gentlemanlike."

"Ally, he's not being polite," she insists. "I bet that if you'd let him, he would like to be very impolite with you," she adds with a mischievous smirk.

"I... he... we don't. It's not like that between us," I protest, while vividly blushing all the same.

"Ally, take my word on this. He's in love with you, there's no doubt about that."

"That's. Just. Impossible." I have to spell it out for her.

"And why is that?" she challenges.

He lives in a jewelry case, he's my personal slave, he was born in the thirteenth century...

"He lives in London, he's an investment banker, and he's still hung up on his ex," I say instead.

"Hmm, so how long ago did they break up? Why? Was it him or her?"

They didn't. An evil witch cursed him and broke them apart because she was jealous...

"It's a long, complicated story. I'm not sure he'd like me to tell you about it."

"That's BS and you know it."

Okay, she's right, but I can't share the real reasons. So I simply sit in silence, sulking.

"Since he's been here he hasn't hooked up with anybody else, has he?" she continues, making me flinch involuntarily. "He hasn't even been on a date."

Actually, he has, only it was with Bruce. I suppress a smile as an image of Arthur dressed in the short pink tunic pops into my head.

"He hasn't so much as *looked* at another woman," Brooke insists.

No, he was too busy being one. I chuckle internally.

"You've basically been spending all your time together—he even came with you to that stupid corporate retreat as your fake boyfriend!" She air-quotes fake.

"Brooke, stop it. Nothing happened."

"So he never tried anything with you?"

"No."

"Not even a kiss?"

"No, sort of... not really."

"Meaning?" She raises her eyebrows inquisitively.

I explain to her about the karaoke kiss. "...but it wasn't like that, it was more like a dare," I conclude.

"Again, clueless," she comments dryly. "And let me tell you that I also think you're in love with him, only you had your head too far up your backside obsessing about James to notice. And that little speech you made about James being too busy regretting the lost love of a romance and not realizing he had a real one in his life... well, you can turn it around and apply it to yourself, missy."

I gape like a fish, shaking my head, too stunned to speak.

"You can stand there shaking your head as much as you want, but I have incontrovertible evidence."

"Okay, let's hear it. The burden of proof is all yours," I say, skeptical.

"My dear, I could spend the whole morning trying to convince you of the obvious by telling you that it's clear how you feel about Arthur because in the past few months you've spent more time with him than anybody else..."

That's only because of the circumstances.

"...that you probably told him stuff you didn't even tell me..."

Just because he was the only one I could tell. It's a rule.

"...that you consider him to be your best friend..."

Not after today.

"...and that you are always yourself around him like you've never been around any guy before..."

Well, he isn't really a guy, so...

"But—" She pauses for suspense. "I'm not going to because the most definite evidence of your feelings is simple and undeniable."

I have no idea what she's going to say next.

"Remember that night we were watching *Star Wars* at my house?"

"Yes?"

"You gave him your last m&m."

Wait for it... wait for it... but when it is clear it's not coming, I ask, "So?"

"Ally, you did it without blinking!" she exclaims. "An unprecedented fact never witnessed on planet Earth. Ally Johnson giving away a perfect specimen of a delicious, chocolate-coated peanut. I didn't believe it when I saw it," she concludes with a smirk.

"That's your evidence, an m&m?" I ask, annoyed. I thought she was going to blow my mind with some life-changing revelation.

"Not just a casual m&m, which per se would have been noticeable, but to give him the last one! If I had asked for it, you would have probably clawed me. Even when it was James asking, you would give him one or two, very reluctantly, and never ever the last one. With Arthur, you didn't have to think for a second."

"Oh please, Brooke, can you be serious?" I'm beginning to get mad. "I had enough of a bad day as it is without you making a philosophical case about candies."

"I am not making it up. You didn't talk to Dave for a week because he finished your m&m's while you were in the bathroom two years ago and don't try to say it wasn't about the m&m's!"

"Okay, okay. It was about the m&m's," I confess for the first time. "But I had half a packet left. And he didn't just take one—he finished the whole thing. That was rude and inconsiderate..."

"He just thought you could fare as well on Reese's or Nestle Crunch like everybody else. He didn't know you had such a fetish for the little m's—which, by the way, proves my point even further. Nobody normal holds a grudge for a week over chocolate."

"Chocolate *and* peanuts," I clarify.

"See, you're crazy about them."

"Oh, I love m&m's. Guilty," I say sardonically, raising both hands in a gesture of surrender.

"You don't want to listen," she says, exasperated.

I glower at her.

"Let's try it this way." She thinks for a second. "How would you feel if Arthur told you he has to go back to England tomorrow?"

He can't.

"He has been transferred here indefinitely. He won't be going anytime soon," I say.

"That's not the point," she insists. "Let's say they untransferred him and that he had to go, just like that."

Hmm. Let's say I was to voice my final wish; he'd be gone for good. I catch my breath for a second. The thought is really upsetting, which is why I haven't expressed my fifth wish. And I have no intention of doing so anytime soon. Or ever.

Okay, I'll admit I've become very attached to Arthur, but that's only because the situation is so unbelievable. I never thought about Arthur romantically; I'm in love with James. My brain goes there on autopilot. *Was* in love with James, I have to remind myself.

Anyway, it has been clear from the start that romance with Arthur is just forbidden, a big veto from day one, no chances there. I knew that, he knew that, there's even a rule about it. And the fact that losing him would make me sad doesn't mean I love him. Losing Brooke would make me sad. I'm not in love with her.

It's not the same, says a nasty little voice inside my head.

"Brooke, don't go there." I don't like the turn this little chat is taking. "Don't make me go there, please. Trust me on this. It's just not a thing. Not going to happen."

"But Ally, why? *Why?*" She keeps asking questions I can't possibly answer, so I'll just shut the hell up while she continues with her sponsorship of the impossible love story.

"He is kind, caring, and…"

Cursed.

"…he's just so out-of-this-world. They don't make them like that anymore. He is from another time…"

Literally.

"…but he's also bright and easy-going…"

Hmm, whatever.

"…you have fun when you are with him. You're relaxed, you're always smiling, and you have this glow about you…"

Do I?

"…he's gorgeous…"

And she hasn't seen him with only a towel on.

"…and don't tell me you don't get a thrill when he stares at you with those blue eyes…"

I sort of do.

I WISH FOR YOU

"...you love spending time with him..."
I do.
"...Ally, you love him!"
I do.
No, wait, she tricked me. I don't; do I? No! I can't, I simply can't. It's unthinkable.

"And look me in the eyes and tell me that you didn't feel anything when he kissed you." She puts the last nail in the coffin.

My knees went weak and my stomach flipped would be the only honest answer I could give her.

No, no, no, please. I can't go from being in love with an about-to-get-married-ex-boyfriend to an even more impossible cursed-king-of-England-gone-genie-of-the-lamp. She must notice the weird range of emotions passing through my face and my final expression of utter desperation.

"I've upset you, I'm sorry," she apologizes. "You're right, I'll drop it. You've had enough turmoil in the past few days."

Oh, but now is too late; she cannot take it back. The seed has been planted in my brain and there's no taking it out now. She kicked open a door that I've kept closed with a thousand locks. And now that it's open, everything that was hidden inside is flooding out.

I think back to the past months, about how despite desperately pursuing James I felt a sense of calmness, of deep belonging. Until now I hadn't realized it was *Arthur* who made me feel that way.

I think about our nights together, how we talked about everything. I would update him on two centuries of happenings, and he would bring me back to other times, making me see the world in a completely different way. It didn't matter if we talked for hours, watched a movie, or simply sat comfortably in silence reading a book; his sole presence beside me made me feel secure and protected.

He knows me better than anyone else does. I have no secrets with him, and I've never felt the need to withdraw something, or to hide. With him, I always feel at home. And when he looks at me with those blue eyes... as soon as I picture his intense gaze, my stomach does a loop the loop and tickles all over. Ah. Are these the famous butterflies? I swear I never felt anything like it before. And if these are indeed the little fluttery love bugs, it could only mean one thing... that I'm in trouble. Serious trouble.

I'm hyperventilating. I feel hot.

"Ally, are you okay?" Brooke asks, worried.

I shake my head, grab a pink paper bag, and start breathing into it.

"I'll get you some water." She hurries inside.

When she gets back, my breathing is close to normal. I grab the plastic cup, remove the lid, and chug half the glass in one gulp. Then I use the remaining half of the water to splash my face. Next, I start crying. Loud, uncontrollable, body-shaking sobs. I even put an involuntary hiccup in the middle of it every now and then. Gosh, I must be quite a sight.

People are staring.

It takes me a good half an hour to calm down, at least on the outside. Brooke keeps throwing me worried glances that are unnerving me. She must think I'm nuts. Well, actually I am.

I need to get out of here.

I reassure her for the millionth time that I'm okay, tell her to stop apologizing, and that I'll call her later. As soon as she's convinced I'm not in any immediate physical danger, I say goodbye and make a run for my car. I need to go somewhere and think. Alone.

***

The lake always calms me. Its perennial rhythm of wave after wave is appeasing. I've chosen a secluded spot, more to the north of the city where I can sit in peace with nobody else around. I remove my sandals and sink my feet into the cold sand. It's early September, but this is the Midwest and the weather is already cooling. I sit hugging my knees, staring into space, thinking and thinking.

It's true that I've never been as open as I've been with Arthur, but that's just because I never needed to impress him. I had all my guys-filters down! The first night I met him, I had him stare at me in my underwear while getting rid of my most hated physical flaws, naming them loud and clear one after the other! How's that for real?

And he is the most wonderful man; he actually is Prince Charming. At least he was up until this morning. But if Brooke is right, he was just being jealous. And what was it that he wanted to tell me yesterday? I should have listened.

To what end? He's cursed. You can't have him.

Right, I can't. Can I?

I don't see how. The only way I could have him would be if we broke the curse, but we already tried everything. Our latest attempts have been an ancient Mayan ritual to chase away evil spirits, voodoo dolls, two different rites for an exorcism, and we went to services in several churches. At one we even ended up being locked inside, not kidding, for an hour and a half with the most rampaging preacher. I'm still not sure what branch of religion it was, or if it was legal for that matter.

But that's beside the point. The fact is that we tried everything that was humanly possible, and maybe that's the problem. I'm not a witch. I can't undo any curse and witches are extinct.

But magic is not, says the little voice in my head.

That's true, but it doesn't help very much. I still have no idea what to do next.

***

I don't know how much time I spend on the beach staring at the waves, but it must be the better part of the day since the sun is already setting when I come out of the water's hypnosis.

I hesitatingly stretch my legs forward; my feet are numb with cold, and I can't feel my buns anymore. I roll to the side, forcing my stiff joints to raise my body weight in a standing position. As I make a couple of tentative steps, a painful tingling spreads in my toes, heels, and calf, signaling the reappearance of blood flow in my lower limbs.

I look at the lake one last time, an air of resolution pervading my whole being. It's time to go home.

Thirty-five
The End

I come back to my apartment to find it as empty as I left it. Sugar must have sensed the atmosphere charged with tension because tonight he doesn't run at my feet asking for his dinner even though he hasn't had anything to eat since this morning. He must have gone into hiding, just like the other male of the house. Arthur is nowhere to be seen. I assume that he's still working that second bottle of whiskey in his box.

Still stiff from my long vigil on the beach, I decide to take a warm shower before facing him. In the bathroom, I turn the water so hot that it is almost burning. I let it soak my skin and soothe my stiffened muscles.

After half an hour of this treatment, I'm calm. I've reached the conclusion that we only have one option: find a way to break the curse. It's possible, and even though we already tried everything we could think of, we must've overlooked something.

We'll have to research, to seek the help of experts. We'll go to the source and travel to France to see if we can find any clues there. We have to find something! I don't see any other way.

When I re-emerge from the bathroom, I'm determined. Arthur is still nowhere to be seen. I don't have the patience for his tantrums; we need to have a serious talk.

"Arthur," I call out loudly.

Nothing.

"Arthur, come out we need to talk," I try again.

You could picture tumbleweeds flying in the desert from the silence there is in this house.

"I summon thee, open sesame, sim sala bim…"

Still desolation.

"ARTHUUUR," I scream at the top of my voice.

I jump back, gasping loudly when I suddenly spot him sitting in his armchair in silence, as sulky and ruffled as he was this morning.

"We need to talk," I announce without hesitation.

"I have nothing to say." He's not going to make it easy.

"I guess you'll just have to listen then." I try to be as conciliatory as he's trying to be infuriating. I refrain from commenting on his appearance, which has declined even further since I last saw him, or on his tardy response to my call.

I am in no-nonsense mode. From now on I'll be direct, and everything will be out in the open.

"Arthur, I know you care about me," I say softly.

"Oh, I always seem to get some degree of attachment for my charges," he answers evasively, returning his vacuous gaze to the wall. "No matter how senseless they are," he adds caustically.

I pretend not to get the insult and persevere. I sit on the coffee table right in front of him, locking eyes with him.

"Arthur," I murmur, "we both agree that this, I mean us, it can't keep going. I am sure you'll agree with me. We have to find a solution. If we stay this way, it would only get worse for the both of us."

He turns his head slowly when I'm finished speaking, grimacing bitterly.

"I understand completely, milady. I will by no means suspend any pleasure of yours. You simply have to express your fifth wish and you will be rid of me for eternity." His tone is so glacial that it chills me to the bone. "I will not impose on you any longer. I will leave you to enjoy your life with Mr. Avery." He takes a bitter pause before adding, "I dare say you deserve each other."

"Arthur, please. James has nothing to do with this. I've said goodbye to him this morning and I'm not going to see him again."

"So he left again?" he asks, derisive.

"It was a mutual decision," I reply, ignoring the sardonic smirk on his face. "We thought we loved each other, but now I know that died a long time ago. I wasn't in love with him. I was in love with the idea of him, maybe, but not him, and for him it was the same. We needed closure, and we finally got it."

"You no longer love him?" he asks, surprised.

"No, I haven't for a long time. I was just stuck in the past."

A big smile spreads on his face. So he was just being jealous!

"I apologise," he says, getting up fretfully. "I am in no fit state to make conversation—I have degraded myself beyond decency. Please forgive me. I am going to make myself more presentable."

"But Arthur, we need to talk."

"There will be plenty of time later. If you will excuse me."

He bows, for real this time, and disappears again.

Ah, men! The moment you try to have a serious talk they evaporate. He will have to reappear sooner or later.

***

A couple of hours later. I'm sitting in the living room watching a "Project Runway" marathon. I love the show and I needed to give my brain a well-deserved pause from thinking.

I decided not to summon Arthur again, to give him a little time to process. He will come out of his hiding hole when he's ready to talk. As if on cue, I hear a polite cough behind me.

I turn around, and my heart stops.

Arthur is standing in front of me wearing a white shirt and beige chinos. He showered, his hair is still half-wet, forming soft, dark curls just above his shoulders. He shaved, his skin is back to normal, and the redness of his eyes is gone. But most of all, he has those deep blue pools fixed on me.

He's breathtaking! Did I not notice before? I mean, I always thought he was good-looking, but the man standing in front of me is… nothing could describe it. You'll have to take my word for it.

"You're back," I squeak, trying to keep it together. "How are you?" I ask awkwardly. I'm not used to being self-conscious around him.

"Much better—I feel completely restored. I apologise again for my previous behaviour. It was foul and indecent. I fell into an old habit of drinking and I am deeply ashamed of myself. Can you find it in you to forgive me?"

"Arthur, I'm in love." Did I just say that?

"Ah." His face becomes serious again. "I see."

"With you, you idiot." Two fat tears run down my cheeks. "I'm in love with you," I howl.

"You love me?" His eyes widen in shock. He seems incredulous.

"I do. I have for a long time." Surprise, elation, and finally, sadness appear on his face. "I just didn't let myself think about it because it was… it is…"

"Oh, Ally." His voice is soft for the first time today, but it has a firmness I don't like. "Do not open doors that should remain locked."

"Why not? You were opening it last night, right? Is that what you wanted to say?"

"No, last night was a mistake for the both of us. We did stupid things that we should have avoided," he sputters frantically.

"What do you mean, a mistake? You're avoiding my question. If you don't love me, you just have to say it!"

"Ally Johnson, I am desperately in love with you! You have opened my heart to a sentiment that I thought lost to me a long time ago. You made me smile again, you made me want to live again. You can be the most annoying person I've ever known, but I wouldn't want to spend eternity with anyone else. You stole my heart, and it belongs to you and only to you," he says, looking at me as if seeing me for the first time.

I WISH FOR YOU

Butterflies? I have a pretty bad infestation.

"But all the love in the world shall be in vain for us."

Ugh? No, no rewind. Let's go back to the part where he tells me how much he loves me.

I try to protest, but he doesn't let me.

"I cannot make you happy," he continues. "And I will not condemn you to live half a life like mine."

"What if I want to?" I ask, petulant.

"My dear, I would never allow it. In time, you will find someone else, a man that is whole. A man that will give you a family. You shall find happiness. Before, I was so incensed because I knew you were making a huge mistake. James was—*is*—beneath you. In my rage, I made a mistake. I have made you see something that I should have kept private. My love for you can bring you no good. I beg you, you have to let go of me."

I don't want to. If he goes, in time I could probably find someone else, but I don't want someone else. I want him and him alone. Everything else would be settling, settling for someone other than him.

"I don't want you to go," I wail. "I can't let you go."

"If I stay, no positive things can come of it... especially for you, my love. You have to use your last wish and start a life without me in it."

"I can't, I just can't," I say, beginning to sob loudly.

I can tell he has to master all his self-control not to come over to me and comfort me. He moves farther away instead.

"There must be something we haven't tried, something we can do." I get up and move toward him; his passive acceptance of our destiny is making me furious. "If the curse can be broken, we just have to find out *how*. There is a way—we just have to find it. We can't give up."

"My love—"

"Don't call me that," I yell, getting even closer. "You don't get to call me that if you're not willing to fight for me! You're giving up so easily; it seems you don't even care."

"Believe me, I have never cared more. I am simply doing what is best for you."

"You don't know what's best for me! If you knew, you would stay and fight for me and not go hide into oblivion. You're just a coward," I add with scorn. "You let go of Héloïse, and now you're letting me go, too."

At the look of deep hurt that appears in his eyes, I wish I could take my words back. But I can't. Unable to control myself, I wrap my arms around him and press my lips to his.

He tries to push me away, but I won't let him.

At once, it's as if I was naked in the middle of the Antarctic. Liquid ice is soaking through my skin where I'm touching him, sending icy waves to the rest of my body. The chill is so intense that it hurts. Every cell in my body is screaming for me to pull away, but I won't.

The cold... it's invading all of me. It feels as if I'm transforming into an ice sculpture, frozen in this kiss. My whole body seems to disappear... everything feels numb.

The air is freezing solid into my lungs, making it almost impossible to breathe. I can't breathe. I'm dying... now, I know it. I am going to die. I don't care; if I can't be with Arthur, I don't care about anything, about beauty, money, life... I'd rather die kissing him than live another day without being able to touch him. It will be over soon. My body can resist much longer. It's so freezing that it burns.

Wait a second, it's actually scorching. It's as if a reverse process has started. The liquid ice has transformed into a stream of lava that's flooding over me, starting from our lips, from our kiss. The cold is being replaced by warmth. A stream of heat is rushing through me, awakening every particle of my being, bringing me back to life, infusing me with a magic glow, the glow of life, the glow of love.

Finally, Arthur pulls me closer, responding to my kiss, and oh my, the man can sure kiss.

I WISH FOR YOU

When we finally separate, I look into those deep blue eyes, feeling the strength of his love for me radiating over me like sunbeams, warming my body and my heart.

"I love you," I whisper, breathless.

"I love you too," he murmurs, nuzzling my neck, sending tendrils of excitement down my spine.

"What happened?" I ask, still shaken.

"Where is the coffer?"

"It's over there," I say, indicating the spot on the kitchen bar where I always keep it.

"No, it is not," he says, turning around to check the spot.

I look over his shoulders and find that indeed the coffer is not there. It has been replaced by a small pile of fine ash.

"It's pulverized!" I blurt, stupefied. "What does it mean?"

He looks at me, bewildered. "You broke the curse," he whispers, astounded.

"I did? You're free?" I exclaim excitedly. "How?"

"It must have been your kiss."

A true love's kiss? Really?

"I thought it was impossible for you to wish me free," he continues, amazed. "What were you thinking while you kissed me? Did you wish I was free?"

"No, I just… I just wished for you," I whisper, choked, trying to find the words to describe what I felt. "I was thinking that I didn't care about anything else, the other wishes. I didn't want any of that anymore. All I was thinking was that I didn't want to live without you."

"Ally, you released me!" he says, taking both my hands into his and kissing my knuckles.

"But I didn't say any abracadabra!" I protest.

"It doesn't matter; your heart spoke for you. You gave up everything for me."

"Did I?"

"Try to make your hair blonde."

"Already playing kinky games?" I ask coquettishly.

"No, silly, I just want to see if you still have your powers."

"But I can see without my glasses, so I must still have my powers."

"Magic does not work backward that way—try to see if you can make yourself a blonde."

"If you insist." I let go of his hands and concentrate hard on my hair color, but I don't feel any prickle flashing through me.

"So?"

"No, still a brunette."

"Oh."

"Are you sad?"

"Sad? How could I be sad? I finally have everything that I need. This is the best day of my life," I say, leaning in for another kiss that I interrupt almost immediately, suddenly feeling very self-conscious. "Are *you* sad I'm going to get fat and have horrible hair?" I ask.

"I'll be happy to see you with a bit more flesh, and your hair was already perfect the day I met you."

"I don't believe you, but I'll take it." I kiss him again.

This time it's his turn to push me away with a worried face. "You have to know that most of your wealth will disappear now."

"But you said magic didn't work backward," I protest.

"No, but what kept your investments solid *was* magic—now it will all crumble. Only the material things you already bought—like this apartment—will stay. Everything financial will collapse. You left your job," he says, worried, brushing one hand through his hair. "And what about your dream of being a veterinarian?"

"Arthur, I don't care. We still have more than we'll ever need. We've bought so many things in these past months, and we can sell this place if I need to go back to school. And my real dream, the most important one, has always been to have a family. And with you that's possible."

"But I don't have any way of providing for you."

I WISH FOR YOU

"Don't worry—I could always go back to work if we need the money."

"A woman providing for me?" he says, outraged.

"Hey, this is the twenty-first century, remember? You can be a boy toy. It's very *in* these days."

"I am not even sure I actually exist in this time."

"We can check that right away," I say, grabbing my bag to see if his passport and driver's license are still in there.

I find them, and I also find something else.

"It seems your papers are still here," I say matter-of-factly, handing them to him. "And about that providing for me thing—" I continue caressing the shiny paper rectangle in my hands. "It seems we just won ourselves the lottery, baby," I add, beaming and showing him the golden winning ticket that he conjured and that I haven't cashed yet.

"Now please, no more talking." I grab him by the collar of his shirt with my free hand and pull him toward me for another long kiss.

The first of many more to come...

Thirty-six
Epilogue

Chicago Tribune

Monday, September 14
Another Collapse in the Banking World

In one of the most dramatic days in Chicago's banking history, Prime Capital National Bank's top management has announced that on Sunday night, at closed markets, an agreement to sell the company and all his assets back to the Van Horn Family has been signed.

After its unprecedented free fall on the stock market that has seen the share value of the bank drop dramatically over the past week, the only option for P.C.N., in order to avoid bankruptcy and liquidation, was to find a buyer.

It found a more than willing one in tycoon Adam Van Horn, who merely a month ago was stripped of the control share of the bank in a reckless financial maneuver. The financial market mogul happily stepped in to regain control of his first company, achieving a substantial profit with the quick maneuver.

Nathan Murphy, the former CEO of P.C.N., allegedly received a severance package close to five million dollars. His thirty-day appointment as commander in chief of Prime Capital, if short, was definitely remunerative, having allegedly granted him a check for roughly one hundred sixty-six thousand dollars per day of work.

The previous owners of P.C.N. Bank, the only true victims of this anomalous financial disaster, remain anonymous; the only available links to the recent takeover lead to an offshore company whose shareholders remain unidentified.

CHICAGO SUN-TIMES.COM

Monday, September 14
Courthouse Wedding for Vanessa Van Horn

Vanessa Van Horn, daughter of Adam Van Horn, tied the knot with fiancé James Avery last Saturday in a subdued ceremony at the downtown courthouse.

After the abrupt interruption of their previous wedding ceremony held at the Van Horn mansion for a total of five hundred guests, the gossip columns said the couple was done for. However, the two lovebirds surprised everyone and, at the sole presence of four witnesses, got hitched in downtown Chicago.

Rumor has it that Mr. and Mrs. Van Horn were not present at the ceremony. The respected businessman has made his dislike for the groom known to the public by delivering a jab straight to his soon-to-be-Son-in-Law's face in the middle of the interrupted function held at his house.

The family has not been available for comments.

Lake Forest Gazette

Monday, September 14
$15 million Lottery ticket sold in Lake Forest, the mystery of the unclaimed prize finally solved.

The fifteen million dollar ticket was sold at Madison Avenue convenience store. It matched the six winning numbers in the drawing—2, 4, 10, 22, 39 and 55—of last month's state lottery and had remained unclaimed up until this weekend.

The winner, Ally Johnson, born and raised in Lake Forest, finally claimed the jackpot of $15,622,000 on Saturday morning. The lucky winner said she had forgotten buying the ticket in the first place. She was about to throw it away upon retrieving it from the bottom of one of her bags but instead decided to check the numbers just in case. And she was in for a big surprise.

Johnson, a former marketing agent, said she plans to invest part of her winnings in education. She will go back to school to earn a degree in veterinary medicine and fulfill her lifelong dream of opening an animal shelter. Johnson promises that Lake Forest will be her first choice location to set up the clinic.

However, winning the lottery was not the sole reason for celebration for Johnson this week. In fact, during our interview, she was happy to share the good news of her recent engagement to British fiancé Arthur Pemberley. The couple said they are planning a summer wedding, intending to return from the honeymoon just in time for the beginning of the school year.

Note from the Author

Dear Reader,

Hello! If this is the first of my books you've read, welcome as well. And if you've read my books before, thank you from the bottom of my heart for coming back. It's so good to see you again and, wow, did you change your hair or something? The new style is fabulous ;)

I hope you enjoyed *I Wish for You*. If you loved my story **please leave a review** on Goodreads, your favorite retailer's website, or wherever you like to post reviews (your blog, your Facebook wall, your bedroom wall, in a text to your best friend...) Reviews are the biggest gift you can give to an author, and word of mouth is the most powerful means of book discovery.

Keep turning the pages for an excerpt of my new novel *A Sudden Crush*.

Thank you for your support!

Love,

Camilla

Excerpt from A Sudden Crush

One

Honeymoon

"Excuse me," I say, trying to attract the attention of the man sitting next to me on the plane.

He ignores me.

I try again. "Um, excuse me?" I have to sort this out before we take off.

Nothing.

Is he brushing me off on purpose?

I decide to gently tap my index finger on his shoulder. "Um, sir, excuse me…"

This time I get a brusque, "Yes?" back.

I start my pitch with a smile. "Hi, sorry to bother you—"

"Then don't."

I'm taken aback by this guy's rudeness, but not enough to desist. "Sorry again. It will take only a minute, I promise."

He rolls his eyes in an exaggerated gesture, but I ignore his body language and continue. *I have to try.*

"I got married today," I say with a dreamy, I-cannot-believe-I-am-this-happy smile, "and we, I mean my husband and I, were held back at the reception for so long, the goodbyes took forever, and then there was an accident on the highway—"

"You have a point?" the man interrupts with the same gruff attitude.

"Yeah, of course." I try to keep my cool as I need to ask this ogre a favor. "My point is that we arrived at the airport super late and there were no seats left for us to sit together, so I was wondering if you wouldn't mind switching places with my husband. He's over there." I point at Liam.

The grumpy ogre takes a casual look at Liam and snorts loudly.

"Was that a yes?" I ask hopefully.

"No, miss, it wasn't."

"It's Mrs., actually, and—"

"He's sitting in an aisle seat," the ogre says. "I want to be in a window one. Anyway, if you ask me, your husband doesn't appear too bothered with his seating accommodation."

"What's that supposed to mean?"

"That he seems pretty comfortable chatting with the top model next to him, not worrying too much about his annoying wife not being there to hold his hand."

"That… you're the rudest man I've ever met!" I'm puffing with indignation; how dare he say those things to me? "You don't know me, how can you say—"

"I've known you the whole of ten minutes, and already I've had enough. I can't help but imagine the poor guy is happy he's having a break."

With that last nasty comment, the troll turns around, presenting me with his shoulders, and goes back to staring out the window.

I turn to look at Liam. Admittedly, he seems pretty engrossed in his conversation. I can't see the woman very well; they're on the opposite side of the plane to the right, four rows down from me, and in first class, four rows is a lot of space. I crane my neck backward, but I see only the top of a blondish head. She must be tall for her head to pop out like that; it's almost even with Liam's, and he's six-foot-two. What are they talking about? And why isn't he trying to have her switch places with me?

I push the request-a-flight-attendant button. This is not how my honeymoon was supposed to begin. So far, this journey has been a nightmare. We left the reception too late, and Liam got mad at me for wanting to say goodbye to everyone. And I will admit that at home my bag wasn't exactly one hundred percent

A SUDDEN CRUSH

packed. I was maybe eighty percent done, at the very minimum. But how was I supposed to know the movers had completely ignored my directions for packing, and that none of my things were in the right boxes at our new house? It took me forever to locate the stuff I was missing.

Then there was traffic. Again, it was hardly my fault that some idiot decided to speed up on I-294, lose control of his car, and create the most prodigious traffic jam in Chicago's history. But Liam is so fastidious about his pre-flight buffer time that, for him, arriving one hour before the departure was almost as bad as missing the plane altogether.

To be fair, when we finally showed up at the airline desk, we were the last two people to check-in, and we had to make do with whatever places there were left. No matter how much I whined with the clerk about it being our honeymoon, she said there was nothing she could do at this point and that we would have to try to switch places with someone else on the plane. Which is what I'm trying to do. Only I'm sitting next to a brute.

I throw a sulky glance at him. He must be a couple of years older than me and looks like a cross between a surfer and a lumberjack. He's probably someone's type, but most definitely not mine... too unrefined, too big, and too dark. He has mocha-brown eyes and longish black hair bleached light brown at the points. His strong jaw is covered by a three or four day's stubble, he has a stubborn mouth, and his face is too rawboned. He's wearing a horrible checkered reddish shirt rolled up at the elbows that leaves his tanned forearms exposed, a pair of faded gray cargo pants, and sneakers. He has a general air of unkemptness or wilderness about him and doesn't look to me like someone who belongs in first class.

Not that I'm a frequent patron; this is my first time. But Liam said we shouldn't settle for our honeymoon, so here we are in plush, bed-like chairs half a plane away from each other. Right now, I'd give up this ridiculously large throne and happily sit in coach if it meant getting to be beside my husband.

3

"Excuse me, miss, did you call?" A smiling stewardess is towering over me.

"It's Mrs., actually, and yes, I need some help. You see, I'm on my honeymoon…"

"Congratulations!" she exclaims, including the brute in her felicitations.

"Don't look at me—I'm not the lucky fella," he says sarcastically.

"So you're not sitting next to your husband?" she asks, the smile evaporating from her lips.

"No." Finally, someone who understands. "And that's the problem. We were detained at our reception…"

"Here she goes again," the ogre grumbles, then resumes his out-of-the-window staring.

I ignore him.

"…then the movers had made a mess, and there was the accident on the highway…" I'm babbling; all the adrenaline from today is making me skittish. "So we were late for the check-in, and the only seats left were these two," I conclude.

"You didn't check-in online?" the flight attendant asks, perplexed, almost shocked.

Am I the only one who didn't get the memo that online check-in is the new black?

"I… should have, but I forgot," I admit, turning scarlet. "With all the details from the wedding to organize, it slipped my mind."

"Madam, I understand completely," she says sympathetically. "And I'm very sorry for the inconvenience, but the flight is fully booked."

"I know, but couldn't we switch places with some other passengers?"

"I'm sorry, madam, but it's too late for that." She puts the last nail in this journey's coffin. "We're about to take off, and the seatbelt sign is already on."

A SUDDEN CRUSH

"Oh." I want to cry. "But this is a six-hour flight!" If it were a one or two-hour connection, I wouldn't care.

"Again, I'm very sorry," she says with a fake smile that I'm sure she reserves for customers she can't accommodate. "Can I offer you some complimentary Champagne before we depart?" she asks, the smile never leaving her face.

Free Champagne, wow! At least she's trying to make up for it.

"Yes, thank you," I say, slightly soothed.

"I will take one too," chips in the troll.

We both glower at him. The stewardess, because he just gave away her game by pointing out that in first class the bubbly is free for everyone, and me for making me feel stupid that I thought the hostess was giving me a special perk.

"I will be back in a minute," she says graciously. She shoots a cold look at my neighbor, her smile changing from fake to "I-politely-hate-you."

As she leaves, the security instructions begin to play in the background. I cross my arms over my chest and look around me only half listening to them.

"...*this aircraft has ten emergency exits...*"

Bored, I automatically reach into my bag to take a manuscript out—I'm a book editor, I love my job, I'm great at it, and I always carry a manuscript wherever I go. But when my searching fingers can't find anything, I remember Liam made me promise to leave all work-related books at home. He's a best-selling author, so we made a deal that he wouldn't write a single word on our honeymoon if I didn't edit a single word. So I left all physical book copies home. Only now we're trapped on this plane for six hours, miles away from each other, and I don't have anything to do. I could try to edit something on my phone, I guess, but I don't want to be sloppy—no author deserves that—and I'm too tired to accomplish anything half-decent, anyway. I even feel too tired to *just* read, which has never happened to me before.

5

"...*illuminated strips on the floor will guide you to these exits...*"

Joan, stay positive, I say to myself. The destination matters more than the journey.

"...*in the event of a loss in cabin pressure, oxygen masks will automatically drop from the panel above you...*"

Tomorrow I will wake up in a five-star resort in a tropical paradise. There's no need to stress about the plane ride.

"...*every seat is provided with a life vest. In first and business class, the vest is located under the armrest. In economy class...*"

"Here's your Champagne, madam." The stewardess is back with two plastic flutes filled with the sparkling liquid. "Sir," she adds curtly. "I hope you have a pleasant flight. Let me know if I can assist you in any other way."

I mutter a thank you. The troll doesn't even bother. So rude.

"...*personal electronic devices may be used during takeoff and landing, providing all transmission functions are switched-off and the device itself is put into airplane mode....*"

I take my phone out of my bag; there's a text from Katy, my maid of honor. She sent me a selfie of us together that she took just before we left. Yes, it was another one of the above-mentioned deferments. I reply with a waterfall of XOXOs and obediently switch the phone to plane mode.

The plane accelerates on the runway and takes off. I calmly sip my Champagne and watch the Chicago skyline disappear beneath us as the plane soars higher and higher in the dark blue sky. Relax, I tell myself. I need to let go of the stress of these past few weeks. After all, from now on this trip can only get better.

Acknowledgments

First, I'd like to thank you for reading my book. It's because of you that I've found the strength to push through every writer's block and inspiration deficit. Thank you for making my work meaningful.

Many thanks to my two editors, Mary Yakovets and Michelle Proulx. Thank you for your thoughtful insights and clever remarks. Your notes made this book so much better.

Thanks to Design for Writers, and to Andrew Brown in particular, for designing the best cover I could have hoped for, and for putting up with my artistic eccentricity.

A special thank you goes to Alex and Desi, my very first beta-readers. Your comments and suggestions were essential.

Finally, thank you to my friends and family for always supporting me. No matter the adventure I decide to embark on, I know I can count on you.

CPSIA information can be obtained
at www.ICGtesting.com
Printed in the USA
LVHW091737251019
635356LV00002B/331/P